Katherine Yorke was born in Cape Town, South Africa, her father English and her mother a New Zealander. Brought up and educated in England, she graduated in Sociology at the London School of Economics and, after taking several false trails in her career, settled down as a writer. For a few years she also worked as a publisher's editor, but since 1975 she has written full-time, also under the name of Nicola Thorne. She lives in St John's Wood, London.

Also by Katherine Yorke

KATHERINE YORKE

THE PAIR BOND

Futura

A Futura Book

First published in Great Britain in 1984 by
Macdonald & Co (Publishers) Ltd
London & Sydney

This Futura edition published in 1985

ISBN 0 7088 2654 7

Reproduced, printed and bound in Great Britain by
Hazell Watson & Viney Limited,
Member of the BPCC Group,
Aylesbury, Bucks

For information on the Falklands War of 1982 the author is
indebted to THE BATTLE FOR THE FALKLANDS by Max
Hastings and Simon Jenkins (Michael Joseph, 1983).

Futura Publications
A Division of
Macdonald & Co (Publishers) Ltd
Maxwell House
74 Worship Street
London EC2A 2EN
A BPCC plc Company

For Vivienne Warszawski,
oldest and best of friends

PAIR FORMATION (syn. Pair bonding)

A pair may form for one mating season or for life . . .

Encyclopedia of Psychology
(Herder & Herder, 1972)

*

I love thee according to my bond;
nor more nor less.

(Cordelia to her father
King Lear Act 1 Scene 1)

CHAPTER ONE

SAM HAHN LOVED HIS WIFE. It would not be far-fetched to say that he loved both his wives, the old and the new. For Barbara there was tenderness, the nostalgia of twenty-seven years of a marriage which didn't end in bitterness because she had gracefully allowed Sam his freedom. For Frankie there was passion, the rekindled excitement and rapture of first love.

The rapture seemed like a never-ending honeymoon, whether they were in Venice or not, Sam thought, stirring the frothy milk into his cappucino coffee as he waited for Frankie on the terrace in front of Florian's. Lifting the cup to his lips he took a tentative sip and then replaced it in its saucer, sighing deeply with satisfaction. He settled well back in his chair and lifted his eyes to the gleaming, golden domes of the Basilica of St Mark, a feeling almost of reverence, of thanksgiving settling over him.

It had been so hard to leave Barbara; but both she and Frankie had made it easy for him, as though neither of them wanted him to suffer. Barbara had made no demands, no claims because, as a self-supporting woman, she was not dependent on Sam and he was more than generous in the divorce settlement – leaving her the Hampstead house outright in which they had shared all those years of diminishing connubial bliss. Barbara had been very dignified about the whole thing.

Frankie, who had already been his mistress for two years when he left Barbara, was equally generous. She hadn't wanted Barbara to feel rejected, cast off. She'd tried to put herself in Barbara's place, although it was difficult because she was then a woman of thirty-four and Barbara, at forty-eight, already seemed to have acquired that venerable, invisible patina of age which Frankie would never have dreamed of associating with Sam. It had been easy to be detached about Barbara, and sympathetic at the same time.

Sam sat up and swallowed his coffee, aware of a faint quickening of the pulse as the tall, slim form of Frankie could be discerned coming out of the narrow entrance to the Merceria, that teeming artery which led to the Rialto where she'd been shopping. She paused, shielded her eyes, though her arms were full, and looked around. Sam stood up, waving his paper, and Frankie began to run across the square towards him. Greeting her, he clasped her briefly in his arms and helped to detach the many little parcels and bags she had strung over each arm.

'Coffee darling?'

'Coffee please!' Frankie, still breathless, nodded her head with excitement and glanced at the gold bracelet watch on her wrist that had been a wedding present from Sam. 'Am I late?'

Sitting down again, Sam stretched his legs in front of him and folded his arms behind his head.

'Darling we have all the time in the world. We have no appointments, nothing to distract us from the pleasure of doing what you want.'

Frankie gazed at him and tucked a loose piece of her ash blonde hair behind her ears. Her face was brown from the hours spent on the Lido in the warm September sun and the tan enhanced the unusual colour of her eyes, which were a very light blue encircled by a dark outer rim. Frankie was an American girl from Pennsylvania, five feet nine in height and with an athletic build that, in the golden age of Renaissance Venice, would have been called willowy. She had a rather sculpted face, not unlike that of a Byzantine Madonna, with deeply recessed eyes that gave her an air of mystery. Sam was terribly in love with her and as he leaned forward she instinctively pursed her lips and their mouths met. Kisses, always kisses. Still passionate lovers after nearly four years.

A waiter stood gazing benignly at them as though, despite the entwined couples he saw daily on the Piazza St Marco, he found this a unique occasion. When the gentle unselfconscious kiss was finished Sam ordered two more cappucinos, his hand remaining linked with Frankie's.

'What did you buy?'

Frankie looked thoughtfully at the many parcels scattered

on the chair beside her and started to count. 'Some handker-chiefs, a blouse, a pair of sandals and something for you!'

She thrust a beautifully wrapped parcel at him, her face alight like that of a child on Christmas morning.

'For me?' Sam pretended surprise.

'For you.' She pecked his cheek again.

'But you give me presents every day.'

'That's because I like giving you presents.'

Sam carefully undid the wrapping as though he too was beside himself with excitement, exposing an Italian silk shirt immaculately encased in polythene, broad grey stripes contrasting with white.

'Perfect,' Sam said admiringly. 'You have such wonderful taste.'

'I could spend all day in those shops on the Merceria.'

'Well you practically do.'

'Darling what about all the sightseeing?' Frankie pretended to look stern and, taking up the guide book on the table before them, shook it mockingly at him.

'I know, we must have almost as expert a knowledge of Venice as John Ruskin and others who have written about it.'

'But you have enjoyed it Sam?' She sounded doubtful.

'Oh I *have* enjoyed it.' Sam squeezed her hand and raised his head as the waiter put two fresh cups of coffee before them, neatly tucking the bill under one of the saucers.

And he had enjoyed it. He had last been to Venice twenty years earlier with Barbara and, although they were then parents of two young children and not by any means old, he couldn't remember getting one tenth of the pleasure he had now with Frankie. It could be he had forgotten; that time had blurred the memory as time sometimes does, playing tricks when comparing present happiness with the past. Also, in those days there was no carefree spending because, as young parents with responsibilities, their respective careers not fully established, they had had to watch the money. They had stayed at a stuffy little pensione off the Campo Santa Maria Formosa with a putrid lavatory at the end of a narrow corridor, containing a shower with an erratic water supply. Their tiny bedroom with its cheap furniture had lino on the floor and at night it was completely airless except for the faint stink of the stagnant canal three floors below.

Now he and Frankie began the day in a luxurious suite in a large hotel on the Lido, and a soft breeze blew in from the Adriatic as they sipped their coffee in the early morning after making love. To begin and end their days with love like this, days interspersed with all sorts of other delights as well, was a perfection he couldn't recall ever having experienced with Barbara.

Like Frankie, Barbara had been a compulsive sightseer, but the shops had never attracted her and, except for a few small souvenirs and presents for the children, they had returned home their cases not much bulkier than they had been on arrival. This time there would surely be an excess charge to pay on all Frankie's purchases: dresses, blouses, shoes, lingerie.

Did he just indulge Frankie because she was almost twenty years younger than he was? A mere girl? An amusing, enchanting companion whose presence was a perpetual adornment to a middle-aged man? Frankie, always vibrant, beautifully dressed, walking by his side, her golden hair bobbing on to her shoulders, heads turning to glance at her. Did he not mind because Frankie, who also had her own income, could buy what she liked, do as she pleased, the personification of the modern, liberated woman whereas, at her age, Barbara had never heard of the term – no one had. It only came into common parlance in the '70s. Was it because the excitement of a new wife had brought renewed life into the body of an ageing man, as though she sent fresh blood coursing through his veins like the leaping waters of the fountains in so many quiet Venetian squares?

Frankie was still studying the guide book, her brow furrowed.

'We should see the Guggenheim gallery.'

'Isn't it full of modern pictures?' Sam wrinked his nose.

'Darling don't be so old fashioned.' Frankie playfully tapped his shoulder with her finger. 'These are the old masters, the Carpaccios, Raphaels and Tintorettos of the future.'

'I suppose they are,' Sam looked doubtful. 'We could, on the other hand, go back to the hotel and have a swim.'

It was very hot. Sam waved a hand in front of his face looking at her pathetically, and Frankie burst into laughter.

'All right, we go back to the hotel and dump the parcels anyway. Have a swim, lunch and then . . .'

'Have a sleep?' Sam said hopefully.

'. . . take the boat and go to the Guggenheim. It's on the Grand Canal.' Frankie ran her finger along the map at the end of the guide book. 'Not far from the Accademia Bridge. If we get off the boat there we can walk to the museum and then afterwards see the Tintoretto frescoes at the Scuola of San Rocco. That's if we have time.'

Sam sighed and grimaced as though preparing to make the extreme sacrifice. He would have been quite happy to have spent the whole time alone with Frankie on the beach or in the large bed in their hotel room. But, falling in with her wishes, willing to be led by her, guided by her, was part of the fun too. He never knew he had such energy. She was making him young again.

He counted out some lire to pay for their coffees, left a generous tip and, seizing Frankie by the hand, jumped up.

'Come on,' he said. 'Don't lounge about. You'll miss the best part of the day.'

Frankie laughingly began to festoon him with parcels as though she were putting the decorations on a Christmas tree.

After the Guggenheim and the Tintorettos they had an aperitif in the Campo San Rocco, which was full of Venetians doing the same thing or merely strolling about with their numerous children, muzzled dogs on leads. There were very few tourists in this part of Venice even though, in September, the tourist season was still under way. The shutters were being put up in the shops and the restaurants were filling up, especially the ones which had tables and chairs outside shielded from the populace by trellis or a row of bushes.

'I prefer the Carpaccios,' Sam said referring to the frescoes in the beautiful little Scuola di San Giorgio degli Schianvoni, founded by the Dalmatians in the fifteenth century, which they'd seen the day before.

'I do too,' Frankie nodded, 'but I'm glad we saw the Tintorettos. I'm even glad we saw the Guggenheim.'

'I liked the *house*,' Sam said, 'though it is hard to imagine it was ever an ordinary home with furniture and books. It looks as though it was made to be a museum. I wonder what sort of woman she was? Another American expatriate.' Sam

11

reached for Frankie's hand. 'Let's go and eat,' he said. 'I've booked at Harry's Bar for eight-thirty.'

'Why Harry's Bar?'

'Everyone eats at Harry's Bar. It's a treat.'

Sam was full of treats, he was the most thoughtful man imaginable – fresh flowers constantly in their hotel room, little gifts by her bedside: a bracelet, a ceramic pill box, a small painting he'd liked of Santa Maria Salute with its dominating position at the entrance to the Grand Canal, its great white dome outlined against the evening sky. Like so many other things it would remind them of the time they'd had in Venice in the years that lay ahead – happy years they would spend together, a lifetime.

Sam's age was something Frankie seldom thought about. He had a quality of youth that so many much younger men she knew lacked. Yet he had the undeniable advantages of age, of experience in making a young woman like her feel that she was precious. She wondered if he'd been the same with Barbara? It was difficult to forget Barbara altogether, though she tried not to think of her too often. Yet the memory of Barbara was never a reproach. She'd been too decent, as if she hadn't really minded giving up Sam.

Frankie knew that Sam had misled her, maybe not delib- erately, but he had. His picture of his marriage was different from Barbara's. It was as though they had both been looking at the same view, but seeing something completely different, like an optical illusion. As though, with the same aspect, one saw a seascape and the other mountains. When she had met Barbara, at last, after she and Sam were married, she saw a woman who wasn't cold or remote at all, as Sam had implied, but someone dignified, compassionate and forgiving. Yet even then she knew that it wasn't possible to be natural with Barbara; that those happy family gatherings, with hatchets firmly buried, that Sam dreamed about, wouldn't be possible.

Frankie and Barbara remained on friendly but casual terms. However, of late Frankie had wondered if it was really necessary for Sam to go up and see Barbara as often as he did. After all, they had been divorced for two years.

Yet what had irritated Frankie more than anything was seeing the change in how Sam spoke about Barbara before he left her, and after. It was as though parting had indeed made his heart grow fonder and that Barbara had become, to him, more precious than before.

Harry's Bar, overlooking the Grand Canal by the Piazza San Marco, was full, lots of English and American voices coming from the crowded tables as they squeezed past to their table by one of the windows on the first floor. It was almost dark outside and the lights from the boats, the passing vaporetti, were reflected alluringly on the water in that enchanting way that was one of the most vivid memories the visitor to Venice took away when he or she left. Opposite the great Baroque church of Santa Maria Salute, built in the seventeenth century by Longhena in thanksgiving for the deliverance of Venice from the plague, maintained its serene vigil just as it did in the picture Sam had bought for her to take home.

Attentive waiters hovered around them and Sam ordered a bottle of cool white Frascati as they studied the menu. They both ordered the same, scallops in white wine, a speciality of the house, and peccatini of veal. Frankie was aware of the slight motion that she felt frequently in Venetian buildings, as though the island in the lagoon was permanently shifting on its foundations. For a long time she'd thought it was her imagination, until Sam had said he felt it too.

As usual she noticed people looking at them, perhaps wondering about their relationship. They seemed to attract curious glances wherever they went. Did people think she was Sam's mistress, a distinguished white-haired man with a much younger woman? Did people care, or were the gazes inspired as much by jealousy as speculation?

'I think they wonder who we are, if we're married.' Frankie giggled.

'Perhaps they hope we aren't.' Sam dipped his bread into the delicious juice, flavoured with cheese, in which the scallops had been cooked.

'Do you wish we weren't?'

'Of course I don't! I had two years of that and it was enough.'

'Still, it was exciting. Affairs are exciting.'

'Marriage is exciting too. To you.'

'Was it to Barbara?'

'Oh darling don't talk about Barbara.'

'I've hardly mentioned her this holiday.'

'Well don't now. Don't spoil it.'

'But why should Barbara spoil it? We both like her.'

'Yes, but . . .' Sam paused.

'But *what* Sam?'

'It's not really the thing for a man to discuss his first wife with his second. I can't explain it.'

'Or vice versa.'

'What do you mean?'

'I know you talk about me to Barbara.'

'We hardly ever talk about you, we talk about the children.'

Sam felt vaguely uncomfortable as though the gentle breeze coming through the window off the lagoon had suddenly turned cold. In fact he talked about Frankie quite a lot to Barbara, whose many years as a doctor and psychoanalyst gave her a special insight. Barbara, in a way, had helped him to settle down with Frankie – to the problems of adjusting to marriage with a much younger woman. Sam remained deeply attached to Barbara. In many ways he wished he could have remained married to both of them.

Frankie put her knife and fork together and carefully mopped her lips with a large white napkin. Then she broke into a fresh roll and played with the crumbs on the tablecloth.

'Do you think we should have a baby, Sam?'

'Baby?' Sam choked on a portion of the succulent mollusc.

'You know, those little creatures . . .'

'I know quite well what babies are,' Sam swallowed his food. 'But I thought we agreed that we didn't want them.'

'I wonder if we were right.'

'I'm quite *sure* we were. Do you think we'd be so happy with babies? Trips to Venice, maybe the Bahamas at Christmas.' Sam made a Gallic gesture in the air. 'All gone.'

'This is really what you want all the time isn't it, Sam? A perpetual holiday with me? You see, that's why I feel so different from Barbara. Even marriage hasn't changed me from being a mistress, a good-time girl.'

'That's awful nonsense,' Sam said crossly. 'You're my wife, part of my life. My goodness, in London our life is humdrum enough.'

'But it isn't, Sam,' Frankie said patiently, tossing back her head. 'We live extravagantly. We go out every night: theatres,

14

operas, concerts. I don't think our life is really normal, if you ask me. It's one long holiday. It lacks reality.'

'And a baby will make it real?'

'Well it would make it into a real marriage – something that's part of us, our gift to posterity.'

'I already have made three gifts to posterity.'

'Yes, but with Barbara, not me.'

The chill suddenly became a gale. Sam thought he had lost his appetite and gazed without enthusiasm at the veal on the plate put before him. Yet only a moment ago he'd still felt hungry.

'I thought we had all this settled Frankie.' He realized the tone of his voice had changed. It was as though he was in the bank, preparing to censure a heavily overdrawn customer. He straightened up and gazed severely at Frankie. 'Has *Venice* made you change your mind?'

'It has made me realize how much I love you.' Frankie saw she'd upset him and groped for his hand lying stiffly on the table, his food untouched. 'I mean really love, not just an affair. I think without a child our life is incomplete.'

'How long have you been thinking this?'

'Some time.' Frankie's face was unusually enigmatic. 'Nothing definite but just there, as though something was missing. I didn't realize I'd feel like this and, I must tell you, it's taken courage to say it. Maybe that's why I've left it until now – to get you in the right mood.'

'You'd never get me in the right mood for that,' Sam said glumly. 'Tom is twenty-six. I find the whole idea absurd.'

'Of becoming a father again? I thought you might like it, really. Anyway, what about me? Am I not allowed to breed because you've got three grown-up children?'

Sam had never thought of Frankie as a mother. She worked in his bank as an investment adviser, a bright young graduate of Vassar and the Harvard Business School. He thought of her as clever, sexy, but not maternal: the ideal modern woman who made sensible rational decisions about her life. He knew that maternity changed women and, at his age, he wanted to be the only thing of importance in her life. He wanted her to belong exclusively to him.

They didn't talk about the baby again that night, but Sam knew it wasn't settled. In a way he felt that it had rather

15

marred the end of their romantic holiday in Venice. It introduced a new dimension, as though the still waters of the Venetian lagoon mirrored what he felt should be the calm contentment of his life, and someone had thrown a boulder into it.

On their last night they travelled on a slow vaporetto up the Grand Canal just to gaze once more on the old palazzi which lined both banks, most of them now turned into flats or municipal buildings but still undeniably romantic, with the soft mellow lights shining from within and the sconces outside illuminating modern anchored motor boats or ancient gondolas gently rising and falling with the motion of the water. They slipped under the Rialto Bridge which was still thronged – as it was all day – with people, making it look very like the market it had been in Shakespeare's day and still was. As they travelled back down the canal the wide expanse of the lagoon came into view, the island of San Giorgo and, ahead but still obscured in darkness, was the Lido. Their hands had remained tightly clasped all during the voyage as though both knew that it was somehow the end of part of their life. Tomorrow it would be an early airplane from Marco Polo airport and the frenetic life of London again.

'We have a very happy life,' Sam spoke quietly. 'You have no idea how constricting a baby can be; and I'm talking from experience of days when nannies were cheap and plentiful.'

'We could still have a nanny,' Frankie's voice was gently pleading as though the decision was still very much up to Sam. 'With both our incomes we could afford one.'

'But would you want to go on working? If so, why do you want a baby? That's what I can't understand. It's not as though you seem to feel instinctively maternal. You said when we married . . .'

'I've changed my mind, that's all.' Sam met her eyes, riveting but strangely vulnerable, lit by the lights of the buildings as they passed slowly along the waterway.

'I feel it's the end of all this,' Sam said, staring helplessly about him.

'It's the beginning of something else. Can't you see it like that Sam? Fecundity, growth, new life? Wouldn't you *like* a child by me?'

Sam looked at her, her pale gold hair, her full sensual

mouth, her large blue eyes gazing directly and rather discon-
certingly at him. He suddenly felt a desire for her that went
beyond normal desire, that was, maybe, a need to implant his
seed in her; to forge a bond with Frankie as he had with
Barbara.

'I simply can't believe it! I can't believe Dad would want to
start being a father all over again.'

Sarah Hahn blinked unbelievingly at her mother, pale
hands nervously fidgeting with a lock of her thick dark hair.

'Your father is rather bemused by the whole thing; but I
can't help feeling he rather likes it.'

'But likes *what* for goodness' sake?'

'Likes his new life. Likes being able to give Frankie a baby,
for instance.'

'But that is mere biology.'

'Oh no it's not darling.' Barbara fitted a cigarette into an
amber holder, lit it and drew on it for a few seconds, squinting
at her daughter through the smoke. Barbara, who had so
much willpower for so many things, needed help to give up
smoking. The cigarette holder came in a packet of various
filter strengths which, in theory, enabled you to give up
smoking altogether by gradually diminishing the amount of
nicotine. 'It's psychological too. A man of fifty plus feels
satisfaction at his ability to impregnate a younger woman.'

'That's childish.' Sarah stared at her plate.

Yet Sarah had seemed more understanding than anyone
when Sam said he wanted to divorce his spouse of twenty-
seven years to marry someone else. Sarah, now twenty-three,
was a rather detached, unemotional young woman in her final
year of medicine. In a spectrum of attractive to plain, her
looks came somewhere in the middle, good features and bad
– large intelligent eyes, overlong nose and a wide mouth –
combining in a rather harmonious yet curious and unlikely
symmetry. Good looking, definitely, but one who was
careless about her appearance so that it seemed an indication
of her lack of self-regard. She did not have her mother's
interest in self-presentation nor Barbara's concern for good
grooming and nice clothes. Like many women Sarah resembled her father, and so features that made Sam handsome had

the opposite effect in his daughter. She had his dark colouring, but also his nose – a beak that gave him a strong masculine profile, but his elder daughter a rather severe, unfeminine one.

Mother and daughter occasionally met over lunch at a small restaurant in Charlotte Street near University College Hospital where Sarah was now doing her midwifery at the Obstetric Hospital. On Tuesday afternoons Babara lectured to the more advanced students in psychoanalytic theory and practice and, Sarah's commitments in the labour ward permitting, they met for lunch on that day. The news of Frankie's pregnancy had been conveyed to Sarah personally by Sam at the weekend at Sunday lunch in the couple's Primrose Hill house. Also there had been Tom Hahn and his wife Natalie, who was also pregnant.

'I thought it ridiculous that both Dad and Tom were expectant fathers.' Sarah took a sip of the water she preferred with her lunch. 'Tom did too.'

'Yes I know Tom didn't take it well. They came over to me in the evening. Tom has had his nose put out of joint.'

'Oh Mother don't be so psychological! Tom was angry. That's what it was – plain anger, and a sort of disgust if you ask me.'

'Did Tom expect his father and Frankie to live lives of sexual abstinence?' Barbara was amused.

'No of course not. He expected nothing of the sort. Oh Mother I can't explain it. *You* should know what I mean.'

'But darling,' Barbara intervened gently, 'the explanation *is* psychological, whatever you say. Why else should Tom feel angry? It's not logical is it?'

'But Frankie was supposed not to want children! Or was it a bait to trap Daddy?'

'I don't suppose it was a *trap*. I don't suppose she knew herself quite what she wanted. She wanted him, he was an attractive man. I wonder if she thought much beyond that.'

'Daddy told us, when he made the announcement about his marriage to Frankie, that he had his family and there certainly wouldn't be any more.'

'He said that to reassure you, especially Amanda. I don't know why, but children are jealous of second families however much they try and rationalize it. Well, I *do* know why, but seeing you don't like me being psychological I won't say.'

Barbara smiled gently as though trying to take the edge off the barb. She and Sarah had never enjoyed an easy relation-ship, maybe because they were very alike: rather intense serious women who rejected the more blatant, stereotyped and obvious aspects of femininity. Of course today it was easier for a woman to be herself than it had been when Barbara had studied at the same hospital in the early fifties. In those days men were still doing their military service and girls were expected – in fact they perhaps wanted – to fulfil the traditional female roles as cooks, cleaners, mothers, whatever their academic achievements.

Looking at Sarah and the life she led Barbara envied her, although she knew very little of what Sarah did with her private life, what men she knew, what interests she had outside medicine. Sarah was very secretive, always had been.

Perhaps because of this subconscious rivalry with her mother, Sarah had always adopted a very practical stance, a pragmatic view of life. Perhaps because her mother had always withdrawn into her inner sanctum where she analysed her patients, that room where the children were never wanted or welcome, that room that they hardly ever saw except when it was being cleaned or redecorated, Sarah had little time for psychological nuances, for things that did not have a rational, verifiable explanation. She intended to be a practical physician, treating ailments with proven drugs rather than probing into the lives of her patients. To her medicine was a modern marvel, and psychology tried and found wanting – out of date. She was convinced about the physical explanation of all human matter; she was a practical woman who read little apart from medical books and thought abstractly scarcely at all.

After lunch the women walked together along Charlotte Street, up Tottenham Court Road and along Torrington Place. There their ways would diverge – Sarah to the Obstetric Hospital in Huntley Street, Barbara to one of the lecture theatres in University College in Gower Street. Her course was not confined to medical students, but was open and optional to any student in the college who was free and could attend it. Needless to say in her final year Sarah had not done so. On the way they discussed other family matters apart from the one that chiefly preoccupied them. Tom, who was in the army, and Natalie, Amanda, Sarah's course. It wasn't until they stopped at the juncture with Huntley Street that Sarah returned to the subject of her father and his new wife again.

'I'm sorry I went on about Dad.'

'I don't mind. You can say what you like.'

'But what do you feel Mother? Really feel?' Sarah took a couple of steps towards her mother and looked into her eyes.

'I feel quite detached, since you ask. I had to cease having personal feelings about your father when he left home.'

'How can you suddenly stop having personal feelings?'

'It's not easy.' Barbara turned up the fur collar of her coat against the keen January wind. Her cheeks had gone the colour of the rather purple lipstick she wore. 'It wasn't easy. Sam and I had grown away, I suppose, as people do when they've been married a long time, but not to the extent that I thought he'd ever want to marry someone else. It was a shock. Of course I still care very much about Sam and what happens to him; but not to the point of interfering, or sharing his life. That is all in the past.' Barbara drew back her glove and glanced at her watch. 'I have five minutes before my lecture starts. Goodbye, darling. Come up for supper on Saturday?'

'I'll think about it, Mum. I'll call you. Bye-bye.'

Sarah kissed her mother lightly on the cheek and sped up to the hospital where a patient of hers was in labour. Two hours later, gowned and masked, Sarah prepared to deliver the baby in the delivery room of the fifth floor of the hospital. A registrar was with her because the delivery might prove complicated, and if forceps were needed it would be the first time she had used them.

Sarah had been up most of the night with her patient, a woman in her mid-thirties having her first baby. Medically speaking this was rather an advanced age to have children and her patient had suffered a good deal. Sarah had the makings of an excellent doctor – unemotional, objective, capable. She inspired confidence in her patients, who trusted her because they thought she knew what she was doing. Sarah thought that this demonstration of capability was far more important than any amount of psychological understanding, though this did not, of course, exclude concern and compassion.

The registrar knew that the patient was in excellent hands and stood at the back of the room while Sarah examined the labouring woman, inspecting the monitor, getting her into the position for delivery, calmly issuing instructions to the nurses assisting her.

The patient was inhaling her gas and air, but it did little to ease her considerable pain. A further examination showed that the baby's head was jammed in the birth passage and, swiftly exchanging glances with the registrar, Sarah took up the forceps while the expectant mother's legs were put in stirrups to ease delivery. Slowly the room filled up with students hastily summoned to see a forceps delivery and, as the registrar stood at her right hand Sarah – who had seen the procedure many times and studied it in detail – gently introduced the pair of tongs into the stretched vagina and delicately probed for the baby's head. She was nervous but she felt confident. Never for a moment did she falter, but worked speedily, swiftly, delicately, her mind on her task, oblivious of the faces pressed closely behind her staring intently at her at work. What mattered was the welfare of the mother and the survival of her first-born baby.

The head turned, the body slipped forward, the mother gave a groan and the registrar reached forward and, with his gloved hand, gently pulled the shoulders of the tiny blood-covered creature while Sarah put aside the forceps and completed the delivery, cutting the cord and giving the newly delivered baby to a nurse.

'Well done,' the registrar murmured. Sarah scarcely heeded him but on making sure that the baby, having the mucus sucked from its nose and mouth, was all right, went over to the panting, exhausted mother.

'She's fine. It's a lovely girl.'

Then Sarah allowed herself to relax and smile and the patient, opening her eyes, grasped her hand.

'Thank you,' she said. Embarrassed, Sarah briefly returned the pressure and went out to remove her gown while the nursing staff cleared up and the students scattered.

Later Sarah was having tea in the canteen when the registrar came over. He was a senior doctor who would shortly be looking for a consultancy.

'You did very well Sarah. I think it's the best first forceps delivery I've ever seen. Usually at some stage I have to take over. You've done your homework well.'

'Thank you Dr Daniel.'

Sarah felt gratified by his praise but not elated. In the practice of medicine there were many milestones and another had been successfully overcome. Dr Daniel sat down and stirred his tea.

'Did you ever think of specializing in obstetrics, or will it be psychiatry like your mother?'

'Oh no!' Sarah gave a short laugh and consulted her timetable for the day. Patients permitting, two lectures and a demonstration.

'You say that very definitely.'

'I am very definite. I like the practical aspects of medicine. As a matter of fact I don't think I'll specialize in anything. I'd like to be a GP.'

'Really? Well you do surprise me. I hear you're quite brilliant.'

Sarah stared at her tea and suddenly she thought of Frankie who, when she had her baby, would be the same age as the patient she had just delivered. Frankie was really too old to be having her first baby in Sarah's opinion. She wondered if her father knew this? At thirty-seven there were risks – a difficult labour was the least of them. She wondered if her stepmother should have an amniocentesis. She was aware Dr Daniel was waiting for an answer.

'I'm sorry Dr Daniel. I suddenly thought of my stepmother who is pregnant. Do you think she should have an amniocentesis?'

Dr Daniel grimaced. 'Any family history of deformity, mongolism?'

'Not on our side.'

'Is she a patient here?'

'Oh no.' Sarah laughed. 'A private Harley Street obstetrician and an expensive nursing home in St John's Wood.'

'I didn't realize your mother and father were divorced?'

'My father married a young American two years ago. She

22

was quite emphatic about not wanting children. Now she's changed her mind.'

'And has your mother remarried?'

'No, nor does she have any intention so far as I know. My mother is, and always has been, devoted to her work.'

'Is that why the marriage broke up?'

Sarah looked at the registrar coolly. Although he was her senior she didn't consider it gave him the right to ask personal questions. Her glance embarrassed him.

'I'm awfully sorry. It's none of my business.'

'I'll have to go and see Mrs Sharp who's expecting twins any minute.' Sarah got up and smiled, consulting her note-book. 'No complications there, I hope.'

'You'll cope Sarah, whatever happens. Think about specializing rather than general medicine.'

'There's a long way to go yet, but thank you for thinking of me Dr Daniel.'

Sarah gave him her appraising look that was neither grateful nor insolent. George Daniel, who was considered a ladies' man though married with three children of his own, found her a chilly, curious woman. It would never have occurred to him to make a pass at her and, in places where men gathered and chatted alone, her name never came up as a candidate for seduction. Considered cold, capable, remote, she was respected, but not desired. He thought she was probably quite frigid in bed.

'Amniocentesis?' Sam said, 'what on earth is that?'

Sarah explained that, by drawing fluid from abdomen of a pregnant woman, it was possible to detect abnormalities, and, if necessary, perform an abortion. 'Frankie is slightly old to be a mother. The chances of abnormalities increase with age.'

'Aren't you being rather morbid?' Frankie, lying on the sofa beside Sam, took his hand. His palm curled reassuringly around hers.

'It's really a question of whether there were any abnormalities in your family, mongolism and such like.'

'Not that I know of.'

'Then the risk is not as great.'

'But there *is* a risk?' Sam enquired anxiously.

23

'There's always a risk.'

Sarah knew she was handling it badly. What had started off as a sensible medical talk after Frankie's latest check with the doctor had begun to look like an inquisition. But to her facts were facts; older mothers ran a greater risk of bearing abnormal children. She had dinner about once a week at her father's house and this conversation took place some days after her lunch with her mother.

'Had you better have it done darling? At least ask Mr Dickens?'

'Certainly not!' Frankie, now four months pregnant, was adamant. 'He said I was getting on absolutely fine. Blood pressure, general health, everything A1. Sarah's letting her newly found obstetric knowledge go to her head.'

'Sarah's being sensible.' Sarah sipped her after-dinner coffee. 'But you're in Mr Dickens' hands.'

Frankie's attitude to Sarah had been to try and adopt the manner of an older sister rather than a stepmother but really to be as natural as possible. The fact that his elder children had been so shocked by their father's decision to marry another woman had shaken her.

The meeting with the children had been very difficult, and she hadn't met Tom until she and Sam had been married for a year. But Sarah, the doctor who saw so much of life, had been, as expected, more tolerant, if not actually welcoming. Although Sam assured her that Sarah and her mother opposed each other in everything, they were very close. Sarah felt that Sam was leaving Barbara in the lurch and when he told her he would never do that she was more inclined to be nice to Frankie; nice, but not warm.

In Frankie's opinion, Sarah was a very curious girl. She found her difficult to make out and certainly to befriend. Sarah always seemed to be watching her, studying her as though making comparisons with her mother. To Frankie this was quite understandable and she didn't act or play a part when Sarah was around, determined to be taken for herself as she was and not as another Barbara.

But that day Sarah annoyed her and Frankie showed it. She went to her room soon after the end of the conversation, leaving Sarah with her father. They had all played down the business of inherited defects but, nevertheless, Sarah had cast

24

a doubt, and that doubt seemed to hover like a cloud in the attractive yet rather antiseptic living room with its low Swedish furniture, its modern paintings and polished pine floor.

Sam felt responsible yet not responsible. He had caused the baby which Frankie wanted. It was rather like the philosophical problem about what came first, the hen or the egg. Sam who did not want a second family, had hoped that somehow Frankie would not be able to conceive; but very soon after the decision was made, she did. He had heard that mature women were not as fertile as younger ones, but she was. He had heard that the sperm of older men might become sterile, but his hadn't. Frankie's pregnancy was a demonstration of his virility, of her fertility. After they knew it both were extremely proud that it had happened, as though there were something unique in pulling off such a coup. Her fecundity made them even closer than before.

Taking their marriage as a marriage – Barbara and his other children apart – it was very successful. Two years old at the time Frankie conceived it had confounded almost all its critics, of whom there were a good number even among Sam's close friends. Barbara had been very much liked and admired and Sam's treatment of her, even by the most liberal standards of a liberal age, was considered shabby. However brave a front Barbara had put on the situation, few were prepared to like Frankie or give the marriage a chance.

Barbara and Sam Hahn had been known as an affectionate couple with three children, a nice home and most things that money could buy: two cars, a country cottage, stocks and shares on deposit and long holidays abroad. Sam was a good looking, easy going man, Jewish on his father's side, so not really a Jew, but with leonine continental Jewish features, a long lean nose, cavernous cheeks, hooded eyes, thick curly hair. Sam had a sense of humour and a zest for life that drew all kinds of people to him. Above all, his charm was overwhelming. He and his attractive, clever wife had seemed to complement each other perfectly.

That the opinion of the critics had eventually been turned in favour of Frankie was almost entirely due to her good sense and personal charm. Despite her natural ebullience she was considerate, polite, even self-effacing. She never flaunted herself with Sam in front of his friends; she was seen not to be possessive. She cultivated, less successfully, good relations with his children and, more important, she was an excellent hostess for a man who liked to entertain, whereas Barbara had had little time or inclination for that kind of thing, and Sam's dinner parties had been few.

In time everyone's views gradually changed. It was wondered if, in retrospect, the marriage of Sam and Barbara had been so happy after all? If, somehow, its failure was due less to Sam than to Barbara, who was a very intense dedicated woman but now, with hindsight, appeared rather selfish.

What could be more natural than Sam seeking happiness in the arms of a warmer woman; one who showed affection, who was clearly deeply in love with him, yet cared for him more than Barbara by the interest she took in his career, his friends, the lavishness yet informality of her American-style hospitality?

For several days after the talk with Sarah Sam felt troubled, anxious about his wife. He wanted her to give up work and take care of herself; he rang the obstetrician to ask about amniocentesis. He had frequent talks with Sarah over the telephone. Naturally, he consulted Barbara.

'Always problems, Sam.' Barbara felt weary after a work day that had begun at seven. In order to greet a patient at that hour she had to be up by six, bathed, breakfasted, carefully made up and dressed in the elegant, tasteful way her patients expected of her. She saw her last private patient at twelve and spent the afternoon in the outpatient clinic of the psychiatric day hospital where she was a consultant. Returning at six she had a light supper and then patients from seven until ten, when she found Sam waiting on the doorstep. 'Where on earth is Frankie at this hour?'

'She's gone to Manchester for a conference. I wish she'd take it easy.'

'But she's not ill, just having a baby.'

She and Sam sat opposite each other in the drawing room with a drink – Barbara a welcome gin and French after a day when, unlike Sam, she could permit herself no alcohol. Sam had his usual whisky.

'But still she *is* old.'

Barbara laughed. 'I seem to remember I was quite "old" myself when I had Amanda.'

'Yes but you'd had two children. I mean a lot of older women have them.'

'Then why worry about Frankie?'

Sam told her what Sarah had said.

'Well Sarah's very keen, being on the obstetric firm. She's right in a way. There was no amniocentesis in my day nor foetal monitoring and very few induced labours, for which I'm grateful. Childbirth was a much more relaxed, easy affair. Today the whole purpose seems to worry the mothers rather than reassure them. I must say I never even considered our children being abnormal. Did you?'

'No, I must say I never did. How far off those days seem.' Sam looked thoughtful, drained his glass and got up, as one familiar in the house, to pour himself a fresh drink.

Looking at him, remembering those days, Barbara felt like a young woman again; the happy mother with three children, a husband who worked at a bank, and the hours she seemed to spend studying. She felt a nostalgic, sad renewal of love for Sam, for the man who had fathered her children, shared her life. How she wished that they were sitting here together as they sometimes used to, he in his chair, she in hers, chatting before they went to bed.

They had married young, she before her medical studies were completed, and Sam had just joined his uncle's firm of Merchant Bankers: Hahn, Peel, Simpson & Co. Sam, being a civilized sort of husband, had wanted his wife to graduate. His mother was a veterinary surgeon so he believed in careers for women. Barbara and Sam had spaced their children carefully to enable her to take the steps she wished up the medical ladder – years of hospital work: houseman, junior registrar, registrar, senior registrar. Long, onerous years when they had a permanent, live-in nanny. Sam had supported her all the time and endured the rather difficult period when, after deciding to specialize in psychiatric medicine, Barbara opted for psychoanalysis and underwent years of individual analysis, a totally new, ruthless, re-examination of herself.

Barbara had good reason to be grateful to Sam, appreciative of his warmth, understanding and love. The advent of Frankie, her importance in their life, the final break, came as such a shock that all her years of training were insufficient to cushion her. She went back for several months to her teacher, the man who had analysed her, for further support.

It was true that in the last ten years of their marriage their sex life had been perfunctory. Barbara had often wondered if Sam had affairs but she wouldn't ask: he wouldn't tell. She had no cause to feel jealous, though the lessening of the sexual bond did seem to coincide with a diminution in their mutual affection, though not esteem. But she supposed this was natural too. The children were growing up, she and Sam were both very absorbed in their work – he a director of the bank, she closeted for hours alone with her patients, often until late at night. They not infrequently took separate holidays, and two years before Sam told her about Frankie they had decided on separate bedrooms.

But there was still love, still fondness and, on Barbara's part, a deep need to grow old with the man she had married when she was only twenty-one.

Sam, his glass refilled, stood looking into the fire. He too seemed possessed of memories and, turning to gaze at Barbara, he thought what a fine looking woman she still was. She had adjusted well; her age sat easily upon her, as though she had absorbed it into her personality, so that one could never recall her being other than what she was now. Barbara had clear white skin with few lines, and fine features: a well moulded straight nose; a firm, though not unhumorous, mouth; clear, penetrating but sympathetic, dark blue eyes. She was tall and slender, with a well-moulded bust and shapely legs. Above all, Barbara exuded elegance from her black hair, flecked becomingly with white streaks, curling naturally around a shapely head, to the tips of her well-polished calf court shoes. Sam sighed. He didn't feel the wish to go back, but there was something natural and satisfactory, something relaxing about being here with Barbara, drinking and talking as they used to. Yet current problems pressed upon him. His brow furrowed.

'Well what do you think I should do?'

'About the amniocentesis? Leave it. Let Frankie have as happy and trouble-free a pregnancy as possible. Let her be guided by her obstetrician and her own natural good sense.'

28

Sam came over to Barbara and touched the top of her head with his lips.

'*You're* so full of natural good sense,' he said. 'A weight's been taken from my mind. I do want you and Frankie to be friends. You're part of my life.'

Barbara smiled and touched his hand with hers, not letting it linger.

CHAPTER TWO

FRANKIE BECAME PREGNANT IN THE winter months following
the holiday in Venice, and left her job at the bank three
months before the baby was due. The plan was for her to
return, but she doubted whether she would. Being Sam's wife
had its disadvantages. She knew she was very good at her job,
but people still seemed to think she was where she was because
of Sam. Financial journalism attracted her. Although she had
no journalistic experience, she was used to making reports in
readable form, to summarizing complicated financial and
economic documents.

Frankie threw herself into being pregnant with gusto. She
was naturally ebullient, entering into each task she undertook
with enthusiasm. The prospect of being a mother – the die
cast at last – absorbed her. It was true that in her younger days
Frankie had never coveted children. But marriage to Sam,
being part of him, changed that. At a deeper level it would
cement their relationship, strengthen the pair bond. She felt
well and her condition suited her. Mr Dickens was reassuring.
Amniocentesis was completely forgotten. The only thing
Frankie had feared was miscarrying, but once that danger was
past she spent a lot of time choosing decorations for the
nursery next to her bedroom, new furniture, carpets, curtains, baby accessories.

Unlike the house where Sam had lived all those years with
Barbara, the Primrose Hill house into which Sam and Barbara
moved after their marriage was modern and elongated, rather
than old and squat. It reached up like a miniature skyscraper
on four floors, standing among others like it at the top of the
hill, overlooking the hill itself, and the beautiful view of
London beyond. There was a tiny garden in front of the
house, and a patio at the back with metal tables and chairs, a
trellis and creeper.

Frankie was a modern woman and she liked bright modern things, Swedish style furniture, abstract paintings, white walls and woodwork, plenty of glass. The kitchen had every gadget that could possibly relieve her of the tedium of work and a well-stocked freezer full of ready-made pre-packed dishes. The large modern kitchen was on the ground floor of the house, sharing the patio with a small dining room which had doors opening on to it. There was also a door into the garage and a small utility room with a washing machine and dryer.

After she left the bank most of the day was taken up with preparations for the baby, antenatal classes run privately by a physiotherapist recommended by Mr Dickens, consultations with the decorator, phone calls to the store from which the baby furniture had been ordered.

Sam's active participation was encouraged, his advice sought. It was important for Sam to feel part of the act, Mr Dickens insisted, and Frankie agreed. Accordingly Sam was dragged along to inspect children's furniture, buy baby clothes and advise on whether modern disposable nappies were preferable to the old style terry towelling. He even went reluctantly to antenatal classes for fathers and was obliged to sit through explicit films of childbirth which he would much rather not have seen. It was distressing to discover how little he knew about small babies, their needs or their care. People deferred to him; expected him to know, but he didn't. Nowadays everything was different, the father's role, before birth and after, more active.

Yet despite it all, Sam enjoyed the whole thing. Above all he enjoyed cosseting Frankie, indulging her, watching her grow larger as the weeks went by. Having a baby would, after all, be fun. Frankie, like Barbara, was a good organizer; all that was required of him was to acquiesce in the experience and pay the bills.

Sam came home one day to find Frankie perched on top of a ladder painting a corner of the room intended for the nursery. As he stared at her aghast Frankie, her face covered with smudges of paint, her hair secured by a spotted bandana, took a few cautious steps down and sat on the top of the ladder,

31

grinning and wiping her face on the back of her hand. Frankie at six months pregnant was quite large and wore a loose blue smock over maternity jeans.

'It's quite all right, Sam. I'm not *ill*.'

'But you shouldn't be up there. What do we have a decorator for?'

'I found a little mark in the corner, so I gave it another going over.'

'You should have left it for him.'

'I like it Sam. I'm very careful, I assure you.'

Sam peremptorily held out a hand for hers, but Frankie sat stubbornly where she was, both arms propped on her knees, her chin resting on her knuckles.

'I have to finish what I was doing.'

'*Please* come down.'

'No.'

Sam stepped back, feeling really angry.

'Frankie you wanted the baby. Why can't you take care of yourself?'

'I do take care of myself. Besides, you wanted it too.'

Looking at her, Sam thought she had never looked lovelier, or maybe bonnier would be a more appropriate word. Her roundness suited her, and her face was vibrant as though an awareness of her vitality made her glow. He realized that Frankie, precious before, was even more precious since she had become pregnant, and was not so only for herself, but for their baby that she was carrying. The thought of the baby inside her, quite large now, made him feel really excited. To this extent they were both right: the pair bond, formed by their marriage, was being cemented. He smiled at her, his anger evaporating.

'I'll watch you while you finish it.'

Sam leaned back against the wall, folding his arms, and Frankie gingerly rose and climbed back again, steadying herself with one hand on the wall while the other wielded the brush.

Later they went out to dinner, Frankie gorgeously clad in a very loose robe, caftan style with a high neck, that floated and swirled about her as she walked. Stephen, the hairdresser in St John's Wood, had done her hair and, as she and Sam strolled into the Lemonia Restaurant in Regent's Park Road, where they were well known, hands loosely entwined, heads turned as Tony the proprietor came to greet them. It was a warm spring evening and Sam felt as though he had shed about twenty years in the last few months. To his intense surprise, the prospect of being a father again had rejuvenated him too.

'You were quite right about the baby. I feel our happiness is complete.'

'Not yet, darling, not until we have it.' Frankie chewed on her kalamaris softly fried in oil. She drank Perrier with her meal, having little inclination for alcohol.

'*We* have it?'

'Yes *we* are having it together.'

'Yes I know, I said I'd be there.'

'It is *our* experience, like we made it together.'

'That was nice too.'

'It's very different, Sam, isn't it?'

'From what?'

Sam knew what she meant and wished she hadn't asked the question. Frankie had talked much less frequently about Barbara since she'd been pregnant and in the very few times that they met — Tom's birthday, a celebration for Sarah's passing of her medical finals that summer — seemed much more at ease with her. Barbara's attitude to the prospect of Sam's new baby was cautious but, as there was nothing much she could do about it to change it, she accepted it with more grace than her children.

Sam, that night, had no thought for his first family, his mind on his second.

'You mustn't think about the past,' he said. 'Not tonight.'

'But I'm interested in what you think about attitudes, now and then. I'm not being morbid.'

'It's like a world away,' Sam said.

'But is it *better?*'

'Much better.'

'Why is it better?'

'Because one is more involved, as you say. Our attitudes in those days were so different, and so were our attitudes towards sex, the place of women and so on. They were bad days, really.'

'I think you're very enlightened,' Frankie said approvingly. 'Most men of your age wouldn't agree with you.'

'That's because they haven't got you,' Sam said. 'I think every male of fifty should be obliged to marry a younger woman.'

Frankie laughed, blushed and looked down at her plate. She was happy, very, but even she wondered about the one that was left behind. When she was fifty Sam would be nearly seventy. It was unlikely he'd be looking around then. Perhaps a second marriage to a younger woman *was* a good thing – the moral being that one should never marry a person too near one's own age. A lot of second marriages were very happy. This was a statistic. Well, she had foregone marriage and a young family in her twenties. She was getting her reward now. She looked up and reached for his hand. For tonight, this moment, their baby, their future, belonged to her and Sam and not Barbara.

It was probably only to be expected that, the fates being so tempted, Frankie should begin her labour in the middle of the night with a haemmorhage, be rushed to hospital before Mr Dickens could be called, and find herself delivered by Caesarian section by a National Health doctor who happened to be on duty when the ambulance brought her in. Mr Dickens didn't even arrive in time to make a single stitch. Sam sat the whole night in the waiting room of the hospital where Sarah, although qualified, had a house job. Only it was not her night on duty. She arrived at five in the morning, by which time the baby, a girl, was safe, asleep in her cot, and her mother asleep in a general ward into which she'd been wheeled after the operation.

'Everyone is absolutely fine,' Sarah said. 'The only thing that wasn't normal was the haemmorhage. It could happen to anybody.'

'It's because she was old,' Sam said. 'I should never have allowed her to have a baby.'

'Dad, I had a twenty-year old mother with the same complication the other day. Frankie was unlucky.'

'What a waste of money,' Sam said bitterly. 'All that care

34

and she has it on the National Health. Dickens should halve his bill.'

'Even Mr Dickens couldn't have foreseen everything. Sister says you can see Frankie, though she's asleep.'

Frankie lay in the corner of the ward, her bed enclosed by curtains. She was so pale that Sam thought she was dead, and a sob broke in his throat. There was a tube running from a bottle by the bed into her arm and a catheter from her body into another bottle hanging down by the side. Her pale fair hair clung damply to her forehead, and the white hospital gown wasn't at all like the frilly nightie she'd planned to receive Sam in, the joyous mother, her baby in her arms.

'She's all right Mr Hahn,' the Sister in charge of the ward said. 'She is conscious but sleeping. Your baby is in the prem unit, but that's just a precaution. I hear she's fine.'

'She's lovely,' Sarah said. 'I saw her. My half sister.'

Convulsively, Sam clasped Sarah's hand.

'She could have died.'

'Not in *this* hospital,' Sarah said proudly. 'We have one of the finest obstetric units in the country. You should have come here in the first place.'

'Next time perhaps?' Sister said encouragingly.

'Not likely,' Sam replied. 'There'll be no next time, Sister. One experience like this was enough. There was no trouble at all with my other children.'

He looked for a long time at Frankie and Sarah thought his gaze was reproachful.

When Frankie woke up Sam was sitting by her side reading the *Financial Times*. The staff had made much of him, brought him breakfast and plenty of coffee. He had been taken to see and admire his new six-pound daughter. The obstetric registrar had been and Mr Dickens had phoned. Frankie held out her hand and weakly clasped his.

'I boobed Sam.'

'Darling you couldn't help it.' Sam rose and sat gingerly on the bed beside her. 'We have a lovely daughter.'

'I know. Still, I'm sorry.' Tears rolled down Frankie's cheeks.

'That it's a girl? That's ridiculous.'

'No; that it didn't happen naturally. After all those classes . . .'

Sam grabbed a tissue from the locker and gently mopped her face.

'Sarah said it could happen to anyone. You were in the best hands. Our daughter is lovely and quite well, though they have her in the ward for premature babies just to keep an eye on her. Oh don't worry darling. She's full term but small. There was something about oxygen deprivation, but she's perfectly normal.'

At the words 'oxygen deprivation' Frankie grew hysterical and began to thrash about in the bed, the tubes wobbling alarmingly. Sam got up and, peering through the curtains, called for Sister. At that moment Barbara walked into the ward, a bunch of flowers in her hand. She couldn't have been more welcome, and Sam called out to her, beckoning her over.

Barbara, concerned at his anxious face, drew the curtain aside, peered at Frankie.

'She's hysterical,' Sam said.

'It's quite normal after a birth . . .' Barbara replied calmly.

'For God's sake will people stop saying everything is normal! Everything is not normal. The birth wasn't normal. I'm not normal, the baby . . .' Frankie started to cry so loudly that a patient could be heard calling for Sister who rushed in as Barbara, thrusting her flowers into Sam's arms, sat on the bed putting her hand over Frankie's.

'My dear, you're tired, you've had a bad experience, but everything *is* all right now. I'm a doctor and I checked. I wouldn't tell you a lie.'

The reassuring presence of Barbara, her soft authoritative voice, had their effect on Frankie who abruptly stopped crying, and stared at her through her tears. The woman she disliked, resented, was looking at her with such compassion, such kindness that Frankie squeezed the hand that held hers, the long, capable beringed hand that had so many times held Sam. But nothing physical between Sam and Barbara seemed imaginable now. Instead of a rival, an ex-wife, a woman who should, by rights, be jealous of her, Frankie thought she saw a friend, a doctor, a psychiatrist, a calm dispassionate woman, someone used to taking charge.

'Did you see the baby, Barbara?' she whispered, feeling like a little girl.

'No, but Sarah saw her. Sarah phoned me and told me what had happened. I felt I had to come, because I know how much the baby means to you and Sam. Besides, I was naturally concerned for you. Sarah met me in the hall and had just come from the prem unit. They only have the baby there as a precaution, but she is absolutely OK. So are you. Congratulations Frankie, and Sam . . .'

Barbara looked up and smiled at Sam who reached instinctively for her hand which she clasped, half shaking it as if aware of the awkwardness and intimacy of the gesture. She quickly let it fall and turned to Frankie.

'I hope you don't mind me coming. It's your moment not mine. I was anxious.'

Anxious for Sam, Frankie knew. But this was not a moment for jealousy. This was a moment to be grateful that she was surrounded by people who cared, to rejoice that she had a daughter who was alive and a husband who had certainly suffered more than she. She looked at Barbara. This woman's husband. Then, for the very first time, she felt doubt about what she'd done.

Postnatal blues they called it. Barbara said it sometimes happened with women when it was least expected; happy, extrovert types like Frankie. Usually the blues came a day or two after the birth, but with Frankie it was almost immediate. Barbara tried to explain to Sam that the trouble was certainly hormonal rather than psychological, though psychological factors sometimes precipitated it. No one really knew the cause. The abruptness of a Caesarian delivery sometimes had this sort of effect.

Frankie remained in hospital, removed to a private ward, and the baby flourished in the nursery for normal babies. Frankie couldn't feed the baby as had been planned. She didn't want to and so her ample milk supply was expressed to help the babies in the prem unit, and then stopped. When the time came for her to go home Frankie wept so much that it was decided to leave her where she was for the time being, but to take the baby home instead.

Sam didn't know what he would have done without Barbara. She organized the nurse for the baby, a live-in housekeeper for Sam and ensured, discreetly and without fuss, that the best treatment was available for Frankie. Above all she reassured Sam that Frankie's trouble would pass; that it was temporary and wouldn't last. She didn't go to see Frankie again because somehow she felt that her presence wasn't the right thing, probably hadn't been right at the time she went, though it was well meant. Being a psychiatrist didn't mean that one's own actions and behaviour were automatically as sensible or rational as they should be. She guessed Frankie would have had postnatal depression anyway, but seeing her hadn't helped. She'd really gone for Sam, to reassure herself he was all right.

The three weeks that Frankie remained in hospital meant that Barbara and Sam saw each other almost daily or talked on the phone. Sam needed her and her advice.

When the baby came home without Frankie it was almost impossible to be in the house without her, with a small creature he hadn't wanted, and now felt he didn't like. Supposing, just, that Frankie never got better? Seven pounds of uselessness as far as he was concerned. He hardly ever went to visit her, pleading work, but Barbara went daily, sometimes twice, cancelling patients. She would hold the baby in her arms, nursing it, loving it, hoping that she would see her, Barbara, as a surrogate mother because of the importance in subsequent development of those early first days of maternal love and care.

Sometimes the whiteness of the walls made her think she was out in the snow; they seemed to press in upon her like a snowdrift, suffocating, reminding her of the tightly-packed snow of the Colorado mountains when they went skiing near Denver in the winter. The room had pretty curtains with pink rosebuds and through the window was an attractive view of Hampstead Heath, many of the trees still thickly covered with leaves of brown, russet and green, though it was nearly December.

The furniture was white too and, though her counterpane was in the same pretty chintz as the curtains, so much white sickened her, reminding her of the hospital. It had been Sarah's room when she was a child. Now it was full of flowers, and a coloured television set sat at the foot of her bed, remotely controlled so that she could turn it on and off when she wished.

Frankie was encouraged to get up, watch TV, sit in her gown by the window. She had the run of the house if she wished. Most of the time she preferred to stay in bed looking at the ceiling, imagining painting it all sorts of different colours to get rid of the white. One day she would draw forests and a river running through the middle like the Canadian Rockies to which her parents had taken her as a child. She dreamt often about her childhood and asked that her mother be sent for to look after her, but her mother was dead, her father remarried. Sam explained it all and then she remembered, wondering how she could possibly ever have forgotten. Who could ever forget the day they told her her mother was dead and would never come home?

The decision to take Frankie to Barbara's house had been Frankie's. It was the last thing Barbara wanted, or Sam if it came to that. They were both shocked by the suggestion, each trying to hide it for Frankie's sake. The hospital had said that, as Frankie's trouble was now properly the care of a psychiatrist, she should be moved to one specializing in the treatment of postnatal depression. But Frankie hadn't wanted to go to another hospital, her own home, or a nursing home. Frankie was adamant about wanting to stay where she was. When it was pointed out to her quite firmly that the hospital would be needing her bed for someone else, she sent for Barbara and, to the surprise of everyone concerned, asked if she could go to her.

Barbara thought that Frankie was trying to sort out something about her and her link with Sam's past, so she agreed; but she was doubtful. The family were appalled. Sarah thought it was quite the wrong thing and Tom wrote that his mother was exposing herself when she had been hurt enough.

Barbara had to rise above it all – calm everyone, assure them that she didn't mind, above all try genuinely to welcome Frankie. She didn't want Sam to sleep at the house, but told him he must regard it as a sort of private clinic and not as his former home. He came as a visitor every day. Barbara called in a colleague specializing in cases of this kind to treat Frankie and gradually, patiently, he tried to discover the reasons for

Frankie's totally unexpected breakdown and help her to recover.

Meanwhile the baby, Zoë, flourished. Zoë had been the name of Frankie's mother and, although she didn't wish to see her baby, she insisted upon her having the name she wanted.

In the weeks after she left the hospital Frankie was taken back to her earliest memories of childhood and slowly returned to the present, past her time at school, at university, her earlier successes in college, her visit to England, her ambition to stay there and work and finally her meeting with Sam. She stuck after the meeting with Sam and would go no further.

'The only one who can talk to her about Sam is you,' Barbara's psychiatric colleague told her. 'I think this whole thing is guilt about you and Sam.'

Barbara said she'd wondered about that too.

'The trouble is,' John Vaughan went on, 'you don't quite fit into the category of the spurned wife. You're too well balanced, too nice. If you were less nice it would be easier for her. I think in a way she identifies you with her mother, which is why she wanted to be here. She's guilty about hurting her mother. Maybe she thought she was responsible for her mother's death, and her own maternity has brought this collapse about. You'll have to talk to her, Barbara. The rest is up to you.'

John Vaughan didn't guess it – Barbara's detachment fooled everyone – but Barbara thought this was one of the most difficult periods of her life. The rest, including the loss of Sam, had been easy. Despite all her experience she didn't feel equipped to deal with a girl who had taken her husband from her, however mixed her motivation. But she did; she had to. If she refused, her vulnerability would be apparent to everyone, and Barbara needed her mask.

Frankie was lying, as usual, staring at the ceiling when Barbara went in. She certainly thought Frankie looked better. There was more colour to her cheeks and her naturally beautiful hair, which had grown lustreless, had begun to shine again. Frankie, unsmiling, turned to look at her as she entered. The distressing thing about the normally ebullient Frankie now was that now she hardly ever smiled.

'What a beastly day it is.' Barbara drew up a chair, crossing her long legs in front of her, taking a cigarette from the pack she carried with her, placing it in its holder. 'Does it distress you if I smoke?'

'Of course not. It's your house.'

'Still, if you didn't like it I wouldn't do it.'

Frankie gave a gesture of irritation and sharply looked away.

'I do irritate you, don't I Frankie? You wish I weren't here? You wish you were in this house with Sam, and I was dead . . . or had never been born.'

'Yes, I wish you'd never existed.' Frankie looked at Barbara almost with despair. 'Does that shock you? Or do you know it all?' Yet having said it, she felt better and watched Barbara form her reply.

'I know that you're very disturbed about me and Sam and it's quite unnecessary. I've come to help you try and work it out because like that you'll get better. You'll want to live again and be with your daughter. Now you want to die like your mother.'

'That's what Dr Vaughan said.'

'Well that's what I think too. You feel you've failed horribly after such a perfect pregnancy, by having a Caesarian section, rejecting your baby. You've let Sam down.'

'You were such a perfect mother. No trouble with the children, combining them with your career, looking after Sam . . .'

'I wasn't perfect at all, although I suspect you've always thought that about me.'

'You gave in so gracefully about Sam.'

'I didn't give in "gracefully" as a matter of fact. I was naturally very distressed at the time.'

'Sam said you were wonderful.'

'Sam certainly helped make *you* feel guilty.' Barbara finished her cigarette and stubbed it out, neatly and fastidiously as she did everything, with precision. Then she folded her arms and gazed at Frankie. 'I accepted that Sam loved someone else. Whatever I did I couldn't get him back, scream, storm, plead. Maybe I'd lost Sam's love years before. We led very separate lives. I think we took each other for granted, or I expected he felt about me as I did about him. I mean I'd

41

never have dreamt of leaving him.' Frankie's pale face flushed.
Barbara hadn't meant to get in a crack and went quickly on:
'You find that men and women are very different as they get
older. A woman is quite happy to settle down, men – some
men – want fresh stimulation.'

'How do I know Sam will settle down with me. Especially
after this?' Frankie looked not so much dejected now as
worried.

'You feel you've let him down again, don't you? "Especially
after this".'

'After what?'

'You've been ill; your illness is partly organic. I think
you're getting better.'

Frankie leaned back against the pillows, closed her eyes and
sighed. 'I'm not.'

But Frankie was. From the day of her talk with Barbara
Frankie became more alert, more interested, she ate better.
The ceiling no longer obsessed her so much and she felt the
need to get out of bed. One day she dressed and came
downstairs. Barbara found her in the drawing room after
she'd finished an afternoon consultation.

'I hope you don't mind?' Frankie plucked nervously at her
jeans. She had fastened her hair back in a pony tail and,
wearing a warm polo-necked sweater, looked very young and
girlish. Yet soon she would be thirty-eight years old.

'Of course I don't mind.'

'This *is* Sam's house after all.'

'You could say that.' There was no rebuke in Barbara's
tone, 'although we bought it together.'

'Sorry, that was a horrible thing to say Barbara.'

'Be horrible.' Barbara sat in a chair facing Frankie, who
was tucked up in a corner of the sofa. 'I'll be horrible back.'

'Is that the psychological thing to do?'

'It could help us both. There is obviously a lot of tension
between us. I didn't really want you here, for instance. I did
it to please Sam.'

'You want Sam to think you're great?'

'Exactly, warm and understanding.' Barbara's smile was
ironic. Frankie was neither a patient, nor a friend. Telling her

42

the truth was not easy. Frankie's role was unique and Barbara's attitude now had to be too. She hadn't been quite in this situation ever before.

'You made Sam feel guilty too.'

'Maybe I did it deliberately.'

'You're not perfect at all, are you?' Frankie looked as though something new had suddenly struck her.

'On the contrary, I'm very devious.'

'You know all the answers.'

'Exactly.'

'You could have been a pain in the neck to Sam.'

'To any man. No one has wanted to marry me since Sam and I were divorced.'

'Don't you have a lover?'

'No.'

'Don't you want one?'

Barbara felt the need to smoke again, but resisted. This girl had to use her for her own therapy.

'I didn't want one at first. Losing a husband, even in the sense that he's still around, is a kind of bereavement. I didn't want physical sex just for the sake of it. I wouldn't mind the company of an interesting attractive man.'

'Like Sam?'

'Well, yes, if you like. Like Sam.'

'Would you go back to Sam if he were free?'

'No. You can't go back in things like this. I'm actually quite happy as I am and I do have colleagues who ask me to dinner; but no one regular.'

'You make me feel sorry for you.' Frankie wriggled in her sofa. 'Sorry again.'

'Isn't it time you thought about your baby?'

Frankie looked surprised.

'You think about me and Sam, but do you think about Zoë? Frankly in all this I think she's the most important. She's lovely. Even if she weren't, she's yours. Your responsibility.'

Frankie got up from the sofa and fled abruptly from the room. She didn't want to think about responsibility. Barbara wondered if she would ever have her house to herself again. How long would this unwelcome guest be here?

But everything that happened to her these days seemed to make Frankie think. She was aware of the positive act of thinking and wanting to know. She was aware of coming to life again, of wanting to live. After this talk she felt more on a level with Barbara, more equal. Barbara wasn't perfect after all.

Two days later she let herself out of the house and went home. Sam found her there when he came in, playing with the baby. She looked rather nervous, not at ease, but glad to be there. The nurse had been absolutely dumbfounded, knowing who she was from the photographs in the house. She wanted to rush out and ring up Mr Hahn or Dr Hahn, but Mrs Hahn seemed quite normal. She held out her arms and the nurse gingerly gave her baby Zoë, now three months old. Her mother had only seen her twice. It did seem a pity, the nurse thought.

Sam got down on the floor beside Frankie and together they looked at her swinging in a contraption suspended from the ceiling, her arms out, laughing with glee.

'Isn't she adorable, Frankie?'

'She's rather nice.'

Frankie didn't sound as though she was talking about her own flesh and blood; but Sam thought it was a start. He looked at the nurse who smiled encouragingly, meaningfully indicating Frankie with a half wink as though they were dealing with someone who had escaped from a lunatic asylum. Sam thought Frankie was better. He hadn't seen her like this for weeks. He put his arms round her and kissed her on the mouth.

'Let's go and have a drink,' he said.

In the days that followed sometimes Frankie was sorry she had come home; but mostly she was glad. She continued to see Dr Vaughan at his consulting rooms and he encouraged her about the positive aspects in what she'd done. She'd made up her own mind to go home; she'd accepted her baby.

'I don't love her though,' Frankie said. 'She's very hard to love.'

'That's natural.' Dr Vaughan always sat half in shadow, his face, like his manner, somehow ephemeral and obscure.

'It doesn't sound very natural to me.'

'Well it's not unusual, let's put it like that.'

'Everyone says she's a very beautiful baby, and I don't even like her.'

'Why did you go home then?'

'To be with Sam.'

'You're improving.'

And on another day:

'Sam and I made love for the first time last night, since Zoë was born.'

'I notice you call her Zoë. Usually it's "The Baby".'

'Yes Zoë. But what about Sam and me making love?'

'That's good.'

'It wasn't very good. I was rather afraid. Please don't tell me it's natural, Dr Vaughan.'

Dr Vaughan didn't reply.

'I haven't started on the Pill yet and we didn't use any precautions. Wouldn't it be a damn silly thing to get pregnant again?' As he still didn't reply she went on: 'I'd have an abortion again.'

'You had one before?'

'I had one in my twenties.'

'You never told me about that.'

'I didn't think it was important.'

'You did. You thought it was important to keep it from me.'

'You psychiatrists talk an awful lot of rubbish.'

'Still, I'd like you to think about the abortion.'

'What about it?'

'How you felt about it.'

'Nothing. I was glad to get rid of it.'

Frankie looked into the shadow that was Dr Vaughan and burst into tears.

The birth of Sam and Barbara's first grandchild had been utterly eclipsed by what happened to Frankie. Three weeks after Zoë was born Tom's wife Natalie had a daughter, Clare. Clare, like Zoë, was a full-term baby but weighed over eight pounds at birth, after an easy, almost ideal, labour. Natalie was twenty-two, almost the perfect age, physically and emotionally, to be a mother.

Tom had decided to be a soldier quite late in life. Sam had hoped that after university he might go into the law or the bank. But Tom first joined the Army, going through Sandhurst as a graduate, and only later on transferred to the Marines. His decision coincided with his father's announcement he was marrying another woman, though at the time no one read any significance into it. Now, at twenty-six, he was a captain fully launched on a career full of promise.

The bond between Barbara and Tom had always been a very strong one despite the fact that, by temperament, they were so different. Tom was a big extrovert chap, games loving, friendly and uncomplicated. He was not insensitive, but he had never been tormented by doubts about who he was or what he should do. Every step in his life so far had seemed to lead logically and inevitably to the next. He had many of Barbara's physical features, the only one of her children to share with her those intensely blue, luminous eyes.

Tom had bitterly resented his father's behaviour towards his mother. His home had always been important to him, not so much a refuge as a symbol of stability and security. The kind of background that stood one in good stead, which one would like to recapture in one's own family life.

In Natalie he had chosen a woman quite unlike Barbara, with no intellectual pretensions at all. She was fun loving like Tom, her father a wealthy gentleman farmer with a large property in Wiltshire. Natalie had even done a London season, various courses in cookery and dressmaking which both she and her parents felt would help to make her the ideal wife and mother. She was a very fresh, pretty, likeable person and popular.

There was only one thing that troubled Natalie about Tom. She wasn't keen on the life of the wife of a member of the Armed Forces. She was a county type, and a man keen on the land, farming and horses, would have suited her down to the ground.

Yet when she met Tom at a friend's party – he was still at Sandhurst – no doubt occurred in her mind as she fell instantly in love. The doubt came later.

But here she was, loving Tom and content to be his wife.

46

One day, though, she hoped she'd get him back into civilian life – a market garden, perhaps, or a farm. Until then, she not only bided her time but played the part of a dutiful, loving wife to perfection. It was known she didn't like Service life – moving about in quarters or rented accommodation – but not how much, although there were occasional rows between her and Tom which most people, Barbara included, considered normal, understandable.

Natalie had arrived in Tom's life before the breakup of his parents' marriage and she gave him the support that he so badly needed, the comfort that his mother, who couldn't comfort him then, used to give.

'It really is quite disgraceful that Dad had that woman here after her baby was born. How can someone be so insensitive?' Tom looked rather aggressively at his mother – almost as though he blamed her.

' "That woman" is called Francesca, or Frankie as she prefers to be known. She is your father's wife and the mother of a new daughter. She was very ill and she needed somewhere to go.'

'But why couldn't she have gone to her own home?'

'She didn't want to and she needed to be looked after.'

'Then a nursing home?'

'She didn't want to go to one. She felt a need to be here and in fact it was very suitable for her, very successful. She didn't trouble me and I didn't trouble her. She had Sarah's old room. She almost grew well on her own.'

Ever since the family had arrived Barbara knew that the subject of Frankie would pop up quite soon. In fact it was at dinner on their first night of the Christmas holiday that Tom voiced his feelings. Tom now sat where Sam used to sit, a reassuring bulk, as Sam had been, someone on whom she felt she could perhaps one day lean. She smiled at him.

'I do agree with Tom, Mum,' Sarah said. 'I think Dad and Frankie put on you. Then I understand she just left, without saying goodbye.'

Barbara shrugged and sipped her wine, a very very pale green Moselle that she had taken from the good stock in the cellar which Sam had built up, and abandoned, though he helped himself to it from time to time. She felt peaceful and at ease, loving her family around her.

'It was of no consequence to me how she left, as long as she was better, and I understand she is quite fit again. We'll soon see anyway. They'll be here for lunch on Christmas day.'

'With the baby?' The normally equable Natalie looked slightly outraged.

'Naturally. Zoë, after all, is Clare's aunt.'

Everyone laughed at the thought except Amanda Hahn, who had taken very little part in the table conversation. Until Sam left home she had been a very normal sort of girl, unremarkable except that she was tall for her age and had striking features that, even then, made her much better looking than her sister – pale, tall, dark, at fourteen she had looked seventeen. Now, at seventeen, she could pass for twenty.

From the age of eleven Amanda had been at boarding school in Somerset. She hadn't wanted to go, but Sarah and Tom had boarded and it was considered sensible with parents who both worked, especially a very busy mother who didn't keep conventional hours. Amanda seemed to resent the consulting room and its secrets more than the others, because she clung to her mother and showed a great need for love. Barbara had sent her away with extreme reluctance.

Amanda bottled up her feelings about the divorce, although she blamed her father and refused to meet Frankie for ages. Now they scarcely ever met and her reaction to the baby had been negative. During the conversation at dinner she seemed ill-at-ease and nervous. Barbara, looking anxiously at her, felt she must devote more of her time to Amanda this holiday.

'Amanda darling aren't you hungry?' Her mother looked at her plate. 'You've hardly touched a thing.'

'I think I'm getting the 'flu, Mummy. May I go up to my room?'

Amanda half drew back her chair and her mother looked at her with concern.

'Oh not at Christmas?'

'I'll take her temperature.' Sarah rose. 'I thought she looked a bit peaky.'

'I thought it was the strain of mock A-levels.'

Amanda had arrived home a few days before from her expensive boarding school in Somerset.

'Go with her darling and I'll come up later.'

48

Barbara looked thoughtfully after them as Natalie began stacking the plates and Tom refilled the glasses with red wine for the cheese.

'How do Amanda and Frankie get on?' Tom asked casually, sitting down and studying the cheeseboard.

'They hardly ever see each other. I must say not too well. It's not Frankie's fault – she does her best. In fact she's awfully nice to her – Frankie is, as a matter of fact, a very nice woman. I wish you'd all realize that.'

'Oh Mother you're just too magnanimous.' Tom cut himself a slice of cheese. 'I have never heard you say one nasty thing about Frankie. It's not natural.'

'Don't forget your mother is a psychiatrist.' Natalie smiled in the rather diffident way she had when the cleverness of Tom's mother was even touched on. Which, unfortunately, it invariably was when Natalie was around. It seemed a sort of compulsive topic of conversation. Compared to Barbara, Natalie couldn't help feeling gauche, uneducated and inferior even though Barbara did her very best to make her feel at ease. But professional women were quite outside Natalie's experience, for the kind of women she had grown up among were all rather well heeled, often with equine tastes, and perfectly at home in the woman's place that their class had been accustomed to for generations. Barbara was very fond of Natalie and considered her an ideal wife for Tom – the sort of pretty, sporty, extrovert girl he liked, full of robust good sense. Nevertheless these frequent allusions to her profession – at least one a day when Natalie was around – irritated her.

'My dearest Natalie, outside my consulting room I hope I am normal and like anyone else. I don't say I expect to be abnormal in my consulting room, but I have to take on an extra dimension. I think it's my experience of life as a woman, not a psychiatrist, that makes me react to Frankie as I do. I was personally very sorry for her when she had such a hard time giving birth to Zoë and then fell into a state of profound depression. It happens to the most surprising people and I must say I would never have thought it would happen to Frankie. But she's perfectly all right now.'

'She had a course of drugs.' Sarah slipped into her place and immediately drained her glass. 'They always work.

49

Mummy had a shrink brought in, needless to say, but the drugs would have worked anyway.'

Barbara didn't reply but drew the cheeseboard towards her and carefully inspected the selection as though it had her entire attention. For many years she had employed a daily housekeeper who, knowing her taste, did all her shopping for her.

'I can't understand why you and Sarah are always getting at each other about medicine.' Tom poured himself more wine. 'You'd think you each had a completely different profession.'

'It's a matter of interpretation.' Barbara kept her tone light. 'It's quite true that Frankie did respond very well to hormonal and anti-depressant drugs and I don't know how I or John Vaughan, who came to see her, helped her.'

'Probably not much,' Sarah said. 'Might I have the cheese?' She smiled brightly at her mother.

Sarah's hostility to psychiatry was unfortunate, her mother thought, as they all stacked the dishes in the washing machine before gathering in the drawing room to watch TV. She thought it might make her a less able doctor than she would otherwise have been, less flexible.

Sam was not analytical either. Psychiatry bored him as much as it bored Sarah; it was as mysterious to him as it was to Tom. She had had little time for the financial world or the trivial talk among the wives at business lunches and dinners. Barbara's apologies were almost always sent, and Sam was accustomed to going alone. In time Barbara's non-appearance at all sorts of functions was automatic. No wonder Sam was seen as a desirable man about town. No wonder she had lost him.

Still, with it all and what it had led to, Barbara didn't regret all the dinners and lunches, parties and functions she hadn't attended. All she regretted, very much, with her children around her and Christmas only two days away, was losing Sam. How nice it would have been to celebrate Clare all together. How very nice it would be – in her heart of hearts she admitted it – if there hadn't been the complication of Frankie and Zoë too. She didn't imagine she would ever be able to think of them as one family.

The dishes stacked in the washing-up machine for Linda to

50

do the next day, they returned to the drawing room and Tom turned on the nine o'clock News. They were just in time. He motioned for his mother to sit next to him on the sofa. As she sat down, smiling at him, he took her hand, gently warming it inside his.

CHAPTER THREE

SAM SAT AT THE PLACE he had traditionally occupied for
Christmas dinner and, seeing him there, jocular, merry rather
than tipsy, with a gold crown on his head, carving the turkey,
it was difficult to believe that anything untoward had occurred
in the Hahn family in recent years. It looked just like a
normal, happy family Christmas; with crackers and champagne, a great fir tree glowing with many coloured lights
brightly behind the table. And so it was, in a sense, except
that Sam could now be said to preside over two families rather
than one: his two sets of children, his two wives, one past one
present – like the ghosts in *A Christmas Carol* – his newly
acquired granddaughter who slumbered upstairs next to her
infant niece.

Sarah was due to go on duty at the hospital that night, as
she had been the previous night but, after sleeping late, she'd
arrived in time for lunch. Linda, the obliging daily, had come
up to help Barbara who had spent the morning in the kitchen,
as she always did, preparing the family feast. Natalie looked
after the baby and helped with household chores, and tall,
pale-faced Amanda who, everyone agreed, was at a difficult
adolescent age, drifted aimlessly round the house with a
duster.

As family occasions went the party, though not an uproar-
ious success, was not a disaster although, in Sarah's opinion,
her mother had stretched herself too far in inviting Sam, his
wife and baby. The laughter was often a little forced, the
gaiety almost too gay as everyone tried their desperate best to
have a good time. It was the first time Sam and Frankie had
been included in the Christmas celebrations since he'd left
home. Barbara was trying very hard to do Sam's bidding and
make a friend of her successor, to make her feel welcome, one
of the family. Looking at her, poised and regal opposite Sam,

in her traditional place, elegantly dressed, it appeared that she was making a very good job of it. Strain, if there was strain, didn't show.

But the strain showed on Frankie. She looked very beautiful, her gold, casually waving hair framing a face that was, if anything, a little over-made up, with perhaps a touch too much rouge and overaccentuated mascara. She wore a white woollen suit and a dark blue blouse with a mandarin style collar, a heavy gold pendant from a gold chain hanging round her neck resting on her breast. Yet she said little and ate little, her face animated, as though from a desire to please; her eyes, perhaps a more truthful indication of her real feelings, listless. They seemed to rest almost perpetually on Barbara and then, with a brief spark of animation, to flick to Sam and back to Barbara, as though to reassure herself that no signs of affection passed between them.

Sam seemed oblivious to hidden tensions. The talk almost invariably, and perhaps unfortunately given the circumstances, dwelt on cheerful family Christmasses in the past. Christmasses spent mostly at home, but there had been two in the Swiss Alps, combined with a winter sports holiday, and one in Tangier to get away from the cold. That was the year Amanda developed appendicitis and the family had to stay an extra week until she recovered. Oh yes and then there was the one . . .

Frankie suddenly put her head on one side and leaned back in her chair, her face turned towards the door. Sam paused at the moment of reminiscence and looked at her.

'I thought I heard one of the babies crying.' She gazed back at him apologetically.

Natalie threw her napkin on the table and jumped up. 'I'll go and see.'

'I'll come with you.' Frankie got up too and, as the women made for the door, Sam, unperturbed, continued:

'Do you remember that marvellous Christmas in Devon? Now what was the name of the place . . .'

Thankfully, Frankie shut the door behind her and followed the younger woman upstairs.

The babies were in Sarah's room, the one occupied for so many weeks by Frankie. Frankie looked around, as though seeing a familiar home, and sat down on the chintz counter-

53

paned bed. The crying baby was Clare, though Zoë had stirred and looked on the verge of wakening.

'She's hungry,' Natalie said after inspecting her nappy. 'She wants some Christmas dinner too.'

Natalie expertly took the baby in her arms and sat down in a chair, unbuttoning her dress and drawing out a heavy breast. Frankie instinctively averted her eyes and, after introducing the nipple into the baby's mouth, Natalie sat back comfortably, and eased off her shoes.

'You can look if you want. I do it quite freely in public, well, you know, discreetly, but I don't think it's anything to be ashamed of.'

'Oh I don't either.' Frankie blushed and then stared almost hypnotically at the bulging breast, as though trying to show she was broadminded too.

'I see you have a bottle for Zoë,' Natalie looked at the impedimenta, the machine for heating the bottle, the various bibs and cloths on the dressing table. 'Did you not want to feed her?'

'I couldn't. I was ill.'

'I'm sorry. I forgot.' Natalie, with the happy glazed look in her eyes of the nursing mother, shifted to an even more comfortable position, and put her feet on the stool by the dressing table. 'Yes I heard you had a very hard time.'

The two women had, naturally, met over the years, but didn't know each other very well. This was possibly their first conversation alone. There were fifteen years between them, the same gap as between Barbara and Frankie and, except for their membership of the Hahn family, they had nothing in common.

'I don't suppose Tom approves.' Frankie felt more at ease now and sat comfortably back on the bed, cushioning herself on the pillows.

'Approves of what?' Natalie's eyes were cautious. 'Of the baby?'

'Of me – *and* the baby.'

'I think he's sorry his parents broke up. Who wouldn't be?'

'Naturally.'

'But I don't think he disapproves of you, particularly. He hasn't said so.'

Natalie studied the baby's head, avoiding Frankie's eyes. In fact Tom had said so long and often. Almost every time he saw his father and his new wife it changed his mood for the day.

'Barbara was very good to me when I was ill.'

Frankie had long ago decided there was not much to Natalie – not much in the upper storey anyway – and she had to be encouraged out of her shell. But because of her insecurity about her place in the family she was anxious to pump her.

'She's amazing really.'

'Do you think she . . .' Frankie sat upright on the bed again, groping for the right word. 'Cares?'

'Cares? About what?'

'Well . . .'

'If you mean that you took Sam away from her, I would think the answer is "yes". But, being the kind of woman she is, with her devotion to her work, she has overcome it, made the best of it.'

'I meant about the baby.' Frankie corrected herself quickly. 'Anyway, I didn't take Sam away from her. He wanted to leave her. He said their marriage was dead.'

'They still get on well,' Natalie said disbelievingly. 'Very well, I think.'

'That's because they're divorced. It's easier to be friends. It wasn't like that before.'

Natalie didn't reply. She knew what Tom would say about that. According to him, his parents had always appeared a harmonious couple.

As she changed the baby to the other breast, Frankie watched it pumping milk from its mother unable, she felt, to keep the envy from her eyes. They had had to take pints away from her because she had so much. Maybe if they had forced her to feed the baby she would care more about her now.

As though by a magic transference of thought Zoë stirred and Frankie got up to test the temperature of the bottle in the warmer, sprinkling a little of the milk on the back of her hand. Then she put the bottle back, sat down again and stared at Zoë.

'Did you love your baby immediately?'

Natalie looked at her in amazement.

'Of course. The moment she was laid on my tummy.'

'I had a Caesarian. It was all going to be so perfect, with

55

Sam beside me, and then it all went wrong . . .' Frankie searched for a handkerchief in her cardigan pocket and wiped her eyes.

Natalie, remembering what she had heard about the depression, felt her amazement change to alarm. 'That certainly wasn't your fault,' she said gently. 'It could happen to anyone.'

'Oh I *wish* people would stop saying that! It happened to *me. That's* what's important! I so wanted this baby . . . and now.' Frankie blew her nose. 'Now I wish I hadn't had her,' she gulped with a noise like a spurting geyser, the tears starting to stream down her face. With the baby in her arms at her breast, tugging away, Natalie didn't know what to do and looked helplessly on, wishing Tom were here. But Frankie rushed on. 'I find that . . . it's very difficult to love her. I want to, but all I can remember is what happened to me when I had her, those awful months of depression when I didn't want to get out of bed. Now I've got her for the rest of my life.'

'I'm very sorry.' Natalie, practical Natalie, for the first time began to feel some stirrings of sympathy for a woman whom, because of Tom, she had very much disliked, although her stepmother-in-law had never done anything to her to fuel this feeling. On the contrary, Frankie always put herself out to be nice to her and Tom.

'It's altered me and Sam too,' Frankie said through a fresh deluge of tears. 'He knows how I feel and he's resentful because he never wanted the baby. I made him. He was quite happy with his family, he said, and with me. When we were first married I said I couldn't stand children. I never had any maternal feelings at all.'

'Then what made you change your mind, for goodness' sake?' Natalie, who had never been troubled by such labyrinthine decisions – and didn't ever expect she would – eased the baby away from her breast and, popping her over one shoulder, began to wind her, gently rubbing her back.

'Barbara.'

'*Barbara?*' Natalie accidentally gave Clare an extra hard pat and the baby's loud burp sounded like indignation.

'Barbara and the family. They were all so close.'

'Oh that! I thought Barbara had talked you into having a baby.'

56

'No, but I resented the hold the family had on Sam. He's forever up here with Barbara, or on the phone talking about them. I thought that as they were all so old he wouldn't. But the family seem to obsess Sam. Either the family or Barbara. I'm not quite sure which. Both, maybe.'

'That's because of the Jewish streak. They're very family minded. His father had ten brothers and sisters.'

'Oh I know that! Some relation or other is always on the phone, though thank goodness most of them seem to live in America. Well anyway all this family thing got me down. I decided I wanted, needed, a baby to bring me close to Sam. If Sam and I had a family he'd have less time for the other one, who didn't need him. So much anyway.'

'Still, it's a funny reason to have a baby you didn't really want.' Natalie felt a bit out of her depth. 'No wonder you can't really love it.'

'But I *thought* I would love it.' Frankie's voice had a pathetic, hopeless note. 'Besides, there's nothing like a baby to create a bond, is there?'

Remembering the look on Tom's face as Clare was born Natalie knew what she meant. She and Tom wanted a large family too. They were family minded, like Sam. Natalie had plans to be pregnant as soon as Clare was weaned. The only thing that threatened a really happy stable family life was Tom's career. He could be sent to any part of the world at a moment's notice. She wished he were a farmer like her father. There was always some fly in the ointment, always some reason to wish things other than they were. However, at least she hadn't Frankie's problems.

Frankie's monologue was uninterrupted: 'You see I was an only child and I had a very unhappy family life. My mother and father didn't get on and then she died in a road accident. My father married again and I didn't like my stepmother. My father sent me to boarding school and that was effectively the end of family life for me. I grew up feeling very rootless. I decided to be a career girl and forget about families.'

Zoë was now awake, looking at her mother. She really was a pretty baby, Natalie thought, prettier than Clare; petite, dark haired and with a skin like Sam's. Tom had his mother's white skin, her delicate looks, though his frame was robust.

57

Zoë gurgled smilingly at her mother, and it was hard to imagine that anybody couldn't love her.

'I think she wants her feed.' Natalie jerked her head in Zoë's direction.

'Oh.' Frankie got up, took the bottle from the warmer and awkwardly removed Zoë from her carrycot. Natalie could tell by the way she handled the baby that she resented her or, more accurately, that she was unused to her. She sat her rather stiffly in her lap to feed her instead of cuddling her, and it was obvious that Zoë was uncomfortable. Frankie stared dejectedly at Natalie.

'I've made a mess of things, haven't I?'

'You're making a mess of feeding that baby.' Natalie put the replete Clare back in her cot and went over to Frankie. 'The way she's sitting makes it hard for her to digest. Look, take her in your arms like this . . .'

Natalie made a move but Frankie jerked Zoë protectively away, forcing the teat out of the baby's mouth. Zoë started to cry and fell backwards on the bed.

At that moment Clare, who needed changing after her feed, started to bawl and Natalie looked helplessly round while Frankie clumsily tried to right the baby, at one moment holding her upside down.

'You'll hurt her!' Natalie cried. 'You've really *no* idea, have you?'

'I wish you'd mind your own business and stay out of this!' Frankie grasped Zoë and stuck the teat of the bottle savagely into her mouth. The baby struggled and went red in the face while Natalie stood looking ready to pounce.

Suddenly vomit started to come out of Zoë's mouth and her eyes rolled as she gagged.

'You'll choke her!' Natalie pounced at last, wrenching the baby from Frankie's arms. Frankie rose and clawed for the baby while Natalie backed away, falling over her own baby's cot. Now both babies were screaming, Frankie distraught and Natalie tearful herself.

'What on earth is going on?'

Tom appeared in the doorway, pipe in mouth, a golden crown similar to that worn by Sam balanced precariously on his head.

'I'm just trying to help with the baby,' Natalie appealed to him.

'She's interfering.'

Frankie tried to grab Zoë back but Natalie held on to her. Now Frankie started to scream.

'Give me back my baby!'

Tom quickly and deftly removed the child from Natalie and restored it to its mother.

'For God's sake let her have her child if that's what she wants.'

The whole thing was too much for Zoë who sicked all over her mother's beautiful blue blouse, the one that reflected the colour of her eyes, while Clare, not to be outdone, let out an enormous bawl and flung her arms in the air.

'For Christ's sake can't somebody *do* something? What is going on here?' Tom's raised voice joined in the general clamour and Barbara swiftly slipped past him, gently took the baby from Frankie's arms, wiped its mouth and, one arm keeping tight hold of Zoë, put a free arm round Frankie and sat her down on the bed again.

'Tom, go and get Sarah, will you?'

The calm authoritative voice had the desired effect of restoring order. Tom went smartly out of the door, Natalie quickly retrieved her baby from its cot and started to change her nappy and Barbara, still clasping Zoë, sat down beside Frankie and put a cool hand over her hot one.

'Sarah will lend you one of her blouses.'

Frankie stared at Barbara, shook her head and once again burst into tears.

'I can't cope, I can't cope.' She rubbed the balls of her palms into her eyes, smearing her mascara, making runnels through the peachy colour of her makeup so that her face resembled the delta of a river when the rains came.

Sarah, Tom behind her, came through the door and Barbara handed Zoë to her.

'I think she needs feeding. You finish that and I'll help Frankie to change. Can we take one of your blouses? You're more of a size.'

'Of course.' Sarah, trained like her mother to coping with emergencies, neatly fielded Zoë as Barbara went over to her wardrobe and began sorting through the garments hanging there.

'This will do.' She held one up against Frankie who now stood in the middle of the room, dazed, tearful, but more controlled. 'Now come with me.'

'I want to *know* what's going on?' Tom insisted, his golden crown looking particularly foolish hanging lopsidedly over one ear.

'Oh Tom, do be sensible. Two young women with two young babies?' Barbara looked at him as though that statement was self-explanatory. 'Now go back downstairs and talk to your father and Amanda, there's a dear.'

'I want to help Natalie.' Tom stubbornly looked at his wife who, flushed, the buttons of her dress in disarray, was nevertheless briskly powdering the bottom of Clare, who had taken her turn to be spreadeagled on the bed.

'Right, Tom, you stay with Natalie and Sarah, and I'll take Frankie to my room.'

Barbara, clasping the blouse to her chest, firmly pushed Frankie in front of her and closed the door gently after them, saying, 'Let's go to my room where there's a bit of peace.' Smilingly, she preceded Frankie along the corridor, opening the door and standing back for her to pass through.

Frankie had never been in Barbara's bedroom, which was a large room, comfortably furnished, overlooking the Heath. In all her five weeks in the house she had never seen it, normally meeting Barbara either in her own bedroom or downstairs. There was something about the fact that it was Barbara's bedroom that made her nervous, that had always made her too timid to knock on the door. Like Barbara it seemed rather too forbidding, that white door at the end of the corridor well away from the stairs and the rest of the house.

'Now let's take this blouse off.' Frankie stood inertly as Barbara swiftly undid the buttons of the blouse and helped her out of it. 'Would you like to wash? You smell a bit of sick. I tell you what, take the blouse into the bathroom and you'll find everything you need.'

Frankie nodded and took the garment, glad to be by herself. She examined her face in the mirror. She looked terrible. Then she took off her brassiere, which too smelled of sick, and looked at her bare bosom, half the size of Natalie's. She squeezed her nipples but nothing came out. Useless. She was useless. She sat on the edge of the bath, leaned over and was sick. Then she slumped on to the floor and started to weep.

Immediately Barbara was beside her, kneeling, pressing a damp cloth to her face.

'You poor girl. I shouldn't have left you. You don't feel well at all do you?'

'I feel terrible. I can't feed my baby.'

'Never mind about that now.' Barbara gently took her by the arm and pulled her up. It was as though she was quite unaware, or at least unconcerned, that Frankie was naked from the waist up.

'There. I'll give you a quick sponge and you can slip into my gown and lie on my bed.' Barbara put in the plug, drew the water, tested it with her fingers as though Frankie too were a baby and, with lightning dexterity, dampened a fresh cloth and sponged Frankie's breasts. Quickly she dried her, powdered her and helped her into a robe which hung on the back of her door. 'Now, you rinse your face, dear.'

But Frankie couldn't move, so Barbara did that for her, carefully washing off the makeup, round the eyes, erasing the white runnels that dissected the peach complexion. She patted Frankie's face with a towel, combed her hair and led her gently back into her bedroom, where she turned back the sheets of the bed.

'If you'd like to take off your skirt and things and get into that . . .'

Frankie looked at the bed, the sheets so invitingly turned back, and flopped on to it. Barbara gently removed her skirt then pushed her between the sheets and covered her up. After swiftly changing into another dress, because her own smelt of vomit, and seeing to her makeup, Barbara crept quietly out of the room.

Downstairs the gathering – complete now with Sarah and Natalie because Barbara had been away a long time – awaiting her were standing or sitting in various expectant attitudes of solemnity, except for Amanda who had gone for a walk.

'Did Frankie have too much to drink?' Sam enquired, helping himself to some more.

'I think she hardly drank at all. I didn't see her.'

61

'Or ate,' Sarah added. 'It was awfully silly of you to bring her here, Dad.'

'But she's been here before. She stayed here five weeks and was at dinner here two weeks ago.'

'But not with all the family.'

'But she *wanted* to come.' Sam looked pained.

Barbara sat down and took a cigarette from an onyx box that stood on a small table. She lit it forgetting about the holder.

'I think she was quite happy, but something happened in the nursery.' She looked at Natalie who, composed now and buttoned up, was drinking coffee.

'Well we had a chat about babies, and . . .' Natalie looked at Tom, 'not only that.'

'Tell them,' Tom said firmly, joining his father in refreshing his glass.

'Well I think Frankie really *is* very unhappy. She says she can't love the baby. She wonders how you all feel about her. She is really quite distressed, I'd say. She poured things out so much I could hardly take in half she said.'

'For God's sake we've been married over three years,' Sam said as if he were talking about a lifetime. 'You'd have thought she would have adjusted by now. As for the baby . . .' He sat down heavily, next to Barbara on the sofa, his drink in his hand, and crossed his legs. 'Yes, the baby was a mistake, much as I love her, and I do.'

'Rather a big one to make, Dad.'

'What can I do about it now?' Sam looked sharply at Tom who had made the remark. 'We can't give her away.'

'I don't know why not if you don't want her.'

'Oh don't be so absurd!' Sarah burst out. 'We're talking about a human being not a dog.'

'There's such a thing as adoption,' Tom insisted.

'Tom, you're talking about your half sister! What has got into *you*?' His mother's tone reminded him of his schooldays.

'Well, Mum,' Tom moved to the fire, either to warm himself or to take a stance. 'This baby *is* a disaster. She can't help it, poor lamb, but she has made Frankie ill, and Dad doesn't seem very happy. In fact he never wanted a baby as far as I know. Why he ever wanted to marry Frankie I can't imagine.'

'Tom, please don't go into all that again . . .' Barbara looked anxiously at him but Tom ignored her.

'Or rather I do know. He wanted a bit of sex. Well he got it. With knobs on.'

Barbara stubbed out her cigarette without her usual delicacy, and stood up facing her son.

'Tom, I won't have you talking to Sam like that here. I know you're not a child but if you go on like this I'll have to ask you to leave the room. Your father could have got "a bit of sex" elsewhere, as he probably did from time to time.' Sam stared at her, but Barbara hurried on. 'He was and is genuinely in love with Frankie. It was time for a change, a new marriage. . .'

'I don't know how *you* can speak like this, Mother . . .'

'Now don't interrupt me. But we can't put the clock back, whatever the reasons. I am deeply devoted to your father and I always will be. I believe he is to me. The fact is he is married to another woman and he now has a child by her. They are having difficulties not infrequently experienced by couples with a new baby . . .'

'Look at Natalie . . .'

'That is entirely different. Natalie is a good deal younger than Frankie. She is not married to a much older man with a grown family, with an ex-wife who is still part of the picture. Sometimes I think I did the wrong thing remaining in the picture. I think now, with the benefit of hindsight – though I had my doubts at the time – that Frankie should never have come here to recuperate. Also I should probably not have asked her today. The tensions are too much for both of us. I am trying too hard and so is she. That's why she broke down today. Sam, I think that . . .' Barbara turned to Sam who, with his head in his hands, was staring at the floor. 'I think, Sam, that you and Frankie must lead your own lives. I must stay right out of it.'

'But we have to see each other . . .'

'And we have to talk . . . as partners who are divorced but also parents have to do. Maybe the relationship has been too close.'

'But I need your help with Frankie. I can't cope with her on my own. I think she's sick. What woman wants a baby and then can't love it?' Sam looked appealingly at Barbara, his hands extended. 'I ask you?'

'It does happen, Dad.' Sarah, looking as unhappy as everyone else, intervened from the corner where she'd been sitting. 'It is to do with the hormones. She needs to see her gynaecologist. It isn't just psychological.' Sarah glanced at her mother, who still had her eyes on Sam wondering if he was the next who was going to burst into tears. His chin seemed to quiver.

'I think it *is* psychological,' Natalie said, unexpectedly and firmly. She was sitting on the arm of a chair holding the hand of Tom who still stood by the fire. 'I don't know a lot about it except what I read in women's magazines; but Frankie was on about being an only child and not being loved by her father. I guess,' she looked anxiously at Sam and then at Tom as though wondering if she dare go on, 'I guess she found a sort of father . . . in Tom's father, in Sam.' Natalie gulped and stopped, her face very red. 'It just came to me now. Maybe I shouldn't have said it.'

'I'm glad you did,' Sam looked at her and smiled. 'Maybe it explains a lot of things.'

He got up and went towards the door. Barbara called after him that he should stay and not disturb Frankie, but he looked back at her, his face regretful.

'Perhaps you're right Barbara, we have our separate lives to lead.'

Sam shut the door and Barbara started to tremble, quickly taking a fresh cigarette which shook in her hands as she lit it.

'What a lovely day,' Tom said. 'Another Christmas to remember.'

Inside the room where he had spent so many years with Barbara Sam stood for a long time looking at the sleeping form of his young wife. The room still smelt slightly of vomit and suddenly his heart ached with love and compassion for her. He took off his shoes and jacket and lay down beside her, clasping her body between his hands. He was excited to find that she was naked, except for her pants and tights. Gently he caressed her breasts and, as she stirred and murmured, he brushed her lips with his. She opened her eyes, blinking in the dim light of the unlit room.

'Sam?'

'Who else my darling?'

'How did you get in here?'

'Through the door.'

'Oh, Sam,' as memory came rushing back Frankie held him and he squeezed her so tightly that her breasts ached. 'Oh Sam I *am* hopeless. What shall we do?'

'We'll make it together,' Sam said.

'But I can't cope. Compared to Barbara . . .'

'The shadow of Barbara is always between you and me.'

'But you need her. We both do.'

'Not if she comes between us. We'll be better without her.'

'She was wonderful today, coping.'

'She is trained to do that kind of thing, Frankie,' Sam released her and moved away so that there was a space between them. 'Can't you realize that I love *you*. I'm married to *you*. I want *you*. I want *our* baby. My other life is part of my life, but it is separate. I didn't realize how much it interfered with us – me always ringing Barbara, always chatting to her about this and that, always asking her opinion, her advice.'

'But Barbara is your wife . . .'

'*Was*. She is the mother of my children but she is not my wife any more. Stop trying to make it with Barbara. You're younger, prettier, you have a baby . . . but you'll destroy yourself if you're always competing. There is nothing to compete with. She has her own life, her career. I think she always preferred it to me.'

'It *would* be nice to be friends with her, though.'

Sam lay on his back and sighed. He wished that someone had shown him a crystal ball and warned him about the future. That way, he might never have married at all. But would he have taken any notice? He felt a movement and there, above him, Frankie's face hovered like an apparition. He clasped her and drew her down to him, measuring his lips against hers. Her naked breasts swung somewhere about his left shoulder and a nipple touched his neck. He reached down and drew her pants and tights over her buttocks in a practised sweep, and then he leaned right over and stretched his body alongside hers. Unfastening his trousers, he kicked them off

65

with his pants and, as she lay spreadeagled on the bed, he mounted her and entered her, humping his back like a rutting stag.

Later, when they had gone, Barbara knew what had happened in the bed. They had taken no trouble to disguise it, and the crumpled sheets and stained dried semen neither disgusted nor surprised her. She removed the old sheets and put them in the wash and then she put fresh ones on.

She felt rather anesthetized about the events of the day – certainly not a Christmas Day to include in the happy family memories. One to forget. She wondered if they would ever have the family round the table again, and thought how stupid it had been to try. Stupid, especially of her.

If she was honest she guessed she was competing with Frankie – trying to show Sam what a mistake he'd made by putting herself in a good light. She had succeeded beyond her wildest dreams; but there was no satisfaction, no victory.

She knew that Sarah and Tom blamed her for inviting Sam and Frankie. They thought she should have known better. And, in the light of what had happened, she felt she should have too. Still, Frankie had got a bit of her own back by making love to Sam in her bed. They probably did it intentionally. She wondered if it had given them particular enjoyment. Barbara tried to imagine Sam in the act of sex – an act which he and she had performed thousands of times together; but now it was difficult. He had, indeed, passed on to another woman.

Barbara sighed and lit a cigarette, carefully fitting it into a No 3 size holder and gazing at it severely for being so addictive, as though she blamed the holder, not herself. She put on her glasses, looked at the clock by the side of her bed and reached for a volume of Freud. It was one o'clock. Sarah had gone back to the hospital, Amanda was asleep in her room. Tom and Natalie were asleep – well, probably that, or making love or talking or reading like her – in Tom's old room next to hers.

Barbara turned the pages, looking for her place. She made a practice of trying to read the complete works of Freud in the course of a five-year period, give or take a year. Then when

66

she finished she started again. Barbara read Freud as devout people read the Bible going back, like them, to the founder of her religion. Like them she took comfort from his works, as well as instruction, perpetually learning something new or relearning something forgotten.

But though her religion was not a belief in God, an intangible infinite Being, it was still something as intangible, as infinite; something that sceptics, too, doubted: the subconscious. She believed, no, she knew with more certainty than many a deist has in the existence of God, that in healthy and unhealthy people alike, human behaviour, aspirations and misery sprang from motivations that were often not part of the conscious mechanism, an irrationality that was seldom known, understood, or appreciated.

Barbara had spent most of her professional life trying to unravel part of the mystery that was the unconscious; trying to do so to help and to heal: to help well people to know themselves and sick ones to get better. Obviously the best subject, both to begin with and with which to continue, was herself. For countless years she had been on just such a voyage of self-discovery.

Yet, in a way that she could still not explain, though she knew it happened in the lives of other analysts too, this voyage had its unsatisfactory aspects. It was full of low valleys and high mountains, and one of the pitfalls was that those nearest to you often reacted against what you were trying to do. Her family were singularly unsympathetic to analysis, and its practice had often prevented her from seeing with her own eyes what was going on under her nose.

She knew now that Sam had had affairs, yet she had never considered it, and the shock of Frankie had hit her as hard as anyone else. The fact of the disintegration of her own marriage, and the reasons for it, had completely escaped her notice, making her wonder if she lived in a world of fantasy like some of her patients. Her idolized son had become a soldier, the last profession Barbara would have wanted for him, and her rather difficult elder daughter, although following her into the medical profession, affected to despise psychology. Then there was Amanda who was a problem – a young girl yet detached and withdrawn, who had scarcely seemed to figure in the day's activities, a nagging worry to

Barbara like a small pain that might grow into a bigger one or a disease that might spread.

Having spent a lifetime trying to help others it was very galling to realize, at the age of fifty-one, that one had cast one's family adrift in alien seas far from home, far from where they were most needed.

Barbara found her place at last but couldn't digest what she was reading. Her mind was too far away. She removed her glasses, put down her book and switched off the light.

Even in the bosom of her family, she realized now that for many years she had felt alone, and probably always would.

CHAPTER FOUR

FRANKIE LEANED OVER THE YELLOW plastic bath tub and pushed the little yellow duck in front of Zoë who bent forward and tried to grasp it, squealing with delight. Behind the tub the nanny, June, a gentle hand on the baby's back, a towel in her other hand, looked on with approval. The duck hit the edge of the tub and rebounded back again and Zoë clasped it in her tiny hands and tried to put it in her mouth. Frankie beamed at June who arranged the warm towel on her lap and reached for Zoë.

'No let me do it,' Frankie said and tenderly lifted her daughter from the water and laid her on June's lap. June wrapped the baby in the towel, then Frankie took her in her arms and gently began rubbing her as she went over to the low chair by the baby basket with its collection of nappies, pins, cotton wool buds and bottles of various kinds: oil, cream, powder and baby lotion. Frankie sat down on the chair, continuing to dry Zoë, under the armpits, over the tummy and between her chubby little legs.

'There, who's a pretty girl?'

Zoë, wreathed in smiles, gurgled and put a hand up to her mother's cheek as though welcoming the compliment. Frankie kissed the hand and held the baby close to her, before lowering her again and powdering her all over.

June got up and emptied the bath in the basin in the corner of the nursery, wiped it and put it back in its stand. Frankie took a clean soft terry towelling nappy from the basket and, spreading it on her lap, started to fold it over Zoë's lower parts with a good deal more skill than she'd shown some weeks before. June passed her a pin which Frankie put in her mouth until she had completed the operation, then secured it carefully into the corners of the nappy which met in the middle of the baby's tummy. She leaned over and implanted

69

a kiss on Zoë's chest, then reached for the nightgown which June held out for her and slipped it over the baby's head. She took a brush from the basket, fluffing up the soft dark hair, and kissed her again.

'Don't babies smell lovely?' Frankie sighed with happiness and, getting up, took Zoë over to her cot and tucked her in. 'I hoped Sam would be home in time to see her while she was awake. He does adore her.'

She stood for a few seconds looking at the baby in the cot, who gazed back at her with wide-awake, serious eyes, a message of love momentarily passing between them. Zoë, as though contented by the message from her mother, gave a big yawn and her eyelids flickered.

On the other side of the room June was tidying up, collecting the used nappies from a bucket and putting the pots and bottles neatly back in their basket.

June, more than anyone, was thrilled by the progress Frankie had made since Christmas when she'd come back in such a state after the lunch at Dr Hahn's. The next day Sam had called Mr Dickens, who came to see Frankie at home and put her on a new course of pills. Sam had asked if she should continue to see Dr Vaughan, and they discussed the business of Christmas Day over sixteen year old malt whisky in the sitting room.

'She just needs pills,' Mr Dickens had said. 'Her hormones are still all to pot.'

'But how long will it take?'

Mr Dickens had been guarded.

'Sometimes days, weeks or even months.' He looked at Sam. 'I've never known it take years, if that's what you're worried about. Medicine is advancing all the time.'

'But what about the psychiatry?'

'Well that's your first wife isn't it?' Mr Dickens had scratched his head. 'I don't go a lot for it myself. Now that *can* take years, and it makes the patient so dependent on the psychiatrist. I never think it's a very healthy relationship even if it achieves anything, and one never knows. I scarcely ever send my patients to a shrink. No need. Besides,' Mr Dickens looked again at Sam, 'is it necessary to see all that much of your first wife? It can't have a very good effect on Mrs Hahn. I was against her going there in the first place. Not natural.'

'But Barbara is a professional woman. She was very good.'

'Oh I know that; but from what I can tell your present wife doesn't like her. She's afraid of her. Why she should have wanted to go to her house, I don't know.'

'Dr Vaughan said she felt guilty.'

'Well I'm sure he knows what he's doing and who am I to question motives?' Mr Dickens' professionalism did him credit and he finished his drink. It was Boxing Day and he had no other calls, but he would put in a very big bill for this visit, coming out at Christmas. He guessed Sam could afford it. 'Look Mr Hahn. I don't know much about psychiatry or psychoanalysis, but I know an awful lot about women. It's my job. It's not easy for an older woman to have a baby, yet even then your wife was unlucky. I can see there are a lot of complicating factors, and I do think your links with your ex-wife are one of them. I appreciate you must have some contacts because of your family; but they're all grown up aren't they?'

Sam nodded. 'Except for my younger daughter who's still at school.'

'Well then keep the meetings to the minimum. Make them business-like. Above all, please don't take Mrs Hahn there for some time again. You'll see, in no time she'll be as right as rain. Now have this prescription made up as soon as you can. There are quite a lot of chemists open today. I passed one in Regent's Park Road on my way up.'

Mr Dickens gave Sam the prescription written on heavy vellum headed notepaper – which was expensive too.

And Mr Dickens was right. June, who knew all about what that eminent and fashionable gynaecologist had said, had seen Frankie progress daily almost from that very moment, obediently taking her pills three times a day together with plenty of vitamins and long walks on Primrose Hill, or around Regent's Park. She rose late and she went to bed early and, gradually, after sitting in the nursery watching June take care of Zoë, she began to look after her herself, although June was always there.

Sam kept all his family away from the house and entertaining down to a minimum. He asked Barbara to phone him at the bank.

It was not the sort of life that Sam had planned when he took on a new, younger wife. Being in love again at fifty plus had been accompanied by a resurgence in his sexual powers, though they had never been given a chance to lie dormant for long. But, accompanied by love, it was much better than mere lust.

For two years they'd had a wonderfully happy time, the best time Sam could recall in his whole life. Being older seemed to give him that extra dimension of experience missing in his younger days. Then an awful shadow had intervened, but now it was clearing again.

Sam got out of his car and opened the garage door, returned and drove it in behind Frankie's small Fiat. He closed the garage and went into the kitchen from which good smells emanated. Frankie was at the stove, a plastic apron round her waist, stirring a pot.

'This is a very domestic scene.' Sam put his hat and briefcase on the table and, going up to her, he kissed her on the side of her face.

'*The* woman's place.' Frankie turned round, her unmade-up face shiny with the heat, and kissed him full on the lips. For a moment they clung together, eyes closed.

'That was a lovely welcome home,' Sam said, as they drew apart. 'How was your day darling?'

'Lovely, how was yours?'

'OK.' Sam went over to the kitchen dresser and poured himself a whisky. 'Will you have wine darling?'

'Not just yet.' Frankie went on busily stirring. She wore jeans and a large fisherman's knit sweater, rope soled shoes on her feet. 'I've just put Zoë to bed, so I'm a little behind.'

'And how is my precious girl?' Sam sat down on the bench that ran alongside the table and sipped his drink.

'Which precious girl? Me or Zoë?'

'Both,' Sam said disguising his emotion by taking another sip of his whisky. 'Both precious.'

'June and I took Zoë for a walk in the park, fed the ducks, the usual thing.'

Frankie added seasoning and tasted the casserole. She hardly ever froze food these days, preferring to buy everything and cook it fresh on the day. Only the day she described wasn't the usual thing, or hadn't been until very recently. What made it now so nice was that it *was* unusual. 'I'm really getting used to being a mum. I don't think I'll want to go back to work.'

'Don't then.' Sam put his arm round Frankie, who had come to sit next to him on the bench.

'Well I must.'

'But why?'

'I think I'll go to seed.'

'That's ridiculous, why you've just got . . .' Sam stopped and hid his face in the wide rim of his glass.

'Well? Is that what you were going to say Sam? I've just got well again?'

Sam put his glass down on the table and loosened his tie. He had in fact had rather a difficult day at work and was tired. The economic climate meant that firms of all sizes were going bankrupt, but the larger ones caused a private bank trouble because they reneged on their debts. A particularly large machinery business in which Sam had been closely involved as an adviser had that day called in a receiver. Sam put his hand over Frankie's.

'Yes, darling. You've just got well again, really well, after five months of hell.'

'We'll say three. I started to get better after Christmas. I guess that was the watershed.'

Sam shivered. 'Please don't talk about that again. What a ghastly day.'

'Still it served its purpose.' Frankie got up and, taking some handfuls of rice from a tin, threw them into boiling water. 'I was in a terrible muddled state before then. I didn't know myself. I wasn't sure of you . . .'

'Not sure of me?' Sam looked at her incredulously. 'It was silly to feel like that.'

'Still I did, I always had. I knew how much you saw of Barbara, the things you asked her, talked about . . .'

'Well I don't now,' Sam said firmly. 'I have not seen hide nor hair of her since that day.'

'But you talk.'

'On the phone only, about business or the children. Amanda is not doing well at school and Barbara is worried about her. She failed all her mock A-levels. It's a pity because she's a bright girl and we hoped she'd follow Sarah to university. But I don't want to burden you with that.'

'But I do want to share it, Sam.' Frankie went to the fridge and got out a bottle of white wine which was half empty. She poured herself a glass. 'I want to share your life, your children, but not Barbara.'

'You never had to share Barbara.'

'I was afraid of her, of her power over you.'

'Well she had none.'

'I know that now.'

'Oh how?'

'When we made love in her bed. It was like you were fucking the past.'

Frankie sat down beside him again and once more Sam encircled her waist with his arm.

'What a very curious thing to say.'

'Well it wasn't tender, it was violent. Screwing me in Barbara's bed. I enjoyed it.'

'Did you now?' Sam raised his eyebrows. 'Well we won't do it again — not there anyway.'

'We've done it — you've done it, and that's what matters.'

The feeling of security had come to Frankie because Sam had made love to her in Barbara's bed, like a dog defiling its own doorstep. He would, Frankie had reasoned, hardly do that in the bed of a woman he still loved. Although not inexperienced in life, Frankie still made the mistake of confusing lust with love. She failed to understand the elemental, primitive nature of a man to whom the act of sex was not necessarily an indication of real affection, wherever it was performed.

'Well I'm glad if it makes you happy, and I don't suppose Barbara minds either.' Sam relished the pleasure on her face.

'Do you think she noticed?'

'Probably not.' Sam looked thoughtful. 'Barbara, despite her undoubted cleverness and intuition, never seems to notice anything going on under her nose. I've often wondered about it. Anyway, my love, don't let's talk about her, but about you going back to work or rather not going. I'd much rather you stayed at home, enjoying yourself, getting to know Zoë.'

'I know her and I love her. The love didn't come to me in

a great flash, but gradually as I got used to touching her, did things with her, played with her . . .'

'I know that. That's how love usually does come, getting to know someone gradually by being accustomed to them. Getting to know a baby, even your own, is like getting to know someone strange.'

'I was frightened at first, Sam.'

His hand closed over hers. 'Now you're not, and you're a wonderful mother, as I knew you would be.'

'Do you think we should have another baby, Sam?'

'Oh God,' Sam raised his eyes to the ceiling. 'Please let's do one thing at a time.'

'I'd hate her to be the only one.'

'She's not the only one. She's one of four.'

'But there's a big age difference.'

'Darling, we'll think about it, but not now. Something's burning,' Sam said, hoping to change the subject.

And so the good days went on, each one blending harmoniously into the next as far as Frankie was concerned. Having June enabled her to see as much of Zoë as she wanted, but did not tie her down. She was able to spend days in town and meet friends, join Sam at night for dinner or the theatre. Gradually they recaptured the days of their courtship and early marriage again, except that now it was better because they had a bond.

But by Easter Frankie was showing signs of restlessness and was looking for work. She discussed this with her friend Poppy, a girl-about-town who worked on a magazine.

Poppy and Frankie had met in the States when they were both at Harvard Business School, both the same age, both unmarried and career minded. Poppy was still unmarried and, to a certain extent, had succeeded in her career.

'At nearly forty one gives up the idea of marriage,' she said to Frankie when they met in their favourite Italian restaurant in Blandford Street, as they habitually did to have lunch and gossip.

'Why?'

'Because who is there?'

'I thought you were never very keen on marriage anyway.'

'I wasn't and I'm not. I'd like someone though. Seeing you with Sam and Zoë sometimes makes me jealous.'

Poppy was a woman of medium height with brown hair casually swept back from a pale, intelligent face. Frankie was very fond of Poppy, with whom she had shared a flat before her marriage. Poppy had been in at the very beginning of the affair with Sam, being involved with a married man herself, so she knew all about these things and was a mine of information. At the time she had informed Frankie that Sam would never marry her, but Frankie was charitable and never reminded her of this. It had amazed and mortified Poppy when Sam did propose.

Although Poppy had been genuinely glad about Sam and Frankie it was only natural that she regretted losing a companion who had shared the miseries and frustrations which even the enlightened, liberated women of the late 1970s had to admit to, if only to themselves.

Poppy attracted married men because she was discreet, undemanding and liked sex. She was also used to all those mysterious phone calls at unusual hours with messages that seemed like a wartime code. Like every other normal girl, Poppy would have liked a boyfriend with whom she could have an open relationship even if it didn't lead to marriage; but, like many another normal girl of her age – the difficult years of the thirties – she wasn't successful. Those who were available didn't attract her, and those who did were married.

Frankie was full of magnanimity when she was with Poppy and listened to her with endless sympathy and patience. She felt she owed her because Poppy had been so kind to her about Sam, so supportive, and had acted as a witness at the Registry Office wedding. So she listened to Poppy's thoughts and feelings about marriage, and the lack of it, and assured her that she wouldn't wish on anyone what she had gone through even though she adored Sam and the baby. All this cheered Poppy up and she was even more cheered by the knowledge that Frankie was beginning to feel bored and wanted a job.

'What kind of job?'

'Anything?'

'Would you go back to the bank?'

'No, not that bank, not with Sam. I was glad to get away anyway. If I went back it would look like nepotism.'

'That's true.' Poppy stirred her coffee and looked at her watch. Besides her masses of brown hair she had a rather freckled skin, a snub nose and large friendly green eyes. She was popular and had a lot of girlfriends. She was out every night with never a moment to spare, unless it was for her lover, when he could spare one for her.

'I thought financial journalism.'

'But you can't write.'

'I can,' Frankie said indignantly. 'I've written masses of reports.'

'It's not the same thing.'

Poppy was a journalist and she knew. In addition she was jealous of her territory. She hadn't spent nearly twenty years grinding away at a career to become senior features writer on a magazine just to have someone, who was really an economist, rush in and do the same thing without the effort, angling and waiting about Poppy had endured. 'Why don't you write about your experience?' Poppy said after giving the matter more thought.

'What experience?'

'The depression? Your feelings about the baby?'

'I couldn't.' Frankie shuddered and the whole thing seemed to come back again. 'I'll have to stick to money.'

Poppy decided to be magnanimous after seeing the expression on Frankie's face. Now that Frankie's normal good looks had been restored Poppy realized how much she had suffered. At one time she had looked like a wraith, her lovely hair – not quite as lovely as Poppy's, in her opinion, but lovely still – quite lustreless. Her curvaceous figure – certainly a factor in attracting Sam because it made her so sexy – had almost whittled down to that of a skeleton and her eyes had been vague when they had not mirrored a desperate expression resembling total despair. At one time Poppy, who had visited her frequently, had been seriously alarmed about Frankie.

But Frankie looked lovely now – like one of the healthy, vigorous All-American girls who got up to such larks in *Charlie's Angels*. Frankie wore Cossack trousers scooped into high leather boots and a Fairisle sweater topped by a camel coat. Her hair was secured at the top by a band, and her skin glowed with vitality that owed nothing to makeup.

'I'll ask my editor if she can think of something. She's a good sort. I must fly now.'

Poppy was always flying, figuratively speaking, taking off to exciting places where, Frankie imagined, there was a lot going on, plenty of action and drinking. Poppy could drink like a fish, and did, with no obvious ill-effects; she was always in a hurry, which made people tend to feel grateful that she could fit them in at all.

'How's Barbara by the way?' Poppy reached for the bill after saying she wanted to pay for the meal. Frankie shuddered again and that nervous, almost frightened, expression once more clouded those clear, healthy eyes.

'Barbara is something we don't talk about.'

At times Poppy wondered if Frankie really and truly was better. There seemed to be so many things that still bothered her, questions that one couldn't ask.

Jennifer Littlejohn was an unusual patient. She was a tall, vigorous, vivacious woman who gave an impression of strength. Yet for much of her life she had been prey to anxiety, feelings that varied from vague, free floating unease to acute attacks of panic. For Jennifer a pain, some muscular spasm or gastric disturbance was never interpreted as something simple, but a presage of disaster – cancer, heart trouble or fatal paralysis. Her bedside table was like the counter of a chemist's shop.

Jennifer's symptoms were sometimes so real that she became actually ill, but their cause lay in her mind not her body. Over the years Barbara had tried, by explanations, interpretation and counselling to guide her away from this morbid preoccupation with herself, and adopt an approach to life that was actually equivalent to the one she presented to the world. To some extent Jennifer had improved. Her anxiety was less fierce, her hypochondriasis more controlled. In many respects Jennifer managed very well, but she was not helped by marriage to an extrovert, insensitive man; nor by the fact that this marriage was childless. Jennifer automatically retreated into herself to cope with this unbearable domestic situation.

Barbara encouraged Jennifer as far as she could to stand on her own feet and make her own decisions, to achieve some kind of balance instead of seeing her life as a leap from one panic station to the next.

Barbara was a very important person in Jennifer's life, a woman whom she admired, with whom she identified. She felt it would be nice to be like Barbara – capable, controlled, knowledgeable. This feeling, which almost amounted to one of love, had been anticipated by Freud who called the irrational preoccupation of the patient with the analyst 'transference'. Through transference a patient was supposed to work through their symptoms in the analytic situation, where the analyst occupied the role of the father or mother figure.

But Jennifer's feelings were even more complicated. As Barbara was a woman very similar to her, in age, social class and the way she dressed, she tended to compete with her – to try and be better groomed, more elegant than Barbara, to impress her with her obvious wealth and range of social contacts. She even bought clothes with the express object of impressing Barbara, rather than her husband. Barbara was an over-riding presence, constantly in her mind. Barbara, well aware of these tactics and complications, ploughed on trying to unravel the multiplicity of emotions that accounted for Jennifer being, *au fond*, a very unhappy, unfulfilled woman.

Today Jennifer was talking about her attempts to find out about John's suspected new mistress, her interception of his phone calls, her inspection of his underwear. Barbara wished she could free this woman from her neurotic obsession with her husband, but so far she had failed. Sometimes Barbara wondered if John actually was the man his wife made him out to be, or if this Don Juan creature was also a projection of her wish fulfilment.

'In a way I'd prefer something I knew, *someone* I knew. Why doesn't he tell me her name . . .' Jennifer went on with the same old story that Barbara had heard so many times before; even the details hardly varied. It was very sad, but it was an obsession, whether based on reality or not, that Barbara with all her skills found hard to unlock. She sat in her chair with her back to the window, her head resting on the palm of her hand, studying Jennifer's tormented face. Yet

79

her mind was not as concentrated as it should be on what Jennifer was saying.

It was three months since she'd seen Sam and she missed him. Coming to terms with losing Sam was as difficult for her, she realized now, as it was for poor Jennifer to take the mat from under John. Thinking, too, about John, her patient's husband, reminded her, as it had in the past, how unsuspecting she had been about Sam. There was a John Littlejohn under her roof and she had never known. Was knowledge better than ignorance? Did it shield you from the sort of shock she'd had about Sam? If John Littlejohn told Jennifer he was leaving her, would she be surprised?

Yet Sam had never really separated in this way before so completely. His obvious guilt about Frankie and the divorce had made him hang around, and it had suited her. There had never been a complete break with Sam, but there was now.

Somehow she had thought that the children and the house and all they shared would keep them attached forever. That they could remain on affectionate terms even when he was married to someone else. It had seemed for a time that they could. She was used to being needed by him even if she was no longer a wife to him. Sam with problems was better than no Sam at all.

'There's someone ringing at your door, Dr Hahn.'

Barbara started guiltily. She had broken the cardinal rule of therapy, that of listening carefully to the patient despite the number of times one had heard what he, or she, was saying before. She had let her own thoughts and feelings intervene between her and her attention to Jennifer Littlejohn.

'The bell?' she glanced at her watch. It was too early for the next appointment, but she pressed the switch which would admit the patient into the waiting room next door. Some liked to come early and compose themselves, but the person she was seeing after Jennifer was usually late.

'Go on,' she said, settling back.

'Then I tell him that if he would be honest about the whole thing I'd know where I stood.'

There was a knock on the door. Jennifer stopped, looking uneasily from Barbara to the door.

'I'm awfully sorry about this.' Barbara got up and opened the door, peering out. Another cardinal rule was that the analytic session should not be interrupted, and she looked annoyed.

Sam stood in the small hall that ran between the front door and the consulting room.

'I'm sorry to interrupt,' he whispered. 'Could I see you for a minute?'

Barbara popped her head back telling Jennifer she would not be long and closed the door behind her, ushering Sam into the waiting room.

'Whatever is the matter, Sam?'

'I tried to get you on the phone but your answering machine has been on all afternoon.'

'Couldn't it wait?' Barbara's expression was severe. She assumed it was something to do with Frankie.

'It's Amanda. The school rang to say she's in hospital.'

'Hospital?' Barbara felt suddenly cold, but she was still mentally inside her consulting room with her patient, even if she hadn't been giving her her full attention. It was positively Freudian to find Sam, on whom her mind had been concentrating, standing here before her, as though she'd wished him to appear.

'She's had some sort of collapse. She's OK but they really want us to go down at once.'

Amanda, very pale, her dark hair somehow shocking on the white pillowcase, her long fingers listless on the white counterpane, lay in the bed of the private ward, her eyes closed. Barbara's eyes closed involuntarily too at the sight of her youngest daughter and she groped for Sam's hand. His fingers tightened firmly, reassuringly, round hers. All her children at various times in their lives, and for various ailments, had spent spells in hospital and, despite her medical training, Barbara still felt the normal maternal anxieties when she saw them lying inert in bed after an operation or an accident. Both Tom and Sarah had had their appendixes removed and Tom had been unconscious for two days after a motor accident soon after he joined the Marines.

But Amanda's illness was nothing like any of these normal, if unfortunate, experiences of family life. She had been found semi-conscious in bed that morning at school and, all attempts

81

to revive her having failed, had been rushed in an ambulance with shrieking sirens through the streets of the market town to the local hospital. Barbara and Sam had seen the doctor who was caring for her before being escorted to her room.

'Acute *malnutrition*?' Barbara had exclaimed. 'But why didn't anyone notice she wasn't eating?'

'Apparently people did, according to her headmistress whom you'll see later on, and some of her friends were worried about her. She weighs seven stone, Dr Hahn, which is very underweight for a girl of her build and age.'

All the serious illnesses which had weight loss as a symptom rushed through Barbara's mind, normally neatly catalogued, but now that her own daughter was involved jumbled alarmingly all over the place.

'We're doing tests of course,' the young doctor said. 'But you must know about anorexia nervosa, Dr Hahn.'

'Of course I know about anorexia nervosa . . . but . . .'

'Anorexia what?' Sam had enquired, and it was explained to him that it was an increasingly common disease among young people, especially girls.

'But Amanda eats like a horse,' Sam had begun, but Barbara shook her head.

'Not at Christmas. I noticed how little she ate. Oh God, why didn't I see it then? I'd actually meant to talk to her but, with all the family around, we had so much to do. Of course you don't know for sure,' she added.

'We're running all the usual tests; but that's my preliminary diagnosis. You'll know, of course, what she's going through. She is conscious now but very sleepy. I should think she's rather ashamed too, and will be shy of talking to you.'

'I know all about anorexia,' Barbara shook her head sadly. 'I have treated a number of people for it.'

'Then she'll be in very good hands,' the doctor said, but Barbara thought he looked doubtful. He probably thought that a mother like her should have noticed something before.

She knew Amanda was awake, but she wouldn't open her eyes even though they'd spoken softly to her for some time. Sam's face was ashen with worry and Barbara sat on the bed holding Amanda's limp hand. She could see movement behind the closed eyelids.

'We really *aren't* angry, darling,' she said. 'Just worried about you. Won't you open your eyes and say "hello" to us?'

But Amanda, perhaps unconsciously to inflict more anxiety upon her parents, kept her eyes firmly shut and at last they crept out telling her they'd be back soon. They knew she could hear.

Later Sam took the headmistress to task, but Miss Evans kept her eyes relentlessly on Barbara.

'You'd think her mother would have known, Mr Hahn. She's both a doctor *and* a psychiatrist. She said she noticed symptoms at Christmas. That was three months ago.'

'I noticed she didn't eat much and I was worried about her being so withdrawn. But she cheered up towards the end and seemed happy and eager to go back to school.'

'Then she failed *all* her A-level mocks, Dr Hahn.'

'We didn't want to come and see her then in case she thought we were reproaching her. I assure you we didn't ignore the situation, Miss Evans. Her father and I discussed it carefully.' But on the phone, Barbara thought, not together. Had we met in person we might have reached another decision. The phone was too impersonal. One had Frankie to thank for that. 'At half term she went to her friend Sandra Baldock in Yorkshire,' Barbara finished lamely.

The expression on the headmistress's face made them both feel very neglectful yet, since Amanda had reached her teens, they often didn't see her during the term. It seemed to make her feel more grown up if they kept away.

'I think the staff should have noticed all this, Miss Evans,' Sam was determined to protect Barbara and himself. 'That's what I find incredible. We leave our daughter in your charge and you can't even see she's lost two stones in weight.'

'Anorexics are very devious,' Barbara observed quietly. 'They pretend to eat but they don't.'

'But she was getting so thin!'

'She's a skinny girl anyway,' Miss Evans said relentlessly, defensively. The parents of her girls paid a lot of money to send their daughters to her school where the ratio of teachers to pupils was high. Anything like this was a disaster for the school, as well as the girl.

'She won't have had periods either for some time; but she could keep that secret too.' Barbara got out one of her

83

cigarettes and fitted it into the holder despite Miss Evans' disapproving look. 'Well we've all failed, Miss Evans.' Barbara inhaled and blew the smoke away from the headmistress's face. 'We'll all have to start again. If she's well enough we'll take her home. If not I'll stay here to be with her.'

'But what about your patients?' Sam said. 'You have a duty to them too.'

'My duty above all is to my daughter.'

It was a terrible dilemma and one which, in all her years of practice, she had never encountered before. Every illness, every disaster – even Sam leaving her – had been somehow endurable, backed by supportive people around her. Now here in this Somerset market town, despite the presence of Sam, she felt terribly vulnerable. There was no one around – no Sarah, no Linda, no Joyce, her part-time secretary. She had never cancelled a patient, never been ill, always had someone else to cover for her. Everything had gone on quite smoothly because people expected it.

This was an unpleasantly unique situation.

CHAPTER FIVE

THE IRONY WAS THAT BARBARA had chosen to specialize in psychiatry all those years ago in order to have more time for her family. She reasoned that if one worked at home one was nearer to them. She had reckoned without the power of, the threat posed to her family by, the secret room.

Barbara's decision to give up many of her patients had only been taken after much thought and rejigging of schedules. In addition to her lectures at the university, she was also part-time consultant to a psychiatric day hospital and at first she thought she would give up the hospital and the university and concentrate on her private patients. But that would have kept her at home all the time and, since the divorce, she welcomed the opportunity that lecturing offered for renewing and increasing her social contacts. Besides, it wouldn't have given her a great deal more time with Amanda – which was the object of the exercise.

In point of fact all the patients Barbara weeded out were the ones who, over a long period of time, had either failed to respond to treatment or were really well enough to be on their own, but lacked the willpower, or needed a decisive push. The really serious, or new cases, she was keeping. Unlike a surgeon or physician who could, with some confidence, pronounce the patient cured after an operation or a course of treatment, psychiatric patients seldom had such certainty. With relatively little outlay, except a couch and a comfortable chair, a psychoanalytic practice was an income for life.

Yet if it frustrated the patient it also frustrated the conscientious practitioner. It was easy to show improvement, but difficult to say for a certainty how long it would last, and almost impossible to announce when a patient was better. Barbara seldom had the satisfaction of knowing she could safely send someone into the world, knowing they could cope with everything, that they would not be back. Those whose psyches had been bruised took a great deal of healing. In many ways they seemed to reject it, as though their psychological misfortunes were of comfort to them.

Barbara practised psychoanalysis on strict Freudian principles, which required those under treatment to come daily for a number of years. However this was reserved for the few who had the time and the money; it was exhausting for the analyst as well as the patient. The majority of her patients came for psychotherapy; a rather vague, pragmatic attempt to unravel the psychological misfortunes of those who felt disturbed enough to seek treatment. The people who came to her had minor neuroses of various degrees of severity and disablement – depression, anxiety, obsessions – or were simply very unhappy. Unhappiness seemed the twentieth-century disease for which Barbara and her fellow therapists were unable to offer an antidote or a cure. Jennifer Littlejohn was really a woman with time and money on her hands who was simply very unhappy because she was childless and her husband was a remote, apparently unloving figure. Or was a very seriously unhappy person fundamentally ill? Unhappiness brought about its own symptoms, its own neurosis.

Jennifer Littlejohn was borderline and Barbara had debated quite a long time over her. Freud recognized that the obsessive neuroses were hard to cure, and Barbara knew that here was a woman who could go on being neither wholly ill nor completely well until the end of her life.

On balance Barbara decided that a push would do Jennifer good. She explained the reasons.

Jennifer Littlejohn was a dignified woman. She listened to Barbara, her expression one of dismay, even devastation; but Barbara knew she wouldn't break down.

'It's been seven years, Mrs Littlejohn, and now I have to give up some patients so that I can spend more time with my daughter. I really think you're one of those who can stand on their own.'

'Couldn't I see you just from time to time?'

A terrible feeling of panic engulfed Jennifer Littlejohn, though she took care not to show it.

'I don't think it would make the break easier. If you feel

86

that you really can't stand it on your own I'll give you a short list of colleagues whom I think might suit you. But I'd like you to give it six months or so.' Barbara smiled encouragingly. 'I have a lot of faith in you.'

'I don't know how I'll feel without you in the background, Dr Hahn. It will be like . . .' Jennifer twisted the handkerchief she had kneaded in her hand all during Barbara's explanation. 'It will be like a death.'

Afterwards Barbara thought, with a flash of startling intuition, that that was how she felt about Sam. Getting used to being without him was like living through a bereavement; slowly, with difficulty, nursing oneself back to normality and health.

'Of course Mummy cares. She really wants to help.'

Amanda's answer was silence and she sat staring in front of her, pulling her gown more tightly around her as though to protect herself from the neglect of an uncaring parent. Sarah sat watching her, willing herself beneath the skin of this troublesome, yet obviously ill and tormented, younger sister.

Amanda had been brought back to London by ambulance and taken to a private clinic in Hampstead specializing in the treatment of this twentieth-century disease. Its causes were complex. In adolescent girls it seemed to spring from low self-esteem, a feeling of inadequacy in one's ability to face the demands of the grown-up world, a fear of life. By starving themselves, victims attempted to become young children again and thus postpone the agonizing process of entering into that adult world.

With the benefit of hindsight Barbara was able to see that Amanda was in many ways a perfect candidate for the slimmer's disease. She came from an affluent, high-achieving family with successful parents, a sister who was a doctor and a brother a captain in the Marines. Amanda, who had been as clever as any of them, who had previously been a high flyer, had started to fail her exams. That, in itself, should have given Barbara a warning.

The whole burden of Amanda's illness had fallen on Barbara because everyone, friends and family, thought that if anyone should have seen the signs it was she. Barbara knew they were right and that her own problems, her own sense of bereavement after losing Sam, had turned her inward, seeking consolation and satisfaction where she got it best – in her work.

Yet in treating her own daughter Barbara found herself in a predicament. She couldn't treat her professionally and from the beginning Amanda had reacted to her with implacable hostility, rejecting all invitations to confide or talk. Barbara had stayed in Somerset for two weeks with Amanda, while Sam returned to London to get on with his life and work.

Barbara agreed that her place was with her daughter; but she couldn't be there forever. She was not helping Amanda, who kept on asking for her father and sister, and needed professional psychiatric and medical help. But although Amanda abused her mother she wanted her near, and she resisted all attempts to be removed to London.

The only thing Barbara could do in the end was to go back to London herself, and after a while Amanda felt compelled to follow.

Sarah sat reflecting on all that had happened, on her own and her parents' dilemmas, as she sat watching Amanda stare at a blank television screen.

'Shall I turn it on?'

Amanda shook her head.

'You've got to get over this Amanda.' Sarah got off the bed on which she was sitting and came and stood by her sister, slumped in a chair. 'You are much better. You've put on weight and the doctors are pleased with you. It's up to you.'

Sarah wanted to tell her that she had brought on her condition and the cure was up to her; it was that sort of illness, unlike a gall bladder or appendicitis where the circumstances were, or seemed, externalized; everybody knew what they were and how to treat them.

Amanda was much better and there was talk of her going home, which had precipitated the conversation with Sarah – the fact that Amanda considered her mother neither wanted nor cared about her.

'Mummy has in fact done an awful lot,' Sarah started again. 'She's given up quite a few patients. What would you say if Daddy worked part-time at the bank?'

'What do you mean?' Sarah had broken through Amanda's reverie and it was her turn to stare.

'Well, why should Mummy give up work and not Daddy? Mummy's is important too.'

'Are we going to have another lecture on feminism?' Amanda gave an exaggerated sigh.

'Well it's a point of view. Mummy has a job as well as Daddy, yet it is Mummy who stays with you and cuts down on her patients. A lot of people depended on her too. How can you say she doesn't care?' Amanda appeared to consider these words and fell into a brown study again.

Sarah had been a feminist from her early days at university, a member of women's workshops, a participant in many of the allied protest movements that stemmed from the women's movement. She attended as an assistant a clinic where medical advice to women was given free outside the NHS. All the members of her family, including her mother, regarded her beliefs with attitudes varying from amused tolerance (her mother) to outright hostility (Tom).

'I'd rather go to Daddy than Mummy, anyway, when I leave here,' Amanda murmured as though talking to herself.

'With *Frankie*?' Sarah exclaimed.

'Well she's all right.'

'*And* the baby? I thought you hated her.'

'I haven't seen her much really. I suppose she's all right too. Mummy can then get on with her work, can't she, without me around?'

'Mummy is quite prepared to have you at home and look after you. She is making arrangements to do just that.'

'Pity she didn't do it before.'

Amanda snuffled and got out her handkerchief, prepared for another good cry. Sarah knelt beside her and put an arm round her.

'Oh my dear you do feel miserable don't you? Unloved and unwanted?'

Amanda nodded her head vigorously and blew her nose hard.

'But you're not. Very much loved and very much wanted.'

'Daddy has his new family, and Mummy has her work. I don't think either of them has much time for me.'

'Of *course* they have. Daddy's new family doesn't mean he loves us less.'

'I think it does.' Amanda looked suddenly wise. 'He has to share us, in a way he didn't before.'

And Sarah, looking at her sister, realized that, as the baby, she had felt more rejected than any of them – though not perhaps as much as Barbara. But Amanda wouldn't understand that.

'Besides,' she continued, as though determined to continue along this preferred path of self-denigration and self-pity, 'you're all so clever.' Amanda kneaded her handkerchief in her eyes.

'But *you're* clever too. You got eight O-levels with four As. It was taken for granted you'd go to Cambridge. There's nothing to stop you going now.'

'It's too late.'

'You can take A-levels next year, even if you don't go back to school. You can go to a crammer in London. Mummy's thought of that too.'

'I'd rather look after dogs,' Amanda said abruptly.

'Be a vet do you mean, like Granny?'

'No, a kennel maid.'

'I never knew you liked animals all that much.'

'Well I do.'

Amanda rubbed her eyes once more and then firmly put her handkerchief away, looking rather pleased at the surprise she'd given her sister.

'A *kennel* maid?' Barbara said as though Sarah had announced that Amanda wanted to go to Mars. 'I never heard that one before.'

'I didn't even know she liked animals particularly.'

'Well, maybe she thinks dumb pets are preferable to human beings. Sometimes I think I agree with her. Some of my patients who no longer really need me have been quite savage.'

'Then why didn't you get rid of them before if they didn't really need you?'

'It's not that easy.' Barbara screwed up her eyes. They were sitting in the garden, in a tiny arbour in the corner of the lawn which was protected from the breeze. It was now June and Amanda continued to be as much a problem as she had been at the end of March. She was now ready to leave the clinic, having put on a stone and a half, but no one could decide where she should go. 'People become very dependent in psychotherapy. It's very hard to terminate without seeming cruel. You can't just say "now you're cured you can go away" because most of them aren't and never will be.'

Barbara looked thoughtful, dejected. Sarah had seldom seen her as low as she had been over the past few weeks. Barbara had lost weight too, the flesh on her neck was rather loose and scraggy. Suddenly, she had begun to look her age.

Sarah held out her hand. 'I think you need a rest too, Mum. Why don't you pack it all in for three months and go away?'

'Amanda *will* think I have rejected her then.'

'Can't you take her with you?'

'You'd call that a holiday? No I could cope with Amanda, just about, here, but not in the South of France or the Bahamas. I need you. I need your father . . .'

Even Sam on the end of the telephone was better than no Sam. She knew Sam was avoiding her and that the cause was Frankie. Sam always took care to ask when she would be visiting the clinic so that their paths didn't coincide. She didn't know what Sam would do when Amanda came home.

Sarah looked at her mother in surprise.

'I never really thought you needed anyone, Mum.'

'Well you're wrong. We all need people, family. Family especially. With a family like ours one can be quite self-contained. Or could be anyway.'

'Do you think, if Dad hadn't left home, all this with Amanda would have happened?'

Barbara leaned back in the deckchair and closed her eyes, feeling the warm sun on her face.

'It's impossible to say. Quite impossible. Anorexia, much illness, even physical illness, is a cry for attention. Somewhere both Sam and I failed Amanda. She was trying to kill herself, starve herself to death. What could be more of a judgment on parents than that?'

Sarah, gazing at her mother lying in the chair with her face to the sun, eyes closed, was appalled to see tears steal from under her closed lids. They were not a demonstrative family

91

so, with some difficulty, she leaned forward and timidly touched Barbara's knee.

'Mum! Oh Mum don't let it upset you so.'

Impulsively Sarah knelt on the grass by Barbara's chair. She had never seen her mother cry, even when her father had left home. She had been obviously sad and troubled but she had never wept. Over the years Sarah realized how much they'd all depended on their mother being a tower of strength, never allowing herself to weep or give in, even to be ill.

Barbara put her hand over Sarah's, which rested on her knee. She opened her eyes, blinking, sat up and ferreted for a handkerchief in the pocket of her slacks. She blew her nose and then, staring at the handkerchief, folded it repeatedly to find a clean place. 'Thank you, darling. I am being rather silly. I'm simply giving in to self-pity and that won't help anyone.'

'Give in, Mum, give in. You never give in. Give in to self-pity if that's what you're doing and have a good cry.'

Barbara smiled and patted Sarah's shoulders.

'Psychologically you're absolutely correct. Why didn't I think of that before?' She blew her nose on the clean place, refolded the handkerchief, and tucked it back in her pocket. 'Tears really are good for one, but they don't solve anything. Whatever mistakes we've made in the past, Sam and I, what we must decide now is what to do in the future.'

'Amanda wants to go and stay with Dad.'

Sarah had been reluctant to say it – coming on top of the blow that Amanda didn't want to go to university – but now that Barbara was determined to face up to things, it seemed the best time. She saw Barbara blench but she didn't reach for her handkerchief again.

'Did she say that too?'

'Yes. Even with Frankie and the baby.'

'I don't know what Frankie will say.' Barbara looked thoughtfully at the grass.

'But don't you *mind*?'

'I don't mind if it will make Amanda happy.'

'You've given up so many patients.'

'Well, some of them had to go anyway. It was a good excuse.'

'But you couldn't go and see her *there* Mum.'

92

'Why not?' Barbara smiled. 'Sam always wanted Frankie and me to be friends.'

Barbara thought that congresses of psychoanalysts were depressing affairs and she did her best to avoid them. Somehow too many of one's own species together made one doubt the validity of the discipline. They were all so obviously imperfect in various ways. She wondered if the same could be said of renal or heart specialists gathering together, or was there something about psychiatry, especially psychoanalysis, that made one unique? The different factions were always quarrelling, especially in America, the supporters of one eminent theorist at loggerheads with their rivals – just as in England the followers of Anna Freud had refused at one stage to talk to those of Melanie Klein. Barbara realized, with some reluctance, that this was also in the tradition of the Master, who had fallen out with more of his followers than he had apparently kept as friends. Yet these congresses met, and she supposed something good came out of them. Anyway, it was an opportunity to get away.

Barbara had really decided to come to this particular meeting in September because the rendezvous was Nice. Sarah had almost pushed her on a plane, telling her to stay as long as she could. Now, preparing for dinner on the penultimate night, she wasn't sorry.

Barbara put the finishing touches to her toilet and looked critically at herself in the mirror. Had she acquired a few more white streaks in the last few months? Not surprising. She brushed her thick curls into place, grateful, as she so often was, for hair that needed such little attention, that could be washed, dried in a towel and look perfectly groomed half an hour later. Sarah, who had been treating her like a patient, watching her diet and pressing various vitamin preparations on her, had also seen to it that Barbara had put on a few pounds after dropping to such an alarming low that Sarah warned her she was in danger of becoming anorexic herself. Barbara rubbed rouge in her cheeks and carefully outlined her lips with her favourite Lancôme red. She had chosen a black dinner dress, scalloped with lace at the sleeves and hem, and a rather daringly low neckline. She wore high-heeled black suede shoes and carried a small black grosgrain bag. Giving a final pat to her hair and making an approving twirl in front of the mirror she slipped on her mink wrap – a twenty-fifth anniversary present from Sam – put out the light and descended in the lift to the ground floor where Alfred Kleber stood waiting for her.

Barbara had known Alfred Kleber for many years. He lived in Vienna, but he travelled a good deal on the psychoanalytical circuit, lecturing and writing books. Barbara felt the few patients he had must have had a raw deal because he was so often away, but he was a clever, amusing man only a little older than herself. They had been members of the same working party and he'd asked her to dinner.

Alfred Kleber, with his cosmopolitan practice and international outlook was a good companion, a man at ease with men and women, but known for his fondness for the latter. Barbara had never heard that he was a womanizer, but there was something about him that reminded her of Sam. Was Sam a womanizer? Looking at Alfred over her langoustines she wondered. He was a rather small man, a lot shorter than Sam, yet he had the same greying, dark Jewish looks and that indefinable air of sophistication that women liked. He knew how to order and what wine to drink. Important at any age, it was vital in one's fifties when one liked to think that those things were under control. It was especially important to a woman who had lost her husband (the image of bereavement had now settled firmly in Barbara's mind) and seldom dined alone with a man these days. Alfred had selected a restaurant out of Nice in the mountains overlooking the twinkling lights in the bay. The restaurant itself had no view – but two stars in the Michelin guide. For Alfred Kleber, gourmet, man of the world, food came before views any day. Besides, he had no idea of seducing Barbara Hahn, who had the reputation of being an iceberg in those circles where male psychoanalysts talked about sex and seduction, rather than the practice of their profession.

Barbara, however, was liked, respected and admired. Everyone felt a good deal of sympathy for the way she had been treated by her husband, although she never talked about it. It was the first time Alfred had been alone with her since

94

the divorce, and for the first half of the meal they talked shop rather than about their personal lives.

'My daughter's going to university in London,' Alfred said as they broke off to consider the cheeseboard. 'I tried to persuade her not to, but she was quite insistent. This looks delicious.' Kleber cut himself a large piece of brie that seemed to have achieved the precise point of perfection, neither too runny nor too hard.

'Why did you try and persuade her not to go to London?'

'Well,' Dr Kleber popped the cheese in his mouth and closed his eyes in an expression of ecstasy. 'Isn't it a city of sin?'

'No more than any other I shouldn't imagine.' Barbara watched his greed with amusement. He was certainly too fat. She had asked his permission to smoke instead of having cheese. 'Then what's so attractive to her about London?'

'English. She wants to study English literature. In fact her English is so good that she has been accepted into University College. Isn't that an achievement?'

'It is. I congratulate you. I don't think you'll find UC very sinful. My daughter Sarah is attached to the hospital, and I have a lecturing job there.'

'I know, Barbara. So my asking you out to dinner wasn't entirely altruistic, although it is *always* a pleasure to be with you. I wondered if Sarah could keep an eye on Madeleine for me?'

'I'm sure Sarah would be delighted, but her plans are very vague at the moment. Both Sam and I have tried to persuade her to specialize, but she wants to go into general practice. She's on holiday in Greece at the moment, thinking about it.'

'Oh dear I'm sorry. What about Amanda, isn't she due to go to university? Cambridge I suppose?'

Barbara looked at the tablecloth. She wondered if she knew Alfred well enough to confide in him or, even if she did, if she should. But he was always a friendly, practical man and his gaze, as she raised her eyes, was kindly, encouraging.

'We've had a great problem with Amanda, Alfred. Naturally I'd rather this didn't get around . . .'

Dr Kleber held up a well cared for hand, as though to indicate shock at the very idea that he could possibly be guilty of an indiscretion.

'The fact is that our younger daughter has become a victim of anorexia. She collapsed at Easter and, although she is now much better, she couldn't take her A-level exams for university. We're hoping she might next year, but who knows . . .'

'My dear Barbara I'm very, very sorry to hear that.' Dr Kleber spread his final piece of cheese on to a piece of bread and popped it with reluctance in his mouth, as though sad to see the last of it. He munched hard on his bread, took a gulp of wine and wiped his hands on his napkin. 'That *is* terrible. But, had you no idea?'

Barbara shook her head, aware of the slight blush that always came to her cheeks when people asked her, as they invariably did, if she'd had any warning. 'It's a reflection on me, isn't it Alfred? Well she was at boarding school, you know. Anyway I should have known, I agree. I've tried now to make amends, to cut down my list of private patients, but it's a bit too late.'

'Why is it too late?' Kleber was all professional concern.

'She has cast me as the villain of the piece, the cause of all this, and she's gone to live, or stay, with Sam.'

Alfred Kleber shrugged. 'She would turn against you because she can hurt you most.'

'I *know* that; but knowing it and doing something about it are two different matters. I have to be very careful with her, and I don't feel very welcome when I go to visit. Sam, you know, has married again and has a baby daughter. His new wife, incidentally, is very nice. She does her best.'

'That's very generous, Barbara. Too generous perhaps?' Dr Kleber leaned over the table, studying her as though she were a patient, his eyes warm, kind, yet probing.

'You mean generous of me about her? Well she *is* very nice. Sam was the one at fault, not her. That I do believe. She had a very different view of our marriage, from what Sam told her, than was actually true.'

'Has she told you all this?'

'Oh yes, we've had many heart to hearts. She once stayed at my house for five weeks when she became ill after their daughter was born. I realized then she felt very guilty about me.'

'And you made her feel better?'

'I tried.' Barbara lit another cigarette from the stub of the

96

first. Not a very elegant gesture she knew, but one to which she often resorted when she was nervous or in a hurry, or both. 'We both tried, but Frankie – her name is Francesca, she's American by the way – didn't really like me in her heart. We had a pretty disastrous Christmas lunch, and after that I didn't see her again until I went to visit Amanda. That was pretty awful too.'

'Why was it awful?'

Barbara stretched out her arms, her cigarette clasped between the index and middle fingers of her right hand. 'I felt I wasn't wanted. Frankie was awfully nice, Sam very considerate; but Amanda sat and stared at me as though I'd interrupted some cosy family gathering. I felt I had. Sarah goes there a lot too now. There's no doubt Sam has become the centre of the family. I feel very isolated.'

'You must make your own life, Barbara.' Kleber's tone had the gentleness that made Barbara realize why he was famous. She thought he had been about to touch her hand and then decided against it.

'I must. I shall; but it isn't easy.' She looked across at him, hoping the dim restaurant light concealed the tears in her eyes. 'It isn't easy, once you've had a sizeable family, to become a single person. It isn't as though they'd died; but sometimes it feels as though they had.'

This time Alfred did extend his hand, and she felt its comforting masculine pressure over hers.

CHAPTER SIX

AT THE TOP OF THE HOUSE there was a small room, next to the guest room, which Frankie used to call 'the tip'. Into it she and Sam had put all the impedimenta from their previous dwellings for which they had no immediate use in the new house. Sam had left all the furniture, of course, at Hampstead, but there were several boxes and suitcases full of possessions that were either personal or sentimental and whose distribution around the new house would have marred its clean, Scandinavian lines. Frankie had a few bits of furniture, a standard lamp and assorted memorabilia, more suited to bed-sitting-room land than the new modern dwelling, only five years old, on Primrose Hill.

When Frankie decided to work at home she cleaned 'the tip' out, gave away or sold much of the stuff neither of them wanted – she was glad to get rid of some of Sam's pieces which had nostalgic associations with his old life – put cases and boxes in the utility room next to the garage, and converted it into a study. She whitewashed the walls, hung curtains, with a contemporary abstract design from Heals, and had Berber carpet laid on the floor. Sam gave her a desk and filing cabinet that were no longer needed at the bank.

Frankie now called this room 'the office', and she had not sat there long waiting for work. Poppy's editor liked the idea of a financial column written for women which neither talked down to them nor tried to exploit them, but kept them informed on current economic matters to do with investment, saving, pensions and the like. The magazine was aimed at the modern working woman, who had money of her own, married or single, and Frankie's ideas were admirably geared to this market. Francesca Hahn's *Money Talks* was an immediate hit and she received a substantial post bag as a result. She decided that she might even start a financial consultancy for women and Sam gave her encouragement, advice and the benefit of his insight and knowledge of the market. It appeared that Frankie would soon be making a substantial contribution to the family budget.

Frankie's new life was abruptly interrupted by the advent of Amanda, who came to them straight from the clinic once she had achieved the goal of nine and a half stones. Of course, there could be no question of refusing to have Amanda, although Frankie, but not Sam, found the whole business very upsetting at the time. Frankie had reckoned with a new baby, but not a new grown-up daughter in the throes of what was apparently a nervous breakdown of some seriousness.

Besides, her own life had just stabilized. Zoë was six months old; she had a new job, and the presence of Amanda threatened to disrupt this domestic harmony. There was also the shadow of Barbara, from whom Frankie at last felt she had well and truly weaned Sam.

But, as with many things that are feared, the reality when it came wasn't as bad. After a holiday without Zoë in Spain, to prepare themselves for what both privately thought would be an ordeal, they returned to collect Amanda from the clinic to find to their surprise, and Frankie's delight, that she appeared well recovered from her ordeal. She was happy to settle down in her father's home with as little interruption to his lifestyle and that of her stepmother as one could imagine.

It was also pleasant to discover that the threat posed by Barbara failed to materialize. By agreement Barbara visited infrequently, and kept in touch with Sam by phone as they had done previously. Another bonus was that Sarah became a much more regular visitor than before, and the relationship not only between herself and Amanda but between all three of them – Frankie, Sarah and Amanda – improved. What was more, both Sarah and Amanda adored their half-sister.

Sam was delighted about the whole thing, and Frankie, sitting now in her office gazing out across the roofs of North London towards Hampstead, felt a deep sense of satisfaction that everything had gone so well – had, in fact, settled down to the sort of peaceful domestic existence that she and Sam had craved all along.

There was a knock at the door and Frankie started guiltily from her happy reverie and quickly began to tap at the typewriter after calling out to whoever it was to enter. She expected it to be June announcing that she and Zoë were off to the park.

'Am I disturbing you?' Amanda put her head round the door.

Frankie sat back, tucking a straggling lock of hair back into place. 'No, of course not. Come in.'

She pushed back her chair and indicated the comfy divan on which she often lay for an afternoon nap or when she wanted to think.

Amanda didn't sit down, but hovered above Frankie looking down at her desk.

'What are you writing?'

'An article for my magazine.'

'What's it about?' She peered over Frankie's shoulder.

'Women and the stock exchange. They used not to be admitted but now they are. It was one of the last bastions of male chauvinism in the City to yield.'

'Are you a feminist?'

Amanda sat down on the divan and stretched out her legs. She wore blue jeans and a check shirt, her short curly hair, like Barbara's, rather tousled and uncombed above her pale face. She still had the pallor of her days in the clinic, but that was mainly because she didn't bother to wear any makeup. She was a naturally pale girl, with Barbara's fine features but Sam's large brown eyes. She was much better looking than Sarah, Frankie thought as she considered the question, though neither of them bothered to make much of themselves. Neither had Barbara's poise, elegance or dress sense.

'Yes I am a sort of feminist,' Frankie said. 'I mean I believe in women's rights, don't you?'

'I don't know. Sometimes I think it's only done women harm.'

'What on earth makes you say that?'

'You have only to look at Mummy.'

'What about her?' Frankie was cautious, feeling that this exchange had been deliberated upon and carefully planned.

'She's too educated for her own good.'

'What about your father? He's educated too.'

'But men are meant to be, don't you think?'

'No I don't.' The lock of hair had fallen back over her face

100

and Frankie brushed it away again. 'I mean I think women have every bit as much right to be educated as men. I am very highly educated, as a matter of fact. I went to university and did post graduate study for many years afterwards.'

'Yes, but . . .' Amanda was clearly on the point of saying something startling, but didn't appear to know how to put it. 'Well . . . you're, I mean, you're much more *feminine* than Mummy. There's the baby and you obviously adore Daddy.'

'But your mother adored your father too . . . at one time,' Frankie added quickly. 'And she had three babies. You can't remember those times, can you? I think your mother's a very attractive, clever, feminine woman.'

'You'd think you liked her!'

'Well I do,' Frankie said carefully. 'I have no reason not to.'

'You must have known she was a terrible mother, and she never made Daddy happy. If she had he wouldn't have gone off with you.'

Frankie swivelled her chair around so that she faced Amanda directly.

'How do you mean she was a terrible mother?'

'She had no time for us, sent us all to boarding school so that she could follow her own career. I bet you'll never send Zoë to boarding school, will you?'

Frankie chose her words carefully.

'We haven't discussed Zoë's education at all yet. I imagine she'll go to a local London school. I was at boarding school too, you see, and I do know what you mean. But there were special circumstances as far as I was concerned.'

'Oh? What were they?'

'My mother died and my father remarried. I wasn't wanted; but I'm sure you were. You see,' Frankie leaned forward, winding the straggling lock of hair in her fingers, 'I think you really have got the wrong idea about your mother. Maybe it's because of your illness, which she really isn't responsible for, though I know you think she is. My hope is that as you get better — and you are improving every day — you will consider your mother as the friend she is and want to go and live with her again.'

Amanda, who had been lounging back against the wall, sat bolt upright.

'You mean you want to get rid of me?'

'Not at all!' Frankie exclaimed. 'That is very far from the truth. We like having you here, we really do. But your mother will be very hurt if you never return home again. I'd like to think that we're helping you get well so that you'll want to. Then you'll have two homes in both of which you're equally welcome.' As Amanda, her mouth turned down in an ugly expression of disbelief, didn't reply, Frankie hurried on. 'As for her not making your father happy I don't think that's true either. For many years they were very happy, and they're years you must remember too.'

'Then why did he leave her?'

'Because . . .' Frankie swivelled her chair right round and back again. 'Because they had grown apart, grown apart enough so that when he met me he fell in love again.'

'Tom thinks you snatched Daddy from Mummy.'

Frankie put her hands on her cheeks to conceal a sudden blush. 'Well, I'd expect a son to think differently. But it's not true.' She stared at her desk. 'I really should get on with some work now, Amanda. What are you going to do today?'

'That's the trouble, I don't know.' Amanda leaned against the wall again. 'Can't I help you?'

'There's nothing you can do at the moment. I've done all my research.'

Amanda's chin slumped petulantly on to her chest.

'I'm quite useless you know. Good for nothing.'

'Oh that's nonsense. Wouldn't you like to start studying again? See if you can take A-levels next summer?'

'The last thing I want to do is my A-levels. The last thing I want to do is be like Mummy. That's a terrible example to any girl.'

Frankie sighed.

'I tried to tell you, Amanda, explain it to you, that it's not. Your mother's cleverness had nothing to do with what happened in her marriage and with her family.'

'It had everything to do with it. There was that horrible secret room for a start.'

'Secret room?'

'Where she sees her patients. It's in a separate part of the house. I hated that room, wondering what went on there.'

'But what did you *think* went on there?'

'Oh talk, I suppose. I think psychiatry is absolutely idiotic.

102

Sarah does too, and Tom. I bet Daddy does too, but he doesn't say.'

'Maybe you think your mother's work excluded you. I'm sure it didn't.'

'Well it did. I'll never go back to that house again as long as she has that room. Never, never.'

Suddenly Amanda got up and bolted for the door, slamming it hard behind her.

Frankie sat for a long time poised over the typewriter, her fingers stiff as though paralysed above the keys. She wondered if the happy, peaceful time was over.

But that night at dinner, at which Sarah was present, it was as though there had been no outburst at all. Amanda had gone to the park with June and the baby and she was full of stories about what they'd seen and Zoë's reactions. Frankie, remembering the outburst of the morning, was relieved.

'Amanda really has a wonderful way with the baby,' June, who always ate with the family, said quietly. She was a sandy-haired Scots girl who had begun to train as a nurse but, because of her devotion to children, broke off her training to become a nanny. Sam and Frankie knew how lucky they were to get her.

'June says I should perhaps work with babies,' Amanda burst out enthusiastically, while the rest of the family silently digested this information.

'Well why don't you?' Sam said. 'For a while.'

'But why only "a while" Daddy?'

'Well,' Sam looked nervously at June. 'You wouldn't want a career in that sort of thing would you?'

'I don't see why not.'

'Just because you're good with Zoë doesn't mean . . .'

'It was puppies a few weeks ago,' Sarah observed dryly. 'You wanted to be a kennel maid.'

'Just so,' Sam looked approvingly at Sarah. 'You're too volatile at the moment, my darling, to make major decisions. We all hope that, eventually, you'll want to go to university.'

'But *why* Daddy? Just because you've all been?'

Sam looked at Frankie for help.

103

'I think your father means . . .' she began, but Amanda interrupted her.

'I want *Daddy* to reply please Frankie.'

'Don't be rude to Frankie,' Sam said.

'I wasn't rude. I was just saying that I would like you to answer the question I put to you.'

Her father sat back scowling.'

'Yes, we've all been to university and we think it's a good background in life for anyone.'

'June didn't go.'

'You were talking about the *family* Amanda,' her father said pointedly.

'Yes but isn't June as good as us?'

'Mr Hahn I didn't mean . . .' June began, but Sam held up a hand.

'Amanda's not herself, June. Please don't take anything she says personally.'

Amanda got up and, leaning over the table, shouted at her father.

'I'm not *insane* Daddy, if that's what you're suggesting. Because I've been in a mental home it doesn't mean that I'm nuts . . .'

'Whoever said anything . . .' Sam half got up and sat down again.

'Yes *I was* in a mental home, whatever you like to call it. And we all know why I was there. Because too much was expected of me by my family – my clever banker father, my brilliant psychiatrist mother, my talented doctor sister, my brave brother the marine . . . *after* a university education of course. Well I'm not brilliant or talented or anything.'

'We just assumed darling . . .' her father's voice was gentle, his face worried.

'Well you shouldn't assume *anything* about people. You shouldn't put them into slots. I want to look after babies or dogs and I don't give a damn which . . . and I don't want any qualifications either. Stuff your qualifications . . .'

Frankie thought that Amanda, leaning across the table towards Sam, her face contorted, would have a seizure. She got up and put her arms around the girl's shoulder, gently trying to draw her back. Amanda struck out and hit Frankie hard in the solar-plexus with her elbow. Winded, Frankie slumped back into her chair and Sam, getting up, reached over and hit Amanda across the face.

'Don't *ever* do that to my wife again, you silly hysterical girl. Go to your room at once.'

Father and daughter stared at each other as the bright red weals started to rise on the surface of Amanda's skin. Sarah, after making sure Frankie was all right, firmly took hold of Amanda's arm and pulled her gently away.

'Come on now. Let's go and talk.'

Gently she drew the girl, who had started to sob, out of the room.

Sam took a deep gulp of wine and went round to where Frankie was sitting bent over in her chair, clutching her stomach.

'Darling are you all right?'

'Perfectly all right, just a bit winded.' White-faced Frankie looked up at Sam. 'What a hellish evening.'

'She'll have to go,' Sam said. 'We can't have this. She's out of control. Think what she might do to the baby.'

'She's perfectly all right with the baby, Mr Hahn. You have nothing to fear from her.' June's soft Scotch brogue was reassuring.

'But she was like a fiend tonight.'

'She was upset,' June insisted. 'She is *very* volatile, you know. Her hormones have all been disturbed. She's very fond of you and Frankie.' She always called Frankie by her Christian name but used his surname for Sam, out of respect for his years.

Sam sat down in Sarah's place, next to Frankie, and took her hand.

'Well I don't know. I'll have to see what Barbara thinks.'

'Oh God *no!*' Frankie, her nerves taut, thumped the table. 'Please for *God's* sake, Sam, don't ask her every time you want to make a decision about *anything*.'

'Yes, but Barbara's a psychiatrist. She's trained.'

'For God's sake she's also the girl's mother!' Frankie banged on the table again and the glasses danced dangerously. 'Sam have you *no* confidence in yourself or me? Can you make *no* decisions without talking to Barbara? I would have thought that she'd failed already with Amanda. The girl didn't even

105

want to go to her own home. How can you possibly ask Barbara what should be done?'

'I still think . . .' Sam began but Frankie got up from her chair and abruptly left the room.

As Sam and June stared at each other the baby could be heard from upstairs wailing loudly.

'Excuse me,' June said and quietly, thankfully, left the room too. Sam crossed his arms, sat back in his chair and stared at the ceiling.

From that evening on the peace in the Primrose Hill house was broken. Amanda either stayed in bed or disappeared on her own for hours. She had nothing to do with the baby and she wouldn't speak to Frankie or her father. Any conversation was conducted through June, who became very embarrassed about the whole thing.

One day Amanda didn't come back at night and Sarah rang, just when Sam was about to call the police, to say Amanda was with her and she'd keep her for a few days.

'That's the best place for her, with her sister,' Sam said, relieved.

'I feel we've failed, Sam.'

'Failed with what for God's sake?' Sam turned to Frankie who'd been listening to Sarah on the extension in the hall.

'Well with Amanda. I felt that I was getting close to her and that she liked me.'

'You just wanted to take the place of her mother. Well you can't do that Frankie. Anyway, she's impossible. I don't understand her at all. She has everything she wanted . . .'

'I did *not* want to take the place of her mother.' Frankie, annoyed, interrupted him sharply. 'I just wanted to help her. She's *your* daughter.'

'God, don't I know that!' Sam helped himself to whisky. 'I only hope that if Zoë turns out like this I'm already dead.'

'That isn't a very nice thing to say.'

'Why not?'

'Because *you're her* father too, and I'd be there coping on my own.'

'I might well be dead,' Sam said as if, not having heard her, he was doing a mental calculation. 'I'll be in my seventies, an old man. Have you thought of that Frankie?'

'We talked about it exhaustively when you asked me to marry you, as you well know. I said I didn't mind.'

'Well maybe you should have thought about it more carefully. An old man with a young daughter of twenty. It seems obscene doesn't it? You'll still be in your fifties when I'm seventy-three.'

'Oh Sam do shut up.' Frankie got up and took his glass from him. 'You're drinking too much too. This business with Amanda has unhinged you. You rush up to the bottle every night and seem to have a glass in your hand until you go to bed.'

Sam snatched the glass from her, spilling some of the contents on the carpet.

'I'll thank you *not* to run my life,' he said. 'Watching my drinking as if I were a schoolboy.' Sam carefully poured another measure into his glass. 'Don't forget I'm not a child. I've got grown up children.' Sam paused thoughtfully. 'I will say this about Barbara . . .'

Without warning Frankie seized the glass again and threw its contents into her husband's face. They both stared at each other, he incredulous, she immediately registering regret at what she'd done. Frankie lowered her eyes then, gently pulling his handkerchief from his breast pocket, began unsteadily to mop his face.

'I'm terribly sorry Sam. I really am. I completely lost control of myself.' She stopped her mopping and stared earnestly at him, handkerchief still in her hand. 'But I tell you this, my darling, and I mean it: if you don't stop bringing up Barbara's name every time we have a crisis in this house, I'll leave you. I will. I really will.'

Barbara was aware of Alfred Kleber sitting at the back of the room during her Tuesday lecture at University College. She was now giving a course on the development of Freudian thought and the practice of psychoanalysis since his death just before the war, and the lecture room was full. Barbara was a popular lecturer; she spoke well and her facts were neatly presented, her theories logically expounded. Quite a lot of the people liked looking at her, too, as she roved around the small podium, stopping now and then to consult her notes.

After the lecture one or two students came forward to talk to her, but Alfred Kleber hovered, waiting for them to go before stepping forward and shaking Barbara's hand.

'Excellent, Barbara. How simple you make it all sound.'

Barbara laughed as she gathered up her notes, tucking her spectacles in their leather case back into her handbag. 'Well it *is* basically simple, isn't it Alfred? The best and most workable theories I always find the least complicated. How nice to see you anyway. Visiting Madeleine?'

'Passing through, really, on my way to New York. Yes I'm spending a few days seeing my daughter, and I saw a notice of your lecture. I personally think you are less than fair to Klein, but still . . .' he gestured vaguely into the air.

They discussed Klein versus Anna Freud and the controversial ideas of R. D. Laing, as they made their way through the college to the canteen where they sat drinking coffee until nearly four, when Barbara glanced at her watch.

'My goodness I have a patient at five.'

Alfred looked regretful.

'What a pity. We haven't really started to talk. You're not free later for dinner by any chance? Madeleine has a date, and I want to hear about Amanda and your family.'

Barbara considered. 'I could be free by seven. Yes, I'd like to.'

'That's marvellous. I have hired a car and I'll pick you up. You tell me a nice restaurant in Hampstead or anywhere you like and we'll go there.'

'I'll think about it.' Barbara shrugged herself into her coat. 'Now I must fly. See you just after seven.' She waved and ran down to her own car parked just behind the college.

The candlelight flickering between them reminded her of the dinner in Nice two months earlier. That was September, now it was November. Alfred had arrived at her house just past seven and, after a drink, they had driven to a restaurant in the High Street only a few minutes away. Barbara was explaining what had happened about Amanda and that she was now living with Sarah.

'So she's rejected Father and Mother?'

'She is certainly rejecting *authority*; but she can't stay with

Sarah forever because Sarah's looking for a job. If she finds some nice North Country practice she'll join it. Naturally I feel Amanda's rejection very deeply. She is my baby and not to have her feel she needs me is very wounding.'

'But you know she's just rejecting you for what you stand for. In time she'll come round.'

'Yes I know that, but still it's hurt me very badly.'

'So what temporary solution do you envisage for Amanda?'

'At the moment Sam is talking to someone in Kent who owns kennels. Amanda has a fixed idea that she wants to be a kennel maid. So, if she wants to . . .' She trailed off, gazing at Alfred.

'You seem disappointed in your children, Barbara.'

'Oh not Tom! I'm not disappointed in Tom. He's a very straightforward young man doing something he likes, married to a nice girl who is pregnant with their second child. He takes his responsibilities seriously. I often wonder if the girls were more affected by the divorce because they were younger. Tom had met Natalie when the news broke about me and Sam. I think she supported him, diverted his attention.' Her expression grew gentle. 'Tom has never given me any trouble. Ever. But I'm not really disappointed in Sarah either. She did very well in her finals and if she decides to specialize there will always be a hospital job for her. I hope that after a year or two doing her own thing she might. It is simply that Sarah and I, being very different, have never had a particularly easy relationship.'

'How are you different?' Alfred rested his chin on the palm of his hand and smiled encouragingly at her. The tone of his voice invited confidences, intimacies. She knew why he was successful with women.

'Sarah is *very* practical; she had no time for the psychological approach. She thinks things – illnesses and so on – have physical causes and there is a practical solution to them . . . pills, fresh air, long walks. Rather nineteenth century really. To the extent that our approaches differ so much there has always been friction, even when she was quite a small girl. With Amanda it was easier, until recently. I think she'll get over that in time.'

'But it's been hard for you this period Barbara, yes?'

'Yes.' She felt close to tears.

Once again his hand closed over hers and this time, looking into his eyes, she thought it was a gesture of invitation rather than comfort.

Barbara hadn't been to bed with a man other than Sam for years. She hadn't particularly wanted to go to bed with Alfred, but he had been pressing and she knew he would think her unfeminine if she refused. She despised herself for such weak logic, but she felt very vulnerable too. Alfred had been so kind and, somehow, to pack him off without giving him what he wanted seemed, at the time, both graceless and ungrateful. He didn't attract her, in fact he rather repelled her, but he was a skilled lovemaker, adept at getting women from the vertical position to a horizontal one in a very short space of time. They had gone back to her house for a nightcap and half an hour later she was in bed, with Alfred's short, hirsute, but enthusiastic little body between her legs, his eyes closed with ecstasy, feeling the base of his penis as though to reassure himself that it was really where it was, well lodged.

'You're beautifully moist,' he said, as if delivering himself of a verdict after a satisfactory clinical examination. 'You know I've always dreamed of making love to you Barbara?'

'Really? You never showed it.'

'I didn't dare, not with Sam around. I thought there was hope for me in Nice; but no opportunity, alas.'

Alfred paused, stared at her, and his mouth bore down upon hers again while his lower parts dived in and out of her like a small but efficient battering ram, not violent, but insistent. As a lover he was expert, his kissing practised and gentle. His hands roved over the right places doing the right things and, as he prepared himself for his own climax, his busy finger massaged her clitoris, bringing her to orgasm too.

She lay there feeling rather astonished at the pleasure this unexpected lover, who lay panting, inert on her body, had given her. The immediacy of such intimate physical contact, the baring of flesh, surprised her once again, as it always had in the past. The fantasies and experiences of her patients absorbed her life so completely that she often forgot she had had no recent direct experience of the sexual act.

Alfred had been sweet with her, gentle, and she was grateful to him for reminding her of the release that lovemaking afforded the taut, nervous human body.

After a while he raised himself and withdrew from her, inspecting his now flaccid penis carefully as he did so. It was obviously a part of himself of which he was very fond. He kept on feeling it, and talking about it, rather as one might about a person – referring to it as 'him' – all the time they were making love.

'Is it all right?' She smiled.

'Of course he's all right. Why shouldn't he be?' He looked at it again, this time nervously as though she'd seen something he hadn't, a concentrated frown on his brow as he wiped it with a tissue from the box by Barbara's bed.

'Well you keep on looking at it and touching it as though you're afraid it might disappear or come out in spots or something.'

Alfred looked at her wisely. 'I *have* come out in spots. One can't be too careful. But with a lady like you . . .'

'Good heavens.' It was Barbara's turn to look startled. 'I hope it's cured.'

'My dear that was years and years ago in Vienna where I was a student.' Alfred produced another tissue from the box and began delicately to wipe Barbara. Then he bent down and kissed her, licking her gently with his tongue. An erotic spasm of such violence shot through Barbara that her legs involuntarily twitched in the bed. She clasped his head and drew it away from her.

'My goodness you liked that didn't you?' He looked at her with gratification. 'Shall I make you come again?' As he bent his head she grasped him sharply by a tuft of hair and pulled him away.

'Please don't.'

He lay down beside her and gazed at her.

'You shouldn't be afraid of pleasure, Barbara. I'm sure you haven't had a man for years, have you?'

'Is it so obvious?'

He nodded and stroked her breast. It was a gesture she resented until she recalled that she had, not a few moments before, allowed him the freedom of the most intimate part of her body.

111

'You were very tight, like a virgin. Very nervous too. I guess Sam screwed you all up, Barbara.'

'With Sam there wasn't much either in recent years. I'm not a very sexy person you know.'

Alfred gave a short laugh. 'That I don't believe. Barbara, look, I'd like to see you again when I come to London, if I may.'

Barbara lay back and closed her eyes, suddenly resentful of this intimacy. Who knew where all this would lead? Would she be Alfred's port of call every time he came to London? Did she want that?

'I'm not sure.'

'But why tonight then?'

'I'm not sure about that either.' She opened her eyes and looked at him. 'Maybe I *was* thinking about Sam, I don't know.'

'But you must have wanted a lover?'

She shook her head. 'I felt dead since Sam left, sexually as well as emotionally dead. It took me that way, like a bereavement.'

'A conscious envy of his new wife?'

'I've had to work on it hard.' Barbara reached for a cigarette, glancing at her watch. 'I've got to be up early Alfred . . .'

'I hoped I could stay the night. There's no one else here is there?'

Barbara shook her head.

'I'd much rather you didn't.'

'I will try again Barbara.'

'I'm sure you'd try all night if I let you . . .'

'I don't mean that. I mean next time I come to London.'

'Doesn't your wife ever come with you?'

Alfred looked offended, as though the mention of his wife was in bad taste.

'She *never* comes to London.'

'But she might now that Madeleine's here. I think we should regard it as a "one off" Alfred. I . . .'

'Then if it is a "one off" let me stay the night. Please?'

'You'll have to be gone by seven.'

Barbara felt rather angry, as though she were being used, and got up to wash and brush her teeth. In the bathroom she examined her face in the mirror, seeing a woman well into

112

middle age with white streaks in her hair and a well-lined skin. It was quite ridiculous to have gone to bed with a man just to prove she was still a woman. Now he was going to be a pest and want to make love at dawn, maybe prod her all through the night as far as she knew. It was so hard to refuse a man, particularly one you didn't know very well, when he was actually in bed with you. She had to work the next day and he didn't. She brushed her teeth, and then she removed her gown and washed her body carefully. She thought she heard a knock on her bedroom door but knew that was impossible, there was no one in the house.

Suddenly a terrible thought struck her and she ran to the bathroom door just as the knock sounded again and Sarah anxiously called out 'Mummy', and almost simultaneously her head appeared round the door.

Sarah didn't seem to see Barbara standing at the bathroom door. Her eyes had immediately gone to the bed where she had expected to see her mother, and remained riveted on the hairy body of Alfred Kleber, who lay propped up on the pillows, stiff and petrified, his eyes wide open with shock, as though he could make her disappear by an act of will. He and Sarah stared at each other for a while; then Sarah's eyes wandered to where her mother was standing in the doorway of the bathroom, clutching a large bath towel to hide her nakedness.

'I'm sorry,' Sarah said and abruptly shut the door.

Barbara ran back into the bathroom, grabbed her gown and rushed through the bedroom towards the door, tying the sash of her gown tightly around her. She could see Sarah's head disappearing at the top of the stairs as she called.

'Sarah!'

Sarah didn't look behind but continued her descent and Barbara fled after her, calling again.

'Darling, please wait.'

When Sarah got to the hall she stopped, as though not knowing what to do. Barbara ran down the stairs and took hold of her arm, steering her firmly into the sitting room, closing the door behind them. Sarah, white-faced, her expression a mixture of shock and disgust, avoided looking at her mother, whose arm still held hers firmly.

113

'I'm sorry you saw that Sarah; but I am quite an old woman, you know, and I haven't got a husband.'

'But *he* has a wife! Dr Kleber. Mummy how *could* you?' Sarah shook as though her incredulity, her sense of loathing were intensified.

'It was something that happened very suddenly. We had dinner and . . .'

'I think it's perfectly disgusting.'

Barbara let go of her daughter's arm, and turned away.

'I am sorry you saw what you did. I know it doesn't look dignified, absurd even, two middle-aged people . . . disgusting as you say. I'm not particularly proud of myself either, Sarah. I mean I didn't especially want to, nor did I enjoy it all that much . . .'

Sarah shook her head and stamped her foot.

'Oh don't go *on* about it Mummy. You make it worse. Dr Kleber. He's quite revolting, a revolting little man.'

'If you compare him to your father he is certainly not good looking; but I don't think he's revolting. He's a very intelligent man,' she added, as an afterthought.

'I don't know how you could.' Sarah looked her mother full in the eyes. 'A woman like you, dispensing advice to others. You make yourself cheap.'

'Only to you, Sarah,' Barbara said sadly. 'No one else will know about it, and I would have thought that you were old enough now to stand the shock.'

'Supposing it had been Amanda who came home?'

'I must confess that when I heard the knock that was the first thought that occurred to me.' Barbara's heartbeat was still fast and erratic because of the shock she'd had.

'But what would you have *done*?'

'I don't know.' Barbara shrugged her shoulders, slumping into a chair and, as she did, her gown fell away exposing a bare leg. Hastily, she covered it up.

'It's terribly irresponsible, Mummy.'

'In *what* way is it irresponsible? This is my own home. I live alone, unmarried. It didn't occur to me that either of you would come here tonight, certainly not unannounced. I am sorry you saw it; but in future I'll lock my door. If there is a future,' she said bitterly. 'I don't intend to see Alfred Kleber again, and I was telling him just that.'

'A sordid little one night stand,' Sarah said contemptuously. 'I don't think I'll ever feel the same about you again.'

'How did you feel as a matter of fact?' Barbara's voice was very low.

'How do you mean?'

'How did you feel about me? You've been very censorious lately. First about Daddy, then about Amanda. I'm just sinking right down the ladder aren't I? A person for whom you'll have very little or no respect.'

'I can't help that,' Sarah said, 'if you behave as you do. When I think that you give counsel to others it makes me laugh. You can't even run your own life. Your husband leaves you, your daughter develops a psychological illness that you're not even aware of, and then won't let you look after her. What sort of mother is *that* to engender such feelings?'

'A pretty poor one by your standards obviously,' Barbara replied. 'But your standards are very high Sarah, and always have been. You could try and be a bit more understanding about people, and you could begin with me.' Barbara suddenly rose. 'Now I must go and release poor Alfred.'

'*Poor* Alfred,' Sarah sneered.

'Well he won't be feeling comfortable either.'

'Don't worry, I won't tell his daughter.'

'I'm sure you won't.' Barbara paused and gazed at Sarah, aware of her feelings of guilt turning to anger. Who, after all, was Sarah to expect her to be Caesar's wife, above reproach? 'What is it you came for tonight anyway, at such a late hour? Is Amanda all right?'

'Now you ask.'

'Well is she?'

'Yes she's all right. I just felt I wanted to talk to you about something. I needed your advice; but now I know what to do.'

'Oh Sarah stop talking in riddles,' Barbara said wearily. 'You found me in bed with a man; you're not pleased and I am sorry the circumstances were what they were. But you are a woman of twenty-five, a qualified doctor and I hope in time you will realize that, although I'm twice your age, I have human feelings and needs too. I'm still your mother and I can still give you advice, if you want me to.'

115

'I don't want your advice any more,' Sarah said. 'Tonight has decided me. I'm going away. I'm leaving the country. I've had such a bellyful of my family that I can't stand it here a moment longer.'

CHAPTER SEVEN

SAM AND FRANKIE, ARMS LINKED, stood outside the wire mesh fence that surrounded the well-spaced dog kennels. Inside Amanda was grooming a handsome red setter who kept giving her appreciative licks with a large red tongue.

'He likes her.' Sam pressed his arm against Frankie.

'She's very happy here, that's obvious.'

'She's put on six pounds in the month she's been here. That's the main thing. She's well on the way to recovery. She obviously has a marvellous rapport with animals, and we never knew that. There's a lot we never knew about our youngest daughter.' Sam's voice throbbed with self-reproach.

They both raised their hands and waved as Amanda saw them. She let go of the dog and, rushing up to the fence, peered through. The dog, by her side, peered through too.

'Are you off now?'

'We said goodbye to the Maxwells. They're very happy with you.' Sam kissed her through the wire fence. 'And you're happy too darling. We're so pleased.'

'Terribly happy Daddy; but don't let Mummy come down will you?'

The smile of tenderness vanished on Sam's face.

'She'd love to see you Amanda. She feels very rejected.'

'I'm not ready for her yet, Daddy.'

'But she does *love* you. You've got to work it out with Mummy sometime.'

Amanda turned away, brushes in her hand, and then knelt down next to the impatient dog who was delighted to have her to himself again.

Sam and Frankie waved again and called goodbye; then they strolled slowly back up the lane to the hotel, where they had spent the night, to get their things and go back to London.

'God knows what we'll do at Christmas,' Sam said. 'It's Sarah's last Christmas too.'

'Don't say it like that Sam, you'd think she was dying.'

'Well I mean we don't know when we'll see her again. Going abroad on this medical relief thing. I'm not at all happy about it.'

'Well *she* seems very happy. She's going to Africa and Asia. It will be wonderful experience.'

Sam looked at her.

'Do you realize, Frankie, that Sarah came second in the whole of her year? Everyone else on either side of her is going to specialize, get top jobs, become consultants. Think how proud we'd all have been of her then.'

He took Frankie's arm and they continued to stroll along in silence until they came to the country inn where they'd entertained Amanda to dinner the evening before. They went up to their bedroom, which overlooked fields of hops stretching as far as the eye could see. Away in the distance a spiral of smoke trailed upwards through the sparse red and brown leaves on the trees. Sam leaned out of the window and sniffed.

'I love burning leaves. Sometimes I feel I'd like to live in the country. Wouldn't you darling?'

Frankie, folding his pyjamas into the suitcase on the bed, shook her head.

'Nope. I'm a town girl. Sam, you promised we could visit the States this year. Well it's nearly gone and we haven't.'

'Well we've had a lot to occupy ourselves.' Sam sat on the bed. 'The baby, Amanda . . .'

'Well that's all taken care of now, Sam.' Frankie shut the case and fastened it with a determined click. 'Zoë is fine, Amanda is very happy here, and Sarah is going to Africa. Barbara has her own practice and her own life, and Tom may be sent to Singapore. What's to stop us?'

'Nothing.' Sam took her hand and brought it to his lips. 'I do love you Frankie. But what about your articles?'

'I'm not talking about going forever.' Frankie laughed and kissed him on top of the head. 'A holiday, two, three weeks. Could we go soon Sam?'

'I'll think about it,' Sam said. 'I really will.'

Sam was very worried about Barbara. She had taken the

news about Sarah's forthcoming departure badly – almost as though, Sam thought, she felt responsible for it – and was more upset about Amanda than he thought she let on. He and Frankie had brought Amanda to this quiet place in Kent, installed her and visited her. She had excluded her mother from her life completely. Sam didn't understand it. Anyone would have thought Barbara had been actively cruel to her and he knew she hadn't. He fretted on Barbara's behalf. But Sam never dared talk about Barbara to Frankie. It was the one subject that was forbidden, except in the most casual reference.

Sam loved Frankie so much; but he wished she'd be more understanding about Barbara, realize how a woman in her early fifties must feel about losing three-quarters of her family in the space of three years. And to the extent she saw Tom she might as well consider him lost too.

On the way up to town Frankie was very silent and Sam kept on looking at her, wondering if she was all right. To his query she replied that, of course she was all right, but one couldn't go on talking all the time. There was something in her eyes though, an expression that worried him. It had been there for quite a few days and it seemed to him that Frankie wanted to tell him something, but couldn't get the words out. He had tried to get her to talk the previous night after Amanda had gone, but all she wanted to do when they got to their room was make love, more vigorously and passionately, with more frenzy than usual. Spent in every sense of the word, Sam had been glad to go to sleep immediately afterwards and when he woke Frankie was out walking in the wood bordering the hotel. After that they'd had no chance to talk, and now she was silent again.

When they got back to town about four the lights were on in the house. They left the car in the garage and walked into the kitchen calling for June. June was upstairs bathing Zoë and Sam and Frankie spent a ritualistic hour worshipping at Zoë's shrine, playing with her in and out of her bath, cuddling her before she was put down for the night. June left early to go out and Sam and Frankie ate a cold supper on their laps in front of the television.

Sam forgot all about Frankie's secretive demeanour until he got up to switch off the television and she suddenly announced: 'I've got something to tell you Sam.'

119

It was the way she said it that made Sam's heart lurch. It was bad news, not good news she had to tell him. Full of foreboding he turned round and looked at her.

'I knew you had something on your mind.' Resignedly he sat down and took her hand. 'Why didn't you tell me before?'

Frankie sat huddled up, her legs tucked under her, her shoulders hunched against her cheeks.

'I couldn't seem to get it out. I hoped that I could tell you in Kent. I wanted to and I tried, but . . .' She looked at him fearfully and Sam began to feel seriously alarmed.

'Are you ill Frankie?'

Frankie smiled, a sort of ironic smile that seemed to say it depended on how you interpreted the word 'illness'. She looked up at Sam, her lower lip trembling.

'I'm pregnant, Sam.'

It really was like announcing a serious illness, even a death, as far as Sam was concerned. He closed his eyes and shuddered, his hand between Frankie's feeling very stiff and cold, like a board.

'I knew you wouldn't like it and I didn't want to tell you. I decided I'd have an abortion and you wouldn't know; but I just can't go through with it.'

'But now what?' Sam felt rage beginning to overwhelm him instead of that awful despair.

'Well I'm careless, aren't I Sam? I don't always use the cap. It's not surprising it happened really. In some ways I think maybe I wanted it to.'

Sam let her hand fall and stood up, his hands on his hips, gazing down at her.

'I think you did this deliberately, Frankie. You were always talking about having another baby.'

She gazed back at him, bolder now than before.

'I didn't do it deliberately, Sam, I promise you. I would never have done such a thing without your agreement.'

'But Frankie for God's sake think what happened last time! You were nearly out of your mind. You're nearly forty. I can't go through all that again. It isn't fair to me, never mind you. I'm sorry, Frankie, you will have to get rid of it. I'll speak to Dickens tomorrow.'

Frankie pursed her lips and raised her chin, an expression of stubbornness with which Sam was very familiar.

120

'You can't force me to have something done I don't want Sam. You can't force me to have an abortion. I've considered it and I've rejected it. I've talked with Sarah about it and she agrees. She has been very supportive towards me.'

'You've talked with *her* and not me?' Sam looked furious. 'How long has all this been going on for God's sake? How pregnant are you?'

'Four months.' The look of defiance was there again.

'Four months, and you didn't say a thing! I suppose you thought that the longer it went on the less chance there would be of an abortion.'

'There is *no* chance of an abortion, Sam.' Frankie's tone was quite definite, almost cold. 'I will, however, have the amniocentesis Sarah was on about last time. There is a chance of a defect the older you get, though I am only thirty-eight and not forty.'

'You're nearly thirty-nine and will be when the baby's born.'

'*Still* not forty. They can't do this until about sixteen weeks, and I'm not seeing Mr Dickens, whom I didn't much like, but I'm going to Sarah's hospital where they're very good on the outpatients and it's all free. She knows all the obstetricians there and I'll be well looked after.'

'But she won't be there.'

'It doesn't matter.'

Sam flopped down in a chair and spread his long legs out in front of him.

'It's all decided then, all arranged.'

'I'm afraid so.'

'And yet you couldn't tell me, your own husband?' He looked at her so sadly that tears sprang to Frankie's eyes.

'I couldn't tell you Sam because I was frightened. Sarah wanted me to tell you and now I have.'

'But I love you, why should you be afraid of me?'

'Because I knew what you'd say, how you'd react. You do love me, I know that; but I'm also rather frightened of you Sam.'

'*Frightened* of me?'

'Yes. You once told me, you remember, about your vast experience, how you were the father of a grown-up family? At times I do feel a gulf between us based on our respective ages. Sometimes I feel like your daughter rather than your wife.'

'That's a very hurtful thing to say,' Sam said, and Frankie got up and went to kneel by the side of his chair, reaching for his hand.

'You know you're paternalistic. You've admitted it.'

'But not to you. I'm your lover.'

'But you're authoritarian Sam, you make the decisions. For a woman like me, perhaps being an American too, it's not easy.'

'But you never *said* anything.'

'You must have realized it, when things went a bit wrong. I felt like a little girl when I had my breakdown, with you and Barbara like my mother and father. Dr Vaughan said that was why I resented Barbara so much. I still think sometimes of you and she as a pair and me as the interloper.'

'You know I hardly ever see Barbara. The only time recently has been to discuss Sarah and Amanda. I am utterly and totally one hundred per cent wedded to you. What you say is very hurtful to me. I am not an old man and I don't feel it. But I tell you this, Frankie, and I tell it to you straight.' He looked at her, lightly putting his arm round her shoulder, but casually not caressingly. 'The thought of having to go through what we went through last time, as well as having a young baby in the house again, frightens me. I don't think I can bear it.'

'I won't be ill again, I know that.' Frankie tugged the lobe of his ear, reached for his hand again and squeezed it, but it remained unresponsive. 'I know why I was last time and I won't be this time.'

'But they said it was hormones.'

'It was also psychological, jealousy of Barbara, the things I've explained to you. I'm strong enough now and we still have June. The new baby will fit very easily into our household and, I promise you, there will never be another.'

She looked up at Sam, willing him to smile; but too much had been said, too many things implied to make him feel happy.

Barbara seldom had time for shopping of the practical kind. She scarcely ever went into a grocer's, a butcher's or a greengrocer's because goods were either delivered to the door or else bought by Linda before she came to work. Barbara, however, had always been a good cook and this talent went back to her youth when, as a young doctor and mother, she did all the cooking, shopping and rearing of the children as well. These days, except for the very occasional dinner party, Barbara scarcely cooked an elaborate meal at all. For herself she preferred a steak and salad, or fish and fresh vegetables, things that were tasty and easy to do.

So when Barbara went to Hampstead High Street it was usually for some other reason than to shop for food. The shops were daily changing so much – boutiques and delicatessens, take-aways and junk food shops appearing and disappearing – that it amused her to wander along when she had the time, usually after collecting books at the High Hill Bookshop or visiting a favourite boutique in Haverstock Hill where she liked to buy tailored shirts and skirts. Barbara's forays abroad took place between seeing patients, or if she had a vacancy or a cancellation, and were usually rather hurried.

One morning Barbara was going quite briskly along the High Street, with two newly purchased books under her arm, because it was very cold and not the sort of day for loitering. She regarded a trip to the High Street as a form of constitutional and this, combined with an occasional swim in the Swiss Cottage Baths, was about all the exercise she felt she had time for. Barbara heard her name and stopped, not sure from which direction the voice came.

'Dr Hahn!' She looked around and saw an upraised hand on the other side of the street. She waved in response, recognizing Jennifer Littlejohn, and wondered whether to walk on or wait. But the decision was made for her as Jennifer, careless of the traffic, came running across the road, her pretty face animated with excitement.

'Dr Hahn I *thought* it was you. What are you doing here?'

'I've been to the bookshop.'

Jennifer looked at the parcel under her arm. 'I'm going to the hairdresser. I don't suppose you have time for a coffee?' Jennifer glanced to a coffee bar just beside them.

Barbara studied the eager, smiling face and felt curious. After all she and this woman had had a relationship for many years. One couldn't cut off a relationship of such intimacy as

123

though with a knife, though psychoanalytic theory advised that one should.

'Why not? I only have a few minutes though, because I have a patient at twelve.'

Jennifer darted ahead of her into the coffee bar, sitting breathlessly down and drawing off her gloves. For a moment the two women gazed silently at each other.

'How have you been?' Barbara put her parcel on the seat beside her and undid her coat.

'I've been quite well,' Jennifer replied, rather guardedly Barbara thought. 'As you said, I needed to be given a push. I mean it hasn't been as bad as I feared, though I've missed seeing you.'

'How's John?' Barbara said.

'Oh about the same. In fact nothing has changed very much. I play a lot of bridge. I do a lot of voluntary work, Oxfam and one-parent families mostly. I fill my mind and time as best I can.' Jennifer leaned forward. 'And how's your daughter? The one who was ill?'

'Oh she recovered completely.' Barbara bent to sip the steaming coffee that a waitress had placed before her. 'She's working in the country with dogs.'

'Dogs?'

'She wants to be a kennel maid.'

'Oh? I thought she was brilliant.'

'Well she wasn't brilliant, but clever. And my elder daughter, who's a doctor, is going abroad.'

'Where to?'

'Africa. She's joining a relief mission run by some American organization. It's not religious or anything, just a body of people bent on helping others.'

'That's very noble.' Jennifer sat back, her hands quietly folded, and Barbara thought she had acquired a quality of repose since she'd last seen her. 'Sometimes I wish I could throw everything up and do something like that.'

'She'll only do it for a year or two.'

'You must feel very lonely, Dr Hahn.'

Barbara found Jennifer's keen gaze rather disconcerting, as though their roles had been reversed in some curious way and she was the patient, Jennifer the analyst.

'I have a very full life. I shall miss my daughter Sarah, though . . .'

'Dr Hahn you know John and I have a little coastguard cottage in Kent? I mean it may be absolutely useless to you, but if you or you and your daughter, or any of your children, would like to slip away for a few days by the sea you'd be very welcome. I thought you looked rather tired.'

'Mrs Littlejohn that is *very* good of you . . .' Barbara began. 'But I can see no reason why I . . .'

'It was just a thought,' Jennifer said hastily. 'You know, you might like to get away and it's very near London, just out of Folkestone. I wouldn't be there of course, nor would John.'

'I'm deeply touched,' Barbara said. 'I'll certainly give it a thought.'

'Well I owe you a lot for all the years you sat there patiently listening to me. I must have seemed idiotic, unable to solve my problems or come to terms with my fears. The same thing over and over again about John . . .'

'You don't owe me anything,' Barbara said gently. 'It was my job to try and help you to understand and, if possible, resolve your fears, and with your husband you felt you had real reason for your misery.'

'I imagine your husband gave you a lot of misery too.'

Barbara didn't reply at once, studying the face of the woman opposite her whose life she knew so intimately; yet hers was supposed to be a closed book. How much had she revealed of her own unhappiness and tension as, day after day, she sat listening to her patients, trying unobtrusively to direct their muddled lives when her own emotions were in turmoil? How many of them had she deceived? She recalled how often John Littlejohn had reminded her of how little she knew about Sam. His exploits always seemed to trigger off her own reminiscences and anxious speculations.

'I'm sorry, I shouldn't have asked.' Jennifer's voice brought Barbara back from her reverie.

'Yes my husband *did* give me a lot of misery. I always felt that you imagined my own life was carefree and perfect. Does it make the help I try and give to my patients any less good if it isn't?'

'I know it seems childish, but one likes to feel that the person sitting opposite you has got their lives all satisfactorily sorted out. I mean they've had so much experience, so many years of learning. I got quite a shock when I heard you were divorced.'

'Because you imagined me living in perfect harmony with some ideal man.' Barbara smiled and drew on her gloves. 'The longer I live the more I feel that one is only qualified to help others if one has weaknesses and imperfections in one's own life. Otherwise we would feel terribly superior wouldn't we?' She stood up. 'It *is* nice to see you again.' She took her purse from her bag but Jennifer said hastily:

'No, let me. I invited you.'

'Let's go Dutch.' Barbara firmly put some coins on the table. 'And if I should ever take you up on the offer of the cottage, and it sounds delightful, I'd like to pay.'

'You don't want to be dependent on anyone do you Dr Hahn?'

'It's not dependence; it's simply not taking favours when there is a semi-professional relationship.'

'I do know what you mean.' Jennifer began to fasten her coat. 'You can rent the cottage for a nominal sum any time you like.'

They walked to the door and shook hands outside on the pavement. Then Barbara started up the hill, while her former patient stood for a long time looking after her until she disappeared round a corner.

The nearer Christmas came the more of a threat it posed to Barbara, who had made no plans and didn't know what to do. A few days after her encounter with Jennifer Littlejohn the idea of the cottage suddenly became appealing. A few days in Kent by herself? It would let everyone off the hook and Sam could entertain the family in his own home without the burden of her presence.

'What a very good idea,' Sam said when she told him the next day, and she could sense his relief on the phone. 'Though Amanda is staying down in Kent . . .' There was a pause. 'Nowhere near you I suppose?'

'I'll be on the coast,' Barbara said. 'Kent's a big county, though I do intend to try and see more of Amanda in the new year. I just feel I need a break to get away from it all.'

'I'll miss our family Christmasses,' Sam said solemnly.

'I won't,' Barbara replied, glad that they were separated by

126

miles of telephone cable. 'The kind you're talking about are gone forever.'

Tom and Natalie squeezed with reluctance into the small bedroom at the top of the house, though Frankie allowed two cots in her study for the babies so that they could be within earshot of their parents next door.

Frankie was very reluctant to entertain the family for Christmas, but it never seemed to enter Sam's head that she should do otherwise. Sam took things for granted where the family was concerned. The expected new baby was to be announced to the family at Christmas and Frankie considered the prospect something of an ordeal. Apart from this she was not having a good pregnancy, with morning and evening sickness and excessive tiredness. Her life suddenly seemed sapped of all joy. Poppy told her she should put her foot down and tell Sam she wanted to go away; but Frankie knew there was no question of such a thing with Sam. Family life, its pleasures and duties, was a *sine qua non* of existence to him.

'It would alienate him more,' she had said when they met in their Blandford Street restaurant before Christmas.

'More?'

'He is very angry about the baby.'

'But, golly, it's his baby! I mean he *did* the bloody thing. He must have known you weren't wearing the cap.'

'No he wouldn't know. Sam wouldn't know. He'd leave that kind of thing to me.'

The coil hadn't suited and Frankie felt she was too old for the Pill. Sam would rather have fathered twenty children than use a condom and twenty more than have a vasectomy. The idea was firmly rooted in men of his generation that the burden of preventing children, having them, rearing them belonged to the woman.

Poppy looked at her watch and said she must fly. Her envy of Frankie was beginning to evaporate. It was quite liberating to feel that, even if one lacked family life and companionship, one did not have the burden of a much older husband and babies one didn't really want. Procreation was fine as a concept, almost mystical; but, in reality, it led to years of stress, work and toil

127

while the much wanted baby grew into adulthood. In an expansive mood, she treated Frankie to lunch.

'You're having a rotten time poor old thing aren't you?' she said grabbing the bill.

Frankie felt the bile rise in her throat as she looked at her plate.

'If only I wasn't so sick. This time I really do feel I'm too old; but the hospital say I'm fine and sickness doesn't mean anything's wrong. But I hate the whole thing. I'm very sorry I went ahead with it.'

'Is it really too late for abortion?'

Frankie screwed up her nose.

'It's kind of repulsive to me, unless I have to, unless the amniocentesis finds the baby's deformed. The thing that really bothers me is Sam. It's changed our relationship. Sometimes I feel, lately, he regrets marrying me, that he'd rather have Barbara, peace and normality.'

Poppy could suddenly see that Sam probably was thinking just that.

'I think it's very irresponsible of you, Dad.' Tom took a deep gulp of his brandy as if fortifying himself against his father's reply. The announcement had been made at dinner and Sarah rushed to the support of Frankie and her father saying how splendid it would be for Zoë to have a playmate. Natalie said she was tired and went to bed early, Frankie soon followed her and Tom, Sarah and Sam sat up talking.

'It wasn't me,' Sam said savagely. 'I didn't want the baby.'

'Then why?'

'It just happened.'

'But couldn't she get rid of it?'

'She didn't want to. I don't understand women. As if she hadn't had a bad enough time when Zoë was born, and now she's nearly forty!'

'Well she doesn't look particularly happy about it if you ask me.'

'She isn't. She's ill most of the time. If we didn't have June I don't know what we'd do.'

Sarah sat like a referee between the two men, her arms linked behind her head.

'You should have known what you were doing when you married a younger woman, Daddy. I have to defend the woman's viewpoint. The urge to reproduce oneself is very strong.'

'You sound just like your mother,' Sam said savagely. 'Why you went ahead and encouraged Frankie I don't know.'

'It wasn't your business, for a start.' Tom looked at her accusingly.

'It *is* my business – as a woman and a doctor and as Frankie's stepdaughter. She came to me in some distress – me mark you, not Daddy – and, after listening to what she had to say, I decided that she did in fact want the baby. To have had an abortion might have plunged her into depression again. She saw our senior obstetrician and he thought that too. Frankie needed a lot of shoring up to face Dad. That's what I find regrettable.'

She turned her formidable gaze on her father who looked away. Tom twirled his glass in his hand studying his father's heavy features, cast in gloom.

'Do you ever regret leaving Mother, Dad?'

Sam jerked himself up as though his son's words echoed his thoughts. He rose, lit a cigar and blew smoke in the air, then refilled his glass and Tom's.

'Well, if you want me to be honest, sometimes I do. I mean I didn't bargain for two babies in quick succession, and a wife who was frequently ill. Goodness, you knew Frankie – she was so full of life, such fun! It's all very different now.'

'I can see that Dad. You made a mess of it if you asked me. You should have kept her as a girl friend.'

'She wouldn't have it,' Sam said avoiding his son's eyes. 'I did think it was the best thing to do. I didn't want to upset Barbara, the family and all that; but Frankie wouldn't have it.'

'I don't blame her,' Sarah said shortly, but Tom interrupted her.

'You mean she actually *demanded* that you left Mum?'

'Oh no,' Sam said hastily. 'Nothing of the sort. She didn't want to break up my marriage, but she said she loved me and would rather give me up than keep on as we were. Hole in the corner. She was planning to go back to the States.' As Tom snorted disbelievingly Sam went on. 'No it's true. She had the ticket. I couldn't bear her to go Tom. I knew I was really in love. That's what did it.'

'That's an old ploy Dad. She could quietly have disappeared and that would have been it.'

'It was love Tom. Mutual love.'

'It was *sex*, Dad.' Tom gazed unblinkingly at his father. 'Love was what you had for Mother and the family. I can't believe you don't love her in that way now.'

'I do,' Sam said, bowing his head. 'I do love her and I miss her. I feel she has had a very bad time recently and I want to go and see her. She doesn't deserve what's happened to her.'

'Then why don't you go and see her?'

'It upsets Frankie.'

'To hell with Frankie.'

'But I'm married to Frankie. She is very jealous of Barbara, frightened of her.'

'She's frightened of Mother's power over Dad,' Sarah intervened. 'She has reason to be. That's not illogical at all. Our mother and father have a very strong bond, based on many years of marriage and three children, now two grand-children. The nicest woman in the world – and Frankie is a particularly nice woman – would fear that sort of competition.'

'If she's "particularly nice" why did she go off with someone else's husband?' Tom enquired sarcastically. 'That's not a "particularly nice" thing to do is it?'

'Tom I'll have to throw you out of here if you talk like that,' Sam half rose in his chair. 'Heavens, the circumstances were explained enough, then and now.'

'Another jolly Christmas.' Tom sighed, pretending to duck.

'Tom always took Mother's part,' Sarah said. 'I could be more detached. As a wife, Mother wasn't really particularly good. I mean she never shared Dad's interests nor invited him to share hers. She had that secret room where she saw her patients, and it really was her life. Didn't you ever feel jealous of the patients Tom?'

'I can't remember. It was such a long time ago.'

'I think you probably were. A busy mother and father threw us on our own resources; a busy wife made Dad interested in other women. Women who are neglected often turn to other men. If I'm as devoted to my work as Mummy is to hers I don't intend to marry or have children.'

'Really?' Sam looked astonished.

'Yes really. I believe in equality, but it's hard in practice, mainly because women are constructed differently from men.'

Tom chuckled. 'Coming from the arch feminist I think that's rich. How are they differently constructed may I ask?'

'A woman carries the burden of reproduction, or the pleasure, whichever way you look at it,' Sarah replied without rancour. 'It's a physiological fact. Anyway what's done here as far as our parents are concerned, is done. It's no good moping about the past, but let's make what we can of the present and the future. I want to try and see you all sorted out before I go.'

'I wish you weren't going,' Sam said. 'I feel I can lean on you, now that I can't lean on Barbara. Frankie doesn't mind that. She needs you too.'

He looked appealingly at his daughter who shook her head. 'We must all stand on our own feet, Dad. I feel others need me more. Here in the affluent countries we are satiated with people who can help us. In Africa there often isn't a doctor for hundreds of miles. Here I don't really know what I want; I'm full of vague unease and discontent. I'm useless to my family really, useless to Mother . . .'

'Why your mother?' Sam said curiously.

Sarah passed her hand through her hair, so reminiscent of a gesture of Barbara's that for a moment Sam saw mother and daughter as one.

'Oh Mum and I had a row about something a few weeks ago. I haven't seen her since then either.'

'She must feel very lonely.' Tom looked at them both. 'I wish I were nearer her. What kind of Christmas is she having all by herself in Kent?'

A silence fell as though each one were seeing that familiar, well loved figure now abandoned and on her own in unfamiliar surroundings.

'If you know where Mum is, Dad, I'll go down and see her,' Sarah said suddenly.

'Oh darling that would be nice of you.' Sam reached for her hand. 'Make it up with your mother, and tell her about the baby. I haven't had the heart.'

131

CHAPTER EIGHT

THE COTTAGE ON THE ROAD between Folkestone and Hythe was, in itself, unprepossessing. It was set in a row of similar cottages which had been built some time towards the end of the nineteenth century for coastguards and others whose work was the sea. A tiny fenced garden separated the cottage from the road and at the back was a paved terrace that looked directly on to the sea. To the right was Hythe Bay and to the left the jutting promontory of limestone cliffs with Folkestone harbour, from which the boats left for France, beneath. None of the cottages had gardens at the back because of the high winds which drove the sea against the cottage walls, and all of the back windows were shuttered against the elements. A path ran the length of the line of buildings, continuing a shore walk, and this was protected by a high sea wall with a parapet.

Inside the house was comfortable enough with storage heaters and open fires, a kitchen with a stone floor and whitewashed walls, a large living room, a combined bathroom and lavatory, and three small upstairs bedrooms. It was a funny sort of place for the Littlejohns to have; Barbara had expected something rather more attractive and, perhaps, a little more luxurious. She found it hard to think of sophisticated Jennifer being at home in the place, or mysterious John whom she knew so well but had never seen.

Barbara had never had such a Christmas on her own and, as soon as she got to the cottage, she realized it had been a mistake to come. She would have been more comfortable at home. She was used to central heating and the convenience of a large house, the comfort of her own bed and, if she wanted to go out, long walks on Hampstead Heath or in Highgate Wood.

But to go home would be to acknowledge her mistake and, besides, the family would be uneasy. Sam would consider it a duty to telephone her, Tom and his family and Sarah to come and see her. It would emphasize the contrast between this Christmas and the happy family Christmasses of the past. That was really why she had gone away.

Happiness seemed to have eluded Barbara and her thoughts were constantly melancholic and nostalgic as, wrapped up against the icy winds that blew almost permanently, lashing the sea against the high wall, she walked along the front between the two towns or up into the woods and fields at the back.

Barbara arrived on Christmas Eve and spent Christmas Day trying to pretend that it was just an ordinary sort of holiday day and not Christmas at all. She'd toyed with the idea of having lunch or dinner at a local hotel, but thought that it would emphasize her solitude, call attention to her remoteness from other people with large happy families enjoying themselves. She cooked a chicken, had some paté to start and opened a bottle of wine. She decided that, having performed this involuntary penance, she would go home the day after Boxing Day.

Barbara returned from her walk on Boxing Day to find Sarah sitting in her car outside the door. She looked cold, as though she'd been sitting there a long time. Barbara stared at the car and then at Sarah who looked at her mother as though uncertain of her welcome. Barbara bent down and smiled through the window, opening the car door as she did. She stood back to let Sarah out and then shut the door and, tucking her arm through hers, led her into the cottage.

'This is a lovely surprise,' she said closing the door behind them.

'I'm glad you don't mind, Mummy.'

'Mind? Why should I mind? On the contrary I'm delighted. Nothing wrong in London I hope, or elsewhere?' Amanda out of sight and out of touch always made her uneasy.

'No everyone's fine; but we were talking about you yesterday and I suddenly felt bad and wanted to see you. We all did.'

She was looking around the living room as Barbara removed the fireguard and threw some logs on the fire.

'You all felt bad? Why?' Barbara straightened up and looked at her.

133

'You know why.'

As her mother watched the flames licking round the dry wood Sarah suddenly thought how much older, and sadder, she seemed than when she had seen her before.

'Because you were all alone, Mummy. We couldn't help remembering Christmasses in the past.'

'Yes, but they're over darling aren't they?' Barbara began taking off her coat, untying the thick woollen scarf which covered her hair. 'Can I take your coat?'

Sarah, her hands bunched up in her pockets, shivered. 'It's cold here isn't it?'

'It is rather cold,' Barbara agreed. 'And melancholy too. It's such a dark cottage. I'm sorry I came; but I'm glad you're here now,' she said brightening. 'And we will go out for dinner. Can you stay the night?'

'Of course, that's why I came. What do you mean "and we *will* go out for dinner" in that tone of voice?'

'I thought of it yesterday, but decided it would be awful on my own. Silly wasn't I?'

With an effort Barbara was making her tone light and cheerful.

'I think you're absolutely right to feel miserable, and we should have come to you. Daddy and Frankie could have celebrated on their own. There was no need to have a repetition of last year. Tom and Natalie are much happier with you than with Daddy. I mean, as far as accommodation is concerned. That house is awfully small for so many people.'

'And how are Tom and Natalie and the babies?' Barbara hung her coat on a hook on the wall.

'Oh they're fine. They sent you their love. Oh Mummy . . .' Sarah took a step forward and Barbara, in the act of going into the kitchen, paused and looked back at her daughter.

'Oh Mummy . . .' Sarah said again and then rushed into the arms that were suddenly opened to her and closed around her shoulders protectively, comfortingly. Barbara leaned her head against Sarah's, feeling the wetness on her cheeks.

'There's no need to *say* anything darling. I know how you feel. Me too.'

Sarah sobbed quietly for a while and Barbara remembered how emotional she had been as a little girl and how, as she'd

134

grown older, she had seemed to withdraw into herself, become quite self-contained and able to conceal any feeling at all. When she took up the study of medicine she never expressed shock or horror at anything she'd seen. Nothing, however grisly, ever upset her.

After a few minutes Sarah broke away, wiping her eyes on the sleeve of her jersey and then, extracting a rather grubby handkerchief from the sleeve, blew her nose vigorously.

'I feel so awful about my behaviour that night.'

'It was perfectly understandable.' Barbara took Sarah's hand and drew her to the sofa. 'My behaviour was pretty despicable.'

'But, as you said, you were old enough to know what you were doing. I'd no right to carry on as I did.'

'But you're my *daughter*, can't you understand?' Barbara looked at her in surprise. 'I would have felt the same if I discovered you in a similar situation. Where there's a blood bond there's always disgust at some demeaning sexual behaviour, and that was demeaning. It also ruined my friendship with Alfred Kleber,' she added regretfully.

'For good?'

'Oh I expect so. I mean I could hardly face him again after I bundled him out of the house half-dressed. I guess he felt pretty demeaned too; not keen to repeat the experience. It taught me a good few things about myself I can tell you.' Barbara looked at her daughter, and the smile that slowly illumined her face made her beautiful again. 'We're always learning, you know. I'll go and make tea.'

Barbara went into the kitchen, her heart so light that it made the dreary Christmas seem worthwhile, one of the best for what it had so far, unexpectedly, achieved. Her self-reproach about her adolescent behaviour with Alfred Kleber had been compounded by misery over her separation from her censorious daughter. The fact that Sarah had made the move of reconciliation filled her with joy and, over tea, they chatted animatedly by the fire, looking upon Sarah's trip abroad as something exciting, a welcome challenge rather than an escape.

Barbara, with difficulty, secured a table for dinner – there had been a cancellation at the Grand – and, as they toasted each other Sarah decided it was time to tell her mother the news about Sam and Frankie.

'Another baby?' Barbara said. 'Well, well.'

'Dad is taking it very badly. He said he hadn't the heart to tell you.'

'Poor Sam,' Barbara smiled and refilled their glasses with the best claret the hotel could offer. 'You know sometimes I really feel sorry for that man and the scrapes he gets himself into. It's as though he's gone back to his youth – a young man trapped in an old man's skin.'

'Is that really how you see Daddy?'

'Oh yes.'

'And how do you see Frankie?'

Barbara looked at her in surprise.

'As a perfectly normal young woman who wants to be loved. Seventeen years' difference isn't a lot except that Sam had so much past compared to her.'

'Do you think you and she could ever just be normal . . . friends?'

'It would be wrong of me to say that I don't see why not. It *is* a difficult situation. I think I tried too hard and she tried too hard. We both wanted to please Sam. Now I think this separation is for the best, except that I wish I saw more of your father. He was my friend and I miss him.'

'He said he still loved you. He more or less admitted he thought he'd made a mistake.'

Barbara was silent, looking at the beautiful red liquid in her glass, swirling it around to catch the reflection of the chandeliers overhead.

'I think you misinterpret him. Naturally, even at your age, you'd like your father and mother together again.' She raised her eyes to gaze at Sarah. 'I think he *is* in love with Frankie and would have been perfectly happy if she'd remained the carefree young woman he married. Sam wanted passion in marriage; friendship and companionship, such as I thought we had, wasn't enough for him. A physically demanding man like Sam needs constant stimulation. It's all this burden of new parenthood that he finds hard. Even new young wives can't be passionate all the time once they have pregnancy and babies to attend to.'

136

'Frankie is having a very bad pregnancy too. She can't work at all. She seems very depressed.'

'I'm so sorry to hear that.' Barbara was quite genuine.

'She says she thinks Daddy does love her less. She feels she irritates him.'

Barbara folded her arms on the table and looked around at the crowded dining room. How much nicer it was to be here with a beloved companion rather than alone. 'Well there is, this time, nothing I can do to help. Hard as it seems, I must say it: they have made their bed and they must lie on it. Now let's talk about you and your plans.'

Sarah, overjoyed at her newfound rapport with her mother, related with enthusiasm her itinerary for the next six months, the people she had met whom she was flying out with, the nature of the work once she got there. As she talked with such animation, Barbara thought that, with very little effort, Sarah would be beautiful. Dressed in one of her mother's dresses and with her curly black hair glistening and springing back from her face – no makeup on, of course, but that was a matter of principle – she had a vitality that seemed new to Barbara, that Barbara welcomed, even envied. Sarah was on the brink of life; in many ways, and despite herself, she felt hers was over.

'Won't you stay a few days darling?' she enquired on the way back along the coast road. 'I can bear it here with you. We haven't had a holiday together for years.'

'I can't remember when we were alone like this,' Sarah replied.

'That's the trouble with families.'

'But then, when Dad left, you were thrown completely on your own.'

'Oh no, not completely; but the family did become divided and I always felt you favoured your father. I don't mind,' she added quickly, 'and it's not meant as a reproach. But you can love two parents equally, you know.'

'And be forgiving,' Sarah leant forward in the dark. 'I realize that now.'

And Barbara realized too that she was going to miss Sarah very much.

*

All night long the wind raged and the sea butted against the high sea wall, sending spray on to the walls of the single row of cottages, the windows secure with their strong iron shutters. Barbara lay in the dark listening to the storm, thinking of the ships that would be making their slow way through the channel buffeted by the huge waves, some remaining safely in harbour and others heaving to until the storm was over.

In the morning the rain was still lashing down and the cottage was cold despite the storage heaters which really afforded very little warmth. She had to put on her raincoat and wellingtons to go and get more coal and wood from the outhouse, and paused with some fascination as well as horror to stare at the boiling sea the colour of mud.

'Thank God the tide's out,' she said to Sarah, who had come down in her gown and was standing shivering by the unlit fire, 'or I'd be afraid of damage to the buildings. Do you really want to stay, darling?'

'Well if we go back . . .' Sarah paused as if considering the alternatives. 'No, let's stay another day and see what happens. I love walks on days like this and the sea air will do me good.'

'In that case let's start with a hearty breakfast.' Her mother finished lighting the fire, rubbing her black hands carelessly on her blue jeans over which she wore a thick fisherman's sweater. Like Sarah she was without makeup and the two women were very much alike, of the same height and build. It was even difficult to tell that twenty-five years divided them because the physical work coupled with the presence of Sarah had suddenly made her mother seem youthful.

Later in the morning, looking through the window, Jennifer Littlejohn was astonished to see two people, two Barbaras she thought. They both wore jeans and fishermen's sweaters, and they both had wiry black curly hair. Only one was attractively flecked with white and the other woman had a very long, large nose which was not like Barbara at all. Jennifer hesitated now as to whether to announce her arrival. Her hand shook as she knocked on the door. There was no answer and she knocked again. The wind howled around and she realized they couldn't hear her. She went back to the window and banged on the window pane, and the woman with the big nose got up with the paper she'd been reading, a startled expression on her face. Then Barbara, looking up from her book, recognized her and beckoned. Sarah went to the door.

'I'm so sorry. Were you there long?'

'A few minutes,' Jennifer said shivering from nerves as well as cold, her hands clasping and unclasping each other. 'I'm terribly sorry to disturb you. Hello Dr Hahn,' she waved over Sarah's head as Barbara came over, her hand outstretched.

'Mrs Littlejohn! This is a very nice surprise. My how cold your hand is. This is a Dr Hahn too. My elder daughter Sarah.'

'How do you do –' Jennifer shyly shook Sarah's hand and then looked fearfully around the cottage.

Barbara was immediately impressed by her demeanour, quickly divining that this wasn't merely a social call. The woman looked terrified. But terrified of what?

'I'm awfully sorry to crash in Dr Hahn. I heard about the storms sweeping the south coast on the radio.'

'Oh but we would have rung you if anything was wrong. We were very careful to batten the hatches at night.'

'I know that,' Jennifer smiled nervously. 'That's not really why I'm here. I'm very sorry, I thought you'd be alone. I didn't really want to come at all. I know I shouldn't but . . .'

'Here, come by the fire,' Barbara said gently drawing her forward, looking at Sarah and then jerking her head towards the kitchen door as though she should make more coffee. 'You're very upset about something aren't you? Is your husband annoyed we have the cottage?'

'Oh it's not about that! It's nothing like that! I know I shouldn't have come. I should have coped; after all these years you'd think I'd be able to. I've abused our relationship – lending you the cottage and now coming here to weep on your shoulder . . .'

'Oh dear, is it as bad as that?'

'I'll wash up and make more coffee,' Sarah said and disappeared into the kitchen, closing the door behind her.

'Now she's gone and you can tell me everything.' Barbara got a cigarette, offering one to Jennifer who shook her head. 'I didn't know if you did.' Barbara lit her cigarette and threw the match into the fire. 'I'm always trying to give it up. Now what has upset you so much?'

139

'It's John.'

Of course it would be John. Barbara blew cigarette smoke into the air and knew she should never have come. Having Jennifer's cottage gave Jennifer rights she would not have had at Christmas time in Hampstead when Barbara never saw patients unless they were on the brink of suicide.

'John's left me,' Jennifer went on. 'He wrote me a note to tell me he wouldn't be there for Christmas and that he was going away with a woman.'

'When did he tell you this?'

'Christmas Eve.'

'Not a very nice time to choose was it?'

'I didn't know what to do. I didn't know where he'd gone. If we'd have had children he could never have behaved like this. Could he?'

Barbara silently shook her head.

'Regrettably I have heard of men who do things as bad . . . with children.'

'Well I don't think he would. Leaving me like this, with so many things planned, dinners and dances and so on. It was so humiliating. I felt I couldn't go on, suicidal. I wanted to get in touch with you, but I felt it was abusing our relationship.' She looked timidly at Barbara. 'The fact that you had our cottage. Then this morning I felt I couldn't go on any longer, Dr Hahn, knowing where you were I felt I had to come. I thought I'd make the storm an excuse. I had to.'

Barbara threw the unsmoked half of her cigarette into the fire and leaned back folding her arms behind her head.

'Then I'm glad you came. You're here now and we can talk about it.'

'Thank you Dr Hahn.' Jennifer looked as though she was about to throw herself on her knees, but Barbara held up a hand.

'Don't be grateful and don't call me Dr Hahn. We have known each other long enough to use Christian names. You have really sought me out as a friend, and that's what I am. A professional friend. Now look, John has gone and that's what you always dreaded, isn't it?'

'Yes.' Jennifer looked at her knees. Despite the holiday she was beautifully dressed in a Shetland skirt and jumper with a pearl choker necklace. Had it not been the day after Boxing

Day and a holiday Barbara would have sworn that, despite her emotional confusion, she'd been to the hairdresser. She had certainly taken a great deal of trouble, as always, both with her makeup and her coiffure. Even in the holidays she couldn't be herself. She always had to dress up as though protecting herself against the judgment of a world which might otherwise see her naked. Barbara was aware that Jennifer's excessive concern for her appearance was to deceive others into thinking she was something she wasn't – a woman in control of herself.

'So now what you've dreaded has happened. Our job, mine and yours, is to make you accept it; to realize that it is the best thing, probably, and that you're better without him.'

'But I love him.'

'It's an obsessional love for a man who isn't worth it.'

'I know that. I'd take him back tomorrow, Dr Hahn . . . Barbara.'

'Well, he may come back tomorrow. What then?'

Barbara spent the rest of the morning closeted with Jennifer while Sarah washed up, swept the kitchen, made cups of coffee and finally went for a walk along the seafront throwing pebbles into the stormy sea, trying to work out her own indignation that the secret room had even invaded her holiday retreat with her mother. Barbara had told her that it simply couldn't be helped and Sarah hissed back in the kitchen that it could.

The day was ruined. It would soon be dark. As she walked and wrestled with her rage, her jealousy of this wretched woman who had interrupted the first holiday she and her mother had ever had alone, she thought back over all the years when her mother's professional life had intervened, spoiling family outings, disrupting family holidays, when it had taken her mother away when she needed concrete help or to confide some fear, some need of her own. Patients always seemed to come first, as now, family second.

And then she reminded herself that she, Sarah, was a grown woman, a doctor, shortly to embark on a strenuous task helping people in underdeveloped countries. Why was she childish, petty and silly about Barbara and her patients?

'Because I don't think she should be here, Mummy,' she said when she got back and Barbara came out of the sitting

141

room to talk to her, the door closing behind her. A new secret room transported from Hampstead to Folkestone.

'But darling it *is* her cottage.'

'But she's a patient. You wouldn't see her at home. You'd be on holiday and your answering machine on.'

'I might have seen her if she were as distressed as she is now. I'd see anyone. She was very dependent on this husband . . .'

'Who treated her disgracefully for years.'

'Yes, but there was still an emotional dependence that you might understand better if you'd ever been emotionally dependent yourself. I have to talk her through it, Sarah. To help her the best I can.'

'Then I might as well go back to London.'

'But that's silly, darling! We won't be talking all day.'

'I can't bear the thought of a neurotic, nervous woman moping around. We were so happy together, Mummy.'

Her mother leaned against the kitchen wall, folding her arms. Her face looked tired and drawn as though she had somehow absorbed Jennifer Littlejohn's sufferings to herself. As though John's desertion reminded her of what Sam had done four years before.

'Sarah you will find that, having embraced medicine as a career, it never leaves you. It is not a job, it's a calling. I should have thought you understood that now.'

'Oh I understand,' Sarah exclaimed bitterly. 'I understand all about medicine and its demands on the family, Mother! I intend to remain single, I can tell you, but if I do marry and have children I'll give up medicine. You talk about me not having been emotionally dependent on anyone. I know what you're getting at – but that's why. Love is a tie, and I don't want it.'

'That's very shortsighted, very silly.'

'It's *very* sensible,' Sarah gestured towards the door. 'Why it's not even as though that woman were really *ill*. She is not suffering is she?'

'Yes.'

'Not physically. She has no pain, no ulcer, no cancerous growth. Why doesn't she take tranquillizers and leave you alone?'

'Oh Sarah . . .' Barbara ran her fingers through her thick

142

springy hair. 'I do wish you wouldn't take it so badly, darling.'

'But how *long* is she going to stay?' Sarah began to feel quite desperate with rage and indignation. The calmer her mother became, the more furious she got.

Barbara gestured again. 'I don't know. I really don't know.'

'Then I'm going.'

'I think I could have accepted it so much better if he'd told me. Don't you think he owed me an explanation?'

'What could he explain?'

'Well the reason for going away this time, and for good. I could have told him I'd accept the sort of life he led, if only he would stay with me . . .'

(Barbara had said: 'Why not have her as a mistress? Please Sam, don't break up our family life.' But he said that he loved Frankie, needed her too much to give her up. Besides she wasn't the sort of woman to accept a life like that, second class, second best. 'Does she want children?' Barbara had asked, but Sam replied it wasn't that at all. It was just wanting to be together. Barbara had her work; she would understand.)

'But you were never really *happy* Jennifer, always suspicious. Maybe without him you can find happiness now.'

'Oh never, never . . . He didn't know how much I needed him, what an empty life I have without him. A bit of John is better than no John at all. He was a great charmer, you know. All the women adored him and I felt proud to be seen with him. Now it's the betrayal, I feel, the humiliation, of people knowing. Didn't he think of this?'

(Barbara had said that if Sam wanted to start life all over again it was his business, but she felt the humiliation too. She often wondered if she'd pleaded with him more, made it more difficult, he would have stayed with her; but it was beneath her pride to beg. She clung on to her pride for dear life, and Sam went. She remembered the emptiness when he moved out of the house with his bags, an expression of anticipation on his face as if he were going on a holiday. Did he know what he was subjecting her to? The knowledge that he wasn't coming back seemed unendurable at one point. But she would

143

close the door of her consulting room and take her place opposite her
patients – listening, counselling, helping, submerging her own grief
in that of others. Compared to her Jennifer Littlejohn had nothing
except a big empty house and hours and hours of time on her hands.)

By four o'clock in the afternoon Jennifer Littlejohn was
calmer; but a new commotion was now at work inside Barbara
who, unknown to her patient, had seen Sarah go down the
garden path and drive off without looking back. She went
into the kitchen to make tea and when she came back Jennifer
was looking at the sea which still tossed and raged against the
high sea wall.

'How angry it looks,' she said going up to Barbara with a
smile and taking the tray. 'Thank you Barbara, you're so
good to me. Where's Sarah?'

'She's gone.' Barbara sat composedly beside the tea tray
and started to pour.

'Gone? Gone where?'

'Back to London.'

'Because of me?'

'Oh no, she was going anyway.'

'But I thought you said . . .'

'She changed her mind. She goes next week and has lots of
things to do before that.'

Jennifer took the cup proffered by Barbara, helped herself
to sugar and stirred it thoughtfully.

'I still think it's because of me. I'm terribly sorry. How
selfish people get when they're upset. Your last chance to be
alone with your daughter.' She looked at Barbara as she
sipped tea. 'It's because I never had children. I don't know
what it feels like. Maybe if John and I had had children
everything would have been so different.'

Always that theme of childlessness.

'It often only complicates things. It didn't prevent my
husband leaving me.'

'And that upset you terribly of course?'

'Of course. We had the children and we have to talk
frequently about them. A clean break would have been much
better for me.'

'Did he leave you for someone else?'

'Oh yes.'

144

'So you have been through it too?'

'Yes.'

'Tell me about it.'

Jennifer leaned back, her attitude suddenly transformed from one who had unburdened herself to one who was now prepared to listen, to absorb confidences, to share her own sorrows with a fellow sufferer. She propped her face in the palm of her hand – Barbara's favourite attitude – her eyes, warm and encouraging, studying the face of the woman opposite her.

Barbara leaned forward and poured herself fresh tea. It was true, she felt an unexpected need not only to talk about herself, but to share part of her life with someone who had known her only as a therapist. In a strange way she felt it might help them both.

'Sam and I were married when I was very young,' she began. 'I was a student and he had just left Oxford. For many years our marriage seemed wellnigh perfect because he didn't stand in the way of my own fulfilment in a career and we, as it were, grew into adulthood together. We appeared extremely compatible.'

Barbara told Jennifer all about those early years, the birth of the children, her progress in the medical profession. When she was thirty she decided to train as a psychoanalyst; but it was several more years before she began to practise on her own, and during her training analysis she worked as a doctor in a family planning clinic. She told Jennifer about the children growing up, about Sam's success and talent as a banker, travelling round the world attending international monetary conferences. Then, very abruptly, she made the years roll forward until the breakup, the sudden revelation that Sam not only had someone else he wished to marry, but that he'd been accustomed to having affairs with other women for years. And his analytically oriented wife had suspected nothing.

'Either Sam was very skilful, or I was very foolish,' Barbara said.

Then followed the problem of how to deal with Frankie. To ignore her, or to accept her? In a way acceptance had been forced upon Barbara, but in the process she tried to show Sam that she was indispensable to him.

'Which is why I am here,' she concluded, the cup of now stone cold tea still in her hand. 'By myself for Christmas until my daughter Sarah took pity on me.'

'And now I've sent her away.' Jennifer, her face contrite, bent forward and pressed Barbara's hand. 'You must hate me.'

The pressure of the hand made Barbara suddenly aware of Jennifer and her surroundings. While she had been recounting the story of her life each scene had presented itself so graphically to her inner field of vision that she seemed to have lost track of where she was, with whom or the time of day. She started apologetically as if Jennifer's personal touch embarrassed her, and Jennifer stood up abruptly and took the cup from her.

'It's cold. I'll make a fresh pot.' Jennifer seemed nervous, as if fearful of breaking some newly created spell.

As she listened to movement in the kitchen, the clatter of cups, the sound of the kettle coming to the boil, Barbara threw back her head and closed her eyes feeling drained in the way that she knew patients must feel drained after a session with her. She breathed deeply for a few moments and, as Jennifer came back into the room with a pot of newly brewed tea in her hands, she opened her eyes and smiled.

'That's *very* good of you Jennifer.'

'A nice warm cup of tea.' Jennifer's voice was motherly. 'It helps to share, doesn't it Barbara?'

'I don't know.' Barbara looked about for her cigarettes and found the packet was empty. 'I shall have to go out for more fags.' She paused again and rubbed her hand over her face. 'I shall have to go home Jennifer, after Sarah. I think the whole purpose of telling you what I have was to decide what I should do.'

Jennifer's expression was startled. 'How do you mean?'

'I need Sarah. She has always resented my work and now, once again, I've put it before her. She's going away, soon. Besides . . .' Barbara stared into the empty cigarette carton as though hoping to find one still lurking in a corner, or halfway down the pack, 'we've spent the whole day together. There's not much more we can do.'

'In what way?' Jennifer now looked seriously alarmed.

Barbara tapped her finger against the empty packet. 'I can't

146

treat you any more, Jennifer. You must see that. Today we became friends, women with similar problems. I am in no position any longer to help you as a therapist.'

'But surely we can help each other?'

'No.' Barbara shook her head and got up leaving the freshly made tea untasted, as though her rejection of Jennifer had to be total. 'That's quite impossible. I'll go back to London now, after Sarah.'

'But what about me?'

'You can come back to London too if you want.' Barbara seemed surprised by the question.

Jennifer replaced her cup and saucer on the small table and sat on the arm of her chair staring at her stockinged knees, her legs carefully crossed.

'You don't really care about me, do you Barbara? What happens to me now?'

'Of course I care.' Barbara looked anxiously out of the window. It was nearly dark. Supposing Sarah went to Sam's and told him what had happened? 'But this day hasn't quite turned out as I expected. Not in any way. I thought I could help you, but instead you have helped me. My place isn't here with you Jennifer, it's with Sarah. Sarah came to be with me and I let her go.'

'But she's a grown woman!'

'Yes but don't you understand? She's a child too?'

Barbara looked at the resentful, downcast face opposite her and leaned down and picked up her bag which lay open at her feet revealing its contents. She snapped it shut and put the strap over her arm. 'I can see that you don't. Call me anyway when you get to London, tomorrow or the next day. We'll both think about what's happened, but I know I can never treat you as a patient again. It wouldn't be ethical. If you need someone, if you can't get over John, I know a very good women psychotherapist who will help you.'

Barbara sat down and, opening her bag again, extracted a card on which she wrote a name and a telephone number. She handed it to Jennifer.

'Antoinette Miller. You'll like her.'

'I shan't like her at all,' Jennifer said, snatching the card, gazing sulkily at the name. 'It's beginning all over again.'

'That may be a good thing. Don't you see that our

147

relationship has become too personal? I shouldn't have told you all about my life today, for instance.'

'I should never have offered you the cottage.'

'But you did.' Barbara looked at her. 'You wanted to become more personal didn't you? To establish a bond?'

'I never dreamed that John . . .'

'You wanted to share something of your own with me.' Barbara went to the window inspecting the dark clouds which hurried across the sky without discrimination of shape or form. 'It's quite understandable. I know what I'm doing seems cruel,' she turned and gazed at Jennifer, 'but I can't really help you if there is some personal involvement. By coming here, meeting like this, using Christian names I have stopped being objective to you. I am subjective. I am a friend.'

'You said a professional friend.' Jennifer suddenly looked distraught.

'That was then. *This* is something closer. I wish you could see it.'

'I can't.' Jennifer, in her turn, went to the window which overlooked the street. 'I just know that I need you, not someone, not anyone, but you. You who understand me, who know John. I can't start again with anyone else.'

'A new beginning often helps, and you now have a new life. Someone who can see it with detachment will be of more help to you.'

'I wish you'd go on letting me see you, Barbara, just for a while.' As Barbara didn't reply Jennifer went on. 'I must tell you, Barbara, I resent your daughter. Your attitude to me now. Sarah is obviously so much more important to you than I am, yet I feel you have a duty to me too. I wish I hadn't come.' Jennifer leaned her head against the window as though to cool her hot skin. She rubbed her forehead from side to side and then pressed her nose against the windowpane, which began to mist over from the warmth of her breath.

'I'll go and pack,' Barbara said abruptly, realizing, too late, what an unhealthy situation she had created.

Jennifer turned, her face stricken, her arms stretched towards Barbara.

'*Please* don't go. Not tonight.'

'I must.'

'I can't bear to be alone.'

148

'You'll be OK. You will. I can't stay here.'

'Please . . .'

'I can't.'

Barbara climbed the stairs to her room and didn't see Jennifer kneel down, put her forehead on the floor and hug her body with her arms as though the pain were too much to bear.

Sam had said she was cold; but it was easy for him to say that. It was a taunt at her failure as a woman. It made it easier for him to leave her. Alfred Kleber had implied the same sort of thing too, that she needed a lot of stimulation. Sam also suggested that her patients would find her cold, because she lacked warmth and understanding. Yet who could give more of themselves than she did? Who would have withstood Jennifer Littlejohn for the best part of a day, and then wrenched herself away while the poor woman tried to stop her going? It reminded her of a parting with a child, Jennifer clinging. Dreadful. But why had she made the mistake of confiding in her? Of treating her as a friend? She felt terribly guilty. As soon as Jennifer called her she would see her again, clarify the whole situation and then she would call Antoinette Miller herself and talk to her about Jennifer.

It was quite dark when she got to London.

She could see the light under Sarah's door as she climbed the stairs to her apartment; she had seen the light from the window outside so knew that she was at home. Sarah looked at her for a long time as they both stood on the threshold, then stood back for her mother to go in. There was no attempt to embrace her this time. Sarah hadn't smiled and Barbara saw once again that familiar judgement in her eyes.

'So you did manage to leave Mrs Littlejohn?'

'Did you think I wouldn't?'

'I thought you'd stay holding her hand all night.'

'She wanted me to, but I wanted to make it up with you.' Barbara turned and Sarah was quite shocked by the stricken look in her eyes. 'I can't bear to have a break again Sarah. I can't bear for you to go away without us being friends.'

'We *are* friends, Mummy.' Sarah smiled awkwardly, flop-

149

ping on a giant bean bag on the floor. Her flat was a typical but rather grander version of a student's bed-sitter with a small bathroom, kitchen and bedroom off the main room. 'I just can't keep up with you and your work. It interferes with everything.'

Barbara sank on to the sofa and lit a cigarette. 'I think I was unwise with Jennifer Littlejohn. I think I got too close to her which is breaking all the rules. I failed altogether with Jennifer. You see,' Barbara fiercely blew smoke into the air, 'we were very similar people, married to similar sorts of men. I couldn't detach my own life sufficiently from hers to give her proper help.'

'So what will you do?'

'I'm referring her to someone else. I shan't see her again as a patient.'

'Did you tell her?'

'Oh yes. Of course she's very unhappy about it.'

'I bet. I don't envy you your branch of medicine, Mummy. Give me the good old pills and pep talks any day.'

Barbara gazed at Sarah and thought how much she loved her – sensible, practical, demanding, muddled, half girl, half woman.

'Talking of pep pills, you can give me a brandy,' she said and she leaned back against the bright blue Habitat sofa and closed her eyes. 'I'm worried about Jennifer Littlejohn. Professionally I'm right; but personally I feel I'm wrong.'

Sarah stared at her mother and suddenly saw her as a vulnerable, middle-aged woman. Not a tower of strength, not a paragon at all; she was young, but not young enough. There were plentiful white streaks in her hair and numerous lines in her strong, youthful face. Still in her jeans and jersey, her face without its customary carefully applied makeup, she looked lonely, fragile almost – a woman in need. Sarah got up and sat beside her, gently taking her long strong hand, flecked here and there with the little brown liver marks of age, her wedding ring deeply impressed in her finger as though it had roots there. As far as Sarah knew she had never taken it off. She put her other arm round her mother and Barbara cradled her head against her shoulder, gratefully squeezing the hand that Sarah had put into hers.

'Let's forget about Jennifer Littlejohn,' Sarah said, 'and

concentrate on us in the few days we have together before I go.'

'I wish you weren't going,' Barbara murmured. 'You don't know how much I need you.'

'I do,' Sarah said stroking her mother's brow. 'I do now and I wish I'd known it before.'

'Would it have made any difference?' Barbara looked up at her. 'I mean you still have to go don't you? It's a good thing.'

'I never thought you needed anyone. You've spent yourself on others and I know now how much you needed us.'

'So much,' Barbara sighed. 'So very much. You're going away and your father's got Frankie and his new family. Tom's got Natalie and his family and Amanda . . .' She sighed.

'Amanda needs you, and you need her. Go down and see her, Mummy, when I've gone and try and make it up with her.'

'You can't do much about a girl of eighteen who doesn't want you around, but I'll try. Maybe she'll feel lonely without you. Sometimes I really wonder what use I am to anyone. A failure, personally and professionally.'

'You know you're very useful, very practical, very brave.' Sarah shook her hand. 'And you've always got me and the family, even Daddy, whatever you say or think now. It's a bond that no one and nothing can break.'

Jennifer Littlejohn stood for a long time at the window after Barbara had driven away gazing into the street at the passing cars, the lorries on their way to the docks at Dover.

Cruel, she thought, cruel to leave me, like John. Everyone drives away and leaves me. She gazed at the paper on which Barbara had written the name and phone number of the new psychotherapist and threw it into the fire. Then she went into the kitchen and poured herself half a tumbler of gin.

The thing to do now was to gather strength. She took the tumbler with the bottle Barbara had left behind back into the sitting room and sat on the rug by the fire. It was quite dark outside and the wind, which had never really dropped, had risen again. The relentless sound of the sea pounding on the wall seemed like a summons.

Her only refuge really had been Barbara. How could

151

someone who knew her so well, profess to understand her, be so cruel and leave her alone? How could John? They'd been married nearly twenty years. What would everyone say – the neighbours, the women at the Bridge Club, the tradesmen, her hairdresser – when they knew he had deserted her? Walked out? They would blame her, not him. For a number of years, when he'd tormented her, she'd had Barbara; imagined that perfect life to which she could aspire if she became like her – controlled, detached, serene. Why had she never gone to university? She was clever. Why had she never tried to make more of her life? Why had she frittered it away on a worthless man who caused her to seek expensive psychological help, which was not of much use either?

She took a large gulp of her gin and poured more neat into the glass. It was a colourless, almost odourless and tasteless liquid, but it fired her gut. After some more she felt she didn't need any of these people who had left her – John, Barbara, the few friends she had – though you could only really call them acquaintances. Barbara had gone after her child, preferring her, though she seemed quite capable of looking after herself. It seemed like a taunt, emphasizing her own childlessness and Barbara's fecundity. No, she was quite alone in the world – a barren woman yet, after all, perhaps quite capable of managing by herself. She would probably go on a cruise round the world and meet a new man who would make her forget all about John.

She poured some more gin and realized the bottle was nearly empty. She would take a walk along the sea wall to the off licence in Sandgate and buy a fresh bottle. Gin was of the most enormous comfort to her, as she'd discovered before. She'd never told Barbara that, what a help gin was. She felt that the fastidious Dr Hahn would very much disapprove of, might even despise, a woman who drank secretly and alone for the comfort no living thing could give her. She didn't even have a cat or a dog.

She realized that Barbara had never really been a friend, just a judge – someone she, Jennifer, wanted to impress with her clothes, her large house and her nice car parked outside in the drive, a sporty Porsche that had cost John a lot of money.

Yet she had plenty of money of her own, she was quite independent. She would use some of it now to buy more gin.

Her father, who had only died two years before, had left her a small fortune. Her father had always given them money to help John in his various business ventures most of which, to be honest, were successful so the money just grew and grew. What a waste to throw it away on Dr Hahn whose own life was so imperfect anyway. What a savage, hard girl that daughter of hers had looked, unsmiling, unfriendly, lacking understanding, looking at her as though she was some sort of nut case. Saying quite clearly, though she didn't put it into words, that she wanted her mother to herself.

Jennifer finished the gin in the bottle and got rather unsteadily to her feet. Outside it was now completely dark and the off licence would soon be shut. She put on her coat and tied a scarf round her head, tucked her purse in her pocket and hurried out the back way, shutting the door carefully after her and then closing the shutters on the downstairs windows. The ones upstairs had been closed all day.

As she turned towards the town the lights were bright and rather friendly as though they were waiting to welcome her. She felt curiously exhilarated, aloof and independent, like Barbara Hahn and, as some spray swept over her from the surging sea, she took off her scarf and let it fly in the wind like a flag. She suddenly jumped on the sea wall and below her the foamy-flecked waves boiled dangerously. The wind tore at her clothes and another huge jet of spray nearly knocked her off her feet, causing her to lurch on the parapet. She was soaking wet now and suddenly sober, the scarf that had been a flag limp in her hands. She stared down at the phosphorescent crests of the waves reaching up to her like huge prehensile fingers, trying to pull her down. Across the bay, round the promontory, were the friendly lights of Folkestone, houses with families, hearths with fires, dogs leaping, children prancing around.

But Jennifer alone, cut off; cut off from the world completely.

CHAPTER NINE

JULIA FAIRCHILD WAS A WOMAN of thirty-five with auburn hair that flicked gracefully round her face, framing it like a madonna in a mediaeval oval painting. Her face was very pale, but freckled, as faces of that kind can be, her lips unnaturally red. Her eyes were a curious amber colour and had a very knowing look in them. She gazed gravely at Sam as though weighing an important decision and said that yes, she would like another drink.

On an impulse Sam had invited Julia Fairchild to go with him to the bar in one of the arches under Blackfriars Bridge, which he increasingly frequented after work and before going home. She was a clerk in the securities department which came under his charge, and she was such an unusual looking woman that she rather intrigued him. She wasn't really at all pretty, not the type that normally attracted him, with that freckled, pasty face, overdone lips and large knowing eyes. The eyes seemed to follow him around all the time he was in the securities room, or gazed solemnly at him across his desk when he asked her to bring something to him. She hardly ever seemed to smile with any degree of warmth or spontaneity. Just a perfunctory little upturn of the lips.

'What time is your train Mrs Fairchild?' Sam enquired, bringing her a large gin and tonic with a bowl of nuts which he placed before her.

'They run every quarter of an hour,' she said. 'Bromley isn't very far Mr Hahn.'

She only answered questions, seeming indifferent to – maybe incapable of – initiating any conversation of her own. He thought that she was very dull and the invitation to a drink had been a mistake. Probably it was better to prop up the bar on his own chatting to the friendly staff, male and female, on the other side. As he sat down with his whisky

154

Sam looked at the table next to him where a man of about his age was chatting to a woman the age of Mrs Fairchild, or younger. Their heads were close together, their fingers lightly touching. Suddenly everyone in the room seemed to Sam to be like him and Julia Fairchild, lonely people on the brink of an affair, or having one.

An affair? He looked at Mrs Fairchild and felt rather horrified at the fantasy this speculation had unleashed in his mind. He could see her very pale body naked on a bed, the legs slightly parted, a little tuft of ginger coloured pubic hair all that protected her genitals from his prurient gaze. Her breasts would be rather flat and her nipples red like her lips. Her lips really were huge – he could imagine them clamped to him like a limpet, emitting marine-like squealing noises as she received his kisses. She didn't move or show any emotion as he lay upon her, and this fascinated him in the way that, suddenly, and in reality, completely unexpectedly, she began to fascinate him now. She was one of the most completely passive women he had ever had any interest in. She stared back at him as though knowing his thoughts.

'Tell me about Mr Fairchild,' Sam said suddenly.

'He drives a minicab. He's never really been very ambitious.'

'Oh? And are you?'

'Not really Mr Hahn, I've been in the securities department of some bank or the other for over fifteen years.'

'And you never had children? Never wanted them?'

She lowered her lids and her very pale cheeks were momentarily ruptured by tiny splashes of colour.

'I couldn't have them, Mr Hahn. There is something wrong with my ovaries.'

'Oh I'm terribly sorry. I shouldn't have asked.'

'That's perfectly all right.' The colour disappeared as quickly as it had come. 'It all happened years ago anyway.'

'And don't you mind not having children?'

'I never think about it.'

Sam wanted very much to know what she *did* think of. What went on behind that tired, emotionless face? She was good at her work, but did she have a mind? A mind like Frankie or Barbara, Sarah or Amanda? Did he really like women with minds? They gave a lot of trouble.

Sam knew that he wanted to go to bed with Julia Fairchild

155

and that their coupling would be free and untroubled by any remorse, guilt or apprehension. They would never become involved – their personalities were too dissimilar – and she could never have children. He could imagine that this cool unemotional woman could be very passionate if she put her mind to it. If he put his mind, his skills as a lover of many years' standing, to it too.

She continued her steady gaze and he knew that she knew what he was thinking. Abruptly they finished their drinks and got up, he holding on to her hand very tightly on the way to the door. Outside it was dark in the arch, empty with only the trains rumbling overhead. Sam looked both ways and then pressed her against the wall. He saw her pale face raised to his as he bent to kiss her, her large red mouth open, like an underwater amoeba. It was suddenly the most enticing thing he had ever seen. He put down his briefcase and undid his coat as his free hand fondled one of her breasts. He unzipped himself to release his penis, which was in an enormous state of erection. Julie put one of her cool pale hands against his chest and gave him a gentle push disengaging her willing mouth as she did.

'I shouldn't do it here, Mr Hahn. Not the whole thing.' For a moment her hand gently alighted on his throbbing penis, her fingers flickering so delicately, so suggestively, that he thought he would spurt all over her. Then, with the ease of a practised courtesan, she crouched, protected by his enveloping coat, and took him in her mouth. He came at once.

It was the most erotic encounter that Sam had ever had in his life.

Rising, Mrs Fairchild was completely composed, her immobile features not betraying by a grimace, by any expression whatsoever, whether she enjoyed the taste of his semen or was repulsed by it.

'I washed in the men's toilet,' he said at last, his heart cantering as he did up his coat.

'I thought you had. You always look such a very clean man Mr Hahn.'

Sam couldn't think of a single thing to say in reply. She had not only apparently anticipated what was going to happen – which he had not – but behaved with the detachment of a professional, whether an accomplished whore or a nurse. He wondered how often she did this kind of thing, and the thought, instead of disgusting him, excited him more. He took her arm and accompanied her to the station, standing by the barrier as she gave her ticket to the inspector. While her ticket was being clipped she looked at Sam and, for the first time that evening, smiled; a reassuring smile that freed him from any guilt she thought he might be feeling. Sam felt a surge of hope, compounded with his fear, remorse and an enormous lust to be with her again. But she gave a little wave and quickly walked along the platform before disappearing into the shabby suburban train.

Barbara stood at the back of the chapel, watching with the other mourners as the simple pine coffin containing the drowned body of Jennifer Littlejohn slid slowly out of view. The hatch that committed her remains to the flames came down and she was gone. Burning, Barbara thought, was a very final, effective way of getting rid both of the loved and the unloved: no grave, no headstone needing upkeep and flowers. No earthly reminder at all that a person called Jennifer Littlejohn, or anyone else, had ever existed. Only by the impact they had made in their earthly lives, the love or otherwise they had inspired, would they be remembered.

The chapel was packed for the short committal ceremony at Golders Green, with the sort of assembly that Barbara, with her knowledge of Jennifer's lifestyle, would have expected: moneyed people. There was not an inch of room and latecomers crowded the door. There were many bowed heads, and perfunctory tears from one or two ladies in enormous mink coats, but no display of what Barbara would have called genuine grief. Some of the ladies would be members of the Bridge Club, the ones who entertained Jennifer to tea, and whom she found so futile and boring. The well groomed men with passive faces, chins slightly raised, hands clasped in front of them, would be their husbands, business acquaintances of John's; men with their minds not on bereavement, but business, their mistresses, golf – glancing at their watches, glad it was all over. The air, perfumed with flowers, with expensive aftershave, exclusive scent, heavy applications of hair lacquer, stank above all of that most pungent of all odours: wealth.

As the sound of the organ ceased, the principal mourners standing in the front row led the exit from the chapel. Barbara was curious to see the husband who had tormented Jennifer for so many years. From the back he looked reasonably nondescript, his greying head bowed most of the time except when the coffin started its final journey, and then he watched her go.

The front of John Littlejohn was as nondescript as the back. He was a man of medium height, slender, with a rather gaunt, careworn face and thinning hair. With him was an elderly woman who was probably his mother – Jennifer's parents were dead – and then a sprinkling of middle-aged men and women who would be aunts, uncles and assorted relatives. There were a few children, nieces and nephews, and one or two ill-at-ease, less well dressed, people who probably worked for John – or represented the charitable causes Jennifer had helped with her money, but with little of her time.

A huge cluster of large, expensive cars blocked the semi-circle outside the chapel – Barbara had had to leave hers down the road. She had been late and only just managed to get a seat.

The wreaths and flowers had been placed outside the chapel, and around these now stood despondent little groups, peering at the cards in an effort to see who had paid the most, or the least, for their floral tributes. John Littlejohn, composed, stood in a receiving line shaking hands with the mourners as they emerged. Barbara was one of the last to leave and he looked up at her, clearly having no idea who she was.

'Barbara Hahn,' she said taking his limp hand. 'I was terribly shocked to read about Jennifer's death in *The Times*.'

It had indeed been a terrible shock, only two days before, and for several hours she had not known what to do. In the end she decided to do nothing except attend the funeral. Consequently she had no idea what had happened – suicide, accident or what.

'Ah Dr Hahn,' John Littlejohn shook her hand and, as she was about to pass on, called rather sharply after her: 'I would like a word, if I may.'

'Shall I call you?' Barbara said.

'Please come back to the house for some refreshment.'

Funerals at Golders Green Crematorium were a very brisk business. There was already a queue forming at the front of the chapel for the next committal, cars blocking up the congested drive. Barbara had not wanted to go back to the house, but was impelled both by curiosity and duty, as well as obligation. She slipped through the mourners, past a hearse carrying another body, through the sleek cars attempting either to exit or enter, and down the tree-lined street to her own small car parked under a tree. Then she drove slowly through Golders Green and Hampstead to the large house in The Bishop's Avenue where Jennifer had lived so unhappily for so many years.

The Littlejohns' was not one of the massive, obtrusive houses that stand in The Bishop's Avenue; it was an ornate, but rather neat house at the end of that long fashionable road. Barbara left her car several doors away and thought that the house rather resembled the crematorium chapel with its false Gothic gables and the cars crammed in the circular drive and outside.

A hired maid stood at the door taking coats, wraps and names and once more John Littlejohn stood next to the elderly woman, her grey hair freshly rinsed with blue, perfunctorily shaking hands. Just as she had been at the chapel, Barbara was one of the last to arrive and the room beyond John Littlejohn was already crowded.

She shook John's hand and that of his mother, brother, sister, aunt, whatever, and moved into the throng. It was a large room, expensively and tastefully furnished with double doors, now closed but that in the summer would lead into a well-tended pretty garden. Another hired functionary approached her with a tray and she took a glass of sherry; at her elbow hovered a maid with a large silver tray covered with dainty little sandwiches. Barbara was already sorry she had come; she didn't know a soul and obviously John would be too busy to talk to her. The well dressed assembly pointedly ignored her as they loudly greeted or addressed one another. Of the shabbier attendants at the funeral there was no sign. Rightly believing themselves to be unwelcome they had kept away. Nevertheless the conversation around her fascinated her because she hardly heard the dead woman's

159

name mentioned. It was the usual superficial claptrap of social functions where the people didn't know one another very well. Barbara doubted if there was one close friend of Jennifer's among them. Maybe, of them all, she had known the deceased the best. A professional friend.

She drank her sherry, ate a sandwich and decided to leave, squeezing past the concourse, some of whom glanced at her with curiosity. Just as she reached the fringe of the crowd John Littlejohn emerged and, taking her arm, steered her into the hall.

'I would like to talk to you.'

'And I to you.'

He opened a door and led her into a small room with used-looking comfortable chairs and a large television set in one corner. She guessed it was here that, when at home, the ill-matched couple had spent most of their time – eyes glued to the box to spare them from having to talk to each other. Even then it bore the mark of anonymity, with the air of a rather exclusive small hotel in some such place as the Cotswolds. John Littlejohn indicated a chair, and Barbara sat down, taking out her cigarette packet as she did.

'Please have one of these,' John Littlejohn sprang forward with a large silver box and, though she would have preferred one of her own brand, she selected a King Size Rothmans. He took one himself, lit them both with an ornate Queen Anne silver lighter, and sat opposite Barbara, his feet spread out before him.

'I often wanted to speak to you Dr Hahn.'

'Why didn't you?'

'It was very much against Jennifer's wishes.'

'You know that she hasn't been my patient for about six months?'

She was convinced the surprise on John Littlejohn's face was genuine.

'No I didn't know that. Well Jennifer was *very* much worse in the last six months. So that explains it. I admit I was going to have it out with you today . . . but this changes the situation.'

'Have what out?' Barbara felt rather annoyed.

'Well the fact that you didn't seem to be doing Jennifer

much good. Frankly, I thought for years she was throwing her money away.'

'Relatives often do think that,' Barbara remarked quietly.

'With reason if you ask me,' John Littlejohn said aggressively – she realized it was going to be a hard interview. 'I got sick of hearing your name. Dr Hahn this and Dr Hahn that. She became obsessed by you, almost as though she *was* you. Did you know that?'

'Patients do become rather dependent on the therapist. It's part of the treatment.'

'Well I think . . .' John Littlejohn frowned and Barbara interrupted quickly.

'How did your wife die?'

'She was drowned.'

'I know that. It was in the paper "from a drowning accident". But do you know . . .'

'If she took her own life? Is that what you were going to ask?'

'I wondered how it happened. I was there only a short while before. You know that she rented me your cottage for Christmas?'

'Yes, I knew. Oh no, Dr Hahn, if there had been any question of suicide the police would have been after you to ascertain her state of mind. I nearly rang you but decided not to because it wasn't necessary. There was a witness to her accident. She slipped on the parapet. Luckily someone saw her slip, a man walking his dog. He rushed over to try and save her and she clung to him and the parapet for dear life before another huge wave washed her away and nearly took her rescuer as well. The man who tried to save her said there were no doubts that she slipped accidentally. She'd drunk almost a bottle of gin and probably didn't know what she was doing or where she was going.'

'Gin?'

'Didn't you know my wife was a heavy drinker Dr Hahn? Not just a heavy drinker. She was an alcoholic. But you must have known that, as you were her shrink for so long.'

Barbara always thought the term 'shrink' offensive, and here it was clearly meant to be.

'I wasn't aware she had a drink problem. If she did she hid that from me.'

161

'Much else too, I bet.'

'But why should she want to lie to me when she needed help?'

'Because she admired you. She was mesmerized by you. I can see now that she even *dressed* like you. Jennifer felt so inadequate that she wanted to *be* you.'

'Why was she so inadequate?'

'You should know that. God knows I don't.' John stubbed out his cigarette, blowing the last vestiges of smoke almost straight into Barbara's face. 'I bet you need another drink. I do.' Taking her glass he abruptly left the room. She knew his aggression was inspired by guilt, but she still minded. He was even more horrible than Jennifer had made her feel he was – a rather ferrety little man whose expensive clothes sat on him uneasily. Lacking style, one was aware that whatever he wore or however much he spent he'd look the same. It was difficult to understand why Jennifer had spent so many years tormented by someone like this, lacking any of the expected charismatic charm that so distinguished that other womanizer, Sam.

John returned with another sherry and what Barbara took to be gin and tonic for himself, putting hers rather gracelessly down before her.

'Jennifer deceived people. They thought she was very strong and she wasn't. I only found that out after I married her.'

'Your wife had a form of what we loosely call anxiety neurosis.'

'Well whatever you call it, it got on my nerves.' He took a sip of his drink and looked at Barbara. 'Always fearful, always expecting the worst – afraid of aeroplanes, long voyages, spiders, strange people, crowds.'

'Then it was a good thing she came to me because in the years I treated her I think I helped her.' John Littlejohn looked unconvinced, his head slumped on his chest, as if ruminating over the unhappy years with his late wife. 'It was because I felt I had helped her sufficiently to stand on her own feet that I ended her treatment in the summer.'

'Well, she never told me that and she wasn't ready to stand on her own feet. Never. She appeared to be, but she wasn't. She never got over not having children, yet she would have made an awful mother.'

'On the contrary, I think she would have made an excellent mother.'

'Oh yes, like you. She was always on about you and your children.'

'Some patients do tend to idealize the analyst. The theory is that in their childhood they somehow failed to relate satisfactorily to their parents. The analyst takes the place of the parent. In my opinion a child would have helped to stabilize Jennifer.'

'Well she never got over it. I suppose she told you too that I was unfaithful to her?'

'Weren't you?'

'No more than the average man of my acquaintance. I mean you can't be faithful to one woman forever. Most of my so-called affairs were figments of her imagination because she couldn't get over us not having children. She thought my object in life was to impregnate women. I tell you, Dr Hahn, I am much too busy a man for that. If I had half the affairs Jenny said I did I'd be dead now.'

He certainly didn't look the type. Sam, now Sam was a sensualist, he looked like one; but John Littlejohn had a narrow mouth, small slanting eyes and he seemed a man who would prefer money and possessions to women. Jennifer, with the eye of obsessive love, had idealized him into something he wasn't.

'Did they do an autopsy?' she said.

'Yes, that's how they found the booze. But they sewed her up and the verdict at the inquest was death by misadventure. It was all over in ten minutes. She had her purse in her pocket as though she was going for some more gin if you ask me.'

'But why was she on the parapet if it was dangerous?'

'Because she was drunk.'

'Yes, I see.'

'Look Dr Hahn,' John Littlejohn paused to take a gulp of his own gin. 'I can see that you never really understood Jennifer.'

'I can't worm secrets from patients that they don't want to tell. She did come and see me voluntarily; yet she never discussed drinking. I can see that, trying to be me, she would think that excessive drinking might disgust me.'

'She drank like a fish and, finally, that was why I left her.

163

She drank more in the last six months than I've ever known, and I was sick of finding the bottles under the bed, in the wardrobe, God knows where else. You know how secretive drunks are, how dishonest.'

'Yes I know,' Barbara said quietly, still unconvinced Jennifer was one. 'Untruthful too.'

'I warned her and I warned her and I told her I'd leave her if it went on.'

'But you did have another girl friend . . .'

John Littlejohn nodded vigorously, a man without guilt. 'I did. She'd been my girl friend for over a year, a very patient, loving woman who would never have taken me from Jennifer if Jennifer hadn't overplayed her hand.'

'But why at *Christmas*? Wasn't that cruel?'

As she said it she wondered if the late Jennifer's husband really knew about cruelty, or would suffer the guilt that went with it.

'I had to go some time. Maria – my girl friend – is unmarried and lonely. She did want me to spend Christmas with her.'

'So you weren't going for good?'

John screwed up his face as if from the effort of recollection, or maybe to try and hide the truth too, just as he accused his wife of doing.

'Well, let's say I wanted to see how Jennifer would take it. If it went well I'd stay away.'

'It was hardly likely to go *well*, especially at Christmas time.'

'Oh I knew there was enough drink in the house.' John's voice was scornful.

'She came to see me in great distress. She wasn't drunk when she arrived and she didn't drink all day.'

'You probably tipped her over the brink then,' John said cheerfully, sitting comfortably back in his chair as though he'd shed his burden. 'You people don't seem to know the harm you do. Why did *you* go back to London?'

'Because I had to. My daughter is leaving for Africa.'

Barbara knew she was telling a little lie herself but she felt that, where John Littlejohn was concerned, her conscience wouldn't trouble her much. The problems would arise when assessing her own part in Jennifer's death.

'Well she got into a right state afterwards. You'd think you would put your patient first. She paid you, after all.'

'She wasn't my patient then and she didn't pay me.'

'She paid you enough over the years, my God.' John Littlejohn looked at the ceiling as though seeking the assistance of the deity in calculating the amount.

'I do find your tone rather offensive, Mr Littlejohn, and your insinuation. Money may be everything to you, but it isn't to me.'

'And yet you charge such a lot – week after week. Sometimes I wish I was in the same business.'

Barbara got up, looking at her watch, thankful that she had allowed enough time to lapse before terminating this unpleasant interview. She picked up her gloves and bag and glanced at herself in a long mirror that hung on the wall. She was carefully made up, the delicately applied blusher on her cheeks fading as it reached her well shaped eyebrows, her lipstick a dark shade of pink. She wore no hat but a dark grey corduroy suit with a suitably toned grey blouse, frilly at the neck in the style pioneered by the Princess of Wales.

'I must go now Mr Littlejohn. I don't think there's much more to say.'

'A lot more if I had my way.' John rose too, wagging a finger offensively at her. 'I don't think you psychiatrists honestly do any good at all. You dismissed my wife when she still needed help and hurried back to London to see your daughter who, I expect, is in good health, when my own distressed wife needed you.'

'Her distress was your fault, not mine.'

She glared at him and he lowered his eyes. Would he weep at night? Would he ever feel that, but for him . . . and would she feel that, but for her . . .

When he spoke again John Littlejohn's tone was more conciliatory.

'I was at the end of my tether too, Dr Hahn. I had to leave sometime. I'd given her plenty of warning. I didn't know she wasn't seeing you. I thought that she'd rush to you and you'd help her. I nearly rang you as a matter of fact.'

'I wish you had; but then, you don't think we do any good do you?'

John raised the admonitory finger again.

165

'Don't be funny with *me* Dr Hahn. You know what I really think about all this psychological mumbo jumbo? I think it's damaging. I often thought that if Jennifer hadn't spent so much time talking to you she would have been a better woman.'

'How do you mean "better"?'

'She would have had more interests, done more things. Do you know the only books she ever read were on psychology? The blasted bedroom was full of Freud . . . Freud and empty gin bottles.'

John Littlejohn strode to the door and flung it open. In the hall others were taking their leave and several people who had obviously been looking for him glanced curiously at the door. He didn't say goodbye to Barbara and she didn't say goodbye to him. Barbara was meant to feel like a disgraced student dismissed from the headmaster's study, but she didn't. Without looking at Littlejohn again she walked slowly through the open door, through the massed cars outside and into The Bishop's Avenue. It was a cold, wet day and while they'd been indoors a high wind had risen. Out at sea a storm would probably be blowing, just as it had on the day Jennifer Littlejohn died.

CHAPTER TEN

THEIRS WAS JUST ONE OF the many groups standing around in the departure hall saying goodbye to relatives, friends, lovers – little clusters of people clinging together, clinging to someone special. Some were couples entwined together; children hung on to the hands of departing fathers; babies were nursed in parental arms or being lifted up for a last kiss.

The Hahn family composed such a cameo. Sarah in their midst, turning first to Tom, then Sam, then her mother and finally saved for last, Amanda, who had clung to her ever since the departure of the plane for Harare was announced.

Sarah had never expected a family gathering. She had spent her last few days at the Hampstead house having given up her own flat, and she and her mother had enjoyed time together talking, mostly about the death of Jennifer Littlejohn, and making plans for the future. What plans? Sarah didn't know when she'd be home again, but plans nevertheless because it is never nice to bid farewell to someone in a vacuum, not knowing when you'd see them again. Then Tom had announced he had to come to London on Marine business and finally, at the very last moment, Amanda had telephoned from Kent. Everyone had thought she and Sarah had said goodbye the previous weekend when Sam and Frankie had gone down to see her as well. Sam had collected Barbara, Sarah and Tom from Hampstead in a chauffeured car which belonged to the bank and Amanda had made her way to Heathrow by tube. She was very pale, stricken, and she hung on to her sister.

'I wish I was coming with you.'

'I do too,' Sarah smiled at her.

'I really do. I mean it.'

'If I get a base you can come out for a holiday.'

The departure of the plane was announced again and those

boarding were invited to pass through Passport Control. But Amanda clung on, preventing Sarah from getting her passport from her bag, looking pitifully up into her face. Tom and his father looked at each other as though wondering what to do, and Barbara stood a little back from the group, uncertain how the situation would develop, feeling anew Amanda's rejection of her as a mother. Sam gently took Amanda's shoulder, attempting to prise her away, and Sarah began to look alarmed as the Tannoy blared out again asking passengers to go through without delay. Then, as Barbara had divined she would, Amanda burst out crying and flung her arms round Sarah, who dropped her bag on the floor to embrace her sister. Tom and Sam scrabbled on the floor for the bag and its contents – tickets, passport, money, the lot – and Barbara put her arm around Amanda's waist and gently tugged her away, keeping her tense body firmly next to hers, the sobbing head against her own shoulder. She signalled to Sarah that, without more words, she should go. Sarah took her bag from Tom, kissed him swiftly, waved and went rapidly through the barrier. They could see her running on the other side.

'Oh Mummy Mummy,' Amanda sobbed. 'I don't want her to go. Don't let her go.'

'There darling.' Barbara felt a surge of love, of relief, of gratitude to hear those girlish words spoken in such a pitiful girlish voice, to feel her baby at her breast again. In departing, Sarah had done her a great favour.

All the way back to town Amanda sat with her head resting on her mother's breast, her eyes closed, emitting little sobs from time to time. Sam sat on the other side and Tom in the front next to the driver.

'Is it all right if George drops Tom in Whitehall and me at the bank and then takes you home?'

'Fine.' Barbara nodded. 'Could you dine with us this evening? Frankie too, of course.'

'That would be nice if you could Dad,' Tom said. 'With the weather so bad at home Natalie said she won't expect me back until tomorrow.'

The country had been having a continuous spell of awful weather, thick snow and high drifts, the countryside particularly badly hit as always. In London dirty piles of sludge lined

168

the main roads but otherwise, except in parts of Hampstead where some roads were still snowbound, the capital was clear.

'What about you darling?' Barbara gently pressed the still form next to her side. 'Would you like to stay the night too? I wish you would,' she added.

'Do stay,' Sam said. 'Kent is full of drifts.'

'It took Peter Maxwell an hour to get me to the station,' Amanda admitted, her voice muffled. 'Maybe I will.'

Barbara squeezed her again.

'I don't know about Frankie,' Sam said after giving instructions to the driver.

'Is she still not well?'

'She's very tired at night. She doesn't want to lose her job so she's been working hard.'

'I heard the amniocentesis was OK.' Barbara said quietly, a little note of encouragement in her voice.

In reply Sam sighed heavily.

It really was lovely having the family all together again though dinner was marred by the news from America that a plane had crashed in the River Potomac, drowning almost everybody on board. The horrific scenes of those who were rescued being dragged by helicopter from the river had reduced them all to silence while they watched the News.

'Sarah's going south,' Barbara emphasized; but it still reminded them all of the uncertainties of plane flying, the chance of a crash, the loss of someone so beloved. Compared to this, the disappearance of the prime minister's son in the Sahara seemed like light relief.

Sam came late because Frankie wasn't well. The amniocentesis had seemed to upset her and one of the hazards of the procedure was that it could induce miscarriage.

'I wish it would,' Sam said as Barbara helped him off with his coat in the hall. 'Save us all a lot of worry.'

'Poor Sam,' she put a hand on his shoulder, a gesture of comfort and affection that seemed natural to her, and ushered him into the dining room.

Amanda had cheered up but was still broody, the news from America depressing her even further.

'Wouldn't it be terrible if we never saw Sarah again?' she said.

'Don't be silly darling. Crashes like that are extremely rare.'

'But they happen. She's going right out into the African bush. Flying by plane all the time.'

'Sarah's doing what she wants to do,' Tom poured wine for his father. 'And I may be going abroad too.' As they all looked at him he went on: 'To Singapore. Of course I don't want to, but I don't have much say in the matter. That's really what I came up about today. It's just a possibility. Some of the chaps in Whitehall, incidentally, are very worried about the situation in the Falklands.'

'The Falklands?' Amanda sound unsure where they were located.

'Argentine is making a lot of noises about getting them back.'

'That's usual,' Sam said. 'Their claim to the Falklands has been going on for years.'

'People think the decision to withdraw HMS *Endurance* was very provocative,' Tom continued. 'That's the Navy survey vessel on patrol down there.'

'Why is it provocative?' Barbara served Sam with meat and vegetables, her mind happily on her family, briefly reunited once more, rather than on some tiny islands thousands of miles away.

'Because it will make the Argentinians think we don't care about who owns the Falklands.'

'*Do* we?' Sam took his plate, with a smile to Barbara. 'Anyway, I think what happens to the Falkland Islands the least of our worries.'

'What are your worries, Dad?' Tom leaned back looking critically at his father. 'The new baby?'

Sam glanced at Amanda whose mind obviously still dwelt on her absent sister.

'Well I didn't want a baby of course and nor I think did Frankie. She's nearly forty.'

'But anyway she's OK,' Barbara said. 'The amniocentesis showed it is not in any way abnormal. That's very reassuring, Sam, and as to the future, you have a nanny, Frankie has a job and you'll just have to take care won't you?' she added lightly.

'Frankie wants to be sterilized.'

'Oh for God's sake Dad!' Tom exclaimed. 'We really don't want details of your birth control methods here.'

'I wasn't talking about . . .' Sam looked again at Amanda. 'Anyway it *is* very nice for us all to be together. The family.' He raised his glass and looked round the table. 'Particularly our dear Amanda.'

Amanda, as her mother knew she would, once again began to weep, not hysterically, but with sad twin rivulets of tears trickling down her cheeks. Tom looked at his parents and, getting up, went over to his youngest sister, putting his hands on her shoulders.

'Come and talk to me, old girl. Let Mum and Dad finish their dinner.' Still sniffling Amanda got up and allowed herself to be led out of the room. Sam refilled his glass and Barbara's.

'She's not right yet is she?'

'I think coming home is the best thing that could have happened. I don't want her to go away for a bit if I can help it, Sam.'

'But don't you think she's all right in Kent?'

'Yes but it's not natural is it? Not natural being alienated from me.'

'I think you feel it more than she does.'

'I do feel it.' Barbara lit a cigarette. 'I feel it very much; it's not right for Amanda to have this block about me. For her sake as well as mine, I want her to get over it. I want to find out the reason for it.'

'Well you mustn't force her,' Sam said doubtfully. 'I'm afraid she can't come to us . . .'

'I don't want her to go to you. I want her to stay here.'

'Sarah said you'd had a lot of trouble with a patient.' Sam looked at her speculatively as though this somehow disqualified her from caring for their daughter. Or maybe he was merely curious. It was difficult to tell.

'Do you mean Jennifer Littlejohn?'

'Someone who drowned.'

'Well she didn't kill herself. It was an accident.'

'Sarah didn't seem to think you were sure. She said you were very upset.'

Barbara leaned back, and tapped her cigarette ash into a tray, trying not to mind that Sarah discussed her with Sam.

'I was, and am very worried when anything happens to a patient. Luckily it's infrequent. But she was no longer my patient. It's simply that . . .' Barbara studied the glowing tip of her cigarette. 'Sometimes I think psychiatry is a bit like religion – no proof that it works, only faith.'

'Well you've had faith for a long time. Don't let it desert you now.' Sam's voice was suddenly conciliatory, the old, cheery Sam who used to shore up the few doubts she'd had as a young doctor, or her misgivings when she began psycho-analysis.

'But you've never really *believed* in it have you Sam?'

Sam cleared his throat. 'It isn't that I didn't believe in it exactly. I feel that, as you say, it *is* like religion. One clings on even when the faith vanishes. But why do you say this now?'

Barbara got up and wandered restlessly round the room, the familiar room with food on the table and her husband there, in the next room their son and daughter.

'Because I was *really* upset about Jennifer. I know she didn't kill herself because I'm sure she was the type who would have left a letter. There would have been a need to explain her action to the world, specially to me. She wouldn't just throw herself into the sea. Anyway, someone saw her slip. She was apparently walking on a stormy evening, and when they tried to rescue her she clung to them desperately. She didn't want to go. What bothered me, still does, is that I wonder if she told me the truth about herself all the years I saw her for therapy. Her husband said she drank and a massive amount of gin was found in her body. If she didn't tell me the truth about herself I couldn't help her, could I? Question: How do you always ensure your patients are telling the truth? Oh they do conceal things, specially nasty, shameful things to do with sex. But why shouldn't she tell me she had a drinking problem?'

Sam shook his head, admiring her as she walked round the room, a slim elegant figure in a blue woollen dress with a mandarin neck. Why had he ever left her? He could have stayed where he was in this comfortable house with their children and had affairs – just as he was doing now.

'She didn't tell me,' Barbara continued as though talking to herself, 'because I don't think she had one. I think her husband made it up. He was the liar.'

'What sort of man was he?'

'Self-made, self-important, aggressive. I didn't like him at all. Jennifer gave me the impression of someone completely different. Someone virile, charming, splendid to look at.' 'Like you' she wanted to add, but didn't.

'Then she was a liar.'

'Uh, uh,' Barbara shook her head, continuing her pacing, eyes to the ground like a bloodhound on the trail of a missing body. 'That was how she saw him. She thought he was unfaithful and he was a bit, but not as much as she imagined. She was a fantasist. I'm convinced of that.'

'It's like a mystery story.' Sam's gaze still followed her. Barbara had been very sexy when she was young. He decided she still was; the years in between had clouded his memory. He wondered what Barbara would say if he invited her to bed. Did she ever get it at all?

Barbara was by now sitting opposite Sam, pouring the remains of the wine into her glass.

'You look very thoughtful Sam. Is it Frankie? I bet you're not so concerned about my patient.'

'My dear all your patients must give you problems of a kind. Always have.'

'They do, and one is supposed not to worry about them. I only worry about this Jennifer business because I think maybe I was wrong. My treatment of her was wrong, and I feel guilt and remorse. I became friendly with her, I told her about you and me. All this was after she had ceased being my patient; but it was still wrong. The analytic situation can never be altered. One can't really be friendly with a patient, and shouldn't be, even with a past one. I made a mistake.'

'Dear Barbara,' Sam smiled fondly at her. 'How would you like us to go to bed again?'

'Oh Sam,' Barbara made a gesture of irritation. 'Trust you to say something like that now. Am I a challenge now that I'm no longer your wife?'

'I'm very fond of you. Sex fell off with us didn't it? Was it the climacteric with you do you think?'

'That sort of remark annoys me,' Barbara replied. 'I get

173

tired of jokes about menopausal women. I know a lot of women of my age, and older, who are very sexy indeed.'

'Then why weren't you?' Sam stared at her.

'Maybe you didn't stimulate me enough. You were too busy stimulating other women.'

'That's your imagination . . .'

(Jennifer Littlejohn used to say: 'He never even tries with me now because he has all these women. I haven't had an orgasm for years. I don't miss it though because it's never meant much to me. I liked sex to please John, not otherwise.')

'You mean you were quite faithful?'

'Not quite, but there weren't a lot. After all, I was a man with a busy life.'

(John Littlejohn said: 'I tell you Dr Hahn I'm much too busy a man for that. If I had half the affairs Jenny said I'd be dead now.')

'It's all very academic anyway, Sam. I wouldn't dream of deceiving Frankie with you.'

'Frankie has changed. I think she's quite gone off sex.'

'But you *love* her don't you Sam?'

Sam looked at her, but didn't reply.

'I think we need more wine,' she said and left the room.

Was her tone ironic? Sam wasn't sure. Neither was he sure if he still loved Frankie. He hadn't wanted a modern house and a nanny and two young babies as well. He wanted to go to the opera and concerts in the new Barbican, to Glyndebourne, and plays at the National. He wanted to dine out and go away for weekends, fly to the continent on an impulse for a week's skiing or some sun in the Bahamas. The first two years of their marriage had been like that. Now they hardly went out at all.

He got up and walked to the window, pulling back the curtains to see if there was still snow on the ground. Yes the snow lingered in the garden, that garden where they'd all had such a lot of fun when the kids were small. That was the time to enjoy children when one was young and could appreciate their games; have fun with them. Now he was too old. He had grandchildren the age of Zoë. It was all too ridiculous.

He heard the phone in the hall and then Barbara's voice as

174

she talked. After a moment the dining room door opened and she popped her head round the door.

'It's Frankie. She's sorry to bother you but she's had a little show of blood.'

'Oh dear,' Sam said going towards her. 'Maybe she's going to lose the baby.' Barbara thought he looked concerned but not, exactly, sorry.

The ten o'clock News showed pictures from the Potomac River again and there was still no information about Mrs Thatcher's missing son, Mark. Mr Thatcher had been despatched to Africa to look for him and Mrs Thatcher was seen showing a rare display of emotion on the television screen.

'Maybe she has a heart,' Tom said.

'Mothers are very vulnerable as far as their children are concerned.' Barbara reached over and squeezed his arm. Amanda had gone to bed and they were vaguely waiting to hear news of Frankie. Sam had said he would ring. 'Even hard mothers like Mrs Thatcher and me.'

'You're not hard, Mum.' Tom returned the pressure, putting his hand on hers. 'You've just always had your mind on something else as well. Like Mrs T. It's very hard for men still to accept this you know, even men like me. I like Natalie being a wife and mother. I like her there, at home, and that's it.'

'Will you feel like that when you're both forty?'

'I suppose so.'

Barbara was thinking of Sam. If Tom was a chip off the old block she doubted that he would; but then he wasn't really like Sam. He was more like her. How absurd of Sam to imagine that, because his own wife had her mind more on her forthcoming baby than sex, he could turn to her. She wasn't even flattered. He still thought he could rely on his former wife for everything.

'Did you talk to Amanda?' she went on.

'Quite a bit. She says she feels no one loves her; we all have other things. You have your work, Dad has his and his new family – she resents them – and I have mine. She feels she'll miss Sarah terribly.'

'But Sarah had her work too.'

'But she had a lot of time for Amanda lately, Mum. She went down to see her a lot.'

After Sarah had found her with Alfred Kleber she hadn't been to the house at all. Had she told Amanda anything about that? She so hoped she hadn't, didn't, in fact, think she would. Sarah wasn't a gossip.

'You know Amanda's rejection of me is part of her illness, Tom. Anorexics often become aggressive towards both parents.'

'What then?'

'It depends.'

'I think your knowledge of her illness makes her more afraid too. She knows she can't deceive you.'

'But she can.' Barbara looked at him with surprise. 'I'm her mother. She deceived me before; I didn't know it was happening. I can't see her in a clinical situation. That's why professional people often make bad parents, they can't see the wood for the trees.'

The phone rang and Tom went to answer it. Barbara sat waiting for him to return, imagining it was Sam. She remembered the expression on Sam's face when she had asked him if he still loved Frankie. He looked as though the question made him wonder himself.

'Frankie seems all right,' Tom said, returning and sitting down. 'The doctor was already there when Dad arrived. He doesn't think she'll miscarry but to be sure she has to stay in bed, maybe for a few weeks. Dad sounded rather cheesed off about the whole thing.'

'I expect he's worried.'

Tom gazed moodily at the blank television screen. 'Dad's fifty-five next month, Mum. What an age to be worrying about pregnant wives.'

'In the Old Testament they did it quite a lot – at least I don't know that they worried – and the women were even younger. Older men have always liked young women; it's a biological fact.'

'It still doesn't seem right to me.' He wrinkled his nose with distaste.

'I think what really doesn't seem right to you is the breakup of the family home. You would like your mother and father together, an established order of things.'

'Isn't it the right order of things?' Tom looked quite anguished now. 'People growing old together, their children and grandchildren around them? You'd have liked that, wouldn't you? When something like this happens – one's father going off with another woman, starting a new family – everything falls apart.'

'Dear Tom,' Barbara tucked his hand affectionately in hers again. 'What you're saying is that it would be nice if everything were perfect in this world, and it isn't. I think that's why you were attracted to the army – establishment, routine. Everything has its place. Yet if there were a war all your world would fall apart again.'

'There won't be a war,' Tom said firmly. 'That's why I'm a marine. To keep the peace.' Tom yawned. 'Time we went to bed, Mum. I've to be up early.'

Barbara woke and lay in the dark, listening. It was never quite dark, as the old gas lights in the quiet street outside gently illuminated her room because she left the curtains half drawn. She liked to wake naturally with the daylight, like the birds. She thought a sound had woken her and, slipping quickly out of bed, she went to the window and peered outside. The wing of the house in which she had her consulting room formed an arm which projected towards the street, being bounded by the garden and a hedge at the far end. Now she saw that a light glowed in the window of her consulting room, through the slatted blinds which she kept down all the time.

She'd had no patients that day because of Sarah and couldn't remember going into her room. Yet maybe she had, or Linda had left the light on when she cleaned, and it only showed up at night because it was a small dim lamp by the side of her chair. Nevertheless, she felt, a tremor of unease because she felt sure she would have noticed the light as she drew the curtains before she went to bed.

Barbara put on her gown and quietly opened the door, peering into the corridor. Amanda's room was upstairs, Tom's next to hers. She thought that if a flushing lavatory had disturbed her she would still hear the sound. She wondered if she should call Tom, but remembered that he had to be up early anyway. It was only 2 a.m. and he needed his sleep.

Feeling curious rather than apprehensive – Barbara often said that if she were a nervous person she wouldn't live in this large rambling house by herself – she crept down the stairs, across the hall and quietly opened the door that led to her wing, a consulting room with a waiting room and lavatory next to it. The door of her room was slightly ajar and that was unusual, so, momentarily feeling fear, she crept towards it and peered inside.

Amanda was sitting bolt upright in her chair, her eyes fixed on the couch alongside. Her hands rested on the arm of the chair as though supporting her taut, tense body. Suddenly her eyes swivelled and met those of her mother; but she continued to stare as though she hadn't seen her and Barbara came gently into the room and then dropped on to the couch and sat there, her arms clasped around her knees.

'Not so terrifying is it?' she said. 'Just a chair and a couch and a filing cabinet. How long have you been here?'

'I hate this room,' Amanda said, ignoring the question.

'It's that part of me you hate. The room itself is quite innocuous. It's what goes on here isn't it?'

'Secrets. We called it the secret room, locked, set apart from the house.'

'It was only locked because I didn't want you, as children, to be scampering in and out all day long. Amanda, if I were an ordinary doctor like Sarah, a GP, would you be so afraid of the room? Would you hate it so much?'

'I don't know.' Amanda closed her eyes as though gripped by a sudden spasm. 'I never know what goes on there.'

'I talk to people and try and help them, or mostly, to be more accurate, I listen to them. They have symptoms of depression or anxiety, fears of various kinds, memories, and we call this a neurotic illness. By listening and counsel I try and relieve them of these symptoms and help them to lead normal lives. There's nothing really secret or frightening about it and yet, if I sat here dispensing pills, you'd think it was quite all right. But why did you want to come here tonight? You need only have asked me and you could have seen it tomorrow. You have actually seen this room a dozen times, perhaps you don't remember, and it isn't really secret at all.'

'It frightened us all as children. Sarah said it frightened her too and Tom hated it.'

'I think it was a sort of game. A "let's imagine" kind of game like Bluebeard's Cave. What frightful things go on there? What does she do, what does she *hear*?' Barbara got up and pointed to the leather couch with a pillow covered by a cloth which was changed every day.

'Why don't you lie there darling and I'll sit where you are and you can see it isn't frightening at all.'

Obediently, and rather to Barbara's surprise, Amanda did as her mother bid, stretched out on the couch, modestly covering her legs with her long warm dressing gown.

'Do I shut my eyes?'

'You can do what you like,' Barbara said gently, sitting down in her chair, 'and tell me what comes into your mind.' She felt tired but also alert, keyed up, apprehensive, wondering if what she was doing now wasn't as unorthodox as telling Jennifer Littlejohn about her own life that day at the cottage; the day when she . . . jumped, fell? Barbara leaned back, firmly shutting out the memory of Jennifer.

'Nothing comes into my mind.'

'I just want you to breathe deeply and tell me the first thing you think of. And if it's about me don't worry, say it still.'

'I think you're an awful mother,' Amanda burst out, as if expecting an immediate reprimand, 'and I don't wonder that Daddy left you. I think he was as frightened of you as we were. We hardly ever saw you; we were at school and then when we came home you were always in here, listening to other people. You never seemed to have any time for us. You pretended to be loving, but you weren't. It was all a sham.' She stopped as though waiting for Barbara to say something, but Barbara was leaning back in her chair, her head resting lightly on a hand propped up by the arm of the chair, trying to imagine that this wasn't her daughter Amanda, but a patient who had come to her in need. It nearly always began with the parents, with the home.

'Even Frankie was frightened of you; it screwed her all up. She told me so when I stayed with her. She says nice things about you, but I know she doesn't mean them.'

'Does *anyone* like her?' Barbara intervened quietly.

'Who?'

179

'Your mother.'

'But I'm talking about you.'

'I know.'

'People don't dislike her, you . . .' Amanda said, her voice strained as though she had got herself into a situation she hadn't bargained for. 'I mean you're very pretty and charming, still. I was even quite proud of you when you used to come and see me at school. People said what a handsome couple you and Daddy were. Yes, I was very proud of you. I wanted to be like you.'

(John Littlejohn said: 'She became obsessed by you, almost as though she was you . . . She was mesmerized by you. She even dressed like you.')

'I felt I was an awkward, stupid puppy and I could never be like you.'

'You certainly weren't stupid. You were very clever, and pretty. Prettier than your sister. You would easily have got into Cambridge. You still could.'

'But I didn't want to go to Cambridge! You're still on at me Mummy! I like looking after dogs.'

'And you are looking after dogs,' Barbara murmured. 'You are a fully independent, pretty girl of eighteen with the world before you.'

'What world?' Amanda said bitterly.

'A world full of good things, life and hope.'

'What about the nuclear bomb?'

'That threatens us all, not just you. We all share in the human condition, Amanda. I think you feel threatened by life and you think the nuclear bomb is aimed at you specifically. It isn't. In the breakup of our family you see the holocaust. It is a holocaust in a way, but we're still all here – the family that is – only fragmented a bit, like we all would be if the bomb fell. I've been fragmented too, did you think of that?'

'How do you mean?'

'When Daddy left me I felt as if the atom bomb had fallen on me.'

Amanda turned in the couch and looked at her mother. 'You never showed it.'

'Did you feel I didn't care? I loved Daddy and I still do. I need you to help me – you and Sarah and Tom. I'm as sad at

Sarah going as you are. You don't know now how much I need you.'

'Me?' Amanda sounded surprised.

'You personally. I need your strength and your youth. Your love.'

'Why didn't you tell me that before?'

'I was always so busy putting on a brave front. When you've lived as long as I have you find that breaking down doesn't help anybody. But maybe if one does show weakness then other people know they're needed. They feel equal. At the time you were a young girl, only fourteen and I felt I had to be strong for you. If I'd been weaker it might have been better.'

'I felt that you weren't moved at all,' Amanda said in a small voice. 'You were nice to Frankie, nice to Daddy.'

'You had to break me to show you that I cared. Well you have, and I do.'

'How have I broken you?' Amanda turned and looked at her again.

'By not wanting to see me; not letting me show that I loved you and needed you. That broke my heart almost more than Daddy leaving.'

'Oh Mummy . . .' Amanda's hand flopped over the couch and Barbara suddenly knelt down and clasped it in her own.

'I'm not the psychiatrist and you're not my patient,' she said. 'What frightened you about the secret room was that you felt I gave more love to my patients than to you. I didn't, and can't. In my relationship, a detached, professional one with them, I can help my patients in a way I can't help you, or my family. I'm too close, too involved. I did this to show you it wasn't a frightening business. But I can't even begin to analyse you. I'm your mother and you're my daughter. We've both had a hard time. Today was hard for us both, with Sarah going. Tomorrow Tom goes back to his family and Daddy has Frankie and his new family. We've got each other. Isn't that important?'

Amanda swung her body right round and clasped her mother's head between her hands. It was the most tender, most spontaneous gesture that Barbara ever recalled Amanda making to her in her life. It was adult, too. The hands that

181

held her, the eyes that looked into hers, expressed more tenderness than she had ever known.

Soon afterwards they left the room that had laid bare so many secrets, so many ghosts, in the small hours of the night and climbed the stairs to Barbara's bedroom, their arms round each other, clinging together, giving mutual support.

CHAPTER ELEVEN

'How long will you stay like this?' Poppy asked, flopping on the bed, the quiet atmosphere of the room suddenly galvanized by her presence.

'Maybe until the baby is born.'

'But that's May!'

'I know. It's either that or a threatened miscarriage.'

'Wouldn't it be better darling?' Poppy moved nearer, her large bewildered eyes on Frankie as though devouring her.

'Better what?'

'Well you didn't really *want* the baby.'

'I do now,' Frankie said stubbornly. 'It will be the last opportunity I have. I'm going to be sterilized when it's born. I can't go through all this again.'

'And what does Sam say?'

'Sam, bless him, accepts it. He's been very supportive and sweet.'

'Well thank God for that anyway. He was horrid before Christmas.'

'He was shocked.'

'You're always defending him.'

'He's my husband. If you had one of your own perhaps you'd understand.'

'Touché darling.' Poppy bounced off the bed.

'Sorry, that was bitchy.'

'You were right. I don't understand a marriage relationship. All I understand are dates hastily arranged on the phone and a quick lunch-time fuck while the wife's away.' She sounded sad. 'It isn't that I wouldn't like to, but I can't can I? I've always been unlucky with men.'

'Maybe one day the wife will lose out. Like Barbara. You'll really fall in love.'

'Oh *I* will; but will he? I can't ever imagine anyone loving me strongly enough to do that. Anyway,' Poppy squared her shoulders beneath the extraordinary cloak she wore over her peasant dirndl skirt and high boots, and gave a brave little smile. She plopped herself down on the bed again. 'Anyway can you go on with the articles?'

'I have to. I want to keep that job and my sanity. Although Sam's supportive, he's not exactly cock-a-hoop. He feels chained being at home every night. He hates it, I know.' Frankie positioned herself more comfortably in the large bed. Lacking fresh air and exercise she was pale, her skin almost ethereal, her long blonde hair tied back in a bunch. No longer bouncing with rude health, as before, as though infused with animal spirits, she looked like some pre-Raphaelite beauty in the last stages of a wasting disease. 'I feel I've failed Sam, you know. He didn't expect this of our marriage. He's in his mid-fifties and he wants to have a good time. He married me for fun, not to be tied down by parenthood and a sick wife.'

'You're not sick!'

'I am sick. I'm still actually physically sick twice a day; sometimes I feel sick all day. I'm lethargic, no energy. I can see Sam's face alter when he comes in to see me, his normally cheerful sanguine expression tinged with apprehension. Yet he's so kind, always bringing me some little gift. We play here with Zoë together, but I notice Sam looking at her doubtfully, much as he loves her, as if knowing that soon there'll be another. Sam, if he liked, could sue me for false pretences.'

'But it's a *marriage*. You have to expect these things.'

'Sam didn't. I was very firm at the beginning about not wanting babies. We had such a marvellous time those first two years.' She sighed, leaning back against the pillows as though even the effort of speaking cost her, or maybe it was the memory of the happy times that were no more. 'I feel if Sam and I were more equal, if they were his first children too, it would be bearable. But Sam is much older than me. His eldest child is twenty-seven. When the new baby is that age Tom will be fifty-four and Sam will probably be dead. I know Sam thinks about that.'

'Would you have done anything different?' Poppy enquired gently.

'I don't think I'd have had the children. I'd certainly have taken more care, had I known I was going to be so unwell, not to have had this one. Who would have expected it of a great big hearty American girl like me? Anyway, it's done now. I love Sam even more than I did because he's so patient and uncomplaining. He is a good man. But still, I don't feel he's part of me any more. I feel I'm in this alone – a slight nuisance, a problem. Sometimes I feel like Sam's daughter, he's so concerned and protective, rather than his wife.' She looked at her friend as though weighing something up. 'Poppy, I wish you'd go to one or two things with Sam, concerts, the opera and so on. He'd love it and I know I can trust you, can't I? I don't think he'd make a pass at you anyway. He'd be too nervous about our relationship, yours and mine, I mean.'

Poppy's eyes grew as large as saucers. 'Of course you can trust me! I'm your best friend. But would Sam really like it?'

'I'd prefer you to Barbara, the other most likely candidate.'

'How is dear Barbara, has she been to see you?'

'She wrote me a little note,' Frankie gave a smile of false sweetness, 'saying if ever she could do anything etc. etc. She's had a great big reconciliation with Amanda so all is well again in her particular nest.'

'The anorexic daughter? Oh? How come?'

'When Sarah went away they decided they needed each other or something. Anyway Sam's very pleased. I must say that when I've had this baby and we can return to normal I'll be pleased too.'

Sam came home at seven and greeted the news that Frankie had invited Poppy to be his escort to the evening events he liked with undisguised mixed feelings. Being Sam, educated at Charterhouse and Balliol, he was too polite a man to show actual dismay, especially as Poppy was staying to supper; but Poppy was one of those rather forceful women with whom he found it hard to feel at ease. For one thing she hardly ever stopped talking; she was almost permanently restless, bobbing about, upsetting things. He could imagine her giving a running commentary on the opera in the middle of the stalls at Covent Garden. He knew it was nerves, but it was still irritating.

Sam had got rather into the habit of being the husband of a woman who for the time being was a semi-invalid. She was

185

supposed never to get up except to go to the lavatory, and Sam had moved into the spare bedroom to give her more room and leave her undisturbed. Besides, sex was out of the question for them until the baby was born. It now seemed to make it much more legitimate with Julia, and any qualms he might have had had gone. She was his sex object and he needed her – a therapeutic human doll who did as she was bid.

As though to confirm his opinion of her, that night Poppy made a great play about getting the supper, and was clumsy and spilled things in a way that showed she was not in her natural habitat. Each catastrophe was punctuated by roars of hysterical laughter and a girlish appeal to Sam to help out. She had far too much to drink with her meal and chatted away nineteen to the dozen to Sam, thus confirming all his worst fears. He usually ate with Frankie watching the small TV set in her room, but tonight he sat downstairs with Poppy. June, the nanny, now went out almost every night because her employers were always at home.

'It must be terrible for Frankie,' Poppy said in between mouthfuls of good red wine. 'And terrible for you.' Her large eyes mooned sympathetically at him.

'It's only temporary,' Sam replied. 'Frankie wants a family and I accept it. But this will be the last.'

'She told me.' Poppy poured herself more wine, splashing a good third on the table. Sam looked pained as it spread, because it was not his habit to serve or drink plonk and here was a woman who clearly had no respect for the grape. Another bad mark.

'Well what would you like to see Poppy?' Sam said apathetically. 'There's *Bohème* on at the opera.'

Poppy clasped her hands rapturously together, nudging her wine glass with her elbow and tipping it dangerously.

'I adore *Bohème*.'

'Then let's make it our first one. Would you like to eat in the crush bar at the interval?'

'*Adore* to.' Poppy leaned enthusiastically over the table.

'Then I'll give you a ring when I've got tickets.' Sam produced his diary from the inside pocket of his coat. 'Can you give me your number?'

Poppy felt a thrill of excitement mingled with apprehension as she did.

'You'll be safe with me you know,' she gushed.

'I'm sure I shall,' Sam replied, shutting his diary with a smile.

Frankie felt isolated in her room away from them both. She ate her meal from a tray, with the television on, but she couldn't have told anyone what the programme was. She listened to Polly roaring away in the kitchen, the dishes clattering, and felt a pang of sympathy for Sam.

She was preparing for sleep when he popped his head round the door.

'Has she gone?' Frankie enquired.

'At last. God how she drinks!' He came in and sat on her bed.

'All women like that drink. It's one of the hazards of the journalistic profession. I'm sorry, I should have asked you if you wanted to go out with her.'

'Did you choose her because she's safe?' Sam smiled and bent to kiss her forehead. His kisses were always very chaste now, as though her condition made her untouchable.

'I thought it would be nice for you to get out occasionally. You can go out with other people too if you like, but you don't know anyone do you?'

'Men or women?'

'Preferably men; but you have no close men friends, Sam. I can't understand men, really.'

'I have a lot of close men friends, but they're married and if I took them to the opera people would either think it very funny or I'd have to ask their wives. Most of the latter I dislike. I'm quite happy, darling, to wait until you're better.'

'I'm not *ill*, Sam.'

'I mean up and about again. Look, I'll just take Poppy to one or two things and then drop her. She really is a bit much for me.'

'I'm sorry. I'm very fond of her. She's been good to me.' Frankie gazed at Sam wondering what really went on in his mind now that this situation had deprived them of their sexual bond. That was important to Sam, she knew. Her situation had seemed to render her sexless, actually and emotionally. All she wanted to do now was to produce her baby and for both of them to survive. 'Don't you miss sex, Sam?'

The room was lit by a small solitary bedside lamp which put his head almost in the dark, so that if he started guiltily Frankie failed to see it. He put his hand over hers.

'I can wait until you're better darling.'

'I'm not *ill*. Please don't keep on saying that. It gets on my nerves.' This emphasis on getting well made her tetchy.

'I mean . . .'

'I know what you mean. I'm sorry.' She was frequently irritated with him, but not really with him, with the situation. She hated herself for it, and clasped him impulsively. 'I don't deserve you, Sam,' she added, tenderly stroking his face. 'You're so good to me. I didn't give you the life you expected, did I?'

'You have and you will.' Sam got to his feet. 'And in the meantime, I love you.'

He bent and kissed her cheek, chastely, like a brother.

For Barbara there was an attraction about Camden Town that defied analysis. It was not the prettiest part of London. It did not have the hilly beauty of Hampstead, parts of which still seemed locked fast in the eighteenth century with tiny cottages tucked at the end of cobbled streets scarcely wide enough to allow a car through. In many ways Camden Town was downright ugly with its huge intersection at the junction of Parkway and Camden Road, the central feature of which were ladies and gentlemen's lavatories surrounded by iron fences and disappearing down holes in the ground. There always seemed to be road works at the intersection, and people scurrying madly through one traffic light or the other to avoid annihilation as the mass of one-way traffic leapt forward north towards Belsize Park or west towards Holloway.

Camden Town was full of shabby buildings, some derelict, tatty cafés, fish and chip bars and take-away Chinese restaurants. A good many tramps took refuge in the doorways of mean miserable buildings, consoling themselves with swigs from large beer bottles which probably contained some other, cheaper, intoxicatingly lethal liquid. Its many public houses disgorged the remnants of a drunken, largely Irish population who seemed to have nowhere else to go as they lurched down the street at closing time.

Yet there was a bustle and energy about Camden Town with its hybrid population, its Japanese school, its many Greek and Indian restaurants. Its fruit market in Inverness Street was patronized not only by the obviously poor, but by the trendy intellectuals who lived in Gloucester Terrace and a shifting multi-coloured population of students, workers, drop-outs and the ordinary men and women who lived locally or on one of the many council estates close by. At one end, near the park, Camden Town was dominated by a convent with a fortress-like wall where the good nuns prayed for the release of those souls committed to purgatory. Up the road from the market was Camden Lock, the basin of the Regent's Canal, which housed another market for potters, bead makers, and purveyors of various arts and crafts from second-hand clothes to finely worked jewellery. There were two good fish shops in Camden Town where Barbara bought her fish, several excellent bakers, where she bought pitta or wholemeal bread, and a number of butchers each trying to undercut the already deflated prices of the others.

The psychiatric day hospital was in an old house near Hawley Lock, through which the canal continued on its way through St Pancras and east London. In the early nineteenth century, before the railway ruthlessly drove its way through this pleasant rural suburb, it might have housed a well-to-do merchant, commuting daily to the city, and his family, because it had a large basement area, and extensive attics where the servants had slept. It had a garden surrounded by iron railings and, since its adaptation as a hospital, the windows had double glazing to muffle the noise of the traffic which rushed south towards the West End outside.

On a sunny spring-like day in March, Barbara finished seeing her last patient, her mind on a walk through the streets of Kentish Town and Belsize Park towards home. Her car was being serviced and she'd taken a taxi to the clinic; but now it was so fine that the prospect of a leisurely walk was enticing after a day listening to the cares of disturbed people.

The psychiatric hospital was largely a labour of love for the people who worked there. In many ways it was a love that went unrewarded. Analysis and psychotherapy were processes that required time; time which the largely middle-class patients who could afford such treatment and came to see Barbara in Hampstead had, or could make, but which those who patronized the clinic had not. They had neither the time nor, sometimes, the insight or capability of understanding their symptoms that would allow them to be alleviated. Conditions of housing, schooling, employment or environment often produced symptoms that would not go away because the factors which produced them did not disappear. There were depressed housewives living in poor dwellings and burdened by too many children and drunken, violent, or absent husbands; the nineteenth century could still be observed alive and kicking in the conditions generated towards the end of the twentieth. There were many teenagers bewildered by the huge comprehensive schools whose sheer size emphasized their rootlessness, despite lip service being paid to pastoral care. There were young men and women who had drifted to London from the provinces and who were simply defeated by life. They had ended up in the courts for offences that were neither serious enough for prison nor light enough to be ignored. Frequently, they were put into the care of a probation officer who found the day hospital his or her last resort.

Many took refuge in the clinic by day, for they found people who wanted to listen and help them. There were counselling sessions, discussions, vocational training and opportunities for play. But at night they returned to their unsatisfactory homes, or the institutions to which the court had committed them, or the mean lodgings in the shabby streets nearby, or maybe the large home for men in Arlington Street whose outside appearance was still all too reminiscent of the workhouse in the times when the young Charles Dickens lived in Bayham Street a few blocks away.

To many, the work of the day hospital would have seemed insurmountable, a hopeless task. But to the members of the staff, the doctors, lay therapists, nurses and counsellors, it was work to be got through; it was an attempt to make a small indentation in the mass of misery that modern conditions, despite the welfare state, continued to thrust through its door.

Since Christmas Barbara had taken on an increasing load at the day hospital to which she was a consultant. Previously it had been two half days a week, but now it was more.

The day hospital was run on a five-day week and if Barbara felt satisfied with her work there, and she did, she felt entitled to spend the weekends with Amanda to whom she could be of more practical help, rather than remaining closeted with a private patient unable to resolve his or her difficulties.

Barbara had a small office on the first floor of the hospital overlooking a carelessly tended garden. Beyond was an assortment of roofs belonging to factories or private dwellings and a railway bridge. It was a pleasant room and she made it as informal as possible. It had no desk, but easy chairs and a sofa, a sisal carpet on the floor. It was the sort of place where those who participated in her group therapy sessions could feel secure and relaxed. The members often drifted up with cups of tea or coffee from the small canteen and squatted round smoking, if they wished, while they helped one another, guided by her, in their mutual exploration of the unconscious mind.

Group therapy was really the best way to deal with the hospital's many patients. Individual sessions were almost out of the question, so there was no analytic couch in the conventional sense. She would have private talks with patients, but largely to dispense practical advice and also, when necessary, medication in mild doses of anti-depressant pills or tranquillizers. The harassed, depressed working mother who had a few days' sick leave on account of her condition, had no time for lengthy probings into her psyche either alone or with others. Patients of this kind fell into a category Barbara felt least able to help. To the working classes there was something rather shameful about psychiatry so they kept away, preferring their GPs who had neither knowledge of nor interest in their condition. Barbara's greatest successes were with young adults, who, whatever their circumstances, enjoyed talking about themselves.

Dr Hahn was very much liked by the staff and loved by many of her patients. She was kind, quiet and uncontroversial. She was not ambitious to be director, or climb higher up in the medical hierarchy. If anything, she climbed down. Those of the staff who knew of the personal problems in her own life only admired the way she could set them aside in her concern for others.

Barbara finished writing up her notes for the day, looked at her list for the next and began to gather her things together, glancing anxiously out of the window to ascertain that the weather was still fine. A good brisk walk up Kentish Town Road and through the myriad of small streets towards Hampstead was just what she needed. There was a tap at her door and she looked at her watch calling to whoever it was to enter. As she looked up, Alfred Kleber put his head around the door.

'Am I welcome?'

Barbara would have liked advance warning of the question, but she was not a person used to controlling her emotions for nothing and she rose, extending her hand with a professional smile.

'Alfred, how very nice to see you.'

He took her hand and gazed around the room. 'I just heard you were still here. I thought you only did mornings twice a week?'

'That was in the old days. I think I can do a lot of useful work here, get through to more people in need than in my private practice.'

'I think we all feel that at times.' Alfred looked pointedly at a chair. 'May I? Or haven't you the time?'

'Do sit down.' Barbara sat too, joining her hands calmly in her lap as she gazed at him. That sordid last encounter with him seemed part of the very distant past, though it was only five months ago. He leaned forward, looking earnestly at her as though he was recalling the same occasion, though whether with more pleasure than she, she couldn't say.

'And how *are* you Barbara? I hope no hard feelings . . .'

'You should have the hard feelings.' Barbara's mouth curled with amusement. 'I remember almost bodily throwing you out.'

'It was very unfortunate your daughter appearing like that. It rendered a very pleasant evening slightly . . . how shall I put it . . .' he searched the ceiling as if trying to find either the right phrase in English, or the right word.

'Sordid?'

'A bit sordid, if you say, yes. Although my memories were pleasant too. How is Sarah by the way?'

'She's gone to Africa. By all accounts she's very well.'

Alfred registered surprise. 'For long in Africa?'

'She's with an American relief agency. She could be sent anywhere at a moment's notice, where she's needed. It looks a bit now as though the Middle East is a possibility, maybe the Lebanon.'

'Oh dear, that's nasty.' Alfred pulled a face.

'She won't mind. She is quite insensitive to personal danger or she wouldn't have gone in the first place.'

'Didn't you hope she'd specialize?'

'We did, but she seems wedded to this work at the moment.'

'Wedded?' Alfred smiled expansively. 'Do I detect a Freudian slip? No man in her life?'

'There never has been, as I seem to recall I once told you.'

'Never?' Alfred, the ladies' man, looked incredulous.

'Not as far as I know.' Barbara glanced again at her watch and out of the window. If it got too dark she would feel less like walking. The shadows were already lengthening on the red brick buildings on the other side. Her mind was more on the walk and the weather than her guest.

'And how is Amanda?' Alfred followed her glance.

'She is much better, much, much better and happier. She really does seem to love working with animals so we've abandoned the idea of Cambridge.'

'And your son? The one in the army?' Dr Kleber continued politely.

Barbara got up; then it would be Sam and Frankie, and his wife and daughter and in no time the sun would have gone.

'Alfred, I do have a *very* pressing engagement. I wonder if you'd be kind enough to excuse me?'

Alfred shot up, his expression registering a kind of false guilt, but also something else Barbara couldn't quite put a name to. Or maybe she could, though she wouldn't know whether to call it hope, desire or mere lust.

'I was hoping we might be able to dine, Barbara . . .'

She shook her head. 'Not now, or ever Alfred. I won't bore you with insincere platitudes. I think once a man and a woman have gone as far as we went there's no going back.'

'I hoped we might go forward . . .'

'I don't want to be your "London lay" if that's what you've got in mind.'

The urbane, cosmopolitan psychiatrist looked horrified at the very idea. 'My wife and I no longer live together. I was going to tell you.'

True or false? Barbara didn't care. 'Then I'm sure you have many other fortunate ladies to choose from.'

She picked up her gloves and bag and looked for the key to the door on her key ring.

'I am really very fond of you Barbara . . .' the anxious doctor continued. Women didn't usually reject him.

'And I am very flattered, but no thank you Alfred. Friends, acquaintances, yes. But lovers no . . . not now or any other time.'

'I can't understand why . . .'

She looked at him and thought that, for a psychiatrist, he had about as much insight into himself as a dog, or one of those species who are said to have no mind. He obviously didn't realize that he was neither welcome, nor wanted, because his instinctively male appraisal of himself was so inflated. Then she realized once again that, where personal feelings were concerned, people who specialized in the mind were as vulnerable as anybody else, maybe more so.

Barbara gestured towards the door and, as he preceded her, she followed him, locking the door behind her. The rooms and corridors were already deserted, though some evening sessions would start in an hour or so. All the day patients had gone. Alfred walked silently beside her rolling the brim of his hat between his hands, his expression mystified. He followed her down the stairs and they stood at the entrance. The last dull rays of the sun were slanting feebly in through the door.

'I do admire you a great deal Barbara, as a woman and a professional.'

'And I'm sure we'll meet again Alfred, as professionals. Thank you so much for popping in today. The work we're doing here is in some ways really pioneering.'

'That's what I hoped to talk to you about,' Dr Kleber said dejectedly.

'Goodbye, Alfred.' Barbara waved as the director of the clinic came round a corner, hands outstretched in greeting to the distinguished psychoanalyst from Vienna. Outside the air was warm, and instinctively Barbara raised her head to inhale. It was not clear and fragrant, being impregnated with car fumes, the smells, flotsam and jetsam of a busily populated part of the metropolis. But it was good. Some blackbirds sang piercingly from a tree in the small garden.

She set off for Hampstead, her briefcase in one hand, a paper tucked under her arm.

For the first time in months she was aware of a feeling of contentment; it was not exhilarating but peaceful. She felt that she was beginning to be her own woman – not Sam's, not her family's, certainly not Alfred Kleber's, not her patients', but her own. She didn't have to account for herself to anyone, or consent to an unwished for sexual encounter just to prove her femininity. The expression of Kleber's face as she escorted him from her office fully atoned for the humiliation of that night in November.

At last, she decided, she belonged to herself, and her destiny was what she, and not others, made it. At the age of fifty-two it was quite a discovery.

CHAPTER TWELVE

THE RESTAURANT IN COVENT GARDEN was crowded despite, or perhaps because of, the lateness of the hour. *Die Meistersingers* at the opera had finished at eleven and there was a rush for the many good restaurants around that were still open. Sam had taken care to book; in fact he had laid his plans very carefully indeed, thus surprising Poppy because they usually had a salad and a bottle of wine in the crush bar during an interval.

But Sam, by not going home, because the performance started at 5.30 and they were eating afterwards, would not see Frankie at all that day. She would thus get used to not expecting him at a regular hour. Anyway her baby was only two months away and she seemed to spend most of the time asleep, when she wasn't working.

They ordered prawns and some white wine, steaks and a bottle of red and, for a while, discussed the merits of the performance with Reiner Goldberg making his debut at Covent Garden as Sachs and Lucia Popp singing Eva for the first time. Poppy thought the whole thing enchanting but Sam was bored by Wagner, always avoided *The Ring* if he could, and *Parsifal* with its pseudo mysticism like the plague.

Sam was a very knowledgeable man, not only about finance, music, especially his love, opera, but life. He was a fascinating man to be with. Because he was so tall and leonine people always seemed to look at him when he came into a room, or made way for him as he pushed their way through the crowd in the foyer at Covent Garden. Poppy had always found him attractive (who, she thought, in their right senses wouldn't?) but as her friend's husband he had seemed forbidden fruit. Now she was not so sure. Frankie had almost thrown them together, as if inviting an affair. Would it be so wrong if they had one, just a teensy weensy one, because it obviously couldn't be for long? Once Frankie got on her feet again the domestic noose would be firmly round Sam's neck.

But Frankie trusted her. Or did she? Poppy decided she didn't know Frankie's mind, certainly not now in this very odd situation thrown up by her . . . well, it wasn't an illness, say indisposition. While Frankie was so indisposed she couldn't have sex – she had made that quite clear, and so had Sam who, when he'd had a few drinks, went on with some bitterness about the limitations of the spare bedroom.

Sam had decided that night to confide in Poppy. He never thought he would. But the Poppy he saw on these evenings out was a much more sympathetic creature than the female, obviously desperately insecure and striving to make an impression, he had known before. It was somehow as though she could feel relaxed with Sam, secure that he was her friend's husband and not a potential lover – or was she? He never quite knew. She was a lot of fun and, despite her bizarre clothes, that impossible hair which she flung about like a mane, and her indisputable plainness, she had an attraction. It was not a sexual attraction, for him anyway – he was fully engaged in that quarter – but a likeability. He felt he could trust Poppy, confide in her like a good friend, as Frankie obviously thought she could and did.

For some reason Poppy was excited that night of all nights, at least their sixth night out since it started at the end of January – almost once a week. She detected something in the air. She had felt the increasing rapport with Sam, as she knew he had, and a little tingling sexual nerve seemed to tell her that something interesting was about to happen. Sam had his arms on the table, his head tossing this way and that as he expatiated, very amusingly, on the absurdities of Wagner's plots, the essential Teutonism of his music. No wonder Hitler liked him.

They could, she supposed as she looked at him, her eyes lighting up encouragingly (she knew) giving him very subtly the come hither sign, go to her flat. It was in Kensington, but only a taxi ride away from her office in Fleet Street and his at the bank. It would not be the first lunch-time assignation she had had there with a married man nor, she conjectured unhappily, the last. But Poppy was a fatalist. After a lifetime spent pursuing the wrong people she felt destined to remain unmarried; that she would probably be childless too didn't worry her in the least, especially since Frankie had had all this trouble.

But to be married would be nice; to have a man, something to hold on to and call one's own. With her luck though, the man that she married (were she to do so) would immediately go off with someone like her on the lookout for a man like him. Maybe, then, she was best as she was – mistress of all and wife to none. She wondered if Sam would suggest tomorrow. She remained permanently, hopefully, on the Pill.

'There is something I want to ask you, Poppy,' Sam said at last having delivered his final scathing verdict on Wagner. Poppy leaned encouragingly forward, carelessly upsetting the contents of her glass over the tablecloth. No matter; the waiter had a fresh cloth over it in an instant, and the white wine was finished anyway. The red was opened with the steak and Sam started again. 'I don't want you to get the wrong idea.'

'Oh I'm sure I shan't, Sam.' Steak forgotten, Poppy leaned her head on her hands, her eyes earnestly fixed on him, and knocked the new glass sideways again. Luckily it was half empty and most of the contents went on Poppy's skirt; but, as it was a richly woven tapestry, made probably in Indonesia or Thailand, no one would notice and the damp pressing on to her thigh made her think of sex. She was really feeling quite randy.

Sam, who had never in his life known anyone as clumsy as Poppy, patiently refilled her glass, putting it well out of arms' way and began a third attempt to explain what he wanted. It was difficult enough anyway without interruptions.

'You know that I am utterly devoted to my wife.'

'You mean Barbara?'

'I mean *Frankie*.'

'Oh sorry.' In her confusion Poppy swept her steak off the plate, but quickly secured it again with her prehensile fork.

Sam observed with a feeling of despair the mass of congealed greasy blood on the cloth next to the many wine stains made by Poppy. How a woman like this survived in the competitive, sophisticated atmosphere of Fleet Street he did not know! Was she fit to be trusted with his secret or might she, in an unguarded moment, blurt it out? 'Frankie is my wife.'

'Yes, but I knew you were very fond of Barbara.'

'I am,' Sam wondered if it was worth going on. 'But what I am saying is that I am very fond of Frankie. I want to emphasize that.'

'Yes I see.' Poppy looked straight at him as though not seeing at all. Her cheeks were very red, but they usually were after the quantities she had to drink.

'Look, Frankie . . . I mean Poppy.' (The confusion was surely significant, Poppy thought). 'I want to ask you a favour that concerns my wife.'

'I see.'

'But I don't want her to know.'

'Is it a present?'

She was decidedly thick, Sam thought. But Frankie said she'd been to Cambridge; or was it Aberdeen?

'No, nothing like that. The fact is, Poppy, I regard you as a very good friend.'

'Oh I am.' Sam quickly whipped the glass out of reach as her elbow lunged towards it. 'Thanks, Sam, I am careless; but I do feel these few outings have brought us together. Nothing disloyal to Frankie, I mean, is there?'

'It's because I regard you as a good, understanding friend, that I wanted to ask you this favour.' Sam made little invisible etches with the fork on the tablecloth. 'You know that I haven't had sex for a long time with Frankie. Not her fault, of course, but I am a very sexual man. Even an orgasm without penetration, the doctor says, might set a miscarriage off, and she does so want that baby.'

'I know.' Poppy's eyes brimmed over with anticipation. Would he consider the journey to Kensington too long?

'So we can't have any sexual activity at all. Not any. They say it's bad for a man, at least of my age. If he goes without it too long, there could be permanent damage . . . so, for one's health's sake . . .' He paused again and looked at her significantly as though inviting her to imagine in what this damage might consist. 'Now, it so happens there is a young lady to whom I have become attached . . . only sexually, I mean. There is nothing to it at all besides that. Sex.'

Poppy was slowly beginning to realize he wasn't talking

199

about her. Incredible. *Another* lady? What sort of man, monster, was this, who deceived a hapless, pregnant wife, apparently with impunity and without guilt?

'What about this lady?' she snapped, sitting up abruptly, the beads around her neck jangling a disapproving tattoo on the table.

'I would like to see her and yet say I'm with you. Only . . . I won't be. You see?' Gazing at her Sam knew he had done the wrong thing. Her outraged expression was that of a Victorian spinster who had been asked to drop her drawers by a perfect stranger. 'You won't do it, I can see that.' Sam took a long sip of wine.

'You mean you have a mistress, Sam?'

Sam put the glass down.

'Well, not . . . yes, if you look at it like that. But a "mistress" is a very silly word, I always think. I mean it's not a permanent liaison or anything serious. It hasn't been going on long, I assure you. Only since Frankie . . .'

'You didn't waste much time,' Poppy said sharply. 'Frankie has only been confined to bed for two months.'

'Well, maybe just a little before then. Frankie has been so busy with Zoë, and her pregnancy.' Sam sighed and looked around as if all those in the restaurant would turn to him with one accord in sympathy. 'She really has hardly been a wife to me for some time now. I married her, you know, not only because I loved her, but her youth was an advantage. We had a very sexual affair and I expected it would last well into marriage. Alas, it never does.'

'You didn't give it much chance if you ask me.'

'I see I shouldn't have spoken, Poppy.' Sam signalled to the waiter for the bill, even though they hadn't had coffee. 'You think I'm disloyal to Frankie and I can see I've compromised you.'

'You haven't compromised me at all. Of course I should never dream of telling her what you've told me. But what exactly is it you want *of me*, Sam?' She leaned across the table and the glass wobbled alarmingly but did not spill. The expression on her face – mystified concern – made Sam begin to hope again.

'I wanted you to alibi me. That is, I say we're going out but I'm seeing, Ju . . . this lady friend of mine. As it is, now we can never get out at all. She's married too. I assure you it's simply sexual, a need for both of us; but it would be nice to spend some more time together. Her husband drives a taxi and often works at night . . .'

'A *taxi?*' Poppy boomed in the tone the immortal Edith Evans playing Lady Bracknell had proclaimed 'A *handbag?*'

'She is a very ordinary woman . . .'

'A girl in your office, I suppose.'

'Yes.'

'Isn't it dangerous? Won't people talk?'

'People don't know, that's why I want us to go somewhere else.'

'Where do you go now?'

Sociologically speaking Poppy was curious; but Sam's modesty, or maybe his shame, forbade him to say.

'I'd just like for me to be able to say that you and I are going out – Frankie accepts that now, and I promise that I'll make it up to you in a very special way.'

'What special way?' Poppy was still peeved but, once again, had succumbed to his charm. Sam would certainly be beholden to her if she did something like this for him – and who knew when one could use a friend?

'Something nice,' Sam smiled. 'A very good meal, a trip abroad . . . you'll see. Will you do it?'

'I suppose I'll have to,' Poppy said grudgingly. 'I don't really want to, but I suppose you'll go on deceiving Frankie anyway.'

'Only for the time being.'

'Balls,' Poppy said. 'I know you men.'

'But we really are friends, aren't we, Poppy? You and I? It isn't everyone I could ask something like this.'

'I should think it isn't,' Poppy said and rose to go to the lavatory. The things that some men got up to really boggled the imagination . . .

In the next month, that is March through to April, Poppy and Sam ostensibly went to *Salome*, *Billy Budd* and *Cav* and *Pag* at the Garden and to numerous concerts on the South Bank and the Barbican. Frankie was beginning to feel suspicious, and wondered if her idea had been such a good one after all. Yet whenever she mentioned Poppy as a possible sexual partner Sam went into such paroxysms of mirth that Frankie was convinced she wasn't. You might deny someone was your mistress, but surely the thought wouldn't reduce you to hysterics? Not with someone as honest and straight-forward as Sam?

One thing that added fuel to Frankie's suspicions was that Poppy didn't come and see her as often, and was awkward when she did. But, apart from saying that she and Sam should stop going out, Frankie, the instigator of the whole thing, didn't see what she could do. She decided to do nothing, because she wanted to trust Sam and she had her mind strictly on the baby that had grown so much in her womb. She was very large, slightly larger than she should be because, being bedridden, she had no exercise. She was on a diet and a physiotherapist came every other day but she felt fat, ugly and repulsive. No wonder this feeling engendered in her suspicion about Sam. He would find almost anyone attractive compared to her.

But on 18 March an apparently insignificant event on the far side of the world had occurred that was to put all the problems currently affecting most of the Hahn family to one side. The Argentinian Navy landed a party of scrap metal merchants on the island of South Georgia, and the ice patrol vessel HMS *Endurance* was despatched to the island. A flurry of almost incredible diplomatic activity and speculation occurred, but nothing could stem what, in retrospect, seemed an irreversible tide and, on 2 April, Argentina invaded the Falkland Islands.

Tom, who had been training in North-West England with the 42 Commando of Marines, was among the 600 men recalled to Plymouth.

Thus on 9 April Barbara, Sam, Amanda, Natalie and the children were standing on the quayside at Southampton as *Canberra*, hastily requisitioned and fitted up as a troopship carrier, took part of the Parachute Regiment, and 3 Commando Brigade of Marines, who included Captain Tom Hahn, apparently to war.

There had hardly been time for goodbyes. Barbara and Sam had travelled down the night before with Amanda, and had stayed at a Southampton hotel with Natalie and the babies. All Tom had managed was a drink with them – too elated, too overwhelmed, too excited, in fact, to share the concern and apprehension of his family. At last there was action and, in a mood Barbara had never seen Tom in before, she realized that he had joined the Army just for this: not only to keep the peace, but to put his years of training as a soldier into practice.

They couldn't see him now as *Canberra* moved out into the harbour, its decks thronged with cheering, excited men. Still they waited until the great ship steaming down the Solent was almost out of sight, little Clare frantically waving the two Union Jacks she carried in each hand.

Slowly, through the crowd of onlookers, many now openly weeping, they made their way back to the hotel.

'I feel quite stunned,' Barbara murmured as they sat in the hotel lounge having a drink before departure.

'Of course it won't come to war,' Sam said. 'The whole thing will be settled long before they get to the Falklands.'

'Tom seems to think it will.' Natalie had been very composed the whole time, showing no sign of agitation, calm with the children. A soldier's wife.

'Tom seemed to *hope* it will,' Barbara corrected, thinking of the ecstatic man the night before. 'That's what astonished me.'

'But why should it astonish you?' Natalie looked at her mother-in-law with surprise. 'All soldiers like the chance to fire guns; that's why they join up.'

'Tom said he joined up to keep the peace.' Amanda alone had openly shed tears.

'Well he *is* keeping the peace,' Natalie said firmly. 'The Argentinians have no right on the Falklands.'

Barbara didn't think they had a right there either, but she wondered if it was worth mobilizing half of the British Navy and Army to get them off. Sam was of the opinion that the whole thing had been bungled at the diplomatic level, and ought to have been cleared up years before. Typical case of official incompetence.

'It should never have come to this in the first place; but, since it has, I don't think our men will get any further than the Ascension Islands. He'll be back in no time, you'll see.'

Barbara wondered if Natalie would like to come and stay

with her for a few days, or as long as she liked; but Natalie, all stiff-upper-lip British, was quite firm about that too. She had her place with all the other wives whose husbands had set out with the Task Force. There would be enough for them to do to keep one another cheerful, the children occupied.

'She really is an amazing woman,' Barbara remarked to Sam on the way back. 'I take my hat off to her. Isn't it funny how soldiers seem to marry women who will be good in this kind of situation?'

'Not all of them were.'

'Well they were upset. It was all so emotional with the flags and the bands; but I bet they all knuckle down like Natalie. Remember the war?'

'Tom'll come to no harm,' Sam said. 'It'll all blow over.'

They took a coastal road because they were dropping Amanda off at the kennels near Dover. Barbara would like to have stayed the night, but Sam wanted to get home to be with Frankie. He really was devoted, Barbara thought. Or maybe Frankie had warned him about being alone with her. When they got to the kennels it was dusk and the sound of barking dogs filled the air. Amanda looked excited as the car drew up in the yard.

'Come and meet George,' she said.

'Funny name for a dog,' Sam smiled at her, pleased to see how she'd filled out, how altogether happy and contented she appeared despite Tom's departure. The whole scene had been all too reminiscent of saying goodbye to Sarah, and he had expected her to be more upset.

'George is a man,' Amanda said.

In the area where the dogs were being fed there stood a tall youth feeding the animals, remonstrating with the greedy ones. Beside him was Peter Maxwell, the owner of the kennels, who greeted Sam and Barbara with a handshake and asked how the day had been, shaking his head as he did so.

'Bad thing this. You must all be upset.'

'We don't know how we feel.' Barbara pulled her thick coat around her, whether from cold or apprehension she wasn't sure. 'It happened so suddenly. We couldn't believe it when the phone call came to say he was going, although we had some inkling when he was called back from manoeuvres.'

'He seems pleased though,' Amanda was tugging the

youth's arm as if she had already forgotten about Tom. There was a familiarity to her gesture that rather surprised Barbara who looked with curiosity at the man – boy, youth, he couldn't have been more than twenty – who stood shyly in front of them, a large dog bowl in his hand.

Amanda introduced him to her parents. 'George is my mate,' she said, taking the bowl from him.

George looked apologetically at his hands and rubbed them on his trousers before taking Barbara's in a steely clasp. They were big and cold and still contained traces of dog food.

'How do you do, George?' Barbara said politely. 'You're new aren't you?'

'Started last month,' George replied in a broad northern accent.

'What happened to Fran?' Fran was the other kennel maid.

'Oh Fran's still here.' Peter Maxwell pulled away a friendly dog who was sniffing Barbara's legs with interest. 'We're taking that many dogs on I'm building new kennels.' He pointed vaguely in a westerly direction. 'I might start breeding. Amanda's very keen.' He looked at her with approval.

'George used to work in the coal pit like his father; but he's bronchial and the dust irritated his lungs,' Amanda advised.

'Fresh air's the thing.' Peter glanced at the ruddy-faced George. George gave a cough as though to demonstrate his bronchitic lungs. The trained ear of Doctor Barbara detected that he was well out of the pits; the cough was a nasty rasping one, obviously chronic.

'Well I hope you'll soon be quite well again, George. You're obviously better off here.'

'I am that,' George said.

'We ought to be going.' Sam looked at his watch. 'Are you sure you don't want us to take you out to dinner, darling?'

'Quite sure, Daddy.' Amanda was eyeing the dogs professionally as if all she wanted was to be with them and, perhaps, George.

'See you soon then.'

More handshakes, kisses for Amanda, and then Sam was driving up the narrow lane towards the main London road.

'Well what did you think of George?' he said, stopping for the turn at the top of the lane.

'Seems a very nice boy.'

'A bit of a clodhopper.'

'I think that's unfair. He was obviously embarrassed.'

'I hope to God she's not keen on him.'

Barbara looked out into the dark around them.

'As a matter of fact I would think he was just the sort of boy, man, she would be keen on.'

'Why, for Christ's sake?' Sam turned on to the main road.

'He's not a threat. He's comfortable. Anorexics like to avoid growing up; they're afraid of sex. There's nothing very stallion-like about George. I should think he's just a nice companion for her. Frankly, I approve if he helps her to develop.'

'Trust you to say something like that.'

'But why?' Barbara plunged in the car lighter to light her cigarette.

'He's totally uneducated for a start.'

'I don't see how you can tell that at a glance. You're a snob, Sam. He might be very educated, like D. H. Lawrence, whose father was a miner too.'

'D. H. Lawrence indeed!' Sam scoffed.

'I'm just saying you can't tell by appearances. I thought he was a nice, quiet, interesting looking boy.'

'Ah, but would you like him to marry our daughter?'

Barbara puffed thoughtfully at her cigarette. Her mind was on the many youthful misfits she saw at the clinic. She'd rather Amanda's first boyfriend were a miner's son, someone who liked dogs and fresh air, than an intelligent middle-class layabout on drugs.

'I don't think we're talking about marriage. I haven't got that sort of thing in mind at all. How's Frankie, to change the subject?'

'Big, bored, a bit frightened. I'll be jolly glad when all this is over.'

'I'll be jolly glad when Tom comes safely home,' Barbara said, almost as though she had a premonition of disaster.

Each had their minds on something important to them, different things. She realized how much their separation had driven herself and Sam apart, and how different it would have been if they were still together, sharing things, shouldering together common family problems like the futures of Sarah, and Amanda, and Tom, instead of talking about them over the telephone.

'It's Te Kanawa in *Simon Boccanegra*,' Sam informed Poppy.

'Never heard of it,' Poppy was a bit tired of the alibi role. She kept well clear of Frankie as though sharing in Sam's guilt.

'The baby is due this month,' Sam volunteered as if divining her thoughts.

'Will you be finished with this woman then?'

Sam's answer was silence.

'All right tell me when it is.' Poppy sighed over the phone, noting the date in her diary. Monday, 24 May. It seemed a long way off.

Yet events moved very quickly during those spring days as the child in Frankie's womb waited to be delivered and *Canberra* made its way steadily towards the Falklands. Shortly after Tom left a letter came from Sarah to say that she was on her way to a hospital in Beirut. The Lebanon had been the scene of sectarian conflict for many years now; but, hopefully, it wouldn't get worse.

Sarah's letters were infrequent, but when they came they were as excited as Tom was about the possibility of war in the South Atlantic. She had already covered vast tracts of Africa, providing her mother with medical details about the effects of malnutrition and poverty that would have been incomprehensible to a layman, except that the results were there for everyone to see in the pathetic pictures that from time to time appeared on the television.

Barbara, working steadily in her quiet way, going to the clinic three days a week, lecturing at the university, seeing her private patients, still had time to feel totally caught up in her children overseas and their lives. There was one letter from Tom written on *Canberra* before it reached the Ascension Islands. It was full of the life on board, the fun, crossing the Equator but, also, the deadly seriousness of their training in preparation for an assault on the Islands.

When Barbara wasn't working she spent most of her time in front of the TV set watching the News as Mr Haig shuttled desperately backwards and forwards between London, New

York and Buenos Aires. The Common Market countries decided to place an embargo on Argentinian goods. The Secretary General of the United Nations stepped in; there were meetings all over the world. It seemed impossible that peace efforts should fail. But there was something about the steely look in Mrs Thatcher's eyes every time she was interviewed that reminded Barbara of a modern Boadicea preparing to lead her peoples to war.

The whole world seemed to be waiting in an almost intolerable state of suspense as negotiations failed and the British Navy, now off the Falklands, patrolled its exclusion zone, tossed about on the mountainous seas in an area rugged and harsh at the best of times, but now preparing for winter.

On 2 May the sinking of the *General Belgrano* by the British seemed to put the lid on any hopes of peace and horrified much of the nation that had been sympathetic to the war. On 3 May came retaliation: the sinking of HMS *Sheffield* by an Exocet missile, a hitherto unrevealed deadly aspect of modern warfare to those who remembered the last one, even if they were children, as Barbara and Sam had been.

Now war was inevitable. Surely a landing was imminent? How long could troops, unused to water, survive in such conditions? What would they be like when they landed? Would they be able to fight? There were no more letters from Tom and none from Sarah. Sam was preoccupied with Frankie. Amanda happy at her job in Kent, maybe, too, with George.

Barbara felt very alone – work, work, the TV News and the mail was all she lived for.

One of Sam's many men friends, the ones who were married, and they almost all were, had a flat in the Barbican as well as a house in the Home Counties. It was a very useful place for Sam to rendezvous with Julia, because it was not far from work and he knew nobody else who lived there. Being Sam, and such a sociable person, it was far too dangerous for him to be seen with her at any public place. He hadn't minded who saw him with Poppy. She had his wife's blessing and, anyway, didn't exude the peculiar sexual aura he felt everyone must notice about the silent Julia. They once had a meal at the

Cut Above, the restaurant in the Barbican complex which Sam liked because he enjoyed good meat and it was a carvery. For the entire duration Sam kept on looking around him, or at the door, as though any moment someone he knew would come in, and eventually Julia suggested that they stuck to eating in his friend's flat. Eating wasn't a very important part of their evening's entertainment anyway.

'But I feel I *use* you, Julia,' he protested.

Julia smiled at him enigmatically. The more he knew her, the more he felt convinced that Leonardo had a Julia in mind when he painted the Mona Lisa; some naughty woman, keen on sex, who kept her secrets about her affairs with married men. Except for her body, which he knew very well by now, Julia was a complete mystery to Sam; and the more mysterious she became the more desirable she seemed.

Sam was used to articulate, intelligent women who applied their gifts to the art of love as well. Because it *was* an art, or so Sam had thought until he encountered Julia Fairchild. Now he decided it must be instinctive, not acquired, not an art at all. Julia was by no means stupid, yet she was completely uninterested in the things that interested Sam, or Frankie or Barbara. She lacked vitality. She had no feeling for the arts, no curiosity, read little and he had the distinct impression that she only knew about the Falklands War because Sam's son was involved. Despite the national euphoria, the extensive media coverage, it would not have surprised Sam had that item of information managed to escape Julia's attention completely.

Sam found himself increasingly wanting to know what went on inside Julia, what made her tick. She enjoyed the bank, and she liked her work. That, she told him. Yet he knew nothing else about her at all – about her relations with her husband, Glen, what sort of family she had apart from him, whether she'd ever been abroad or had any hobbies, or what she did with the rest of her life. You had to ask her these things to find out, and they seldom had much time.

Julia was the most vacuous and, it seemed, the least demanding woman he had ever met and yet she had a quality of sensuality, perhaps because of this, that thrilled him to the core. He was so hungry for Julia, so greedy, that he knew he would never give her up, as long as she was willing, even after the new baby was born.

One thing that Julia was very good at was being domestic. Despite the fact that she and Sam spent their evenings in the flat of someone she didn't know, and in an environment that was quite alien to her, she settled in at once, taking care of the stove and the bed in that order. She shopped in her lunch hour for items of food she knew Sam liked, both delicacies and simple dishes because he was always watching his weight. Sam would give her the key and she would be at the flat, which was ten minutes' walk away, half an hour before him so that they were never observed leaving the bank together.

There she served up a beautiful meal to accompany the wine Sam brought. They usually had it in front of the television and then she neatly washed up before they went to bed. Often, though, they talked – it was the only time they did – but only after they had seen the TV News.

On 21 May the British landed on the Falkland Islands at San Carlos and, despite its apparent success, a string of disasters followed in the sinkings of HMS *Ardent* and HMS *Antelope*, and the damaging of a great number of other ships.

'Did you have any news of your son?' Julia enquired over the smoked salmon which they ate from plates on their laps as they watched the news.

'None at all,' Sam said, his eyes on the screen, though there were no current pictures from the Falklands. 'He'll be there somewhere though.' He gestured towards the screen, showing a map of East Falklands where the Task Force had landed, and popped another piece of salmon into his mouth.

'You must feel very proud.' Julia neatly put her knife and fork together and wiped her bright red mouth. She was a clean meticulous person, obviously careful about personal hygiene, for which Sam was grateful.

'I feel very worried.' Sam sipped the Chablis he'd brought already chilled from a fridge in the boardroom of the bank. 'My wife is too. I mean my ex-wife.'

'I should think she is,' Julia said. She seemed to consider the two Mrs Hahns about equal, and mentioned them with respect, never calling either of them by their Christian names nor, for that matter, any of Sam's children either. It was 'your son' or 'your daughter the doctor', or 'your daughter who likes dogs'. She seemed to regard Sam's family, as indeed she regarded Sam, with a certain degree of awe – as though she were in an inferior, almost domestic position *vis à vis* them. She was never really familiar with Sam, deferential towards him as though permanently aware, despite the intimacy between them, that he was a senior official at a bank where she was a very junior one.

'I got some of that nice rare beef you like.' Julia removed Sam's empty plate and put a new one before him. He looked at her appreciatively and helped himself to salad from a small table nearby.

'You're very good, Julia. You know, I feel utterly relaxed and happy here with you.'

He put his plate on one side and got up to switch off the brief News on BBC2, which was all they could see until 9 o'clock when there'd be a fuller bulletin. He bent over to kiss the back of Julia's neat little neck as she helped herself to salad from the table. Then he poured red wine for them both and brought her glass with him as she sat next to him on the sofa, a napkin tidily over her knees which were pressed close together.

'Do you feel happy with me?' Sam asked when she failed to reply, her right hand going mechanically from plate to mouth, back to plate again. 'I never know about you, Julia.'

'What is there to know, Sam?' She shot him a sidelong glance. 'Not much.'

'I know that you're very sexy. Were you always like that? Who was your first man?'

'My husband,' Julia said primly. 'I've told you that before.'

'And I don't believe you.'

'Well he was.' Julia took a sip of wine, then carefully swallowed what she had in her mouth, as though the wine had helped wash it down.

'And how many since?'

'When do I have the opportunity, Sam?' Julia looked at him reproachfully. 'I'm hardly likely to meet someone like you every day of the week.'

'You mean you never had a lover beside your husband?' Julia shook her head, her eyes on her plate. She was wearing green today and it suited her. Chaste little green goddess, Sam thought. Little siren. 'I find that incredible,' Sam went on. 'Sex to you must be absolutely instinctive. I never came across it like that in a woman before.'

Julia knew about his girl friends as well as his wives and was very awed by his experience. Everything about Sam awed her until they got into bed and then a gorgeous feeling of voluptuousness overtook her and she forgot he was Mr Hahn, one of the heads of the bank, and she was Julia Fairchild, securities clerk who lived in Bromley, Kent, in a semi-detached house she shared with her husband, with the taxi parked outside when he was home.

Because she was such an inarticulate person, given to few words, it was difficult for her to tell Sam exactly what he had done to her; how he had liberated her, excited her for the first time in a way that Glen – that 'bang-bang-thank-you Mam' man – had never done. She thought it was truly a miracle that Sam brought out the unexpectedly sensual side of her, that theirs was an encounter of such mutual pleasure. She sighed as Sam's jaws clomped silently beside her, and a delicious feeling of sexual anticipation began to surge through her loins.

'I'll get the cheese,' she said, taking their plates and smiling down at him. She could see he had an erection already.

'We can't be too long tonight,' Sam felt his crotch as he followed the direction of her eyes. 'Frankie's baby is absolutely imminent.' The way he said it you'd think it had nothing to do with him. 'Frankie's baby', not 'our baby'. Julia noted that at once.

'Oh dear,' she looked away from his crotch to the floor, her shoulders drooped.

'It doesn't mean we'll finish, Julia.' Sam got up to take her in his arms and she snuggled up to him like a little waif, the empty plates still in her hands.

'We can't come here though,' she said in her little voice. 'You won't be expected to go out with that friend of your wife's, will you?'

'We'll find a way.' Sam began to be overwhelmed by his desire for her. 'I'm going to try and sort out something long-term. Don't think I ever want to finish with you.'

'Long term?' A faint blush came into Julia's cheeks as she looked at him, speculatively.

'I'm going to try and get a room somewhere where we can

spend more time. Maybe a flat of my own here at the Barbican.'

Julia gazed at him with wonder. She knew they were expensive and he had money, but . . .

'I'm on various committees and things to do with the City, you know. We'll be able to get away quite often, maybe at lunch time too; but I can't always use this place of Tony Green's.'

'What does he think you want it for now?'

'Oh he knows what I want it for.' Sam smiled at her.

Later, in bed, Sam held her thin body in his arms; held tight this frail, undemanding little creature. All the women he'd known – his two wives especially – had never needed to be protected; but this fey, shy, animal–like quality that Julia had made her vulnerable, as though she were an outcast from the pack. On the one hand she could protect herself quite well; on the other, she needed him. She sheltered in him. She was a kind of quintessential Victorian woman, who needed a man the way most modern women didn't. He knew Barbara and Frankie would be quite disgusted by this attitude, which is why he felt that Julia's attitude to him, and his to her, was precious, unique.

'You're very precious to me, Julia,' he said. 'I don't just want you for sex, you know. I'll never get tired of you.'

'I'm glad of that,' Julia replied. 'I didn't expect it, but I'm glad. You see,' she hesitated and then put one of the fingers of her narrow little hand with their almost childish nails, rounded and completely unsophisticated, on his broad, hairy chest. 'I'm very fond of you too, Sam. I love you.'

Sam never thought such words would have the power to thrill him again. He felt a lump in his throat that deprived him of speech, as he pressed her to him and buried his face in her curly red hair.

CHAPTER THIRTEEN

FRANKIE HAD BEEN CONSCIOUS OF faint contractions in her abdomen since late afternoon, just a flicker of feeling, like small unseen waves but, as she was half asleep, she wondered if it was her imagination. At five she looked at her watch, felt her stomach and thought maybe she should call Sam. But she knew how he adored the divine Kiri, how upset he would be if she called him home on a false alarm when Te Kanawa was singing in a little-performed opera, one he hadn't seen before.

By six Frankie felt definite discomfort, but she knew it was now too late to get him at the bank. The opera started at seven, and he and Poppy always had a drink beforehand. There was no cause for alarm anyway.

And as soon as she had made that sensible decision, she was overwhelmed by a sense of catastrophe and rang the bell which would summon June, who was putting Zoë to bed, to her side.

'I think I've started,' she said as June came in.

June had her sleeves rolled up and her arms, still wet, were red. 'I'm in the middle of bathing the baby, Frankie. I had to put her on the mat. Mr Hahn will soon be home won't he?' She looked anxiously at the clock by the bedside.

'He's gone to the opera.' Frankie reached for June's wet hand. 'I know it's silly, but I feel very scared, June.'

'I must go Frankie. I hate leaving Zoë. Goodness knows what she'll get up to. I'll call the doctor and be back as soon as I can.'

June, a sensible Scots girl who liked to do one thing at a time, rushed out and, as the door closed, Frankie felt, however irrationally, that it was like the dying of hope. Waves of genuine fear engulfed her, and the terror of the last delivery and its aftermath seemed as vivid to her now as it was when it was happening. She clutched the bedclothes as her whole,

214

seething body perspired. Then she had a giant contraction which made her give one long scream that was both a bold cry of pain and a call for help.

June, Zoë wrapped in a bath towel in her arms, came back into the room.

'It really *is* happening,' Frankie gasped. 'Please call the doctor.'

'I called him. He's having his evening surgery. He said we should call the hospital and an ambulance.'

'Oh God,' Frankie sank back. 'Oh June I am so frightened, I don't feel brave at all. Please help me.'

June sat on the bed and took her hand while Zoë clapped hers together with a pleased expression, little bubbles of soap clustered about her neck. She had Sam's dark hair and dark skin and she had a roguish, gypsy-like expression as she now gazed thoughtfully at her mother, as if comprehending her distress.

'You'll be absolutely all right, Frankie, if I call an ambulance . . .'

'Please come with me June. Please.'

'I *can't* leave Zoë, Frankie, you know that. Now who is there . . .? Dr Hahn?'

'She's in Beirut.'

'I mean the mother.'

'Oh I couldn't possibly . . .'

'She was very good to you last time.'

'But I haven't seen her for . . .' Another spasm came and Frankie held on to June's hand, pressing hard. 'Call her. Call her, June.'

Barbara was seeing out her last patient when the call from Sam's house came. Within five minutes she was in her car heading down Haverstock Hill without bothering to ask herself why she did these things. She was a doctor and someone was in distress, though she knew, and knew of, a good few doctors who would not take such a Samaritan-like point of view. Frankie was Sam's wife, expecting Sam's baby. She turned right through Englands Lane, across the traffic lights and up to Primrose Hill where Sam and Frankie lived.

June was waiting for her at the door, Zoë, now in her nightclothes, still in her arms.

'Did anyone try and get Mr Hahn at the opera?' Barbara said at once. 'Does anyone know where he's sitting?'

'I don't think it's that much of an emergency, Dr Hahn. I mean she's not in danger. She's just very frightened because of what happened before.'

'That's perfectly understandable,' Barbara said with a sharp look at June, who obviously felt Frankie was making a fuss, and started up the stairs towards Frankie's room.

Frankie had just finished a contraction and was lying looking exhausted when Barbara came in. Barbara went at once to her side and sat on the bed taking her pulse.

'I'm not a real doctor now you know Frankie,' she said gently. 'It's decades since I dealt with maternity cases. We'll have to get you to hospital. Have you any idea where Sam sits in the opera?'

'I don't know. He's with Poppy, you know, my girl friend. I mean it's quite all right. I said they could go out together. They usually have dinner afterwards.'

'Does Poppy have a flat mate?'

'Why?'

'She might know where they're going.'

'Poppy does share with another girl, but I doubt if she knows. It'd be very unlikely.'

'It'll be worth a try, while June gets you ready. The ambulance should be here soon. I'll come with you to hospital. Don't worry.'

'You're very, very good, Barbara. I feel ashamed.'

'Forget it, no need.' Barbara got up briskly, knowing that the gratitude, though real enough now, would probably be short-lived and Frankie's old resentment of her would return again. It was inevitable. That's when the real, Good Samaritan bit came in; with the knowledge that when this crisis was over everything would be just the same as before.

'It's under K in the book,' Frankie said, 'Poppy Kessler.' She gave another grimace of pain and gripped the bed sheets.

June rushed in to say the ambulance was coming up the hill and Barbara took the telephone book as she went downstairs to make the call. Kessler, Poppy. It was very doubtful if anyone would know but it was worth a try.

Someone answered immediately and Barbara went straight to the point.

'I understand Miss Kessler is at the opera with Mr Hahn. You wouldn't have the slightest idea of where they're having dinner afterwards would you? There's an emergency.'

'Who is that?' the voice said after a pause.

'I'm a friend of Mr Hahn's wife . . . in fact I'm his first wife, but that's neither here nor there. The current Mrs Hahn has gone into labour and we're trying to contact her husband. We could ring the restaurant if we knew where they were going.'

Barbara heard a distinct gulp on the other end of the phone. 'I don't know . . .' the voice said, then, 'Mrs Hahn . . .'

'Yes?'

'It's Poppy here. Poppy Kessler . . .'

'Oh you didn't go . . .'

'Are you alone? Is Frankie there?'

'No the ambulance is just coming to get her.'

'Is she all right?'

'She's quite all right, but she wants Sam.'

Barbara now had a definite suspicion that something odd was going on.

'Sam isn't at the opera Mrs Hahn. He's . . . Oh I can't explain. I feel so awful.'

This girl was having an affair with Sam; so much was obvious.

'Is he with you?' Barbara asked patiently.

'No . . . with someone else.'

'Do you know where by any chance?'

'No I don't know who she is or where she lives.'

'She?' Pause again. 'I'd better hurry you,' Barbara went on. 'The ambulance has arrived.

'I feel terrible about this,' Poppy blurted out. 'I knew it was wrong. Frankie trusted me. I know you're a psychiatrist so perhaps you'll understand.'

'Sam used you as an alibi to go out with someone else?'

'Yes.'

'A girl friend?'

'I think so.'

'And he doesn't go to the opera at all? It wouldn't be any use going there?'

'No.'

'And no one knows where he is?'

'No.'

'How very irresponsible. Never mind, Miss Kessler. If he does call or anything tell him will you . . .'

'Please keep the secret Mrs Hahn. I feel terrible . . . for Frankie.'

Barbara, replacing the receiver as Frankie was carried down the stairs, thought that it was a bit late for sorrow now; but then it nearly always was. People rarely thought through the consequences of their behaviour. Sam was having an affair while his wife was lying in bed waiting for their baby. It was a sad, some would say disgusting, state of affairs.

'Did you get the girl?' Frankie asked as she was carried past Barbara.

'She doesn't know.'

'Perhaps someone should go to the opera. I'm sure it's the stalls.'

'We'll talk about it later.'

Barbara followed Frankie into the ambulance and stayed with her during the short journey to the hospital.

'You must despise me for needing you now.' Frankie studied the ceiling of the moving van.

'I don't at all. You had to turn to someone and you turned to me.'

'But I haven't been very nice to you; very ungrateful for what you did the last time when I was ill.'

'That's what you're afraid of now isn't it?'

In reply the expression of terror returned to Frankie's face.

'There's no need,' Barbara went on soothingly. 'There is no reason at *all* for the pattern to recur. Believe me.'

'You're just saying that.'

'I'm not. I know there were all sorts of factors before. They can dose you up with extra hormones after the birth and, psychologically, you're more secure now, secure in Sam.'

Barbara realized the irony of what she was saying, but tried to put thoughts of Sam and his disappearance out of her mind. After all it might be conjecture; just possibly there was another explanation.

'I've just remembered,' Frankie said suddenly. 'Poppy's flat mate's left.'

'Well there was someone there; probably a friend staying.'

Barbara hated to lie, especially to save Sam's skin. Another

218

long contraction came and Frankie clutched the hand of Barbara who leaned over her, gently stroking her brow, murmuring words of comfort. This girl could really be her daughter. In a way she was like her daughter. They were related whether they liked it or not. Her children and Frankie's children were related by blood. There was certainly a bond.

When they got to the hospital Frankie was taken straight to the labour ward where an examination showed that her labour was quite far advanced, the cervix almost completely dilated. Frankie was given gas and air and, as the contractions grew more frequent, Barbara sat by her side, talking, helping, holding – the two Mrs Hahns united in giving birth to the child of Mr Hahn who was probably making love to another woman. It was almost medieval, Barbara thought, recalling a time she'd joked to Sam that he should have a junior wife and a senior wife. Well now he had.

'At about eleven,' Frankie said, as though counting the hours, 'the opera will be over. They usually have dinner late. They didn't used to. They ate in the crush bar at the interval. For some reason it changed.'

'How long have you known Poppy?'

'I knew her in the States.' Frankie looked at Barbara. 'Why?'

'I just wondered.'

'Do you think I was silly suggesting she and Sam should go out together?'

'Not at all, if you trust her.'

'Sam was getting very agitated staying at home all the time.'

'He would.'

'I thought going out with Poppy was better than . . .'

Frankie was prevented from finishing 'going out with you', by the consultant obstetrician who had been called in case Frankie's confinement was a complicated one, in view of the time she'd spent in bed. Barbara was asked to leave while another examination was made. She stood in the corridor smoking, listening to the cries of the other women in the labour ward, the bustle of trolleys and clatter of a busy maternity hospital. She leaned against the wall, reflective, detached, but rather sad. She was glad she wasn't Frankie, going through this all over again with a husband who would obviously never change, who would always find the lure of another woman irresistible and, despite his sterling qualities, would always be weak because of this.

She felt that in many ways she, Barbara, had had the best years of Sam; or maybe they would come again when he was very old, and the fire in his loins was quenched.

The baby was born at two a.m. and, shortly afterwards, Sam arrived. He looked composed, collected, only slightly har-assed, as though he had passed an enjoyable night at the opera. The birth was an uncomplicated one and, apart from the mother and medical attendants, the first person to see Sam's new child was his first wife Barbara. The two Mrs Hahns gazed at the baby lying in a crib by its mother's side.

'Another girl,' Barbara said. 'Sam will be pleased.'

'Why should he?'

'He likes girls.' Barbara realized she had been guilty of a Freudian slip, but hoped Frankie was too bemused to notice.

'I thought he wanted a boy. I'm going to be sterilized you know.'

'Quite right. You don't want to be having babies in your forties.'

'Two's enough, anyway.'

'Quite enough.'

Barbara sat by Frankie's side, their hands joined, until Frankie fell asleep. The lights in the ward were low as the other recently delivered mothers slumbered, their babies in the nursery off the ward to allow them a good night's rest. The new, unnamed Baby Hahn was taken away too. She was a pretty girl, dark like Zoë was when she was born. Barbara heard Sam's footsteps in the corridor and went to the door of the ward to greet him.

'Congratulations Sam, you have another daughter.'

Sam peered over her head into the dark, not even surprised to see her.

'How's Frankie?'

'She's fine. She's just gone to sleep. She had a very easy delivery.'

'Not a Caesarean?'

'Not necessary.'

220

'Thank God for that, after all these months. How does she seem?'

'She seems fine.'

'I hope we don't have the trouble we had last time.'

'Don't even think of it Sam. Now you go and see Frankie and I'll go home.'

'Oh let's have coffee or something,' Sam said. 'She's asleep anyway.' He sounded very offhand for a new father. But, after all, it was his fifth child. Perhaps one grew blasé after a time.

The sister on night duty, recognizing the name and remembering young Dr Hahn, was only too delighted to provide coffee, and stood with Sam and Barbara in the waiting room for a while chatting, asking after Sarah. Then she left them alone. Barbara poured more coffee, looked at Sam while she stirred it.

'How was the opera?'

'Marvellous. Kiri was in fine voice.'

'What would you say if I told you I knew you weren't there?'

He gazed at her and, for the first time that she could ever recall in all the years she had known Sam Hahn, she saw fear in his face.

'Does Frankie know?'

'Not yet; but she might learn it from her friend Poppy.'

'You spoke to Poppy?'

'Only by a whisker. Had I been a moment or two later Frankie might have rung her instead of me. She wanted to know if anyone knew where you ate.'

'It sounds a very long shot to me, as if she were suspicious.'

'When people are desperate they try anything. Frankie was desperate for you. Why do you think she called me? What if it had been Frankie and she asked Poppy where you were, Sam?'

'Poppy doesn't know.'

'Very despicable of you.'

For answer Sam stared ahead as though, just possibly, thinking the same thing about himself. Suddenly he said: 'But Poppy doesn't have a flat mate. Who does Frankie think you spoke to?'

'A friend, but I really think Frankie had her mind on her baby. She might want to know a bit more later, when she's had time to mull it over. You must give this woman up Sam, whoever she is. Frankie is too astute.'

Sam shook his head. 'I can't. I thought I could, that it was only sex and so on. She's just a woman in the office, married, unhappy, not especially intelligent. Well she's intelligent, but not like you and Frankie. Yet she has something. I'm obsessed with her.'

Barbara felt very sad. 'Oh dear God. Why did you have to get into this mess Sam?'

'I never thought for a moment that it would be serious. If you only met her you wouldn't know what I saw in her.'

'Then maybe you will get over her. You must, Sam.' Barbara got up, putting her empty cup back on the tray. 'I feel very tired now. Look, I won't come and see Frankie until she asks for me, not like the last time. But if she does want to see me and I can ever do anything, let me know. I hope all goes well Sam.'

Sam shook his head and looked at the floor, his hands loosely joined, his attitude one of despair. It didn't even seem to occur to him to thank her for what she'd done. Barbara left him like that and stepped into the cold air of Huntley Street, taking a deep breath. She was free, independent. She'd done her duty by society: borne three children, helped many people. But still she was always learning; there was always a lot to learn. Somewhere in the hospital a newly delivered baby gave a despairing cry.

Barbara was glad she wasn't the mother of that baby. Glad she wasn't Frankie; glad, very glad, she wasn't Sam.

Tom Hahn lay with a group of his men, his ear pressed to the mountain as though listening to the beat of its heart. His own heart knocked against his rib cage, but with exhilaration, not fear. Since the landing at San Carlos Tom had enjoyed every moment of the Falklands war, though much of it, spent in mud, driving rain, sleet and intense cold, was reminiscent of the conditions in France in 1914–18. The trenches that the soldiers had to dig were full of water which froze at night, making their clothes adhere to them, shrinking their webbing. Not surprisingly the principal medical problems were those of the '14–18 war too, trench foot, diarrhoea, exhaustion and exposure.

The marines had marched every inch of the way from San Carlos carrying all their equipment, except for some that was taken on by helicopter and Volvo truck. They had captured Mount Kent and secured the adjoining ridgeline of Mount Challenger. Between them and Port Stanley now were Mounts Harriet and Longdon, Two Sisters, Tumbledown and Sapper Hill as well as an estimated thirty-three enemy company groups in a garrison of 8400 men, well armed and dug into fortified positions they had been occupying for six weeks. Not only did the men have to contend with the cold, wet and lack of regular food, but they also had to explore the land around them on foot by sending out advance parties, using their bayonets as prodders. More than once, Tom had seen bearer parties carrying back a soldier with his foot blown off.

On the morning of 11 June the decision had been taken to attack the mountains and the men of 3 Commando Brigade were briefed for battle. Models of the terrain had been created, with ponchos to represent mountains and string and tape to show the possible routes through them. They were told it was to be a decisive battle of the war. After the victory at Goose Green, the loss of so many ships, and the disaster at Fitzroy when 51 men had been killed and many others terribly wounded, as their boats lay in the bay waiting to land, there was no question in the minds of those present about winning.

Snow lay on the hills and all day the helicopters had moved backwards and forwards, ferrying ammunition to forward positions from which the commando would march out. All afternoon the men had waited, stamping their feet to ward off the cold and drinking tea, viewing through their binoculars the landscape in front of them; a strange, treeless yet beautiful country, parts of it resembling Wales, yet so far from home.

At nightfall the long line of heavily armed figures moved forward. The assault had begun. The British guns set up to harass the enemy, supported by ships at sea which had their guns trained on the coast, begun to pound from all directions. Flares sent up by the Argentines caused the men to freeze where they stood or crouch, before they resumed their stealthy walk in the track of the man in front, a single path that had been swept through the minefield.

Mount Harriet had been well reconnoitred in advance by patrols from the Commandos and the Welsh Guard, and now 42 Commando were in position. Tom's corporal was listening to his radio, passing on commands as they came from headquarters, receiving brief replies and instructions from Tom. The blast of the guns, the flares lighting the skies, the chill of the night, impressed on Tom something he knew he would never forget – the anticipation of danger, a sense of the inevitable. He gave the corporal a cigarette and lit one for himself, looking through his night binoculars towards the summit where the Argentinians were dug into the rocks and crevices in the mountain. Then, as men do when they are about to enter battle, as he had before the skirmishes with the enemy during the long yomp across East Falklands, Tom thought once again of his family – of his wife and children, his mother, his sisters, one also now in a foreign land, and finally of his father. They were his family – not Frankie, or Frankie's baby or the new baby Frankie was expecting (about whose birth Tom as yet knew nothing). The family as it had been was fixed in his mind, and he knew once again as he looked into the darkness that he could never forgive his father for what he had done. A stickler for order, Tom felt his father had disobeyed the rules.

But this bitterness, made perhaps more poignant, more irrational and intolerable by the circumstances, soon passed and he ground out his cigarette as the order came over the radio to advance up the hill. They were within a hundred yards of the summit when the Argentinians detected them and opened fire. The Commandos rose as a man, breaking cover, and, backed by 66 and 85mm rockets, leapt forward flinging grenades into the enemy bunkers, raking the hapless occupants with small arms fire. Tom knew that hand to hand combat like this would probably never happen again in time of war. The enemy, trying to escape from the terrifying impact of the British commando troops, were savagely bayoneted or shot or taken prisoner. Then Tom saw the trooper in front of him fall with a bullet in the neck and knew that there was nothing between him and a machine gun post. He took the pin out of the grenade in his hand, ducked and threw it for all he was worth. But the gun went on firing and

Tom prepared to charge the post single-handed with only his revolver in his hand.

Suddenly he saw himself looking down the barrel of a rifle; he wrenched the gun away, firing at the same time into the stomach of his assailant. Then he felt the rifle, the barrel still in his hand, go off, and there was a searing pain in his knee. As he fell to the ground, taking the gun and its owner with him, the rifle went off once more into his leg. Next to him Tom's assailant lay dying, his entrails slowly oozing out of the jagged hole in his stomach.

In his last moments Tom, fighting off unconsciousness, put his arm around him as if to comfort him, to ease his passage from the world. He was about Tom's own age, a strong, fighting soldier. Instead of elation Tom felt racked by remorse. With men all around, alone he clung to his enemy in the dark, as if begging forgiveness. 'Sorry, lad,' he said. 'Sorry.'

The transformation in Frankie was almost unbelievable. After so many months in bed with nothing to do and only her fears and memories for company she seemed to have been recharged with a supernatural energy. She came home from the hospital a week after having her baby, a perfect little girl to be called Elizabeth and, from that moment, the transformation began. No lying about the house, no depression. She didn't even feel tired as most new mothers do.

'Really amazing,' Poppy said as she balanced Zoë on her knee while Frankie breastfed Elizabeth. 'And you feel absolutely fine?'

'I feel marvellous. I think I'm so relieved. I dreaded the baby, dreaded depression, dreaded Sam's reaction. But there was nothing to worry about at all. It shows how unnecessary all this worry is. They knew from the last time, of course, that I needed hormones. And hormones it is.'

Elizabeth was even more contented a baby than Zoë and sat with her eyes closed, her little feet stuck in the air, toes wide apart, sucking contentedly. Poppy, who had previously decided motherhood was not for her, felt a pang of envy again. It was her first visit to Frankie since she'd had the baby.

'Sam's O.K. about it then?' Poppy hoped Frankie wouldn't be able to detect any tremor in her voice.

'Sam's ecstatic. I think Sam is really relieved that the baby is fine and I am, and I've been sterilized. Now we don't ever have to worry about that horrible cap again. How was the opera by the way?'

'Opera?' Poppy looked guiltily at Frankie whose eyes however were fastened adoringly on her baby.

'Kiri Te Kanawa.'

'Oh beautiful. She's a wonderful singer.'

'I think Sam has a crush on her.'

'He has. Everyone has. I have too.'

'I can't remember what she was singing in.' Frankie raised her eyes and gazed enquiringly at Poppy, who knew she was blushing. Could Frankie possibly *know*? Yet if she did suspect her husband of infidelity how could she appear to be so happy?

'I can't remember either,' Poppy said. 'It was just before I went to Italy.'

'*Simon Boccanegra*,' Frankie said snapping her fingers.

'Of course.'

'If it was a boy I'd have called him Simon. Oh how I needed Sam that night.'

'I felt terrible when I heard about it.'

'Not your fault; and Barbara *was* marvellous. Not patronizing at all. Sheer kindness. There's something about that woman I really like. I can't think why Sam left her for me.'

'Oh don't go over all that *again*,' Poppy said. 'Enjoy your baby.' She knew then that Frankie had no idea, and that if she guessed or found out she might well be precipitated into another nervous breakdown. To Poppy her happiness, apparently so secure, seemed fragile.

'I bet you'll miss Sam,' Frankie said tactlessly, moving Elizabeth from one breast to the other. 'You can borrow him from time to time. I'm not as keen on the opera as you are.'

'Oh I don't think I will,' Poppy said. 'People might talk.'

'Talk? Talk about what?' Frankie looked amazed.

'I really had to see you Sam. I'm so worried about Frankie.' They were lunching in a restaurant in the City which catered for affluent businessmen with little time but lots of money. Poppy didn't care. She wasn't paying the bill. Sam owed her.

226

'Frankie's absolutely blooming,' Sam said with surprise.

'Supposing she finds out about . . . you know.' Poppy looked at him meaningfully. 'I think she might kill herself.'

'Oh Frankie would never do anything like that!'

'How do you know?'

For a moment Sam looked unsure too. 'Well how could she find out?'

'If you go on seeing . . . this woman. If you take risks like you took the last time. It's none of my business, I suppose, Sam, but you've made me feel very guilty about the whole thing.'

'I wish I'd never asked you.' Sam earnestly applied himself to the asparagus.

'I wish you hadn't too. You've involved me in something I'd no wish to be involved in.'

'Why can't you just forget about it?' Sam mopped the last of the butter with a piece of French bread.

'Sam how good to see you! And Poppy!' Neil Featherstone was a financial analyst who worked for a City newspaper and knew both Sam and Poppy; Frankie too of course. 'I thought Poppy was only on loan until the baby was born?' Neil who, had he not been an economist, would have made a very good gossip columnist, looked from one to the other.

'This isn't the opera.' Sam sat down after shaking Neil's hand. 'She's a friend. I simply owe her a good lunch.'

'One day you must tell me why,' Neil said skittishly. 'Excuse me, my date is waiting.' He pointed to a pretty woman sitting in a corner of the restaurant and made his way jauntily over to her.

'There.' Poppy's face was scarlet.

'There what?'

'We immediately meet someone we know.'

'We met a lot of people when we went to the opera and the Festival Hall. Neil among them, if I remember. We saw him at *La Bohème*.'

'That's *just* the point. Supposing you're seen with *her*?'

'She and I are never seen in public together. Look Poppy,' Sam leaned forward and touched her hand – a gesture that was not lost on Neil Featherstone greeting his lunch companion on the other side of the room, his eyes still on Sam and Poppy. 'I am very careful. I am very sorry about all this,

227

Poppy. I love Frankie and look, I tell you what,' his eyes gazed into hers, 'I will do what I can to finish it. I really will try.'

'Oh will you Sam?' Poppy convulsively returned his clasp. 'Then my mind would be at rest. Yours too.'

'Well, well,' Neil Featherstone said to himself, ordering drinks.

Karol Lenárt was a man of fifty-five or thereabouts, Eastern European in origin but who had settled in England after the war because he disagreed with the Communist government that ran his country. He had been married twice and had three grown-up children. Now, though officially unencumbered in the legal sense, he shared his favours with a number of women each of whom had the misfortune to believe she was the only one.

It was difficult to put a label on Mr Lenárt. The unkindest, and they included some of his women friends when they discovered to their shocked surprise that they had rivals, called him a lecher, a womanizer, plain and simple. His male friends called him a lucky dog because the success he had with all kinds of women was clearly phenomenal. They included the young and the not so young, English and foreign – and all of them found Mr Lenárt irresistible. Yet Mr Lenárt was not a happy man. Years before he had decided the solution to his insatiable need for women lay in psychoanalysis. He felt he was in the grip of something which, although pleasurable, was also compulsive and possibly ultimately fatal as he rushed round London servicing all the women to whom he had pledged himself, attending to his family and to his considerable business as a public relations consultant. To say nothing of the effort involved in avoiding the wrath of deceived husbands, and preventing all the women finding out about one another. In this he was not entirely successful because he often forgot where he was meant to be; a bad memory was not the least of Mr Lenárt's many problems.

Mr Lenárt was not really ill, but he caused a lot of unhappiness in those unfortunates unlucky enough to fall under his spell, be taken in by his charm, his promises and his honeyed words. It was for this reason that Barbara tolerated him, out of a sympathy for women rather than for him.

In time Lenárt came to respect her; he was careful what he said to her and how he put it. Her stern authoritarian gaze rather quelled him, made him less sure of what he was about. Gradually she was teaching him humility and, maybe, when he learnt that he might be able to control the wayward manifestations of his libido. But Barbara suspected he would manage to resist therapy because the cure would be worse than the disease.

So on this day in June Barbara sat and listened as Lenárt, leaning forward – he sat facing her – his brow furrowed in earnest concentration, explained how difficult it was to understand why he behaved as he did. It appeared he got no enjoyment out of it, absolutely none.

'I find that difficult to believe.'

'Do you say I'm lying to you Dr Hahn?'

'I say I find it difficult to believe, but go on.'

A knock on the door now interrupted this exchange.

'Excuse me.' Interruptions were unusual and Barbara got up and popped her head round the door.

'Phone for you Doctor, very urgent.' Linda stood on the other side.

'Who is it?'

'It's Mrs Hahn.'

'Tell her I'll ring back.'

'*Captain* Hahn's wife, Doctor. She said I had to call you to the phone, no matter what.'

Now the apprehension, the fear, that had lain near her heart ever since that day they'd stood waving goodbye to Tom at Southampton seemed a certainty. However she composed herself for her patient: 'Will you excuse me Mr Lenárt? Something very urgent has cropped up.' She closed the door behind him, following Linda through the house to the telephone in the lounge.

Afterwards she sent Linda to tell her patient she had been detained and she remained in the room, trying not to break down; to retain that control which was part of her, which was vital to her in whatever happened in her life. After a while Linda brought in a tray with a teapot, two cups and saucers,

229

sugar and a milk jug. Tenderly she put it down beside Barbara looking anxiously into her face.

'Is it very bad Dr Hahn?'

'He's lost a leg. He was shot taking some mountain or other. He lost so much blood he nearly died and is still in danger. Poor, poor Natalie.'

Linda put a cup in her hand.

'Poor you, Dr Hahn. Recently you've had more than most women are called upon to bear. Will you tell your husband?'

Barbara nodded. It was still quite natural for Linda, who had been with them since the children were small, to refer to Sam as her 'husband'. 'I have a patient at five whom I must see, and then I'll go round to the house. Now, of course, we'll both worry about Sarah, more than ever.' At the beginning of June Israel had invaded the Lebanon and, despite its professed intentions of merely ousting the PLO, seemed all set, in the eyes of many observers, to press on to Beirut.

'I think Sarah can look after herself.' Linda helped herself to tea with the familiarity of someone who had known Barbara for so many years.

'We thought that about Tom, yet I knew.'

'You couldn't have known. It's natural for women to worry when their men go to war. My mother said she never had a moment's peace while my father was serving in the last one.'

Barbara nodded. 'I know. Every time a stranger came up the drive mine thought it was a telegram from the War Office.' Barbara's father had been an Army surgeon, a country doctor from Devon translated into the thick of the war.

'There, you see.'

'I had a foreboding about Tom. I don't about Sarah. Like you I think she'll be all right, but Sam worries. Anyway Sarah isn't in the front line and we knew Tom would be once the landings took place. Sam will need a lot of support, even with Frankie there.'

Gratefully she put the cup Linda had poured to her lips. The strong, sweet tea had never seemed so good, or so necessary.

For Frankie those first days at home with the baby exceeded in happiness any she had ever known, even the first two years

230

of her marriage. She felt so well and Elizabeth was so easy, a full term baby, larger than Zoë had been when she was born. Frankie never had a moment of depression or doubt or even unease. Being a mother the second time seemed as natural to her as it had been awkward and difficult the first.

That day she was contentedly feeding Elizabeth, her feet up in front of the television screen because there was a report that the Argentinians had surrendered. June came into the room – Zoë toddling beside her.

'Any news yet?'

'The air is thick with rumour. Won't it be wonderful if it's over, June? Sam will be so relieved, and Barbara.'

'There's someone on the phone for you, a Mr Featherstone.'

'Oh good. I asked him to find me some facts about the effect of the cost of the war on the economy. Could you take Elizabeth and wind her for me? I'd just finished.'

June took the baby, humping her over her shoulder. She was so happy and relieved to see how well Frankie was coping, and thinking of her work too.

'Neil how are you?' Frankie sat on the stairs with a pad on her knees, chewing an apple. 'It's very good of you to call back.'

'Delighted Frankie and pleased to know all's going well.'

'Very well.'

'And you're thriving?'

'Me, and the baby.'

'Very soon to be getting back to work isn't it?'

'I can't do it soon enough. I feel I've been an invalid for months.'

'Right,' there was the sound of a rustling of papers. 'Let's begin . . .' He went through the figures which were tentative because no one yet knew precisely how much the war had or might still cost. 'But there was a reserve fund anyway for things like this, even on such a scale.'

Frankie jotted all the details down. She thought it would be an unusual and topical item for her column which would appear, hopefully, when the war was over.

'I bumped into Sam and Poppy at lunch in the City the other day,' Neil said conversationally. 'Is she still "on loan" as it were?'

Frankie looked at the core of her apple as though she'd suddenly seen a worm.

'When was this?'

'Yesterday or the day before.' He sounded almost deliberately casual.

'Oh yes Sam told me. He's very grateful to her for looking after him. But I shall have him firmly back in harness now. Poppy is a great friend of us both.'

'Cheerio then!' Neil said, but the line was buzzing for quite a long time before Frankie replaced the receiver. She went slowly back to the sitting room and sat staring at the children's programme that came on just before the evening News at 5.40.

At half past six Barbara arrived. Frankie knew at once there was bad news.

'Tom?'

Barbara nodded. 'Not dead but badly wounded. I want to tell Sam myself.'

'Of course. Would you like me to go upstairs?'

'No you stay here,' Barbara took her arm and pressed it. 'You're part of the family too, Frankie.' She looked at Frankie and, to her chagrin, Frankie burst into tears. Barbara supposed it was postnatal blues, and helped her to a seat, looking at the TV as she did so.

'Isn't it ironic that the day we hope to hear about victory we hear about Tom too. But don't let it get you too much Frankie. He went to war knowing what he was about.'

'It's not *that*,' Frankie rubbed her knuckles into her eyes then blew her nose hard. 'It's Sam.'

Barbara sat beside her, unbuttoning her coat. So Frankie knew.

'What has Sam done?'

'I think he's having an affair.'

'How did you know?'

Her tone made Frankie look at her. 'Did *you* know?' When Barbara didn't reply immediately Frankie was more worried than ever. 'I suppose you never trusted him after what happened with me. You're not surprised, I can see.'

There was something wrong about the conversation that counselled Barbara, with her well-developed sixth sense, to be cautious.

'I must confess I don't actually know what you're talking about,' Barbara said, and quite truthfully. 'You may have misunderstood me. I asked you how you knew Sam was having an affair and that seemed to imply to you that I knew he was. Who is he supposed to be having an affair with?'

'Poppy!' Frankie burst into tears again.

Inwardly Barbara felt relieved. 'Did Poppy tell you?'

'Someone saw them recently having lunch in the City. I should *never* have thrown them together.'

'You didn't throw. You suggested they went out to a few concerts. Nothing wrong with that. Anyway I think you're wrong.'

Despite herself Frankie looked at Barbara hopefully. 'Why?'

'Poppy is decidedly not his type. Not the girl who flopped into the ward that day you were in hospital.'

'Are you sure?'

'Quite sure.'

'Then why were they lunching . . .'

'Ask him. There will be some quite simple explanation.' Barbara lifted her head and listened. 'There's Sam now.'

'You go and greet him Barbara. I don't want him to see me like this.'

'I'll take him on to the hill for a talk. Have drinks ready when I get back.'

As soon as Barbara came to the door Sam knew there was something wrong.

'Frankie OK?' he enquired, getting his briefcase from the seat next to him and closing the car door.

Barbara took his arm and looked up into his face.

'Frankie's fine; but Tom has been wounded. He's alive. He's OK.'

Sam leaned briefly against her. 'How bad is it though?'

'Bad. Let's take a stroll.'

'He *is* dead; that's what you're trying to tell me?'

She was conscious of Sam's weight, literally leaning on her. 'No he's alive, Sam, I promise you. He was when Natalie got the message which was earlier today. He's been operated on. He's lost a leg.'

Sam sagged against the wall of the garden, and Barbara wondered if they should go in and have the drink now. But she held on to his arm.

233

'Come on let's have a little stroll on the hill.'

'I need a drink.'

'Frankie's upset too. She's getting drinks. We'll only be ten minutes.'

They walked for a while in silence, to the top of the hill where they sat on the bench and looked towards St Paul's, a very tiny white speck in the distance. Much nearer was the Post Office Tower and nearer still the many green acres that formed Regent's Park, with the lake curving in the middle. Sam tucked his hand into Barbara's.

'Just when there's rumour of victory.'

'As long as Tom is alive I don't care.'

'But without a leg.'

'He's not blinded or brain damaged. It could have been worse, Sam.'

'Why did he have to join the bloody Marines?'

'Why did there have to be a war?'

Sam threw his arm round Barbara's shoulder and, leaning his face against hers, wept. It was almost as though he felt their son's injury more than she did. This wasn't true. She had been too busy with the practicalities to cry. She put her arm round his waist, pressing him close, wishing they could go home together and share their grief, drive down to Natalie and comfort her, united as a family. This was the worst moment she could remember since the parting with Sam. She bent her face towards him and whispered into his ear.

'It's a bad time I know, a very bad one; but I have to talk about Frankie. That's really why I wanted to get you alone.'

'Don't for God's sake tell me there's something wrong with Frankie.'

'She thinks you're having an affair with Poppy.'

'Poppy!' Sam threw back his head and actually laughed. With the tears streaming down his face it was an incongruous sight.

'Someone saw you having lunch with her in the City.'

'Neil Featherstone.'

'Why didn't you tell her about the date?'

'Poppy wanted to talk to me about . . . Julia.'

'This other woman's name is Julia?'

Sam nodded. 'Though Poppy doesn't know that.'

'Why did she want to talk about it then?'

'She said Frankie was so happy it would kill her if she knew.'

'I think she does know,' Barbara looked at him gravely. 'Poppy or anyone, she knows, or guesses, there's someone. She's too emotional.'

'But how can she know?'

'I think she knows by your manner. If you're as involved as you told me you were she'll be able to tell. She's a very perceptive woman.'

'I don't want to make her unhappy.'

'Then you must give this Julia up.'

'I can't.'

'You must. You have ruined too many lives Sam . . .'

'Ruined?' Sam looked indignantly at her. 'Ruined whose lives?'

'Mine, if you want me to be truthful. I won't say the children are unscathed by what happened. You like to forget it, don't you Sam, but it's true. Would Amanda have developed anorexia if you'd stayed at home? Would Sarah now be in the Lebanon? Would Tom, even, be in the Falklands? I don't know.'

'You can't blame me for Tom. He was in the Marines already.'

'He was in the *Army* already, but not the Marines. He applied to join the winter you left home.'

'That had absolutely nothing to do with me. He wanted a more active life than the artillery offered. You can't pin that on me.'

'I don't want to pin anything on you Sam,' Barbara said patiently. 'But you do seem to forget, because you want to, that our actions have unforeseen consequences. If you continue to have an affair with a woman, for whom you obviously feel a great deal, sooner or later Frankie will find out. Frankie is insecure enough, as it is. She now has two babies and she wants all the help she can get. She has always been jealous of your other family and me. I think it's time you stopped fucking around, Sam, if you'll pardon the expression, and applied your full attention to your marriage. We'll have to give Natalie all the support we can when Tom comes home. As for Sarah in the Lebanon, who knows where that will end? If you can't get out of this relationship, then you've only

235

yourself to blame for the consequences. It's a matter of responsibility and if this woman, who you said was married, cares for you you should explain it all to her. You haven't time for an affair and, with a wife like Frankie, you shouldn't need one.'

Barbara suddenly thought of Mr Lenárt and the parallel attitude which Sam was all too clearly demonstrating now: as if something he couldn't control had overtaken him, left him powerless before a vengeful Fate.

Suddenly Sam leaned forward and ran his hands over his face, his fingers lingering on the stubble on his chin. 'I think I need a psychiatrist,' he said. 'I really need help on this one.'

When they got back to the house there was news of the fall of Port Stanley, and Frankie stood ready with the champagne they had kept for the celebration.

CHAPTER FOURTEEN

IT WAS IMPORTANT TO BE brave, necessary too for medical as well as psychological reasons. It was to do with glands and adrenalin and the useless consumption of nervous energy if one allowed oneself to be overpowered by fear. Fear meant lack of sleep and exhaustion which prevented one carrying out one's work the following day; fear meant a diminution of one's self-respect. Above all, fear meant loss of control, an abnegation of responsibility, of service to others.

But lying alone at night in her small apartment in the Ras Beirut, the centre of the Israeli bombardment, Sarah found that fear came very easily as the large modern building shuddered and it was so light outside that she could see the gleam of the sea half a mile away. She tried to apply herself to a consideration of the interesting patterns made by the flares and rockets, the tracer bullets in the sky; but the steady thump of the shells thudding into targets, any target because the aim of the guns, despite what was said, was indiscriminate, was too audible a reminder that one might oneself be next. Only the day before an apartment block, similar to this one in Sadat Street, had fallen like a pack of cards, killing many of those in the upper stories and everyone in the basement, which was said to be one of the local headquarters of the PLO. When she had come home that night Sarah had seen the rescue workers still digging for survivors, could smell the stench of decomposed bodies.

It was important not to give in to fear because her family would not expect her to be afraid; her family grieving for Tom, who had been brought home from the Falklands by air and was still in hospital. She couldn't imagine Tom giving in to fear, nor her mother whose equanimity in the face of hardship should be such an example to her.

But still she trembled as she lay covered by a sheet, and

even that was not necessary because the nights were so hot and the windows had to be shut to keep out the dust and acrid smoke that rose from West Beirut, day and night. The sheet seemed like a protection, and she clung to it as a child hangs on to a beloved rag or blanket, as she lay sleepless, paralysed by the dread that the next shell would be for her.

They would never know that she died a coward.

Any sense of peace had been a stranger to Sarah since she'd lived in Beirut. It was as though the American Relief Mission that sent her had foreknowledge – as many claimed the Americans had – of the Israeli plans to invade the Lebanon. Already, when she arrived in April, Israeli planes were bombing the Lebanon and Arafat was challenging them to embark on an outright invasion.

To arrive in the beautiful city of Beirut, as she had done that first day, and to see the blue sea on one side and, behind, the snow-capped mountains from which Lebanon got its name – Aramaic for white – was to be reminded of Switzerland. But to remain there for any length of time was to know what it was like to live partly in hell. Even before the Israeli invasion something was always happening in Beirut. Car bombs were forever exploding, planted by one or another of the many factions, and the sound of gunfire, near or far, ricochetting off walls, splattering across streets, became so familiar that one scarcely stopped to listen.

The Lebanese, who had known this sort of thing for years, never did, but went about their everyday lives as though entirely unconcerned by the dissensions not only between Muslim and Christian but between people of the same faiths, as factions split into other factions and divided the country. Lebanon, that beautiful Biblical land lying between the mountains and the sea, had been torn by strife for most of its history; the Lebanese had scarcely ever known anything different.

In time what amazed Sarah was how accustomed one became to it and how, despite everything, life went on with bathing parties to the sea, meals in restaurants on Hamra Street or in the still splendid hotels which remained on the sea front – the St George, the Vendôme, the Holiday Inn or the newly built, sumptuous, Summerland. Social life was quite frenetic and, within days of her arrival, Sarah was being entertained on a scale she had never seen before by a cosmopolitan group of people she scarcely knew but who received and treated her like a friend.

There were few barriers among the medical community. Educated Muslims and Christians mixed freely together, all united in decrying the harm that the war was doing to their country, while at the same time doing their best to remain unaffected by it.

As a doctor and a stranger, Sarah found it impossible to ignore, as every day brought to her clinic new victims of sectarian warfare and, now, of the Israeli bombardment. You could scarcely avoid taking sides, even if the PLO presence had contributed to the disintegration of the Lebanon, as indeed it had. You could hardly help being affected by the plight of the refugees living in squalid conditions who had lost not only their homeland, but their pitiable homes, their few possessions, their limbs, their loved ones, sometimes their lives.

By the morning the fear had evaporated. The sky, though flecked with little wisps of smoke that were like tiny clouds, was clear. The water ran in the shower, the milk for her coffee was still fresh from the fridge which worked and, incredibly, the building and those around still stood. When Sarah got to her clinic, not far from where she lived, a longer line of people needing attention stood outside, or crammed into the small waiting room, than the day before.

What she needed now was to be an efficient administrator of first aid, an experienced dresser, rather than a qualified doctor, as she cleaned wounds, bathed damaged, suppurating tissue, treated burns and made out a list of those who should be admitted to hospital for further urgent treatment.

Working with her was a young Lebanese doctor who had qualified at the American university and then London. She had intended to go on to the US for further study, but the situation at home seemed to her more important than her career. Between Sarah and Amal Saliba a friendship had grown from the day they both met, new to the clinic, equally lost, equally appalled, wondering where to start, what to do. Compared to the desperate urgency of Beirut, Africa had had a quality of timelessness, albeit hopelessness, that was almost peaceful by comparison.

That evening Amal said: 'Why don't you come home with me tonight? We have plenty of room. I would be terrified if I were you, night after night with the shelling.'

Did it show? Sarah never talked about it during the day, of her apprehension, her fear that the following day she would be dead.

'I couldn't possibly,' she replied. 'I'm not at all afraid.'

'I'm sure you're not afraid,' Amal said, her own pale face darkly shadowed, 'but you look tired. In East Beirut we're well away from the shelling. At the weekend we go up to our villa in the hills.'

'I'd like to come then,' Sarah was helping one of the voluntary European nurses to clear up before the cleaners came in. 'I can't come tonight. Thanks all the same.'

'But why not?'

Sarah threw a bloodstained bowl of water down the sink and smiled. 'I can't explain. It's a battle largely with myself.'

But by the weekend she felt she could give herself a break, even though the battle against fear was not entirely won. The mountains behind Beirut, well away from the depredations of the Israeli army, had traditionally provided refuge over the centuries and were full of large villas well protected from the heat and out of range of the noise. From the terrace of the Saliba house it was, however, still possible to see the Israeli jets streaking across the city, the resulting balls of smoke as the bombs fell, and to hear the crunch of gunfire from the American built mortars strategically placed among the hills on the south side, from which the Israelis were advancing.

Sarah had never met the whole Saliba family, though she had dined at their apartment in East Beirut a number of times. As well as grandparents who lived there permanently, there were the father and mother, and Amal's brother and sister, Halim and Aida. Amal's father, Samir, was a wealthy merchant, a man with business interests in Damascus as well as Beirut, and many European connections as well. He was a stocky, handsome man, his thick hair still black and his jolly, well-cared-for face betraying few of the worries that afflicted him, together with the majority of his fellow countrymen. Her mother, Huda, was a small, well-preserved woman

240

always beautifully and daintily dressed, who managed her homes and her family with a similar apparent lack of concern. They were very interested in Sarah and questioned her about her own family, especially her brother who had served with distinction in the recent war.

'To find England engaged in a war in the middle of all this is ironic.' Samir gestured towards the city as they sat on the terrace which had been laid for dinner because the heat inside was still oppressive.

'But our war was thousands of miles away,' Sarah helped herself to the delicious fragrant *tabule* made of finely chopped parsley, tomatoes and corn which was served as a side dish. 'Except for those of us who had family there, it hardly concerned us at all.'

'But this war hardly concerns us either.' Samir sat back with a gracious smile on his face as the servant waiting on them carefully poured white Lebanese wine. 'Whatever we do we cannot affect its course. Our businesses still run, the shops and cinemas are still open . . .' Once again Samir's elegant hands took in the city. 'This devastation will be repaired and one day Beirut will be whole again, now that the Israelis are here. They will get rid of the PLO and everything will return to how it was before 1975. We had nearly twenty years of peace when Beirut was a thriving city until Hussein kicked the Palestinians out of Jordan and they started to mass here.'

'But where else can they go?'

Amal's brother Halim shrugged. 'That is not our business. We don't want them in the Lebanon and we are grateful to the Israelis who have promised to drive them out.'

Halim was in the Army. It was understandable that he might feel like that, but what did Amal think? Amal who worked indiscriminately with Muslim and Christian, Lebanese and Palestinian victims alike.

'It is true we don't want the PLO,' she said. 'But, unlike Halim, I don't welcome the Israelis. I think once they are here they will never leave.'

'The Israelis don't want to stay here!' Halim protested. 'They have enough to do protecting their borders. They are here to make them safe. Theirs is not an army of occupation.'

'We Christians have always had to look to outsiders for

help.' Aida, Amal's younger sister, was still studying at the American university. 'The whole of the Arab world unites to help the Muslims, but we are Arabs too. The Maronite Christians have been here in Lebanon since the fifth century. What we want is to live in peace with our fellow Lebanese, but we have no room for the Palestinians. With their feuds and their guns, their differing sects, they are destroying our country.'

Indeed, since she had been in Beirut Sarah had found that there was an almost universal desire on the part of the Muslims, as well as Christians, to see the Palestinians go. 'But the Palestinians have no homeland,' she protested. 'It was taken from them by Israel. As the Jews were formerly the wandering people of history, now it is the Palestinians. Israel should return to them the West Bank.'

'Israel never will,' Halim shook his head. 'Never, never, never. It would be like admitting the wooden horse into Troy. They want them dispersed throughout the Arab world.'

'Whose side are you on?' Sarah looked at him coldly. He resembled his father, though he was slightly taller, but he altogether lacked his father's air of tolerant bonhomie. He looked like a thinker, a fighter, a man dedicated to a cause. He reminded her a bit of Tom.

'I am on the side of free, independent Lebanon,' Halim replied gravely. 'I was with the Lebanese Army until I realized how ineffectual it was, how powerless to do anything. Now I am with the Keta'ib the Christian Phalange. It is the only way for us true Lebanese, and Bashir Gemayel, our Commander in Chief, is the only possible leader to unite the whole of Lebanon.'

Samir Saliba looked rather nervously at Sarah. 'You must not think my son is a fanatic. Like your brother, he is in the army to preserve peace.'

'The only way to peace is to fight.' Halim thumped the table, interrupting his father. 'Your brother will tell you that too.'

Later that night when the parents and grandparents had gone to bed, and the two young women were inside watching television, Halim and Sarah remained on the terrace outside watching the flares, the spasmodic fires, which still illuminated parts of the city. Sarah had been talking about Tom, how he had always wanted to be a soldier and how, when their parents had split up, he had applied to join the Marines.

'If he hadn't have been a Marine he wouldn't have gone to the war,' she said. 'The company that he was with before were not involved in the Falklands.'

'Do you regret that he was in the Marines?'

'I regret he has lost a leg. How can he be a man of action now? My mother says he is very brave and unembittered; but I feel bitter, for Tom.'

'You don't think there should have been a war?'

'No I certainly don't – a tiny community on a windswept piece of land thousands of miles away from England? What did it serve *us* to defend them? At what cost?'

'It was to establish the principle of freedom.' Halim, given, Sarah noticed, to gestures, banged his fist into the palm of his other hand. 'To resist invasion, that is the conquest of one country by another force.'

'But that is what the Israelis are doing.'

'It is *not* what the Israelis are doing.' Halim jumped up, staring at her furiously. 'They are helping to destroy the enemy of the Lebanese people, the PLO. Look, Sarah, one day when you are free I will introduce you to my company of soldiers. You will see that they are all really like your brother Tom with the same ideals. Would you like that?' He wanted passionately to convince her of the justice of his cause.

'I would like to understand,' Sarah said quietly, 'but I must tell you that I am a pacifist. My brother and I have never agreed on that.'

'Then I will convert you.' Halim bent sharply forward, smiling into her eyes. 'I will bring about what your brother failed to do. You can never resist aggression by peaceful means; only with the bullet, only with the knife.'

It would never in a thousand years have occurred to Sarah that her first lover could possibly be a soldier, one whose views, whose whole ethos was completely foreign to hers. Later she decided that it was the attraction of opposites which had brought them together, the fact that in every way Halim was completely unlike her. But then she loved Tom, and he wasn't like her either; so she understood.

After that weekend she'd spent with the family Sarah saw Halim practically every day. He would call at the clinic for a coffee, watching her receive the countless patients that sat waiting in line. He would collect her at night for a drink in one of the bars at the Summerland Hotel. He would take her to a cinema or a restaurant and he would see her home.

'Sure you're not afraid?'

'Sure.'

They would say goodnight and she would close the door, weak with apprehension, never letting on to Halim. How he would despise her if he knew.

But then came the night that she was more afraid than ever. At the beginning of August the Israelis had entered Beirut, and a few days later there was a ten-hour Israeli air attack on West Beirut, during which Sarah felt the whole of the apartment block shudder and some of the plaster from the ceiling fell on her bed. The clinic narrowly escaped a direct hit.

'Come and stay with us,' Amal said the following day. 'You have won the battle with yourself. You are very brave. My brother thinks you are.'

Amal smiled, unsure whether her friend and her brother were lovers or not. She knew what a lot of time they spent together. But she also knew how much Sarah disapproved of what the Israelis were doing, how much she blamed them for the escalation of the war. She could imagine they spent their time together arguing rather than making love.

'I won't stay,' Sarah shook her head. 'Halim says the bombing will stop as soon as the PLO leaves, and that's supposed to be next week.'

Negotiations to remove the PLO from the camps had been going of for weeks with President Regan's envoy, Mr Habiba, shuttling between America, Israel and Beirut in a manner reminiscent of Mr Haig when he tried to prevent the Falklands war. For some days Sarah hadn't seen Halim, but she knew that he was very busy helping the Israelis to make a count of the Palestinians in the camp, pinpointing their exact positions. That night he came again to the clinic just as she was leaving.

'I want you to meet some Israelis,' he said. 'You'll see what nice people they are.'

'I *know* they're nice people. I know many Israelis at home,'

Sarah replied, 'but I don't like them here, occupying the Lebanon.'

'Come. Amal is coming too.'

They ate in a restaurant in Hamra Street, which had the cosmopolitan air of every smart restaurant in almost any part of the world. There were wealthy Lebanese businessmen and their wives, there was a sprinkling of Lebanese army personnel, there were many foreigners – journalists reporting the war, members of the American university and hospital – and there were a number of Israeli officers scarcely distinguishable in looks and behaviour from their Lebanese counterparts.

In the happy atmosphere of the restaurant it was easy to believe that the war would soon be followed by a united Lebanon, that outside there were no refugee camps packed with children and sad men and women, specially women who were preparing to bid goodbye to loved ones they didn't know when they would see again.

An officer called Aron had a lot to tell them about the dispersal that would soon take place. How an international force was on its way to supervise the departure of the fighting men of the PLO. How the Israeli military, supported by the Lebanese Army and the Phalange, would ensure the complete evacuation of the camps.

Sarah wanted to know what would happen to the women and children?

Aron shrugged. 'Who cares?'

'I care, Amal cares. I'm sure you all care really.'

Sarah's reply was heated, but Amal, clearly fascinated by an Israeli captain who had his arm round her waist, paid little notice.

'We don't care about these people,' another named Aviv said. 'We don't think they're human.'

'That's what Hitler said about the Jews!'

Sarah's raised voice stopped all conversation at the table and everyone stared at her as though they had found themselves in the presence of an enemy. Halim's face was troubled.

'Aviv doesn't mean exactly that Sarah. But in many ways these people have become savages. Look what they did to our people.'

'Look what you're doing to them now! They have suffered so much. They go from country to country, from camp to

245

camp. No one wants them. They marry, they make love, they breed, their children grow up . . .'

'That's the problem . . .' the officer with his arm round Amal's waist began, but she gestured to him to be quiet and he stopped.

'It seems to me,' Sarah went on heatedly, 'that as long as one half of the human race thinks the other half isn't human, you'll never have peace. You'll go on fighting and killing one another. All you do is make war.'

She pushed back her chair despite Halim's restraining hand, which she impatiently brushed aside. She looked around her at the laughing faces, the open, eager mouths crammed with nourishing food. She remembered a little girl she'd had committed to hospital that day who had lost every member of her family in a bomb blast and whose eyesight was now threatened. Alone in the world, sightless, what chance had that tiny little Palestinian girl got? In Beirut that day she had seen Belsen, and to her now the two were indivisible.

Sarah went to the door without looking back and, once outside, she ran all the way home, fleeing from terror, fleeing to terror. There was terror all around her in the streets and inside the buildings, under the rubble of the bombed blocks of flats, inside the camps, the pathetic homes of the refugees. Just like in any big city the poor lived side by side with the rich. But then bombs did not discriminate when they fell; they could not tell the difference.

Inside her third floor apartment more plaster had fallen from the ceiling on to her bed. A pane of glass that had cracked during the night had now dropped out of the window, and lay shattered on the tiled floor. The water from the shower came in a thin trickle, then stopped altogether. She was trembling so much she knew she was close to hysteria. Suddenly she longed for her mother, for the warmth of her family, the companionship of Amanda, the wise uncritical love of her father, Tom's chaffing about the Peace Movement, women's lib and the CND. How safe it seemed in London.

She undressed, flung herself on to her bed and, as she did so, there was a sudden rumble and the building shook. The lights went out, emphasizing the strange glare over the city. It was not the pleasant glare of moonlight or sunshine; it was unnatural, like the stillness before a tornado.

She lay on her back and put her hand in her mouth, biting it hard. 'I must control myself. I must.'

She knew that if she went on like this she would have to apply to be sent home. She had lost her personal battle. Beirut was too much for her. The divisions inside her mind were almost as deep and as stressful as those inside Lebanon itself.

For a time she lay there, feeling the jagged pieces of plaster under her, yet untroubled by them, careless of the shelling that had started up again outside. She was too frightened, too unnerved to sleep, yet she might have dozed. Suddenly an insistent banging at the door made her alert, sit up on the bed clutching the sheet to her as though that thin piece of cotton could protect her from whatever was outside. The banging stopped and her name was called.

'Sarah are you there?'

It was Halim.

She quickly got off the bed and went for her robe in the bathroom, tying the belt tightly round her waist as she ran into the little hall, listening as she unlocked it, peering round, still afraid.

'What is it?'

'Let me in Sarah.'

Halim stared at her and she stared back, her fingers still tugging at the belt. He pushed open the door and she moved away. As he came into the tiny hall his hand fell on the light switch, clicking it up and down.

'There's no light.'

'Sarah you can't stay here.' Halim continued on into the large room that was her bedroom and sitting-room combined – what was known as a bachelor apartment with a small hall, kitchen, shower and toilet, the inevitable balcony outside. 'The Israelis are going to shell this area all night. There is a PLO office in Sadat Street.'

'They hit it the other day.'

'When one PLO office goes another starts. My friends were horrified when they learned where you lived. They liked you, by the way. They were interested in you.'

Halim casually pulled a cigarette case out of his breast pocket and selected a Gitane, which he lit with a plastic lighter before replacing case and lighter in his breast pocket. She seldom saw Halim in uniform, which made her wonder if he was in Intelligence. The two chairs in the room were arranged on either side of the open French windows and, selecting one, he turned it so that it faced her, and sat down. Sarah came casually over and sat on the edge of the bed, aware of his frank appraisal, his eyes running over her slim body. His manner had changed completely.

'You really look beautiful tonight, Sarah.'

'I'm not beautiful, Halim.' She ran a finger along her nose. 'I never have been.'

'The Israelis thought you were Jewish.'

'My father's family were Jewish. Hahn is a Jewish name.'

'That's what they thought. They couldn't understand your attitude. I told them you were a doctor.'

'And did that explain everything?' Her tone was deliberately sarcastic.

'They understood. They are a very understanding people.'

'You keep on talking as if I hate Jews. I don't. As you say I look Jewish and I have Jewish blood in my veins.'

'Is your mother a Jew?'

'No.'

'Then you're not Jewish.'

'Neither is my father, nor was his father. But his father's father was, my great-grandfather.'

'Many Muslims in the Lebanon became Christians too.'

'There's nothing shameful about conversion.'

'I didn't say there was.'

Halim abruptly got up and went out on to the balcony. She sat watching him, uncertain what to do. Then she got up and joined him. He leaned over the balcony, his hands folded casually as though he were enjoying the air on a calm summer's night.

'It *is* such a beautiful city, you know.'

'It is, even now.'

'It will be again.' He moved closer to her, as though for companionship. 'I find you very attractive, Sarah, your mind, your looks. I admire your independence. It may sound strange, because we argue a lot, but I like women of character.'

'I'm glad, because the women in your family are strong characters.'

'That's why. I was well brought up. The Muslim women, you know, are often very timid, subservient. Not ours.' His

248

manner changed again, becoming more personal, even intimate. 'Do you care a little for me, Sarah?'

She did care for him, but the disagreements they had worried her. 'Of course I care. I like you very much, but we have so many arguments.'

'Disagreements are nothing.'

'They are very important things we disagree about.'

'It comes to the same. We both want peace.'

He was about to kiss her when a flare suddenly lit up the whole area, showing people running below in Sadat Street, and once again the intermittent bombardment began. Halim used the opportunity to hold her tighter to him for a few moments, and she could feel his heart hammering under his thin shirt. Was it fear or was it desire? She wanted Halim but she, herself, was frightened; she was frightened of commitment and of the thing itself, of sex. She didn't know just then which frightened her more.

'You can't stay here tonight Sarah. I'll take you to my home.'

'The streets will be bad.'

'Less risky than here. That is unless . . .'

'Yes?' She raised her head looking into his eyes.

'Unless I stay with you. You'll be quite safe then.'

'Oh?'

'The Israelis would never touch me. I'm their friend.'

By some magic chance or calculation, or maybe Halim knew the bombardment would only last a short time, just after midnight the shelling did stop and some time after that, in the unnatural peace of a Lebanese night, Sarah gave herself to a man whom she desired, but whom she didn't think she loved and whose views she strongly disagreed with. Sex, however, is not inhibited by any such demarcations and, in the full act, she managed to forget what reservations she had. But, for a woman of twenty-six who had never slept with a man before, the best part of the night was actually *sleeping* with him, feeling his bare body next to hers, his arm around her waist.

When she woke up the sun had already risen, turning the yellow walls of the room to a curious shade of amber. His curly, close-cut hair was neat, as though he had just combed it, and the stubble on his chin made him look even more dangerous than she knew he was. When he became aware she was awake, his arm tightened round her.

'I'm very flattered,' he whispered in her ear. 'I was the first, or was it a long time ago?'

'You were the first,' she said, 'as if you didn't know.'

'Was that why it took so long?'

'What?'

'For you to let me make love to you.'

'You mean was I afraid?' As he didn't reply she went on quickly. 'Yes I was a little afraid, but not physically.'

'You're afraid of emotion Sarah.'

'Is it that obvious?'

'To me, yes; you see I know you are a very emotional person. You are so involved in the war and the plight of the Palestinians.'

'I am emotional about a lot of things, things I believe in.'

'But, tell me seriously, you have never loved?'

'No.'

'Why?'

'I don't know.'

'Did you prefer women?'

'No!'

'I thought not. Was it, then, maybe, because of your parents, your mother?'

'Why?' She looked at him with surprise.

'I often find with women who have difficulty with sex that their mother is the reason.'

He 'often found' . . . He had had many women. Was that why she had been reluctant to make love to him?

'I'm very fond of my mother. She's most understanding, a psychiatrist as I've told you.'

'But do you see her watching over you when you make love?'

'No!' Sarah got up and shook her hair impatiently. 'Please don't start being all psychological, Halim. I have enough of it at home.'

'Then it is your mother.' He looked at her happily. He was very charming, most seductive. He gazed at her breasts, breasts that were full but taut, with hard prominent nipples.

Sexy breasts. He pulled himself up and began to suck the one nearest to him and Sarah experienced a sensation in her loins that made her cry out.

Skilfully, gently, Halim laid her on her back and, after careful preparation, made love to her again.

CHAPTER FIFTEEN

'SARAH HAS A BOYFRIEND.'

'Thank God for that,' Sam said. 'I was beginning to think she must be a lesbian.'

'Don't be absurd Sam. Anyway, even if she was . . . but I'm glad all the same.'

'Who is he?'

Sam kept his eyes on the busy road that was leading them to Plymouth to see Tom.

'He's a Lebanese army officer called Halim. His family are Maronite Christians. She says they have nothing in common, but the whole thing is tremendous.'

'Sounds good,' Sam said.

'She sounds very serious, though she hasn't known him long. Being Sarah, having waited so long, she would be.'

'She would,' Sam agreed. 'Do you think she was a virgin?'

'I'm practically sure of it. Now I wouldn't be surprised if she married him. She loves the country and hates the war. It would be a cause for Sarah.'

'Our children do give us problems, don't they?' Sam glanced at her, smiling.

'I think they've turned out quite well. Even Amanda is very happy in her kennels.'

'With George.'

'I agree, George has something to do with it.'

'Would we mind if she married George?'

'Let's cross that bridge when we come to it.'

Barbara noticed how frequently he said 'we'. When she was with Sam, like this, she felt they were a family again.

'Incidentally Frankie would like to ask you to lunch.'

'That's very kind of her. When?'

'She says if you're agreeable to ring her.'

'Can't I fix it with you?'

'She wants you alone. She would like to get to know you better.'

'Oh?'

'Is that all right?'

'I expect so. We're trying again are we? Hadn't we better let it all rest, Sam?'

'Frankie is really very fond of you. She hasn't forgotten how good you were to her when Elizabeth was born.'

'Yet she waits nearly six months to ask me to lunch.'

'Darling . . . Sarah,' Sam sighed impatiently. 'We have had the war; Lebanon; you have been to the States . . .'

'All right I'll ring her. Incidentally, have you finished with that woman?'

'What woman?'

'You know who I mean Sam.'

'Oh her? Yes. That was just a little thing.'

'I'm glad.'

Barbara looked at him closely, but his features gave her no clue as to whether or not he was telling her the truth.

Despite the war, both wars, Barbara felt she had, indeed, begun to settle down. Although it was nice to be here now with Sam there was no longer that yearning for him. She accepted, at last, that they were separate people – parents of the same children, but no longer married. She was very caught up in her family once again. The support for Amanda had been shifted to Natalie and Tom. Sarah was written to frequently. The trip to the States had been to yet another congress at which, of course, the ubiquitous Dr Kleber was present; but she was never alone with him for a moment. It was odd to reflect that, although she was quite old as far as years went, in so many ways she was discovering new things – a self-possession she thought she had already, a readiness to admit mistakes, even juvenile ones like going to bed with the wrong man. But, more importantly, to forget about them too. In the old days she would have clung to her sense of mortification that she'd made a fool of herself. Now she put it all down to experience.

Tom and Natalie had a small house in a village on the outskirts of Plymouth where Tom had been stationed before the war – and still was. Natalie had remained there while he was in hospital, as she had during the war, looking after the babies, keeping cheerful, doing her bit to help other service wives. Sam and Barbara were to pick her up and take her with them to the hospital in Plymouth to which he'd recently been transferred.

Natalie was a wonderful girl, everything they could have wished for for Tom and, now that he needed her more than ever, she was just the sort of kindly, extrovert person to help a grievously injured man.

The door to the house was open as they drove up and then, suddenly, a man appeared in the doorway and started to walk slowly down the garden path towards them. As he got to the garden gate he leaned over it.

'Hello Mum and Dad. Good journey?'

Barbara grasped Sam's hand and he put his arm round her waist to support her as they got out of the car and Natalie emerged from the house smiling broadly, Clare running in front of her and the new baby in her arms.

'Oh Tom,' Barbara leaned forward, stroking his face over the garden gate. 'I can't believe it.'

'It was a surprise. Isn't it marvellous?' Tom stood upright, shaking his artificial leg.

'I thought it wouldn't be for months!'

'So did I.' Tom stood back to open the garden gate for Sam and Barbara. 'But they said the stump was in good shape and the sooner I got used to it the better. I can't keep it on all day, but it's a start.'

'He's been practising for you,' Natalie came shyly from behind and kissed her parents-in-law.

'It's the nicest surprise we could have had.'

Tom tucked his arm through his mother's and slowly they began to walk up the path, Barbara conscious of the extra weight on her arm as he leaned on her.

'Well some of the chaps who've lost limbs are pretty low. The doctors said I'd cheer them up if I could set an example.'

'Trust you to think of others, Tom.'

'And myself. It helped me Mum.' Tom pushed her forwards into the house. 'I've had to come to terms with all this and the prospect of a desk job. But our Captain General, Pringle, has a gammy leg too, blown off by the IRA. One thing I know is that I'll be safe in the Marines and not made redundant. We might come to London if I'm posted to HQ.'

'Will you like that?' Barbara looked at Natalie as Sam swung his youngest granddaughter into his arms. Sam seemed surrounded by baby girls these days, all related to him.

'*I* will hate it,' Natalie said firmly. 'I'd hoped we'd get a little farm near here, or a market garden . . .'

'You mean for Tom to *leave* the Marines?'

'Yes.' Natalie looked at them in her open, honest way. 'I'd like that. He has done his bit for his country and he would retire with honour, but he doesn't want to.'

Tom began to look uncomfortable and Barbara could sense that instead of relief and optimism in the house, there was tension. Lots of it.

'I'm not attracted to the land,' Tom began, but Natalie went on.

'I've suddenly noticed that Tom is very selfish, Mother. Because I've given so much of my life to him he now thinks I should give the rest in doing what he wants. I'm a country girl. I hate the town and the thought of Tom spending the rest of his days working in an office while we stew in some horrible little suburb . . . with all the problems with the schools and so on . . .'

Barbara could see Natalie was close to tears. She put her arm through hers, trying to draw her from the room, saying: 'Let's have a little chat while Sam and Tom . . .'

'No, Mother!' Sharply Natalie withdrew her arm and stood her ground, looking at Barbara. 'You think I'm wrong don't you?'

'I think it's a bit soon . . .'

'But they're talking about it *now*. We might be in London in the New Year.'

Barbara looked at Tom, who nodded his head.

'All able-bodied men will return to duty.' He tapped his leg. 'This makes me able-bodied. Natalie simply doesn't want to leave here. She says that once she does she won't come back. It will be the city for good.'

'Well then, what will you do?'

'Tom might go up for the week and come down at weekends . . .'

'It's a long way,' Sam said.

'People do it, Dad. I see Natalie's point, but I don't share it. I might have been posted to HQ even with two perfectly good

255

legs and given a staff job. I reckon Natalie knew what she was doing when she married me, but she's forgotten.'

'You weren't in the Marines when I married you. We never thought in terms of a conventional war.'

'A soldier has to think of everything, and so does a soldier's wife.' As Tom looked at Natalie, Barbara, to her sorrow, saw what hostility this differing point of view had engendered between them. When she thought of how much Natalie had endured for Tom it was, indeed, very sad. 'I'm to be promoted to major by the way,' Tom went on as an afterthought.

'That's wonderful darling. Congratulations.' Barbara kissed him again, but the news somehow didn't seem as good in the face of this crisis, this totally unexpected crisis in a once happy home.

'I think it would be a good thing for a while to see how it goes,' Barbara said cautiously, catching her eldest grand-daughter, who was scampering about, and putting her firmly on her knee. 'In time . . .'

'I shan't budge,' Natalie said. She looked in turn at them all, staring boldly at one, then the other, especially Tom's parents, 'and Tom knows it. I can't understand him even contemplating spending the rest of his life behind a desk. Daddy's offered to set us up on a farm. It's a wonderful chance. I can't understand Tom turning it down. Frankly I'd rather divorce Tom than go and live in London.'

The advent of a new television station was an exciting business, especially for those who were being given fresh opportunities because of it. Frankie had received a phone call one day from a company engaged in making documentaries for Channel 4, which had resulted in several interviews, and a pilot run giving a commentary on financial news in a new current affairs spot.

With her soft American accent, her confidence and her long blonde hair, Frankie seemed a natural for the medium and everyone asked her why she hadn't thought of it before. Frankie said that no one had thought of her before and asked how they came to hear of her name. The answer was as she had expected: Poppy.

Poppy was into everything to do with the new television

station, and someone knew someone who knew someone else who knew Poppy who said that Frankie would be ideal for the job.

Frankie couldn't begin to thank Poppy enough, but not enough to want to see her. She wrote her a little note of thanks and Poppy promptly rang up and asked her to lunch. Despite all her protestations Poppy pinned her down and they met, as in the old days, in the trattoria in Blandford Street, chatting about this and that before they came to the point.

'I don't know why you put my name forward,' Frankie said after she'd told Poppy about the screen tests and so on. 'Why not yourself?'

'They wanted someone to talk about money. Besides I don't have your looks, even if I knew how many pence there are in a pound, which I don't.' Poppy's self-deprecation was hard at work again.

'There must have been other people. Why me?'

Poppy looked at her speculatively. 'Why shouldn't I mention you, Frankie? We're friends.'

For an answer Frankie went on eating her meal, eyes staring at the plate.

'We're friends Frankie aren't we?' Poppy repeated.

'I don't know.' Frankie wiped the grease on her plate with a piece of bread which she popped into her mouth.

'But why shouldn't we be friends?' As Frankie still kept silent Poppy crossed her arms and leaned heavily on the table, her face a few inches from Frankie's. The fringe of the beaded shawl she was wearing trailed in what was left of her Spaghetti Bolognese, but she didn't notice it. 'There's something wrong isn't there Frankie? You never call me and when I call you you're evasive. Why is it?'

'You know.' Frankie suddenly stared at her.

'*I* know?' Poppy pointed indignantly at her breast.

'I think you're carrying on with Sam. I think that's why you got me the job, because you feel guilty. I can't think why on earth you'd do it otherwise.'

'Oh I see,' Poppy sank back in her chair, arms still akimbo, Spaghetti Bolognese sauce dripping on to her skirt. 'I'm supposed to be having an affair with Sam?'

'That's what I think. Sam's changed, Poppy. He's not the man he was when we first married.'

257

'Few men are. He's been through a lot. Two babies.'

'Yes, and Tom and Sarah, and Amanda; but it's not that. It's the way Sam is with me. He doesn't want me as much; the sex isn't good. There was no need for that to change. I know he has someone else.'

Poppy studied the people passing in the street through the windows of the restaurant. 'But why should it be me?'

'I can't think who else it could be. I threw you and Sam together. Then someone saw you having lunch in the City after Elizabeth was born. Sam said it was just to say "thank you", but I didn't believe him then and I believe him even less now. I even thought of having a detective trail you I felt so jealous. I feel poisoned, Poppy, I really do, poisoned about the whole thing.'

'But supposing I told you I'm not having an affair with Sam,' Poppy said quietly. 'Would you believe me?'

'He's having an affair with someone. I'm certain of that.'

'It's not me,' Poppy said. 'I can promise you it's not me.'

'But you sound as if you know who it is.' Frankie leaned urgently forward as if looking for clues in her friend's face.

'All I can say is that it's not with me. If Sam is having an affair it's not with me.'

'It's easy for you to say that.'

'It's true. I swear to God it's true.'

Frankie, beginning to doubt, leaned her arms on the table and stared at the light grainy wood. There were two things wrong: one was that she believed Poppy; the second was the inflection in Poppy's voice as if trying to suggest to her that she was on the wrong track. She seemed to be saying that there was a girl, but she was not Poppy. She smoothed her hair with her hands and straightened up again.

'Do you know who it is?'

Now it was Poppy's turn to look down. 'I don't know her name. It's someone at his office. Oh God, now what have I done?' She reached over the table and seized Frankie's hand. 'What *could* I do? I knew you thought I was carrying on with Sam from the way you've behaved towards me. I knew what was the matter.'

'Then why didn't you tell me before?'

'Because I felt guilty.'

'But why should you feel guilty?' Frankie scrutinized her face.

'Because Sam asked me to cover for him. *That's* why I've been ashamed to speak to you. I hardly went out with him at all. That day when you had the baby we weren't together. Barbara spoke to me on the phone . . .'

'*Barbara* knows?'

'Barbara's known all the time. I think Barbara knows who it is.'

'Christ, I thought she was a friend,' Frankie said bitterly.

'She may be a friend if she's covering up for Sam.'

'She's no friend to me if she's covering up for Sam. She's probably glad.' Frankie reached for the bill and studied it closely, yet the figures on it were obliterated by her tears. She looked at Poppy. 'Do you realize Poppy that I have two young babies and an unfaithful husband and I'm nearly forty? What am I going to do for the rest of my life? How am I going to sort it out?'

'I'd talk to Barbara first before you do anything rash.'

'I won't live with Sam if he has another woman. I'll never share him.'

'The reason I saw him that day was to beg him to give this other woman up. I'd been to see you at home shortly after you left the hospital and I could tell how happy you were. I knew that if you suspected Sam it would be the end of your happiness.'

'It is. It has. I did suspect him; but I suspected you. I felt you were avoiding me because you were guilty.'

'I was guilty . . .'

'Yes, but not for that reason. What you did was wrong . . .'

'I felt terrible. He said it was only for the time being. He'd give her up.'

'Well he didn't and he hasn't. I'm sure of that.'

Poppy's hand tightened on Frankie's arm. 'Please don't do anything rash, Frankie, until you've seen Barbara. See her as soon as you can.'

'I had to see you before I saw Sam.' Frankie felt awkward, standing at the door. 'I'm sorry if you're busy.'

'I've just got in.' Barbara, surprised, stood back.

'I know. I waited for your car to arrive.'

'You've been waiting in the road?'

'Yes.'

'Come in, come in.' Barbara, sensing her reluctance, put her hand out and pulled Frankie through the door. 'I nearly went to the cinema. What a lucky thing I didn't.'

She could tell by the way that Frankie stood in the hall that something was very wrong. She had the pinched, cold look that people have who are suffering from shock. Barbara took her into the living room and poured her a whisky without asking what she wanted. Then she poured one for herself, indicated a chair for Frankie and sat opposite her. Frankie perched rather than sat on the chair, her blonde hair falling on to the shoulders of the jacket of a blue suit, classic in style with a plain silk blouse underneath. Her navy calf shoes had medium size heels and there was a navy calf bag on the floor by her side. Her only makeup was a pale pink lipstick which enhanced her pallor rather than diminished it. Barbara had talked about nothing in particular as she got the drinks, but now she looked at Frankie, inviting her confidence.

'It's about Sam,' Frankie began . . . then hesitated. 'You remember I once said to you he was having an affair, and you asked how I knew?'

'I remember.'

'I said I thought it was Poppy and you dismissed this. At the time however I thought, from something you said, or the way you said it, that we were talking about different things, and now I know we were. Sam is having an affair with someone else and I believe you know about it.'

Barbara, who was used to the circumlocution of her psychiatric patients, was momentarily disconcerted. 'May I ask how you know?'

'It's no use beating about the bush Barbara.'

'But tell me how you know.'

'Poppy told me. How she covered up for this . . . woman. How you spoke to her on the phone. I know everything except her name.'

'I don't know her name either.'

'You must.'

'I don't. I only know about her because, as Poppy told you, I spoke to her that night. I too asked Sam to give the woman up. When we went to see Tom the other day he told me he had.'

'Well he hasn't.'

'Are you sure?'

'Quite sure.'

'How are you sure?'

'Oh I'm not going on about lipstick on the collar or anything ridiculous. I know Sam. I'm not sharing him with another woman, Barbara.'

'I don't blame you.' Barbara was about to add: 'Neither would I' and then she remembered she was talking to the 'other woman' in her own marriage collapse. How quickly people forgot their own guilt.

'I'm quite firm about this. I've made up my mind. But I wanted to see you first. Poppy said I should.'

'When did you talk to Poppy?'

'I had lunch with her today.'

'You didn't waste time.'

'I can't pretend with Sam. I'll have to come straight out with it.'

'Are you going to ask Sam to leave home?'

'I might.'

'Supposing he says he has given up this other woman?'

'You *must* know her name.'

'I assure you I don't. I know she works at the bank.'

Frankie got up and wandered over to the French windows. Already the leaves on the trees were beginning to fall in the garden and over on the heath. There was a desolate, autumnal air about the scene. She felt very tired.

'I envy you Barbara. You've been through it all haven't you?' As Frankie turned to stare at her, Barbara nodded. 'Losing your husband, readjusting. I know now what you went through. I'm sorry. The only thing was that when Sam left you, your family were grown up. My children are eighteen months and six months respectively. I'm on the brink of a wonderful job with Channel 4; yet my life seems in pieces.'

'Sam can put all that right.'

Frankie swiftly crossed the room and knelt on the floor by Barbara.

'But will Sam *ever* change? Will he ever be faithful to me? You must know, you're a psychiatrist.'

'Unfortunately I'm not clairvoyant as well. I can't tell you for sure what Sam will or won't do. I would never have thought, for instance, that he would have had this affair.'

'Do you know anything about her?'

'Nothing.' Barbara reached for a cigarette from the box on the small table by her side. 'I didn't want to know.'

'Did he say how involved he was or anything?'

'You'll have to ask Sam. Only last week he told me it was over.'

'Hm.' Frankie remained on the floor, seated now with her arms round her knees. For all her distress she looked remarkably composed, yet Barbara was very sorry for her; sorrier than she'd ever been for herself. Forty was a particularly vulnerable age. By the time she was forty she herself had made it professionally and two of her children were nearly grown up. In many ways Frankie was on the threshold of a life that seemed to have little of the promise it might have had ten or fifteen years ago.

'Where will Sam go if he leaves you?' Barbara asked the question that had been at the back of her mind ever since Frankie made her statement. 'He can't come here.'

'Wouldn't you want him back?'

Barbara shook her head. 'Never. Our children will always have a place in my home, but not my ex-husband. Never.'

'I think you understand him better than I do,' Frankie said sadly.

'Maybe I did. I don't know; but I don't want him round here again. If I were you I'd try and sort it out, Frankie. Give Sam an ultimatum.'

'I'll have to see this woman.'

Barbara reached down and put a hand on her arm, a gesture prompted by compassion rather than calculation. 'Frankie, don't demean yourself. A confrontation between wife and mistress would be undignified. I would never . . .' She checked herself. Really it was hard to imagine now that she and Frankie had ever been rivals for the same man. Her feelings towards her were those of a sibling rather than an enemy. She was now so detached from thinking of Sam as a husband and lover that dispensing advice to his present wife in this clinical fashion came to her with surprising ease. Moreover she genuinely pitied Frankie the predicament in which she found herself. She felt they had an important relationship, based not on blood but on kinship. 'I would never advise you to do that.'

'How can I know Sam will give her up?'

'He'll have to promise. You'll have to trust him.'

'Things will never be the same between us,' Frankie said. 'I can see the change already.'

As Barbara saw her out she spontaneously kissed her on the cheek, holding her briefly in her arms. They had never embraced before.

'Good luck,' she said.

They occasionally continued to meet in the flat belonging to Sam's friend in the Barbican. With his increasing guilt Sam had never had the heart to try and get a place of his own, and perhaps he knew, too, instinctively, that the span of the relationship was limited.

He had stopped humping her at work because it seemed so undignified for someone he loved, the way you treated a casual lay or a whore. Now, although the fun had not gone out of their sexual relationship, the passion was too profound for fun and games.

Julia could tell by his manner that something had happened; knew it even in the office when they bumped briefly into each other in the corridor. She could sense his unease as, instead of wolfing his food, he pecked at it but drank a lot. Then peremptorily he pushed his plate aside and suggested they go to bed.

'There's something wrong isn't there?' Julia looked sadly down at him, as though she guessed its nature, as she took his plate.

'No, nothing. I'm tired.'

'I know you Sam.' She carefully put the plates on the table and came back to sit by his side.

'Everyone says they know me,' Sam said bitterly. 'I'm sick of it.'

'Your wife knows. That's it.'

'She thought it was Poppy, the one who covered for us.'

263

'I thought it was silly to tell her at the time.'

'She suspected Poppy and nursed a grudge; Poppy seemed to avoid her and Frankie thought it was an admission of guilt. Poppy did feel guilty so she stayed away.'

'Now your wife knows.'

'Your wife', sometimes 'Mrs Hahn', but never 'Frankie'.

Sam nodded his head and, with the final nod, his chin remained sunk on his breast.

'I hate to make a woman so unhappy. She must be frantic.' Julia touched his arm.

'If only she knew you . . . You've never wanted anything from me, no money, no good times out, no holidays . . .' Sam started to sob and Julia slid her arms around his body, placing his head comfortably on her bosom.

'You were the best thing that happened to me Sam. I knew I wouldn't last.'

'But I *love* you.'

'It could never last and I knew you'd never leave her for me. I wouldn't want you to anyway, with two small babies. It wouldn't be fair. We came into each other's lives too late Sam.'

Would he have married her? Sam opened his eyes, his tears gone, his head resting on her breast conscious of her even breathing, calming, soothing. After the sudden storm he felt peaceful. No, he could never have married her; but with Barbara as his wife, undemanding, detached as she always used to be, he could have had an affair for many years, perhaps until the end of his life. He and Julia growing old together . . . Nice.

'I should never have left Barbara,' he murmured. 'She would have understood. She *did* understand. Why on earth did I leave her?' He gazed enquiringly at Julia as if her wise, knowing eyes held the answer to his problem. 'We had a grown up family, all we wanted. I didn't want more babies . . .'

'But you do love them surely?' Julia's rather high voice, as she grew anxious on this score, rose almost to a squeak as though, in her barren state, she couldn't bear to think of baby girls unloved by their father.

'Of course I love them! I love all my children . . . but two

264

less wouldn't have made any difference. Do you realize what my life with Frankie will be now?'

Julia shook her head.

'Suspicion. She will always be wondering about me; but she says that if she ever knows I'm having an affair she will leave me for good and make me regret it for the rest of my life. I believe her. And I will regret it. I can't leave her, you see. It's such an awful failure to have to admit you made a mistake the second time. Two little girls, what would my friends say? You see that don't you?'

'What do I have to do?' Julia was docile to the last.

'She wants you to leave the bank.'

'Of course.'

'She says she has to know that, and your name and everything so that she can check.'

'You said I would?'

'I said I'd ask you,' Sam lied, his confidence returning.

'I wouldn't want to break up your marriage, Sam. Of course I will.'

'I'll give you references, everything . . .'

'I'll say I need something nearer home.'

'I told her you lived in Bromley. She knows I won't go skating out to Bromley every night.'

He smiled, as though the whole thing was turning into a bit of a joke. Looking then at Sam, a director of the bank, his face stained with tears, Julia thought that, though she loved him, she rather despised him too. She knew too that in six months Sam would have forgotten her.

'Let's go to bed,' he jumped up, kissing her.

Julia, neat, unfussy, rose to clear the plates and wash the dishes. Despite her feelings, the years in front of her seemed very empty now.

CHAPTER SIXTEEN

HUDA SALIBA, EYES BRIGHT WITH pleasure, kissed Sarah on both cheeks, standing tip-toe in order to do so.

'So pleased,' she murmured warmly, 'so very pleased.'

Samir shook her by the hand and held her momentarily in an embrace, and then the younger sister, Aida, came shyly forward as if uncertain what to do.

'I'm very pleased too,' she offered her hand, but Sarah impulsively stooped and kissed her. She still clung to Halim's hand as she had when he stood proudly in the centre of the room after making the announcement:

'We're to be married.'

In Sarah's ears it had seemed such an extraordinary statement that she could hardly believe it herself, as though she shared the surprise of the rest of his family.

'When did you decide?' Samir had called for a bottle of chilled French champagne which he was now uncorking.

'Last night,' Halim said. 'I asked her and she said "yes". I knew long ago that I wanted to marry her.'

'Long ago!' Aida gave her shy laugh. 'You have only known each other a short time.'

'It is long enough,' Halim looked at Sarah, 'when you're sure, as we are.'

Huda seemed to have doubts too. As glasses were raised to toast the couple she said, 'Why decide to marry now? Why not wait a little?'

'We need a bond,' Sarah replied simply. 'In this war-torn city, in these turbulent times, we need something positive to hang on to.'

'We don't *need* marriage,' Halim smiled at her. 'But we wish it. We are both Christian and there is no obstacle.'

'Then when will it be?'

'Soon. As soon as Sarah can get the necessary papers, birth certificate, and so on from England.'

Throughout the meal the lovers kept glancing at each other, feeling for limbs under the table, touching feet, touching hands, anxious to be alone. For the last few weeks Sarah had been in the grip of a passion so strong that nothing outside Halim's arms seemed real; not the continual peace negotiations, the election of Bashir Jemayel to the Presidency, the expulsion of the Palestinians, or the care of the sick and wounded in her charge.

Sarah knew that it was said that when women like her, controlled, seemingly passionless creatures, fell they fell hard, and it had certainly happened to her. This man of average height with his lean, dedicated face had conquered her completely; and she realized how sharing his body made her share his mind as well. Like him, she had come to believe that the salvation of the Lebanon lay in the new President-elect and the continuing strength of the Phalange and their Israeli allies.

Not that she had seen a lot of Halim, except at night when he faithfully returned to her flat in Sadat Street, often to disappear before dawn. Whatever he did was very secretive, and she scarcely ever saw him in the Israeli-style military uniform with the inscription 'Keta'ib Lubnaniyeh' embroidered on the pocket, together with the cedar, to indicate that he belonged to the Phalange and not the rival army of Major Haddad, or the impotent Army of the Lebanon. She knew that he worked with Elie Hobeika, head of the Phalange Intelligence section, and that they were closely in touch with Israeli Military Intelligence. Apart from that he told her little of what he did, but only about what he wanted to do one day soon when the Lebanon would be free.

'Even of the Israelis?'

'Of course. The Israelis are our friends. Now that the Palestinians have gone they want us to be independent and free.'

'Have they all gone?'

'Not all,' Halim replied enigmatically. 'But they will.'

They were talking that night as they returned to the flat, walking through the city streets, arms entwined.

'When will the Israelis go?'

'As soon as Bashir is firmly in command. When he takes office.'

'Bashir seems like a god to you.'

'He is. The only man in Lebanon capable of uniting us. Even the opposition voted for him. He is young, he is enthusiastic, and very capable.'

'I heard that he is very ruthless too.'

'Darling, you have to be ruthless to get what you want in this country, in these times. But look how many world leaders have turned into peaceful statesmen once they have got what they want.'

'Like Hitler?'

'Like Begin.' Halim stopped and faced her, roughly taking her arms. 'Sarah you know I love you; but we cannot spend our lives arguing. What you say is ridiculous. It really makes me angry. Bashir is not like Hitler, nor is Begin.'

'But Halim we do disagree,' she said, quietly disengaging her arms from his. 'We have agreed on that fact, and when we are married you can't expect me to agree with everything you say. I won't. You know that I share with you your ideals for the Lebanon. I want it to be peaceful too; but I am *not* going to be a simpleton.'

'You aren't a simpleton darling.' Halim kissed her hard on the mouth in the public street. 'That's why I love you. I love your spirit; but I hope, in time, you will feel convinced that everything I say is true, because I am going into politics in this country to help to build the Lebanese nation up again.'

'You won't stay in the army?' His statement, unexpected like so many things about him, disconcerted her.

'Bashir asked me only recently to join him when we can safely disband our army. I said I'd think about it.'

Sarah was thinking too that in England, or anywhere in the west, a man would probably consult, or at least inform, his wife before making a decision as important as this one. She was about to make some retort, but decided not to. Her heart and her hopes were wholly with Halim and, although he would not turn her into a mere echo of his own ideas and points of view, she felt that tonight was not the time for argument. Tonight was for the celebration of their engagement, and for love.

Later, as she lay in bed, conscious of the sounds of the city through the open window, it was very hard to think that Lebanon was a country that had recently been at war. The Israelis still surrounded Beirut, but the Palestinian guerrillas had been shipped, or sent overland, to other Arab countries willing to receive them. There was still rubble in the streets and occasional sporadic firing; but the nightmare shelling of only a few weeks ago had stopped. There were no clouds of smoke in the sky, no Israeli Phantoms streaking across, preparing to unload their bombs. Through the window the velvety night sky with its few twinkling stars seemed a harbinger of peace.

Lebanon: land of the Bible, land of contrasts, of strife and beauty but always, for her, Sarah Hahn, the land where she had finally found love.

She turned and tenderly embraced the sleeping body of Halim her lover, her husband to be. Then, her head touching his, she fell into a peaceful sleep.

When Sarah awoke in the morning Halim had gone. They were to rendezvous again in the evening at the flat and go out for dinner with a group of his new Israeli friends. It was still dark, because the day started early in Beirut, and she showered, had her coffee, made the bed and left for the clinic where, as usual, she put in a full day's work because, despite the truce, there was still a stream of sick, needy people to be cared for. In the afternoon she took a taxi to the American hospital with blood and urine samples for tests and microscopic examination. She had just arrived at the hospital and was paying the driver when a rumble like an underground explosion caused the driver to look up, exclaim and rapidly pocket the money as he put the car into gear and accelerated away.

Inside the hospital the rumour soon gained ground that the building in the Ashrafiyeh where Bashir was meeting with a group of commanders from the Phalange had been blown up. First nothing was known, then it was said that the President-elect was safe, and finally that he had emerged from the ruins unhurt. The relief was universal, even among the Moslems and foreigners on the staff. It was known, however, that the blast was severe, the bomb that had destroyed the building huge.

There was no reason why Halim should be with Bashir but, not knowing his whereabouts, Sarah found that she needed all her dedication to maintain her composure. She chatted to various doctors and lab technicians, looked into one or two of the crowded wards preparing for possible casualties; and phoned his mother who was at home alone. She too shared Sarah's sense of apprehension, but told her not to worry. But a gradual unease seemed to spread in Beirut as the extent of the tragedy slowly unfolded, and it was acknowledged that there was no certain news about Bashir or the senior colleagues with him. Some people said they'd seen him, but others said he was still under the debris. There were all sorts of stories about the origins of the blast; that it was the work of the Palestinians, the Muslims who opposed Bashir or even, and more fancifully, the Israelis who had supported him. Once more the outlook for peace in Beirut seemed uncertain.

Early in the evening Sarah, thankful to have had her mind occupied, collected the reports from the laboratory and hurried back to the clinic where a few people still hung hopelessly about, waiting to be seen by a doctor, not ill enough to be treated as an emergency, yet not well enough to go home, if they had homes to go to.

'What a thankless task this is,' she said to Amal who was washing her hands in a makeshift basin in the corner of the room in which they saw patients. 'Did you hear anything from Halim?'

'Halim is all right,' Amal came up to Sarah, drying her hands on the towel. 'He phoned a few minutes ago. He says Bashir is truly dead. Thank God, Halim wasn't in the building, but he went to the scene at once. He knows.'

'Oh my God,' Sarah sank down on a rickety chair by a table they used for minor operations.

'It isn't generally known yet,' Amal went on, 'because they want to prevent a massacre.'

'A massacre? What sort of massacre?'

'Of the Palestinians of course.'

'You think they blew up the block?'

'Who else?' Amal's lips curled with scorn. 'It is in revenge for the deportations. They're still here you know, skulking in buildings, in the camps.'

'Someone said the Israelis may have done it.'

'The Israelis had no reason to kill Bashir. He was their ally, the only hope for Lebanon. Besides, the Phalange is hand in glove with the Israelis. Where do you think Halim spends his time?'

'He never says.'

'With the IDF, the Israeli forces. He is one of the main liaison men between the Phalange and the Jews. He knows the Israelis don't want Bashir dead.'

'Halim is a very mysterious man to me,' Sarah said, pulling a pile of cards towards her and noting on them the results of the various tests carried out that day at the hospital. 'Sometimes I wonder why he wants to marry me.'

'Because he loves you.' Amal sat down beside her. 'He admires you.' She put a hand on her friend's arm. 'But, Sarah, in taking on Halim I hope you realize you're taking on the future of Lebanon too.'

'Oh I know he wants to go into politics.'

'Will you like that? To be a politician's wife?'

'I shall have my work in the clinic,' Sarah said, avoiding Amal's eyes. 'I intend to continue to practise, whatever happens. Only I wish I were a surgeon. How helpless we are,' she gestured round the empty room.

'Why helpless?'

'Because we can do little more than first aid. It could be done by practically anyone. I even wasted my time this afternoon going to the hospital. I hope, when peace has come at last, and if Halim has settled down to his politics, that I may take some time off to specialize, become a surgeon. My mother always wanted it.'

Thinking of her mother, home seemed very far away. By now they would be learning the news about Halim. Because the mail was so bad she'd sent a long cable asking for the papers she needed.

'What about a family?' Amal gave her that meaningful, slight prurient, smile that some people reserve for subjects that are regarded as intimate.

'Well, my mother had a family and specialized. I can do it gradually. Whatever Halim wishes . . .' She paused and

271

looked at Amal, whose blue eyes suddenly took on a mischievous look. 'I mean when Halim and I have had the chance to talk about it.'

Sarah realized, with a shock, that already she was thinking like a Lebanese woman who would naturally defer to her husband. 'Whatever Halim wishes . . .' had come out quite spontaneously. What would her friends in the Women's Movement think if they heard such a statement, which certainly wasn't like her. In loving Halim she seemed to have yielded more than her body. Hastily she added: 'Did Halim say anything about when he'd be home?'

'He said to tell you to expect him when you saw him. Now that Bashir is dead the whole situation has changed completely, and he has much to do.'

During Wednesday and Thursday of that mid-September week, as the news reached the world of Bashir's death, the Israeli forces remained outside occupied West Beirut to prevent, it was said, further disturbances, particularly the retaliation that one Lebanese side might try to exact from another for the death of Bashir. A forward command post was set up on the roof of a five-storey building just on the edge of the Chatila camp that housed the remnants of the Palestinian refugees, mostly the women, children and old people who had been left behind. Visible too from the roof was the Sabra camp bordering on Chatila, only slightly larger, with a similar pathetic, dispossessed and harmless population. The camps consisted of low ramshackle buildings bisected by narrow alleys and streets. Nearby was the Gaza hospital run by the Palestinian Red Crescent and staffed mainly by personnel sympathetic to the Palestinian cause.

Sarah had often been to the hospital during her stay in Beirut because most of the Palestinian patients who came to her clinic and had to have further treatment wished to be taken there. There were several foreign doctors and nurses working there, many of them known to Sarah. Sure enough, as soon as the Israelis occupied Beirut the bloodshed began again as the various factions – Christian, Muslim, Druze and Palestinian – took the opportunity afforded by the chaos of the occupation to settle old scores with one another and make new ones.

During those days, when her worry about Halim was mingled with anxiety and horror at the renewed manifestations of violence about her, Sarah felt it almost impossible to believe that anything could ever be well in the Lebanon again.

Halim rang her twice at the apartment and once at the clinic. He also spoke to his parents, but he remained mysterious about his whereabouts and his movements, even to his future wife, or, perhaps, especially to her. Amal reported that a friend had, seen him with a newly arrived contingent of Israeli officers and suspected that he was working closely with them.

'I thought he was meant to be with the Phalange?'

'The Israelis support the Phalange. And they look now to them to get rid of the remaining Palestinians in Beirut, those who killed Bashir.'

'You're really talking about revenge?'

'We're talking about revenge,' Amal agreed, as though it were the most normal thing in the world. At Bashir's funeral the air had been full of the same word, as grief-stricken friends and mourners accompanied the bier of the assassinated leader: Revenge. It was then that Sarah realized how truly different these people were from any she had known before; ties of race, blood and religion were more important than life itself and, even for a doctor like Amal, took precedence over humanity.

On Friday Sarah and her fellow workers at the clinic heard that the Gaza hospital was reporting a number of cases of badly injured civilians who claimed that a massacre was taking place in the camps among the desperate, poverty-stricken refugees. Amal said that the workers at the hospital were so partisan they would exaggerate, an attitude which shocked Sarah.

'The only people we want to get rid of are the terrorists not the civilians,' Amal said dismissing the reports.

But rumours that something terrible was happening in the camps spiralled like wildfire through Beirut, and not only in the camps. Throughout the city there were fresh outbreaks of violence, little pockets of armed fighters potshotting at one another. On Friday night Sarah had dinner with her future in-laws, Halim's parents, who told her that this was the sort of life Halim had lived for years, ever since he joined the army and she should learn to live with her worry.

'I have,' Huda said smiling at her, offering her more *tabule*, 'believe me, in time you won't think about it.'

'But Halim won't always live this life : . .'

Huda smiled her mysterious smile with her slanting kohl-ringed eyes. 'Halim will never change. You must know what you're taking on Sarah.'

For the first time Sarah was conscious of a constraint between her and Halim's family. Though smiling, their expressions lacked sincerity, and she wondered if they really welcomed her as a daughter-in-law, or if they had pretended, for Halim's sake.

After dinner, as they sat on the balcony of the apartment drinking strong black coffee and looking at the sparkling lights of Beirut which disguised so much that was ugly taking place in the city streets, Sarah announced:

'I've decided to qualify as a surgeon after we're married.'

'Does Halim know?' Huda looked surprised.

'I really only decided this week, and I haven't seen him since Bashir's death. They need surgeons, not physicians, in places like this.'

'He is busy with the IDF,' Samir said, and Sarah looked at him sharply.

'How do you know that and I don't?'

'Maybe he thinks you don't understand; but he speaks such good Hebrew that he interprets for the Keta'ib who don't speak English in dealing with the Israelis.'

'I don't see why he couldn't have told me that.'

Huda leaned over and touched her hand. 'It's very early days for you, my dear, yet. Though you and Halim love each other – I know that – you don't know each other very well. Maybe he thinks he has too many things to explain to you, and so little time to see you. When he is with you he would rather talk of other things.

'But, seriously, if you want to do further study you must ask his permission. He is twenty-eight, you know, and is anxious to have a family.'

'Ask his permission!' Sarah felt outraged. 'Am I not to make my own decisions when we're married?' Samir and

274

Huda exchanged glances, the latter keeping her hand firmly on Sarah's.

'In Lebanon, my dear Sarah, indeed throughout the Middle East, women are accustomed to defer to their men even though enlightened people, such as we are, believe in love and equality between the sexes. It is a custom we women find it very hard to drop and, indeed, many of us do not wish to do so. Some do and do not consult their husbands; that is the modern trend, but not in our household. I think you would be very wise to learn that before you marry my son.'

There was a note of censure in Huda's voice and she gently withdrew her hand.

That night Sarah lay awake in her own bed acutely aware of the stir in the city as though something secret and sinister were afoot. The restaurants were full, the pavement cafes thronged with people, the cinemas were open and the bars and discos in Hamra Street blazed with light. But still people seemed to move stealthily about, shadows flitting between buildings, and there was a large number of armed patrols, both on foot and in armoured cars.

Sarah had gone to bed early after leaving her parents-in-law, feeling depressed and pleading a headache. She had, after all, known Halim less than three months and already his parents were giving her well-meant advice – she must defer to him, ask his permission. She felt as though she were being groomed for her subsidiary role as his wife.

She might have ignored all this if Halim had taken her more into his confidence that week; but she hadn't seen him. That very day, Friday 16 September, he hadn't even telephoned her. Yet his parents knew things that she didn't.

What was Halim, her beloved, hiding from her?

The next day she thought she knew.

All day Friday and during the night the casualties from the Sabra and Chatila camps began to stagger in increasing numbers into the Gaza Hospital. Everyone in Beirut knew there had been a massacre. Early on the Saturday morning the foreign staff of doctors and nurses were marched out by a group of soldiers past the Kuwaiti embassy, through Sabra Street, past the corpses lying by the side, and interrogated in a building formerly occupied by the UN. Finally they were released after the intervention of the Israelis. Beirut by now was full of detailed reports of the atrocities that had taken place in the camps, of the mounds of dead and dying that lay stacked in the alleys, or putrefying under the rubble. There were terrible stories of children trying to escape and being clubbed or hacked to death, as though the massacre of the innocents two thousand years ago was happening all over again, here in the land of the Bible. No one had been spared; neither the elderly, the sick nor the very young. The news bulletins on the television were full of horrible pictures which were being beamed to an incredulous world which already felt it had had its fill of horror from the Lebanon.

Yet all day on Saturday Sarah was too busy to watch the TV screens. An emergency call had gone out to all the clinics and hospitals in Beirut and as she bound the wounds or tried to staunch the blood of the pathetic victims of the massacre, as well as victims of fresh outbreaks of violence in the city, a terrible suspicion kept gnawing at her mind.

Sarah worked late into the night in the clinic, making frequent trips to the Gaza hospital, which looked like a battleground. She heard how the soldiers had occupied the hospital and how one young victim, who had sought medical aid, had been clubbed to death by the military under the gaze of the helpless doctors. The Gaza hospital had already been damaged by the Israeli bombardment and was full of wounded people, its inadequate facilities stretched to breaking point. One or two of the tiny children who came were taken, after treatment, straight to orphanages, having seen their entire families massacred before their eyes.

Who was responsible? Here the stories were as contradictory as the reports of the number of dead. The Keta'ib were the most favoured, out to secure revenge for Bashir. But also in the running were the Israelis; the left wing Militia; the Mourabitoun who supported the Palestinians; the soldiers of Major Haddad who had been in Beirut only the day before to pay his condolences to the Gemayel family, or any one of an amalgamation of a number of small armies, were they

276

Christian, Muslim or Palestinian. The only certainty was that no one really knew.

It was well after midnight when Sarah got home to try and get a few hours' sleep, and at once she knew he was there. The lights were on, there was a smell of frying and Halim was sitting in the chair by the open windows smoking a cigarette and reading a paper. He looked clean-shaven and fresh as though he had recently taken a shower. As she entered the room he jumped up and came towards her, his hand outstretched, but she brushed him aside and sat on the bed where the rumpled sheets told her he had also rested or taken a nap.

'Sarah?'

'You were there weren't you?' she said, her tired eyes resting on his smiling face.

'Where?'

'In the camps. The massacre . . .'

'I was not in the camps.' He bent to extinguish his cigarette in an already full ashtray by the bed. 'And the reports of a massacre are exaggerated.'

'I've seen them with my own eyes, Halim. People with terrible wounds. There are mounds of dead by the sides of the streets.'

'They were caught in the cross-fire. Do you realize, Sarah, that there were still over two thousand terrorists in the camps, shooting at us and the Israelis and shelling us with heavy guns supplied by the Russians?'

'You'll always find an excuse won't you, Halim? What a good thing the foreign forces who supervised the evacuation of the PLO have left, or doubtless you'd blame them? There were women and children with their throats cut, old men hacked to death.'

Halim frowned. 'There *were* a few incidents, but the object was to clean out the camps and that was done. The Israelis supervised the while thing.'

'There was a *massacre*,' Sarah said angrily. 'Some reports say that hundreds, perhaps thousands of civilians have been butchered.'

'This is the work of the enemy to discredit us.'

'Halim you know you're telling lies! Why do you try and hide it?'

277

'Because I wasn't there. I don't know. Neither do you.'

'Then where were you?'

'With the Israelis on the command post outside the camp. Do you think we would have let a massacre take place if we'd known about it?'

'Who was it then?'

'Haddad's men were there for sure, maybe the Mourabitoun . . .'

'The Mourabitoun support the Palestinians.'

'Yes, but they wouldn't hesitate to commit atrocities on their own people to make it look bad for us.'

'They'd cut the throats of their own people?'

'Yes, they would.' Halim stared hard at her and lit another cigarette. 'You don't understand this war, Sarah.'

'I understand revenge. Everyone says the Keta'ib did it to avenge Bashir.'

Halim's eyes showed pain and he slumped into his chair again with the attitude of a weary man for whom effort had suddenly become too great. Smoke from his long American cigarette curled up between his fingers.

'You can't imagine what the death of Bashir has done to me, to us. It has destroyed years of work, of hope. I tell you I hate the people who killed him, but I would not slaughter innocent civilians because of it. Don't you understand, Sarah, his murder was the work of the Palestinians? They never meant to leave Beirut and there are still thousands here hiding in the camps, among their people in these apartments in the city. We have to get rid of them, whatever the cost. The Israelis wouldn't go into the camps, the Lebanese Army refused. Our men, the Keta'ib, did go in, but only to ferret out the terrorists and destroy them. They use their own people as cover, you know. It is they who are to blame for the massacre, not us.'

'Then you acknowledge there was a massacre?'

'I know a lot were killed. But from the command post we could hear and see nothing.'

'I find that difficult to believe.'

'I swear it to you, Sarah. Many of the Israeli High Command were there too. Do you think they would have let a massacre continue had they known one was going on? It would be foolish because of the bad publicity. Elie Houbika was on the roof too, in touch by radio with our men. He told them not to touch the civilians. The Phalange doesn't want this sort of blood on its hands though I tell you, Sarah, frankly, they are all bad. Palestinian women breed male children and male children grow up to be terrorists.'

'You don't think of them as human. You never have.'

Halim drew on his cigarette. 'I don't like them it's true, but I wish you could understand about the Palestinians. They have no respect for life. They are not like us, that's for sure. Do you know in Damour in 1976 they massacred *thousands* of Christian civilians? They butchered them all in the most terrible way, and these were people whose home it had been, who had lived there for centuries. I was in Damour soon after the killings and I can't tell you what it was like. This little thing is *nothing* compared to what happened then.'

'I don't call it a little thing.' Sarah got up and poured herself some water from a bottle on the table. 'I tell you it will finish Israel's credibility, and that of the Keta'ib too. You will never have peace in Lebanon, Halim. I know that now.'

She sat down again holding her glass in her hand, sipping the tepid water. Halim got up and put an arm round her shoulder, pressing her to him.

'Sarah you're tired now, and shocked by what you have seen today.'

'Do you know they came into the Gaza hospital and killed people in their beds? They shot down wounded people in the corridors? Everyone who saw them says they were crazed with so much blood-letting. They took away the medical staff because they supported the Palestinians and threatened to kill them too. And they were *all* the Phalange with insignia on their pockets, like yours.'

'Haddad's men have a similar badge to ours; their uniforms were also supplied by the Israelis . . .'

Sarah threw down her glass on the floor and turned to face him. She could feel his warm breath on her cheeks.

'Halim why don't you take the responsibility? You wanted to kill the terrorists and you butchered their families too. Why don't you admit it?'

'Because it's *not* my responsibility,' he replied angrily, abruptly removing his hand. 'You can't blame me for that and you can't say I was responsible. I'm only one man. I'm not

279

even senior command. Yes I was on the roof and I knew our people were there; but I didn't know what was going on. No one did. No one really knew. If anyone is responsible it's the Israelis who didn't want to do the job themselves. They surrounded the camp on three sides. If they knew what was going on they could have stopped it and they didn't. But if you ask me, Sarah, I'll tell you the truth. I'm glad that whatever happened happened, because the fewer Palestinians there are in this world the better. They are bad people, deep down, and you with your vague humanitarian sentiments won't see it.'

'I only see people,' Sarah said, looking sadly up at him. 'I see people sick and dying, children orphaned, horrible things happening which no one wants to take responsibility for. If you call that "vaguely humanitarian" then I'm glad I am. I can only see evil about me here in Beirut and as for you, Halim, you'll never change and you'll never learn. I made a mistake. It breaks my heart to say it, but there is no place for me here with you. Your parents know it and now I know it. When this latest mess in Beirut is cleared up I'm going home. I would never make you a good Lebanese wife, not now, not ever.'

'Sarah's coming home,' Sam said, putting down the phone.

Frankie looked impatiently at him because she was in the middle of giving him instructions about what to do while she was out, and was short of time as she usually was these days. Always busy. She had rehearsals at the studio before the programme went out live in the evening. It being a Saturday, June had the day off and Sam was once more being instructed in the art of being a father. She had to say the same thing every week.

'Zoë has had her main meal and she'll sleep until about four. With any luck Elizabeth will too.'

'I wish June wouldn't take the day off at the weekend. It's very inconvenient,' Sam said sulkily.

'Don't you think you should have *some* responsibility, Sam, for your children? It's the only day you do.'

Sam cast her a reproachful glance and, sitting down, shook out the paper. He dreaded these days when he was alone with the children, expected to feed them and bath them, put them to bed. He loved them, but to look at, to play with. He didn't feel natural or at ease with very young children. It was an awful chore to feed them and change nappies, put them to bed. He'd never had to do that with his first family and he felt he was too old to learn. Anyway, he didn't consider it was a masculine role. 'I think you deliberately plan it. You didn't say anything about Sarah.'

'What is there to say?'

'Well she was supposed to be out there getting married. Barbara had sent her birth certificate by special courier. I'd expect you to be interested, Frankie.'

'Darling, I *am* interested, but I've a lot on my mind. I'm late already. Perhaps she's coming here for a honeymoon.' Frankie agitatedly checked a list in her hand. 'Now I won't be home until about ten and if you can't be bothered to cook your own meal there's cold ham and salad in the fridge and . . . Sam are you listening?'

Sam was reading the Saturday Review page in *The Times*.

'I know exactly what to do,' he said without looking at her. 'I sit here until one of the children cries and I then get up and hit her until she stops . . .'

'Oh Sam be serious!'

'Well I know what to do.' He glanced at her as he turned over the page. 'I've done it often enough since you turned into a TV star.'

'Then I'm off.'

'Have a good time.'

Frankie ran downstairs into the garage and reversed her car, angrily changing gear as she drove down the hill towards Regent's Park Road. What sort of life did she and Sam have now, since she gave the ultimatum about that woman Julia and threatened to leave him? Perhaps she should have left after all.

In many ways she wished she hadn't confronted him about Julia, maybe asked Barbara to do the dirty work. Perhaps they should never have discussed Julia at all, but at the time Frankie needed to get it out of her system. She was too angry, too fraught with worry to be strictly logical. She had supposed it would straighten out things between them, give them the chance of a fresh start; but it hadn't. Close friends she discussed

281

it with said that kind of thing never did; you could never begin again.

After Julia left the bank she and Sam went on the much promised visit to the States for a holiday, but it hadn't been a second honeymoon. The feeling of betrayal she had went too deep. She couldn't put it out of her mind and all the time he knew what was upsetting her. He didn't seem to try very hard to woo her either. She felt he nursed a grudge because his feeling for Julia – though he denied it – had been too deep. When they came home she flung herself into her work: she needed it to take her mind off her marriage.

Frankie enjoyed her work. The programme was a success and, as these things do, had led to all sorts of other offers. She was already contemplating moving from Channel 4 to the new breakfast television when it started the following year, but that would give her more time alone with Sam and she wasn't sure it was what she wanted. Now, the nights when she didn't have a programme were spent socializing with all her new-found friends from the TV, Sam hovering on the periphery, bored and showing it.

These days, apart from work, she didn't know what she wanted from her life at all. She was thought of as a successful woman with an attractive husband and two beautiful children. People imagined her to be rich, happy and contented. In fact she was more discontented than ever because marriage, children and career didn't exactly gell.

People never really looked beneath the surface and she knew that, superficially, she tried to conform to the image others had of her. For that reason she had no intention of parting from Sam.

Frankie stopped at the traffic lights in Swiss Cottage and turned right by the Odeon cinema towards the north London studios where the programme was rehearsed.

Looking at the screen she didn't seem like his wife. For one thing she looked much more beautiful; she was volatile, too, and full of laughter despite the grim nature of the economic news. Had she been a stranger he would have fancied her.

Did he fancy her now? He drew his chair nearer to the screen and examined her close-up features dispassionately.

Yes, he fancied her; but he knew too much about her, and she had found out too much about him. If only there hadn't been Julia. Julia was the most incredible folly of his life, more of a folly than getting married to Frankie. To involve Poppy in the whole thing had been asinine. Now Poppy was no longer a friend to either of them, Julia had lost her job and, as far as he knew, hadn't found another. It was very difficult these days to get work in the suburbs for a woman with only a limited experience of working in a bank. His friend who owned the flat in the Barbican said he was lucky Julia hadn't tried to extort money from him. But he knew Julia. She might not love him any more, she might nurse a grievance against him, think that she had been badly treated, and she had; but she would never stoop to extortion. He knew he would never hear from her again.

Frankie finished the economic summary and started questioning a well-known financial journalist about the implications of the news. Christ, it was Neil Featherstone! What a lot that man had to answer for. Sam slumped back and watched the two of them together chatting away, smiling, mouthing platitudes. It was really a ridiculous programme which skated only superficially over really important issues: rising unemployment, lack of investment, lack of all sorts of incentive and the real implications of continuing recession.

Sam closed his eyes to shut out Frankie and Neil, who had caused the whole crisis between them. He felt he was imprisoned by a nubile young woman who made him account for every move, watched him like a hawk. Yet what did she get up to? He opened an eye and looked at Neil. Maybe they went out to dinner after the programme. It ended at eight and she said she wouldn't be back until after ten.

Did he care?

Elizabeth started to cry and he got clumsily to his feet, flicking off the TV programme as he did, which was being videoed anyway so that she could see it when she got home. Gaze at herself, fishing for compliments. 'Yes, you looked lovely dear; you're very clever.'

He should never have left Barbara.

At this time of year, late February, Barbara always felt a lift in her spirits, as though she could already sense spring. She looked around her with pleasure as she walked up the path and let herself in by the front door. Tom was just taking his coat off and turned to greet his mother, kissing her affectionately on the cheek.

'Had a good day, Mum?'

'Not bad. Did you, darling?'

'Quite good. I think I'll enjoy being up here.'

'It's going home at weekends that's the problem.' She linked her arm through Tom's and they went slowly into the sitting room because, although he walked well, he still used a stick. Since Christmas he'd gone home every other weekend. 'I wish Natalie would come up here Tom. It's so unlike her, this attitude, after years of devotion.'

Tom went over to the drinks table, putting his stick over the arm of a chair, and poured whiskies for them both. He held his glass up to the light and added Perrier to it. 'Good colour this whisky.' He gave his mother her glass and sat down opposite her, his gammy leg stiff before him. Apart from that he looked fit, strong and handsome in his uniform, with the crown of a major now on the epaulette.

'I think Natalie had enough, Mum. The war took an awful lot out of her.'

'Yes, but it took a lot out of a number of women, and many of them, too many, didn't have their husbands come home to them.' Barbara knew her tone was censorious, sharp.

'Natalie just snapped. She always hated the Army anyway.'

'Then why did she marry you?'

'Love.' Tom smiled. 'You should know that, Mum. Love is all right to start, but after two babies and a war it isn't the same, unless you really share common interests. She hates the Army and I hate agriculture. Natalie should have married a land-owning gent. That's what she was brought up for.'

'I still don't think it was asking much to live in or near London for a time. You could have bought a place in the Home Counties; very countrified, if you ask me.'

'You're beginning to sound like a mother-in-law.'

'Well I am, and I love my son. I don't think Natalie's doing the right thing by you. Not at all.'

'Well she won't come up here. She couldn't now, anyway.'

'Why?'

'Because she wants to sell the house and buy a little farm and run it herself. She has a place in mind.'

'Oh God, then there will be a divorce.' Barbara put her glass to her lips and took a long drink.

'I'll go on commuting in this fashion as long as I can.' Tom picked up the *TV Times*, and started flicking through the pages, ignoring Barbara's observation. 'Good Lord, Frankie's on again tonight.'

'Sam'll be pleased,' Barbara grimaced. 'Tell me what you mean by "as long as you can"?'

'I mean just that.' Tom leaned forward to put on the TV. 'I don't know how long a man can remain this celibate. Do you?'

He didn't seem to expect an answer and Barbara finished her drink and went upstairs to repair her makeup before getting the dinner. On the way past Sarah's room she stopped and knocked on the door.

'Come in,' Sarah called, and Barbara put her head round the door to find her daughter lying on the bed reading a book.

'OK?' Barbara smiled.

'OK, Mum. How was your day?'

'Fine. How was yours?'

'Elementary surgery is like doing elementary anything. Boring. I dissected a frog's leg.'

'Well done.'

'It will take years and years, Mum.' Sarah put her book on her stomach and her arms behind her head. Barbara went right in and sat on the bed next to her.

'But you knew that.'

'Oh I knew it, but . . .'

'Do you really know what you want Sarah?'

Sarah studied the ceiling, her brow furrowed. 'When I was in Beirut I wanted to do surgery. But it's like studying for first MB again. I'm nearly twenty-six, Mum. I'm a doctor. I've seen the world. I've been in love . . .'

'Do you miss Halim?'

'Not a bit.' Sarah had that thin grim line of determination about her mouth.

'Truly?'

'Truly.' Sarah gazed at her mother for a moment as though trying to decide whether or not to say more. Then, when she did speak again, the words came out in a rush. 'My intense physical desire for Halim blinded me to everything else about him that didn't fit. I felt it was so important to love and be loved that I tried to disguise from myself the fact that we really had very different points of view. I suppose I lacked insight, Mother, which is what you always used to say to me . . .'

'I didn't mean . . .' Moved by compassion, by a sense of inadequacy, Barbara took her daughter's hand.

'But you were right,' Sarah insisted, 'and it showed in my relationship with Halim. As you know I've never loved anyone before, and it seemed so miraculous that someone as vigorous, as sexy as Halim could care as he did for me.'

'But I've always said you were attractive darling . . .'

'Yes, but not the sort of woman men automatically desire. Not obviously, anyway. I mean I don't mind admitting that, despite my loyalty to the principles of feminism. It's the truth.'

'Frankly there are very few beautiful women around who are "automatically desired". You're certainly no less good looking or desirable than most of them.'

'Anyway . . .' Sarah swallowed, clearly almost overcome by emotion. Rarely had she talked to her mother as honestly as this, even when she had first arrived home from Beirut. 'The point is that Halim, this man I loved so much, was a terrorist at heart. He was as bad as any member of the PLO whom he hated. He didn't care at all about the population in Beirut who didn't share his beliefs. Even if he didn't physically kill those women and children in the camps he did in his heart. He was on the roof of the command post with Elie Houbika, he told me that. What he didn't know was that the Israelis would be forced to have an enquiry, the results of which would be made known throughout the world. And in that enquiry, the Kahan Report, it was stated that Elie Houbika was in radio contact with his men in the camps and when they asked him what they should do with the women and children he told them they shouldn't need to ask! Raucous laughter followed, we are told, among the Phalangists present, and who was with them, one of them, laughing with them . . .?'

As she stumbled on her words Barbara leaned forward and

tenderly stroked her hair back from her brow. 'You're needlessly distressing yourself, Sarah . . .'

'*Of course* I'm distressed!' Angrily Sarah brushed away a tear. 'Halim, whatever else he was, was also a liar who could not even tell the woman he was going to marry the truth. I could never have married anyone whose beliefs blinded him to all considerations of humanity. I wasn't sorry I left him when I came home, and I'm not sorry now. Really I'm not.'

There were no more tears but the pain, the anger showed in her eyes and Barbara felt pain and anger on her behalf too. The trouble was that Sarah had come rather late to an experience most girls went through in their early twenties, if not before. She had no yardstick by which to judge her feelings for Halim, no former lover to compare him with.

'I'm glad you came home, Sarah, and I'm glad you talked to me now. There will be other loves, you'll see.'

'Not for a long time for me, Mother; a long, long time.'

Were there tears in her eyes again? Barbara wasn't sure. She bent and kissed her daughter, lingering just for a moment longer than necessary to show how much she loved her, how she could always be sure of her support.

But was the love and support of a mother enough?

'Tom's in,' she said, 'and he says Frankie's on the TV again tonight.'

'Not again! Dad must be getting fed up.'

Sarah didn't know about Julia and neither did Tom. According to what Sam told her, and they spoke often, he was quite glad to be alone in the house, or at one of his clubs with his friends, or the opera by himself. At least, he said he was by himself. Who knew?

At dinner the three of them chatted about the day – the Marines, the hospital, Barbara's clinic, Frankie who was becoming a TV star, and Amanda who was talking about marriage to George. She couldn't decide. Barbara was against it on the grounds of age, and Sam because he felt George wasn't good enough, rich or intelligent enough, for his daughter. The next family crisis therefore promised to be about her.

The next? Barbara smiled to herself and sipped her wine. She sat between her eldest children – both wounded by war in a single year, the one emotionally, the other physically.

But now at least they were safe and together and she, Barbara, felt complete.

They might go away from her again and, for their own sakes she hoped they would; that they would both find the happiness they sought. In the meantime to have part of the family close to her again, under one roof, was better than the solitary life which Sam's departure had begun for her.

For the pair bond, however strong, whatever its length, had a weakness: it could be broken at anytime. But its power, which went beyond the mere mating of man and woman, was the generation and creation of life. Thus the real bond, Barbara decided looking at her two loved ones, was between people of the same blood: parents and children. Whatever happened it could never be broken.

It was the one enduring bond, this love, the only one, perhaps, that truly mattered.